Nestor M. Kaminski

Mission Capri

Mission Capri

Originally published in Serbian by Albatros Plus, Belgrade, Serbia as
Misija Capri ili Opklada, Blackbird i Beogradski gambit
Copyright ©2018 Neven Krešić and Marin Krešić
ISBN 978-86-6081-290-4

English Paperback Edition
Copyright ©2021 Neven Kresic and Marin Krešić

Published in the United States by Blue Ridge Press

Library of Congress Control Number: 2020953044

ISBN 978-0-578-83047-6

Front cover photo of schooner *Blackbird* courtesy of Allan Bezanson
Back cover photo credits: William Culhane (photograph of Miles Davis);
National Park Mljet, Croatia; Chess Club Svetozar Gligorić Gliga

Chess Story

A well-known but never explained story, heard by everyone in the world of chess, can today be found in many versions including on the Internet. However, here is the original.

During a tournament of the world's best chess players at the time a mysterious man approached Capablanca and told him, not more and not less, that he solved chess!

The great Cuban thought the man must have been crazy, but the stranger produced twelve large gold coins and offered a bet that he will always checkmate him in twelve moves.

"He may be crazy, but twelve gold coins are twelve gold coins" Capablanca thought to himself and accepted the bet.

The game started normally as usual but, after several strange moves, the champion's position became terrible and he was checkmated in the twelfth move.

Capablanca was in shock but requested a rematch. The game started with a completely different opening but, after several strange moves, Capablanca again faced a checkmate.

Something was obviously wrong, but the champion could not figure out where he made mistakes.

He then called Alekhine and Lasker and asked them to play with the stranger.

Lasker played a defensive opening, but he also was defeated in twelve moves.

The same destiny unfolded for an astonished Alekhine.

"It was horrible and shameful" the chess players later told a friend "but whatever we played, we were always checkmated in twelve moves! We asked ourselves what we, the best chess players in the world, would do from now on because, suddenly, chess is solved and makes no sense any more..."

"But I never heard that chess has been solved! What happened then? What did you do?" the friend asked.

"Well, we removed him, of course!"

Contents

Part Two

Introduction

This story wrote itself, after long and difficult research. It gathers characters separated by decades and thousands of miles yet connected in unexpected ways. Everyone mentioned existed and was real, no one was invented except for me. I did not make up sources of information and documents. The names of only a very few characters were changed, and only because they are still alive. I did not want them to experience anything unpleasant.

It all started with one of my visits to the Thompsons' house in Maine. Peter is a colleague of mine and our work on several projects made us friends and brought our families close together. The Thompsons have one great passion – sailing. A long time ago they bought, at a rather high price, an old wooden schooner, once a beautiful sailing boat, with the name *Blackbird*. For years they have been spending all their free time, literally thousands of hours and a significant budget on restoring it, often with help from their friends. Finally, it seems they see light at the end of the tunnel, as the restoration is nearing completion.

I cannot say they are angry when I ask them why they went to all that trouble and expense, although both have a strong urge to explain themselves:

"Because it is just the right thing to do! She is such a beautiful boat and deserves to sail as long as she can. We have great plans for her and the two of us. And once we are gone, someone else will get to enjoy and admire her."

I bluntly, and perhaps quite rudely, continue:

"So, you are not doing it to better sell her and make some money?"

"Not a chance!" they exclaim in unison. "No money can buy what we have in her. She is not for sale!"

A few months later, during my September 2013 visit to the Thompsons, I saw on the wall of their family room an old, framed and discolored photo of a drawing of a sailing boat anchored in a bay with a rocky shore. The shore was lined with old pine trees. Sandy found the photo in a hidden compartment behind *Blackbird's* kitchen wall during the cabin restoration. The shore on the drawing did not look like anything one would associate with the coast of Maine where the Thompsons reside. I told them the framed photo of the drawing was very similar to something I had seen quite recently. I closed my eyes to concentrate and tried to remember where I had seen the same drawing. Then it all came back to me. Few months earlier, I had been transferring video tapes to my external hard drive. I filmed the tapes during one of our family trips to the most beautiful sea in the World – the Croatian Adriatic. The scene in particular that I am remembering was of our son fooling around while attempting to eat a squid meal in a small family restaurant on the island of Lopud. As the camera panned the restaurant, it stopped briefly on a drawing strikingly similar to the one hanging on their family room wall. Yes, it was the same drawing, without any doubt. So, I asked the Thompsons if, by any chance, they sailed *Blackbird* to the Croatian coast. They both laughed:

"*Blackbird* never sailed to Europe, let alone the Adriatic!"

"I am certain that I know where the drawing was made and I am certain that *Blackbird* was there, on the Croatian coast." I said. "If you still believe *Blackbird* never sailed to the Adriatic, then she must have a twin there." (I did not know at the time that there is a specific nautical term for a twin – *sister boat*.)

The Thompsons chuckled and went to great lengths explaining how that would have been impossible. They insisted that they knew everything about every single wooden schooner designed by John Gale Alden, the famous naval architect from Boston, and all of *Blackbird's* sister schooners, also designed by Alden and built by the Goudy and Stevens shipyard in East Boothbay, Maine. The Thompsons were adamant that none of these boats ever sailed to the Adriatic.

Patiently listening to this rather long explanation of why *Blackbird* or any other similar-looking wooden sailing boat could not have possibly been in Europe, I simply said, once they finished, they were wrong. This really got on Pete's nerves especially because I noted that he, as a geologist, should have noticed the difference between the white limestone on the drawing and any Maine granite.

The argument ended up as quickly as it started after I proposed a bet: If I am correct, Peter will send me a pack of their favorite IPA beer and a bottle of the most expensive aged Kentucky bourbon, regardless of how difficult that might be considering more than complicated regulations of the inter-state commerce of alcoholic drinks. Peter promptly accepted the bet, with a condition that I must do the same if I lose. Also, it would not be enough to just send them the video clip of where I saw the schooner, but I would have to provide additional, irrefutable evidence that it was indeed *Blackbird*, and that she was indisputably anchored off the Croatian coast in the Adriatic.

Needless to say, Peter and Sandy and *Blackbird* were the reasons and the inspiration for the quest that I undertook to understand the past of their beautiful sailing boat. The quest lasted five years and is chronicled in this book. I could not have imagined where this obsession of mine to win the bet would later lead me. Everything that followed, all my discoveries, could not be compared with any life experience I had before.

As it turned out, many others were unexpectedly drawn into the complicated chain of events that was to follow as well.

And now, without further ado, please join me on this secret voyage, in the order the puzzle was solved, piece by piece.

Details of the *Blackbird's* deck, made of painted white pine,
during and after restoration.

Blackbird in Casco Bay, Maine, in July 1994.

Thompsons on *Blackbird* "anchored" in the backyard of their family home.

Peter on *Blackbird* (coming out of the cabin) while the schooner is being lowered to water in Freeport Marina, Maine, in fall of 2015.

All restoration work completed; *Blackbird* is waiting for her masts and sails.

PART ONE

Mission Capri

Chapter 1

Vinko

I am aware that many describe me as a stubborn perfectionist, which has no basis in fact whatsoever. It may be because I usually insist I am right when engaging in a polemic with anybody. But because I always am right, there is no single reason why I would give in just to avoid someone becoming frustrated. It is true that I myself sometimes feel frustrated when this is happening, but by no means am I going to admit that; all I care about is proving that I am right, at any cost. This means that I must win the bet with the Thompsons, also at any cost.

For this and a few other reasons it was only natural that on my first trip to Europe and Croatia in June 2014, after we made the bet, I used the journey as an opportunity to gather the evidence needed to secure a win over the Thompsons. Therefore (and very logically), I put aside a few free days and dollars to go to Dalmatia following business meetings in Zagreb. Although some also maintain, completely unjustifiably, that I am not a spontaneous person, in this case I can thank my very meticulous planning skills for reserving a return flight to Washington, D.C., one full week after my official program in Europe was over.

Upon arriving to the island of Lopud, which lies just off the Croatian coast, I learn about the artist of the original drawing of *Blackbird*. The owner of the small family restaurant where I filmed the video clip knows the artist, Vinko Lovrić (to whom he refers as "dear barba Vinko"), a close relative of his uncle. After I ask him where I can find Vinko, expressing a desire to meet him as soon as possible, the restaurant owner sends me to Podgora. Before I leave, he gives me a bottle of domestic grape brandy called lozovača, with a kind request to take it to his beloved barba Vinko.

I find Vinko in Podgora, as it turns out only three days after his 87th birthday. A picture of vitality and with a great sense of humor, he was still fully active, painting scenes from the picturesque little town on the Dalmatian coast where he lived. He tended a small vegetable garden and fruit orchard in front of his spacious old family stone house. Several seasonal hotel workers moved in few weeks earlier, at the beginning of the summer tourist season, providing him with a modest income.

After introducing myself and explaining how I found him thanks to his relative in Lopud, I show Vinko the photograph of his drawing of *Blackbird*. This moves him to the point of tears. I quickly open the bottle of lozovača and ask for two glasses so we can toast, "as the good old custom dictates." Vinko quickly replies that he just picked some fresh figs from his orchard (proudly pointing a nice grove of fig and almond trees) which he will fetch together with the glasses as he cannot wait to taste his favorite drink, "from the best vineyard there is." After several glasses of lozovača and more than a handful of figs, Vinko calms down and tells me how he travelled around the world, as did his father and grandfather and many other seafaring men of his family. Vinko is obviously enormously proud while reflecting on this family tradition and his own boundless love of the sea and sailing boats, his eyes sparkling as he speaks.

Vinko then tells his life story (before asking me to do the same). He was born in early twenties of the last century on the island of Lopud, in the country that changed its name many times. As long as he can remember, he has been drawing and painting for his own pleasure. He joined the war effort in World War II by helping a Swedish couple on a spy mission, sailing as their mate on a wooden schooner, exactly this one on the drawing. Vinko clearly remembers when he made the drawing of *Blackbird*, which he calls *Swarttrost* – in September of 1943. Aha! Enormously surprised, I repeat to myself *Blackbird* was sailing the Adriatic during WWII. Continuing to listen to what Vinko was saying, I already start thinking of the next steps required to solve the puzzle of *Blackbird*.

After the mission with the Swedes ended, Vinko was in hiding for a while and then briefly joined Tito's partisans, a resistance movement against the Nazi occupation. Right before the war was over, he somehow managed to return to Lopud where he witnessed the end of German occupation and the fall of a short-lived Croatian Nazi puppet state. He finished college in Zagreb and left for Belgrade where he married and had a son. For years he earned a living as an elite member of Tito's Secret Service and followed the Marshall on his many trips abroad. Then he retired prematurely for reasons he did not want to discuss. Because of the time spent with partisans during the war he was able to retire as early as 1980, with full benefits. Vinko's love of the Adriatic brought he and his wife back to Lopud, the choice wholeheartedly approved by their son Teo who would therefore be able to spend summers on the coast which he loved as much as his father, if not more.

Vinko still has the family wooden sailing boat and wants me to see it, kindly asking if I would be willing to drive down to the port, which I gladly confirm. As we are approaching a small stone church, Vinko reluctantly asks me if we could make a short stop there so he can visit his family tomb – the trip from his house is now too long for his aging legs and he does not make it as often as he would like. At the tomb, Vinko's eyes tear up when he points to the name of his late son Teo. He quickly apologizes and then a smile appears on his face when he starts talking how much Teo loved sailing on the Adriatic with their family boat which we were about to see. We parted that late afternoon with me promising I will come again to visit him as soon as possible and with my family, at Vinko's insistence.

I again visited Vinko the following year, in the summer of 2015, with my wife Joanne and son Eddie as promised. Vinko insists that we stay for dinner as he finally managed that very morning to get freshly caught squid thanks to strong family connections ("Everything goes to damn tourists."), chard is always plentiful (he proudly points to his garden), and there still is some good wine left from last year.

After a delicious dinner, glasses refilled with the magic wine (Joanne is in seventh heaven!), Vinko suddenly starts to talk, in English, about the mysterious death of his son Teo, which still eats him alive, day and night. I quickly send Eddie to pick some figs from Vinko's orchard.

Vinko stops for a moment to tell a story of how Teo, at the time a young and upcoming artist, was hired to replace a model of Grace Kelly in Madame Tussauds wax museum in London. The Grimaldi family was very dissatisfied with the existing model and made a request of a trusted family friend, one Stefano Ristorcelli from Genoa, to find an unknown but excellent artist who would correct the unacceptable "error". Teo, after suffering for a long time over the sculpture, realized that nothing could compare with the beauty of the famous actress, and suddenly started to languish, likely mortally falling in love with the princess.

With tears in his eyes Vinko tells us how his son disappeared: during one of Teo's summer stays on Lopud. On September 9, 1980, an accident happened. Teo was swimming after the sunset, which he liked the most, when a ferocious storm appeared out of nowhere. Teo simply vanished and only his clothes, sandals and a metal ball, which he always carried with him, were found on the beach. After an unsuccessful search for the body by the police and the Coast Guard, the investigation concluded that Teo drowned. He was declared officially dead.

Vinko and his wife could not bear the weight of all the memories and the inexplicable misfortune that struck them. They left the island and moved to Podgora, where Vinko's maternal grandfather was from and where his family tomb was.

Seeing Eddie returning from the orchard, Vinko quickly wipes away his tears and manages to cheerfully ask:

"Hi young man, what nice things did you bring us?"

Eddie, very embarrassed, shows a woven basket with only a handful of figs and admits he ate most of them on the way back:

"They were so yummy I just could not stop. I am so sorry."

Vinko laughs wholeheartedly and replies:

"Don't you worry young man, don't you worry. There are so many figs in the orchard. We could not eat them all for days, even if we wanted to!"

Visibly cheered up (to our great relief), Vinko takes a small painting of a flower vase hanging on the wall and gives it to Eddie:

"My son Teo painted it when he was about your age. I want you to have it."

Then he invites us to all go to Teo's room where there were more of his son's paintings. The first thing I notice after entering the spacious, sparsely furnished room, is a photograph standing on a piano. In the photograph is Grace Kelly with a model of schooner from movie *High*

Society. Next to the photograph is an impressive knife for which Vinko says it is a Viking one, and a nicely carved large wooden box.

Joanne, Eddie and I left the Croatian coast two days after that visit with Vinko, full of memories, both nice and sad.

Vinko and Eddie on the roof of Vinko's house in Podgora, summer of 2015. Dalmatian islands are visible in the background.

Chapter 2

Mission

Back at home, it did not take me long to realize how solving the puzzle that is *Blackbird* will not be easy. The war archives I searched were not readily accessible and were scattered at various institutions depending on the degree of confidentiality. All of them also proved to be incomplete, regardless of the country where they were housed. Nevertheless, after countless meetings, (both official and unofficial), as well as various written requests, filled-out forms, and personal appeals, I finally managed to reconstruct the key events and stitch them into a consistent whole. Now, as I look back at this effort from distance, probably the most important realization I have is that it could not have succeeded without help from the friends of friends' friends. Since I have promised complete confidentiality to those that needed it, I will omit some (or more) details where and how certain information was obtained.

Although I was only at the beginning of my research of WWII events in Europe, I rather quickly (and miraculously) remembered my high-school history classes where we learned about the connections between the British and the Marshall Tito's partisans, mainly communists, who were fighting the German occupation of Yugoslavia. I did not remember that we heard anything about a possible Allied invasion of the Yugoslav Adriatic coast, either as an alternative to the invasion of Sicily and Italy, or as an additional invasion aimed at cutting German withdrawal from Greece and The Balkans. The invasion that would, at the same time, stop the rapid advance of the Soviet Army.

Only in January 1943 did the Americans finally comprehend the grave seriousness of the civil war that was raging in Yugoslavia between the communists, royalists, and Croatian Nazis and would lead to an inevitable breakup of the Yugoslav Government-in-Exile in London. This understanding was based primarily on the reporting of a secret agent, with a perfect British accent and identity, who was part of a mysterious British agency operating in the Yugoslav lands. The agent, without British knowledge, communicated directly with American intelligence in Washington, D.C. Nevertheless, the Americans did not show much interest in actively and directly engaging in the Yugoslav chaos, leaving every initiative to the British. From the beginning of the occupation and division of Yugoslavia by the Axis powers, the British started sending various spy missions there. First, they did it in cooperation with the Yugoslav Government-in-Exile (YGE), and later alone.

The first completely independent official British mission to join Tito's partisans was led by colonel William Deakin, close friend of Churchill's. This six-men mission, named *Operation Typical*, was flown from the Libyan town Dern and on May 28, 1943 parachuted near Black Lake on the Montenegrin mountain Durmitor. The mission was composed of the members of British military intelligence and a super-secret agency, named Special Operations Executive (SOE), which Churchill personally established in 1940. The spies and commandos of SOE, of which very little was known even in the intelligence circles, were involved in numerous secret operations across Europe including the Yugoslav coup d'état of March 27, 1941. One of the leading SOE agents, with a reputation for his wild imagination, often bordering on the absurd, was assigned exclusively to the Yugoslav territories for which he had great personal interest. Although he was officially subordinate to Bill Bailey, officer in charge of The Balkans, he was pulling all the strings from behind scenes. His name was Larry Neal.

By all accounts, the first Yugoslav operation in which Larry was intimately involved took place in second half of January 1942. SOE secured cooperation of General Simović, Prime Minister of YGE, in organizing a secret mission in which elite Yugoslav spies were to be transported from Egypt to the Adriatic coast. As always when Larry was involved, the mission got a somewhat peculiar name – *Operation Henna*. Although today everyone can search the internet and find out details about the evergreen bush with an enchanting fragrance and of the same name, it remains mystery to this day as to what was Larry thinking when he chose that name for the mission. Was it simply because of the beauty of the bush? Or because the ancient Egyptian Queen Cleopatra decorated her body with henna pigment? Or, perhaps, because Hindu brides paint their skin with henna paints to celebrate joy, spiritual awakening and, at the end, a complete surrender to the groom? Or because, during a stay in Morocco, Larry saw front doors of houses painted with henna to bring felicity and scare evil spirits away?

In any case, the official documents of the British National Archives on *Operation Henna*, including one designated as ADM 199/1218, refer to a class T submarine, named *HMS Thorn*, which left the Egyptian port of Alexandria on January 17, 1942 on its fourth war patrol in the Yugoslav Adriatic. One of the *Thorn's* tasks was the top-secret *Operation Henna*. None of the documents describe what happened when, few hours before dawn on January 27, 1942, and in a ferocious storm with freezing rain, the submarine disembarked two members of the Yugoslav Royal Army at a sandy cove, Saplunara, on the Adriatic island of Mljet.

After the landing, both men, Lieutenant Stanislav Rapotec, and former police agent Sargent Stevan Šinko (the radio-operator of the mission), both Slovene, were supposed to find their way to Split, the largest Dalmatian port city, where they would connect with the royalists' resistance led by General Mihajlović. Their assignment was to send a report to the office of SOE in Egypt, via a strong radio tower on Malta. The report was to be based on comprehensive and objective information about the situation on the ground.

Unfortunately, as often happens, *Operation Henna* started with difficulties. After landing and as planned, the two Slovenes buried most of the equipment they brought from Egypt including two short-wave radios. They kept a few personal items, small guns, and some money (Italian lire and British gold coins.) Problems began when poor Stevan, already with high fever from likely food poisoning on the submarine, got even more ill thanks to the freezing rain and wind which mercilessly pounded the two secret agents on their way to a house in Babino Polje where a local liaison was waiting for their arrival. Unable to continue because of the high fever and overall weakness, Stevan stayed on Mljet whereas Lieutenant Rapotec did manage to reach Split and, over the next several months, collect valuable information for the British and

YGE. The resourceful and undoubtedly brave Rapotec reached Kairo and the SOE Headquarters for the Middle East in July 1942, after travelling via Belgrade and Istanbul.

The destiny of Sargent Stevan Šinko, on the other hand, was quite complicated and a lot more interesting for our story. The secret documents I was able to see, as well as personal interviews I had with several locals on Mljet during the last two years, allowed me to reconstruct the key events linked to Sargent Šinko. These events, as it turned out, influenced the secret mission of schooner *Blackbird*, our main hero, and the subject of this story.

Šinko spent seven full weeks recovering at the home of J.H. (I promised my source I will not reveal the real name) in Babino Polje under the care of his host's entire family. J.H. was, together with literally all other inhabitants of the island, a fierce opponent of the Italian occupation and an enemy of the Croatian Nazi puppet state established by the Germans. He blamed the Croatian Nazi führer Pavelić for the betrayal and surrender of their beloved island to the Italians. Without any hesitation, J.H. joined the resistance, which was spontaneously organized on Mljet in summer of 1941. He then later agreed to help with the *Operation Henna* when approached by secret channels connected with the Yugoslav Royal Government-in-Exile in London.

One night in March, Šinko was urgently taken from Mljet to the island of Lopud to avoid an Italian raid and almost certain death. J.H. found out about the raid from his cousin who was assigned to a stationary Italian army unit in Polače on Mljet. In an incredibly short time, J.H. was able to secure Šinko's stay at the house of one of the most respected Lopud families. The head of that family was Captain Ivan Lovrić who, by agreeing to take in Šinko, put at risk everything he ever had. Only thanks to Captain Lovrić and J.H., Sargent Šinko succeeded in eventually reaching Split, where more misfortunes awaited him, but on that perhaps some other time. The most important thing in this story of Sargent Šinko is to realize that, in the bloody civil war that butchered Yugoslavia, there were still people who could not betray their deep personal feelings of what is truly just and right. People like Captain Lovrić who, for that very reason, was, in the summer of 1943, approached by the British, through their secret agent, one Giuseppe Ristorcelli from Genoa who persuaded him to again help fight Nazi evil. Captain Lovrić never found out the name of the man that played the crucial role, pulling strings from a safe distance. The one that liked conceiving secret missions and giving them peculiar names. The lead agent of the mysterious SOE, Larry Neal.

Larry, thanks to the extraordinary connections he established during studies at Oxford, managed to personally present his plan for yet another secret mission on the Yugoslav Adriatic directly to Admiral Dudley Pound. This presentation took place on May 2, 1943 during an informal lunch in the large dining room of the Naval and Military Club in London which, at that time, was housed in the famous Cambridge House at the north end of Piccadilly. Admiral Pound was, from July 31, 1939 until September 20, 1943, First Sea Lord and Chief of Naval Staff. As such, he enjoyed the complete trust of Churchill with whom he closely cooperated on virtually all naval strategies, earning the nickname *Churchill's Anchor*. Before the promotion, Admiral Pound served as Commander-in-Chief of the Mediterranean Fleet, the most prestigious unit of the British Royal Navy. This post enabled him, one fall, to visit the Yugoslav Adriatic where he was served with the most extraordinary wine he had ever tasted in his life. The wine about which he later, whenever an occasion presented itself, told fairytales, including from his deathbed at the Royal Masonic Hospital in London where he passed away on October 21, 1943.

During the lunch, which lasted a little over one hour, Admiral Pound and Larry, as gentility demanded, first touched on several general themes, not connected with the main subject of their meeting. Among other things, they spoke about their shared love of sailing, the game of bridge, grog, and Shakespeare's plays. When they finally turned the conversation to the possible secret mission, Pound gave the following long monologue, after which the two men devoured their favorite jam roly-poly dessert and parted in good spirits:

"Young man, the Old Fox is undoubtedly obsessed with this crazy idea of invading Dalmatia. The Americans refuse to even discuss it, so it will probably end up going nowhere. I don't know what to think myself. Damn Russians are destroying everything in their path, and nothing will stop them. They will cut through The Balkans like through Swiss cheese and, if we do not do something, no one knows what will happen next. I pray to God every day that the Italians will capitulate before we invade Sicily. You certainly know that we are secretly negotiating with them about it. If everything goes according to the plan, then it may make sense to cross the Adriatic and at least try to advance into the Yugoslav interior before the Russians arrive. But Germans are Germans, and I am not sure if the price we will have to pay is warranted. The Yugoslavs are another story. They are madly slaughtering each other, and no one knows who is drinking and who is paying the bill. I am equally not sure if any of the parties involved would even help us. On the contrary. Churchill seems to increasingly believe in Tito's communists, who in their souls are completely devoted to the Russians. The men around that bearded General, who is subordinate to the Yugoslav King here in London, are unpredictable; and the Croatian ustashas owe everything they have to Hitler. An absolute chaos in which we should probably not enter, because no one can be trusted. But then again, should we leave everything to the Russians?

One small sailing boat in the waters that boil with different armed vessels and submarines? Crazy! But ingenious for that same reason. If the Americans approve and those adventurous Swedes do not change their minds in the meantime, then why not? On the other hand, even if they manage to somehow reach the Adriatic, it will already be too late because the Italians will fall apart by then and the Germans will quickly take over. But then again, the Germans and the Swedes do not have anything against each other, so there should not be a problem in that respect. Yes, crazy but ingenious. Yes, ingenious! Young man, you have my full support!

And don't let me forget! Please tell the Swedes they must sail to the Pelješac peninsula and taste wine from the monastery there. They will not regret it, I promise. I can still feel its incredible taste. Tell them to bring us some if they manage to survive. And if I am not alive to taste it again, which is almost certain, share it with someone you love. They will be enormously grateful to you!"

The only remaining task now left for Larry was to convince the Americans of the need for the spy mission on the Adriatic including its key aspect: securing an American wooden schooner for the journey.

Admiral Pound and Winston Churchill in London, 1939. Courtesy of WWII Database (WW2db.com.)

British Royal Navy submarine HMS Thorn, which on January 27, 1942 brought two Yugoslav Royal Army intelligence officers to the Adriatic island of Mljet during secret Operation Henna. Thorn was built in the Cammel Laird shipyard in Birkenhead and launched on March 18, 1941. It was sunk on August 6, 1942 by the Italian torpedo boat Pegaso southwest of Greek island Gavdos during an attempted attack on the convoy Istria. Courtesy of uboat.net.

Large dining room of the London Cambridge House where *Mission Capri* was born on May 2, 1943, forever changing destiny of the beautiful schooner *Blackbird* and lives of many known and unknown players. Courtesy of e-architect.co.uk.

Chapter 3

Plan

The scene is of a private but rather large room with windows on three walls and nice views from the third floor of The Congressional Country Club in Bethesda, Maryland, just a few miles northwest of downtown Washington, D.C. A group of four distinguished-looking but not-so-quiet gentlemen in their forties are enjoying themselves sitting at a round table, chatting and occasionally laughing. The table is full of tasty looking snacks with drinks being refilled by a couple of attendants. There is no single reason for the gentlemen to behave or feel any differently even though the times are all but jolly – it is Saturday, May the 29th, 1943 and the United States is in full preparation for another bloody episode in the war – the invasion of Sicily, Italy. The four men all belong to the Special Operations' Maritime Unit of the Office of Strategic Services, OSS (predecessor of CIA), and enjoy the benefits of a more than healthy budget secured by their Big Chief, Brigadier General William ("Wild Bill") Donovan, the head of OSS. While doing so, they are waiting for their boss, Dr. James Wallace, eager to learn from him why this impromptu working lunch has been arranged.

The main door to the room finally opens which causes a welcome breeze and the trembling of long curtains that frame large open windows. Dr. Wallace (it must be him since all the men quickly jump from their chairs) showcases his wide unapologetic smile (he is almost an hour late) while approaching the table:

"Gentlemen, I am a bit late because Bill wanted me to check one last time about this mission."

The men all nod and smile back, still not having a slightest clue what the mission is all about.

Twenty five minutes into the official part of their meeting, the buffet lunch is brought in and all the men, including Dr. Wallace, stand up to

14

stretch their legs and informally show their amusement with the affair by shaking their heads and repeating to each other: "Those crazy Limeys…", "They must be kidding us…", "Common!" and similar soundbites.

After filling their plates full of goodies courtesy of Wild Bill, and attendants gone, the men sit back at the round table and the expression on Dr. Wallace changes to one of serious concentration:

"Gentlemen, now that you know why we are here, let's get down to business and figure out if there were any fatal flaws in what you heard from me."

For those of us who still are puzzled with the scene, an explanation is in order before we can fully understand their business. Other than belonging to this fancy part of OSS, the men share more than just a few additional things in common. They all come from wealthy New England families, are raised in a traditional way (one may perhaps use the term conservative), have something to do with seas and oceans including enjoying their own family sailing yachts when feeling like doing so, are not afraid to speak their minds no matter what the company or the subject of a conversation are, and they all are alumni of Ivy League schools except for Dr. Wallace who is a graduate of MIT. Combined, they know just enough about weather patterns in the Atlantic, boats in general, the state of European affairs, communications, mathematics, physiology, psychology, and a few other "logy" words. For these and other reasons, they will now have the pleasure of tearing apart this crazy plan proposed by one Larry Neal, a British MI6 liaison to their London OSS office. That of course includes the very name of the affair: *Mission Capri*.

Following are some very brief notes on a few more interesting topics and the conclusions of the group's lively but systematic deliberations. Also, in the interest of complete transparency and to avoid any misinterpretations about the graduates of Ivy League schools, here are the names of four gentlemen deliberating with Dr. Wallace: Benjamin Forster, natural scientist of Dartmouth; Nicholas Ballard, oceanographer and medical doctor of Yale; Joshua Hyde, social scientist and psychologist of Princeton; and David Price, mathematician from Harvard.

The easiest thing agreed upon by all the men discussing the top-secret mission, was the selection of a sailing boat. As far as they were concerned, Dr. Wallace did not even need to elaborate much longer after stating it was an Alden schooner, but he did it anyway:

"I went to Boston to ask my former professor at MIT's Pratt School for advice and he directed me to go and talk with Alden downtown, and he provided me with the address."

It also turned out that the professor confided to Dr. Wallace how he was now occupied with other interests and rather unenthusiastic about keeping up with the advances in naval architecture, but was nevertheless very frank about Alden:

"The fellow is the best there is. Certainly, better than I ever was, but don't spread this around too much…"

Alden received Dr. Wallace very nicely and, after learning the mission's basics, immediately recommended the boat with an interesting name *Blackbird*. At the same time, he committed to giving her a full inspection himself before the trip.

The next item on the meeting's agenda was not up for much of a discussion because of the destination of the Atlantic crossing – Sweden. The Great Circle route along the coast of Maine with stops in Nova Scotia and Newfoundland therefore had to be taken by default. Everyone was fully aware of the dangers involved. The route is a very rough journey, often stormy and foggy, with deep depressions, cool weather, and plenty of icebergs floating around. The timing was, however, pretty good. Sailors generally do the route starting at the end of April through early June to avoid hurricane season. Because of the logistics involved, however, the departure date could not be set earlier than June 9th which increased the sailing hazard – later in the season the weather is warmer, and icebergs melt and break away more often. Once off Newfoundland and into the Atlantic, the plan was to stay just far enough south to avoid the Gulf Stream which creates unexpected eddies and meanders, and where thunderstorms can quickly develop without any warning due to temperature contrasts. The departing port was the *Blackbird's* own – Essex Yacht Club in Connecticut, up the Connecticut River from Long Island Sound.

When Dr. Wallace started to explain the question of the radio to be used on board, all four men kept their interest in for a while. They were quite puzzled when Dr. Wallace, uncharacteristically, scolded a "bloody Limey" who made jokes about American short-wave radios and told him one will have to be flown over from England for the mission. So, Dr. Wallace went to MIT again because of that and asked Alfred Loomis, the head of the Radiation Lab, is there anything they can do about this humiliating situation with the damn radios. Loomis, a bit puzzled because his focus was on radars, simply said that the radio they developed at MIT is the best, years ahead of any radio out there, and that he was not even aware of some problematic issues because British were our allies. However, when Dr. Wallace turned to David (the mathematician from Harvard) and started elaborating on what he learned in MIT's Building 4 where Loomis sent him to check out the radio, the remaining men quickly turned their interest to a bottle of 16-year old Scotch malt brought to the table courtesy of the very healthy budget secured by the Big Chief.

"David, you remember that lecture we attended together where Henry tried to explain the Wiener's solution with class L2 functions contained in Theorem XII of Fourier transforms in the complex domain? Well, it turned out these two kids at MIT, to whom Loomis sent me, came up with a fantastic transfer function filter. They then used their solution and actually built both the transmitter and the receiver with independently scrambled-jammed signals with final frequencies no one on Earth can even detect, except for the two of them. They threw in a brand new high-capacity, self-contained, miniature lumped generator-transformer-amplifier unit with power provided by a small hydraulic turbine that can be mounted underwater on just about any moving object. Incredible! They got quite excited when I told them I could use their invention on a sailing boat crossing the Atlantic: "That is exactly what we need to fine-tune the filter! No rumbling of a motor, stray frequencies, no induced white noise, just the wind!" By the way, at the time I still did not know that the mission headquarters would be at MIT itself."

After finishing the sentence, Dr. Wallace notices the object of the undivided attention of the other men and scolds them:

17

"Gentlemen, I thought you would be much more interested in the subject! This stuff they are doing at MIT is what is winning us the war. Our mission may help the scientists a great deal. The boys will connect their equipment remotely to LORAN and achieve the spatial accuracy of less than 1 inch. I mean, do you folks get that?!"

A reply comes from Joshua (social scientist and psychologist of Princeton) who is well versed in human nature, knows how to quickly diffuse tension by momentarily switching the subject of conversation, and knows how to do that in a sly way so no one gets offended:

"Dr. Wallace, I can speak for others when I assure you that we all are well aware of the magnitude of this incredible mission, so please let us recoup and comb through any remaining possible flaws. But before we do that, please taste this outstanding malt – it is even more incredible than the mission."

Dr. Wallace looks at slightly mocking expressions on the gentlemen's faces, gets it, and says through a smile:

"What the hell, you are right!"

For those of us who could not possibly know what LORAN stands for, here it is: Long Range Navigation, or a hyperbolic radio navigation system developed at MIT's Radiation Lab and first used in WWII for ship convoys crossing the Atlantic. The addition to the system, conceived and built by the two postdoctoral students from MIT, remained a secret until now. But, more on the incredible details a bit later. For now, I will just uncover the identities of the two MIT students – Edvard Neumman and Svetoslav Belov.

The next item that came up at the meeting was the name of the mission. Joshua (social scientist and psychologist of Princeton) was again wondering why "Capri" when the boat was clearly supposed to be Swedish:

"Not consistent, suspicious, everyone on the Mediterranean knows where the island of Capri is, especially the Italians!"

The gentlemen all shared the same bewilderment with the choice of the name, but they could not do much about it according to Dr. Wallace. He more than once asked the same question of Larry Neal, who apparently came up with the name. The last time Dr. Wallace asked the same question, he experienced something close to wrath from the

"Limey", who was otherwise very polite in every sense. This time around, quite aggravated, the Limey reiterated that the name was written in stone:

"That is the name, period! There is nothing in the World that could change it!"

And then mumbled something about this very wealthy Swedish industrial magnate who owned an incredible villa on Capri and was well connected with various equally wealthy Italians, owners of equally incredible villas on the beautiful island of Capri. To end this rather fruitless discussion, Joshua almost yelled: "To hell with damned Capri and the Limeys, and…." at which point he managed to compose himself and then empty the bottle of malt into his own glass, quickly grabbing another bottle (courtesy of Wild Bill) to serve his mates as he was a well-mannered gentleman.

Now, in defense of the esteemed Mr. Larry Neal, one must understand his reasoning: the schooner *Capri,* after sailing from Sweden, will spend some time on the island of Capri before refueling and sailing to the Yugoslav Adriatic. To his Italian friends, the wealthy Swedish industrial magnate will proudly parade his brand-new schooner that was sailed from Sweden by his nephew and the nephew's wife. By doing so, he will establish even more companionship with the Italians who will greatly appreciate the name of the beautiful boat while sailing on her a little bit, for fun. I personally don't see anything wrong with this reasoning, but then what do I know about social sciences, psychology, and such?

The sun was already low on the horizon when the five gentlemen concluded their deliberations giving the final approval for the mission. All in very good spirits, for one reason or another, they were more than ready to go downstairs to the grand ballroom to a welcome party for new staff of OSS. Then out of the blue Mr. Benjamin Forster, natural scientist of Dartmouth, triumphantly raised his hand and exclaimed:

"The fatal error – there is no one to sail the boat!"

Except for Dr. Wallace, the remaining gentlemen all widely nod with the approval, grinning and not quite stable on their legs as a result. Dr. Wallace, grinning even more, has an exclamation of his own:

"Gentlemen, I took care of that! I will elaborate downstairs."

Benjamin (a bachelor), not entirely satisfied with the answer but eager to join the company of new staff (some of which were nice-looking young ladies), fires back:

"Better tell that Limey the woman must be young, pretty, and certainly blonde, otherwise the mission will be sunk!"

This stirs up new and quite passionate deliberations, and no one listens to Dr. Wallace who tries to infuse some sense into the situation by repeating that the Swedish crew is none of their business and the two Americans who will sail the boat to Sweden are top notch. Nevertheless, the jolly men wholeheartedly agree with Benjamin who keeps repeating his warning and then expands on it, using somewhat disconnected train of thoughts courtesy of the Scotch malt:

"You know, pretty...the Italians...if something goes wrong...she will take care of it...everyone likes pretty blondes...young...the Italians..."

Once at the welcome party for the new OSS staff, and in a very good mood, all the men, except Dr. Wallace, quickly forgot Mission Capri as they looked around, mingled with young friendly folks, and enjoyed various drinks and other delicacies courtesy of Wild Bill. As far as they were concerned, it was now in someone else's hands.

Chapter 4

Schooner

John Gale Alden, a naval architect from Boston, is regarded by many as the greatest boat designer who ever lived. Sailing boats designed by Alden, including those he personally owned, won all major races in the United States, including multiple wins at the most prestigious race of all – the Bermuda Race.

Sailing boats with two masts were, until early 1930s, the most popular type of yachts among wealthy Americans with a surplus of money. Gradually, they were displaced by sailing boats with one mast or *sloops*. *Blackbird* is a typical *schooner*, a sailing boat with two masts of which the main, taller one, is placed closer to the stern as opposed to a *ketch* where the shorter mast (mizzen) is closer to the stern. The helm is behind the rear mast in both cases. A *yawl*, another popular two-mast boat, is similar to a *ketch* except that the mizzen is much shorter and very close to the stern, with the helm between the two masts. Racing yawls became more popular than schooners – they were easier to handle by a small crew and performed equally well on all points of sail.

In 1930, at the time when *Blackbird* was built in the Goudy & Stevens Shipyard in East Boothbay, Maine, she had an official designation of *Auxiliary Center-Board Schooner, 43 feet 3 inches long, design No. 309Q*. Alden brought his unique skill to perfection and was ahead of everyone else in solving the many mysteries of successful sailing. The 309 was the realization of one of the most important of Alden's goals: that one can sail the schooner alone and still be safe while thoroughly enjoying the whole experience, no matter where in the world one was doing it.

While Alden oversaw the entire design of *Blackbird* and her sister schooners, he also had first-class designers working at his small office.

The schooner's hull and lines were designed by Aage Neilson; Clifford Swain designed the accommodation plan and Carl Alberg her sail plan.

In concert with the schooner's flawless design, the very dense old growth wood used for building it was of the finest possible grade, harvested from untouched ancient forests. *Blackbird's* scantlings and timbers are oak, while the planking is made of long leaf yellow pine and oak butt blocks. Long leaf pine is the longest lasting planking wood ever used in boat construction, as it has excellent strength properties and is highly worm resistant. The decks are of painted white pine and the interior is of mahogany. The most impressive parts of the boat, the masts and booms, were made of Oregon pine supplied by the famous Oregon-American Lumber Company in Vernonia, Oregon, which operated from 1922 to 1957. Alden personally selected an old growth tree grove of pine within the company's landholdings and recommended it for building full masts of his boats. The original sails were made by McClellan, of Egyptian cotton duck.

Alden had moments of movie fame – his schooner *Vennona II*, commissioned in 1925 by Elmer J. Bliss and built in 1926 in Wiscasset, Maine by the Pendleton Brothers Shipyard, made her movie debut in 1940 in *The Philadelphia Story* as the *True Love*, where she appeared as miniature model of herself.

Things seem quite complicated in the movie. Tracy (Katherine Hepburn) has three men courting her and she cannot make up her mind to whom she should give her attention. They are her charming ex-husband Dexter (Cary Grant), designer of sailing yachts; her well-mannered, aspiring fiancée George (John Howard); and her present love Mike (James Stewart). Dexter asks Tracy for an acknowledgment of his wedding present (Tracy is just about to be married to George). Tracy learns that Dexter might sell the boat which two of them enjoyed tremendously when they were married. Tracy and Dexter go on to create one of the most famous sayings in modern sailing circles:

Tracy: It was beautiful - and sweet, Dex.
Dexter: Yes, yes. She was quite a boat, the True Love, *wasn't she?*
Tracy: Was, and is.
Dexter: My, she was yar.

Tracy: She was yar alright. I wasn't, was I?

Dexter: Not very. Oh, you were good at the bright work, though.

Tracy: I made her shine. Where is she now?

Dexter: I'm gonna sell it to Ruth Watrous.

Tracy: You're gonna sell the True Love, *for money?*

Dexter: Sure...Oh well, what's it matter? When you're through with a boat, you're through. Besides, it was only comfortable for two people. Unless you want her.

Tracy: No, no I don't want her.

Dexter: Well, I'm designing another one anyway, along more practical lines.

Tracy: What'll you call her?

Dexter: I thought the True Love II. *What do you think?*

Tracy: Dexter, if you call any boat that, I promise you I'll blow you and it out of the water. I'll tell you what you can call her if you like...in fond remembrance of me, the Easy Virtue.

Dexter: Shut up, Red! I can't have you thinking things like that about yourself.

Tracy: Well, what am I supposed to think when I - Oh I don't know. I don't know anything any more.

Dexter: That sounds very hopeful, Red. That sounds just fine.

Sixteen years later, in 1956, *True Love*, in her life-size glory, appeared in the sequel, *High Society*, starring Grace Kelly, Bing Crosby and Frank Sinatra, and featuring Louis Armstrong and his band. In a famous scene Bing Crosby serenades Grace Kelly with the song "True Love", composed by Cole Porter, while onboard *True Love*.

While writing these lines I often thought how some unnecessary effort during my research could have been avoided or vague tracks should not have been followed ("after the battle all generals are clever."). However, I don't regret even a tiny bit the effort I put into uncovering a small little story, probably of not much importance to anyone, about a model of the schooner in the movie *High Society* (although one can never be sure if something was just pure coincidence or maybe some other forces were at play.)

Dick (Richard) Pefferle of Sidney, Ohio was the worker-bee set decorator for *High Society*, given full trust and autonomy by the chief set designer, eight-time Oscar winning Edwin Willis. Both worked under the art direction of Cedric Gibbons who won 11 Oscars and was also art director for *The Philadelphia Story*. Gibbons decided that a new model of the sailing boat should be used for the famous pool scene with Grace Kelly instead of the model from the original movie. Dick Pefferle, a perfectionist, having learned of Alden, started looking for a model of a real Alden sailing boat hoping to avoid building one, but with no success. Starting to panic as the shooting schedule tightened, he stumbled upon a beautiful model at a party given by Frank Harris, a distinguished member of the original California Yacht Club. To Dick's enormous surprise, he learned that the model was made in Alden's shop and sent to Harris in 1930, to show how the actual boat Harris wanted to build would look. Harris immediately agreed to lend the model for the movie, which was not a hard decision at all given the role Grace Kelly had in the whole thing. A minor problem was easily solved in the MGM workshop – the ketch was quickly converted into a schooner by switching the masts. The 309R was never built but was nevertheless immortalized in the hands of the beautiful actress-princess.

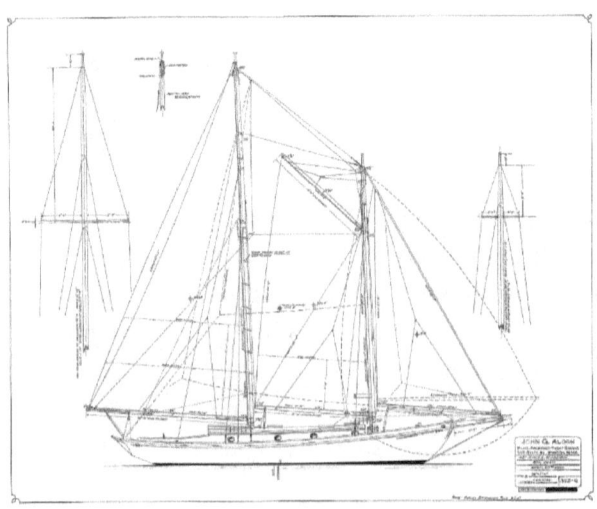

Original sail design for *Blackbird* by Carl Alberg, John G. Alden Company, April 23, 1930.

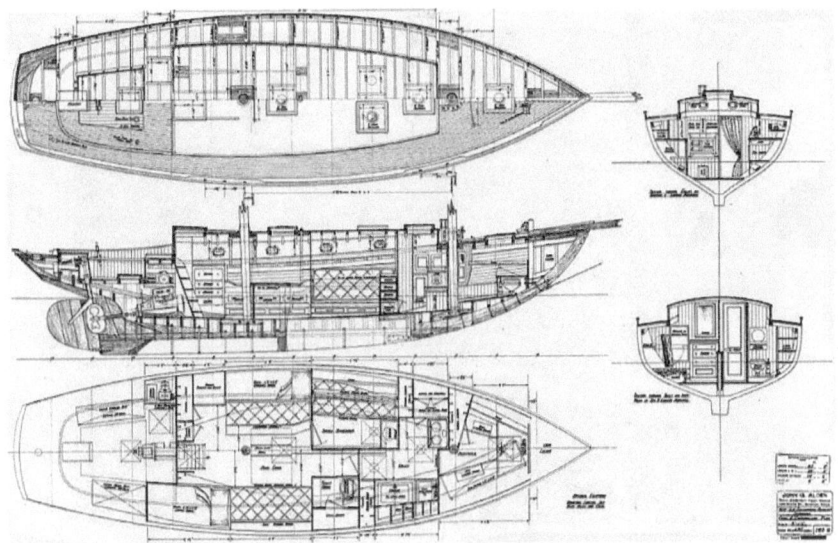

Blackbird: Alden Design 309Q. Courtesy of Hart Nautical Collections, MIT, Cambridge, Massachusetts.

John Gale Alden, naval architect from Boston, chief designer of schooner *Blackbird*. Courtesy of Hart Nautical Collections, MIT, Cambridge, Massachusetts.

Katherine Hepburn in the movie Philadelphia Story with a model of schooner *True Love*. Screenshot Copyright ©1940 MGM.

Grace Kelly in the movie High Society with a model of Alden sailing boat. Screenshot Copyright ©1956 MGM.

Chapter 5

Ocean Race

One of the first clues that would help solve the puzzle and win the bet literally tripped me. I was rushing to obey an order from Peter regarding some stupid rope, when I stumbled on a wooden block on *Blackbird*'s rear deck and fell fully stretched, still somehow managing not to fall overboard. Ashamed, and while still lying on the deck, I angrily looked at the hostile object from up close and noticed a detail on it that immediately caught my attention.

Later that evening, after a delicious lobster meal, Peter showed us an amateur film which former owners of *Blackbird* took a very long time ago, in 1939. In one short scene a gorgeous yawl briefly passes across the screen. Then for about four or five seconds, the camera focuses on a flag at the top of its mizzen mast. As the wind lashed the flag, the camera lingered long enough so that one could recognize the symbol on the flag: it was a swastika. Peter saw my surprise and explained:

"That is the famous *Nordwind* after arriving from Europe to compete with our boats in the *New London–Annapolis Ocean Race*."

This prompted me to mention a puzzling detail on the *Blackbird's* hostile object, a block, that tripped me – a German iron cross. I asked Peter for its origin. Apparently, Peter never paid any attention to it. Intrigued, he immediately brought up the name of *Nordwind's* designer and, over the next couple of weeks, helped my investigation by providing every document about *Blackbird* he had, as well as advice how to proceed including phone numbers of people that may be able to help with certain information. As a result, we solved the mystery of the German cross relatively quickly and, along the way, inseparably connected the two boats.

Heinrich (Henry) Gruber, *Nordwind's* designer, learned his craft in America during the golden age of yacht design, the 1920s and 30s, and returned to Germany in 1935 to start his own business. From the beginning of his career, Gruber admired Alden but never succeeded in working for him despite multiple attempts. He was not a Nazi supporter and because of his American experience was always suspect in Germany but was nevertheless highly respected due to his exceptional talent and hard work. This respect was partly due to unwavering support from Admiral Dönitz, the future commander-in-chief of the German Navy.

Perhaps the most important project accomplished by Gruber was the design and building of two Bermuda yawls for the German Navy with which the Nazis wanted to prove their engineering and other superiority. According to the plan, *Nordwind* and its sister boat *Ostwind* were to compete in all major international races and spread the glory of Third Reich. Gruber decided that the first such race should be in the United States, the country where he learned naval design and from which he wanted the final recognition. Thus, soon after its completion in the Burmester's Bremen shipyard, *Nordwind* crossed the Atlantic in June 1939 and sailed to New England where it was going to compete in the prestigious 465-mile long ocean race between New London, Connecticut and Annapolis, Maryland.

At a reception before the race Gruber met *Blackbird's* owners and, after learning who designed their schooner, he expressed a wish to have a tour of the boat. The friendly owners granted Gruber's wish and, in addition, invited him for a short sail the following morning. To Gruber's delight, they also introduced him to his hero Alden who would not miss the race by any chance, as he had several boats he personally designed in it.

The next day, while touring and sailing on *Blackbird*, Henry Gruber could not hide his admiration for the boat's craftsmanship whereas the *Nordwind's* Nazi skipper Hans Schmelz, who joined Gruber, displayed arrogance and other hints of his unpleasant nature. Despite Hans's wild objections (in barking German), Henry Gruber gives the *Blackbird's* owners a present – a wooden block with the German iron cross. The block is apparently a unique piece of equipment approved by Admiral

Karl Dönitz to be used as gear exclusively on *Nordwind* and her sister boat *Ostwind*.

After returning from the short sailing tour, Gruber abruptly withdraws *Nordwind* from the race to the complete astonishment of the German crew and the enraged Hans who does not stop barking until Gruber addresses him with a firm raised voice:

"Shut up, you are getting on my nerves! I cannot risk and lose my first race. Don't you see that incredible schooner?!"

Gruber himself is bewildered the following morning after all the excitement with the start of the race is over, and seeing *Blackbird* anchored and cheerfully rocking on playful waves, gloriously illuminated by the sun as the last boats disappear from sight. Later that day Gruber learns that *Blackbird's* owners never intended to be in the race and just wanted to have fun with friends and family. After hearing the explanation, Gruber slowly turns his head towards the horizon and his eyes remain anchored to it, while everyone present is silent, including Hans, for what seems an eternity.

For those curious as to which boat won the New London – Annapolis ocean race held on June 24-27, 1939: it was the full keel yawl *Estrella* designed by Alden.

After returning to Europe from the United Sates, in August 1939 *Nordwind* won her first race, the famous *Fastnet* organized by the Royal Ocean Racing Club of the United Kingdom. She set a speed record that held for the next 24 years. The beautiful yawl is still sailing today.

Nordwind filmed by an amateur on June 24, 1939 before start of the New London – Annapolis Ocean Race.

The block on the restored *Blackbird*, given as a present to the schooner's owners by Henry Gruber on June 23, 1939 in New London.

Chapter 6

Preparations

It is Sunday, May 30, 1943. Dr. Wallace, still suffering from a hangover from the previous evening's welcome party for the new OSS staff, and after gulping three cups of strong black coffee, walks to his study and makes a phone call to the Boston office of OSS. This call starts a series of tasks which, we can freely say, were flawlessly executed. A carefully chosen special agent, with a friendly and gentle demeanor, an incredibly honest smile and extraordinarily polite manners, that very day visits the *Blackbird's* owners who did not know anything about the secret mission. After a very long persuasion, which awakened the strongest patriotic feelings in the owners, the secret agent secures their agreement to lend *Blackbird* for the mission. At the same time, another agent manages to locate Alden in Boothbay Harbor, Maine where the famous naval architect was enjoying the weekend sailing with family and friends on one of his own boats. The agent informs Alden that he was expected to show up the next morning, at 9 o'clock sharp, in the town's shipyard where he will receive further instructions.

Meanwhile, on Monday morning, May 31st, immediately upon their arrival to Building No. 4 at MIT, Edvard Neumman and Svetoslav Belov were, without any explanation, escorted to Loomis' office where, frightened, they waited for him. The same day, at four o'clock in the afternoon London time, Dr. Wallace informs Larry Neal that *Mission Capri* has been approved. After doing so, he could not resist telling Larry that it was unnecessary to send a short-wave radio from England because "We have the best navigation instrument ever built, which, at the same time, serves as a multifrequency radio, with a crystal-clear sound, incomparably better than anything you have over there."

Dr. Wallace had a very good reason to annoy Larry about the radio. The two postdoctoral students from MIT, as they were demonstrating their invention to Dr. Wallace few weeks ago, tuned into a direct radio broadcast of the Vienna Philharmonic performance of the Mahler Symphony No. 2. What he heard and the exhilaration he felt would remain etched in his memory forever.

After his first inspection of *Blackbird* and short sail on the bay, the perfectionist Alden is startled with the revelation that something is not quite right with the schooner. He immediately demands an explanation from the chief engineer of the shipyard, with whom he collaborated for many years on building excellent sailing boats. The seasoned master builder could only shrug his shoulders and reply that the schooner's repair, after the Great Hurricane of New England damaged it seriously in September of 1938, probably was not perfect, noting that he was not in charge of the repair anyway. Conquering the rage that consumed him (Alden loved all sailing boats he designed like his own children), the famous naval architect issues simple but firm order, using somewhat unusual language for him:

"Please replace everything according to the original design, down to the smallest detail, and use the best possible materials. If there is an obstacle, call this number and ask for Dr. Wallace. I will be back in three days and if everything is not finished by then, both you and I will be in such a deep s..t that even God will not be able to help us!"

Exactly at noon, on Thursday, June 3, 1943, a large black Packard, followed by a truck with the sign "MIT Radiation Laboratory", stops at the administrative building of the Goudy and Stevens Shipyard in East Boothbay, Maine. From the Packard step out Dr. Wallace and David Price (mathematician from Harvard), and from the truck Edvard Neumman and Svetoslav Belov. After short gathering, they all enter the building where the receptionist directs them to a small conference room. In the room, at a long table, they see the chief engineer sleeping with his head resting on his arms stretched on the table. Alden quickly glances the faces of the men accompanying him and then loudly clears his throat. This momentarily awakens the chief engineer from a deep sleep. Somewhat dazed and confused, he nevertheless quickly gathers himself and rubs his eyes under which there are enormous bags and apologizes to everyone present. Then, with a deep sigh of relief, he looks the naval architect right into his eyes and slowly says:

"Mr. Alden, everything is finished, early this morning, with God's help."

"Excellent, I expected nothing less. Please make sure these two young gentlemen get all the help they need for installing on *Blackbird* the equipment they brought. Even if something looks strange to you, please do what they ask you to do. Unless, of course, it hurts the structural integrity of the boat. In such a case, please contact me immediately, together with the two of them, so we can resolve any issues without delay. I emphasize that time is of the essence here, it is absolutely critical. The boat must sail out for a trial no later than next Monday, which, I believe, you all know very well."

At that moment, poor Edvard and Svetoslav stare at each other in disbelief because it is the first time they hear anything about the Monday deadline. Not knowing what to say or do, and not in a position to ask for the help of Loomis (who obviously forgot to tell them about the schedule!), they secretly hope it will be possible, somehow, and without any serious consequences, to avoid Dr. Wallace's wrath come Monday. Namely, only two of them know that the critical part of the equipment they are about to install on *Blackbird* is not yet finished and can possibly arrive on Monday at the earliest. Even that required lots of effort, and their personal persuasion skills down south in Atlanta, Georgia, where the most critical link of their invention is being created.

Why Atlanta? Because in this charming capital of the South is Atlantic Steel where one Nicholas J. McMillan, chief of the company's Research Laboratory and graduate of The Georgia Institute of Technology, works. And because Mr. McMillan succeeded, back in 1931, to build a literally unimaginable object, at the request and under the guidance of one Nikola Tesla from New York. And how is it possible for you to learn of this fascinating fact? Well, thanks to me managing to dig out, in the archives kept at the Historic Center of Atlanta, a hand-written short note with the initials "NJM" and stored in Box No. 8 of the Atlantic Steel documents, in which one can read the following:

Received ten thousand dollars in cash from Mr. Tesla for a steel container without openings which I will make from a special new steel alloy using original technology and verbal instructions from Mr. Tesla. For the work on the order I will be using Lab No. 2 in the reinforced concrete building, annex to our new Blast Furnace B, during the next three months. I ordered the metals for the alloy from our regular supplier in New Mexico. Date: December 9, 1930.

For those that may have missed it, it is important to note that the same special steel alloy is being currently used by Mr. McMillan in Atlanta, where he is making long spiral coils and a container similar to the one he made for Tesla in 1931.

The explanation how the two young researchers from MIT came up with the idea in the first place, including the engagement of Mr. McMillan, Chief Research Engineer at the Atlantic Steel Company in the city of Atlanta, the connection between Edvard, Svetoslav, Mr. Tesla, the mysterious object from 1931, and the last critical part of the instrument which will be installed on *Blackbird* in just a few days (hopefully by the Monday deadline), I managed to comprehend only in the fall of 2018, and only after all the incredible events of which you are about to read settled in my head.

It is time to return to Goudy and Stevens shipyard in East Boothbay, Maine, where it is already dawn on Monday, June 7, 1943. Filled with caffeine, poor Edvard and Svetoslav, running out of patience, eagerly wait for a Navy hydroplane that left Boston right before dawn. The precious cargo from Atlanta arrived in Boston on an Air Force plane at 3am and was then urgently transported to the hydroplane which immediately took off. At that point the Navy dispatcher radioed the *Mission Capri* headquarters at MIT and confirmed the departure. In turn, the Headquarters, using a special landline, immediately informed East Boothbay that the cargo is on its way. After hearing the news, the two postdoctoral students are finally able, if just for a moment, to relax a bit.

The incredible weight finally lifts off their shoulders when the hydroplane, at six hours and seventeen minutes in the morning, docks at one of the shipyard's piers and two large wooden containers are carefully unloaded. Approximately three hours later the same black Packard stops by the main shipyard building. From it step out two portly men in their twenties, David Price (mathematician from Harvard), Dr. Wallace and Alden. Seeing the schooner tied at the auxiliary working peer, Dr. Wallace momentarily loses his mind and starts to run towards the boat, cursing loudly (in respect to young readers, I will not disclose his words in their entirety):

"God damn it! Are the two of you normal?! It is not a Christmas tree! It is supposed to be an inconspicuous sailing boat, not drawing any attention whatsoever! You are out of your minds! Immediately take all that crap off her before I go completely crazy and throw you into the fucking (again, a big apology to young readers) sea!"

Now, with all due respect to Dr. Wallace, the beautiful schooner could not possibly be inconspicuous, with or without the things that caused this incredible rage. What was that all about? With the help from the Chief Engineer, who gave instructions to three craftsmen, Edvard and Svetoslav managed, during the previous three hours, to install four densely coiled and intertwined long cables, made of an unknown metal alloy, along the entire lengths of the two masts, and connect them with the equipment already installed in the cabin. Similar cables were also visible along the booms and, if it were not enough, the two postdoctoral MIT students were themselves attaching the last few vertical metal strips that were hanging, a foot apart, from the booms. This array of vertical and horizontal metal cables and strips emitted an unearthly glow that overshadowed everything in the vicinity and afar.

Half an hour after his incredible burst of rage, Dr. Wallace did calm down somewhat, to the great relief of everyone who witnessed this unfortunate episode. It later became apparent that Edvard, well-known for his lucid actions, managed to convince Dr. Wallace of the irreplaceable importance of the installed assembly, but only after agreeing to remove all vertical strips, the condition Dr. Wallace presented as non-negotiable, to the point of severing all collaboration with the two postdoctoral students.

Slightly after one o'clock in the afternoon, the Chief Engineer and Alden declare that the schooner is ready to sail to its home port, which reminds the inspired Dr. Wallace to introduce the two young men to the rest, almost poetically:

"Gentlemen, it is my great honor to introduce to you the crew of our beautiful boat, which they will, safely and with God's help, sail to Europe, across the magnificent Atlantic which lies in front of you! Our fearless Marines and sailors, Mr. Cole and Mr. Masters, are chosen as the best of the best, among thousands of brave patriots which, selflessly, defend our beloved homeland!"

Precisely at 8 o'clock in the morning, on June 9, 1943, after a successful test sail along the coasts of Maine and Connecticut, *Blackbird* leaves her home port, Essex Yacht Club on the Connecticut River, and sails on to her secret mission across the Atlantic, to Sweden, the Mediterranean, and its final destination – the Yugoslav Adriatic.

Photo from the December 1938 issue of the journal Yachting. Damaged *Blackbird* stranded on the Essex Yacht Club dock. Photo taken day after passage of the Great New England Hurricane on September 21, 1938. Recorded peak wave height was 50 ft. at Gloucester, MA.

Chapter 7

American Crew

As we already learned from Dr. Wallace, the American crew will be comprised of two top sailors and brave seamen. Here are a few more details about them that I was able to find. *Blackbird* will be sailed to Sweden by Michael Cole born in 1916 in Paterson, New Jersey, and Steven Masters, born in Flint, Michigan in 1920. Both were recommended by Hollywood actor Sterling Hayden who was born in 1916 in Montclair, New Jersey.

Hayden was addicted to the sea from his childhood. He had such a love and knowledge of sailing that by the time he was 20, he became first mate on the world cruise of the schooner *Yankee*. By the time he was 22, he was awarded his first command, skippering the square rigger *Florence C. Robinson* 7,700 miles from Gloucester, Massachusetts to Tahiti in 1938. This voyage was the fulfillment of Hayden's dream which began when he first heard of the heroic sailing adventures of one William Albert Robinson, known simply and famously as Robbie in sailing circles. He gave Hayden command of the rigger named after his wife, Florence. Robbie's fame began after he purchased a 32-foot 6-inch, 3-year old Alden ketch named *Svaap*, which means "dream" in Sanskrit, for $1,000. He departed New London on June 23, 1928 as an entry in the Bermuda Race of that year. All along he was planning to continue from Bermuda around the world in the smallest yacht ever to attempt the journey. Robbie achieved his dream including stopping in Tahiti and circumnavigating via the Panama and Suez Canals with another crew member. He arrived in New York on September 24, 1931. For this achievement *Svaap* and Robinson received the Blue Water Medal from the Cruising Club of America. The award has been given annually since 1923 "to individuals and man-wife crews from around the world who through outstanding seamanship have exemplified the goals of the club, regardless of their nationality or whether or not they were members of the club."

In 1940, Hayden became a model and later signed a contract with Paramount Pictures in Hollywood, for which he made two movies before enlisting in the Marine Corps under the name John Hamilton. In 1942, Private Hamilton attended boot camp at Paris Island, South Carolina where he met Masters. After the Paris Island boot camp, Masters was sent to Guantanamo, Cuba, and Hayden to Officer Candidate School (OCS) at Quantico, Virginia where he encountered his old friend Cole. There he was selected as one of only three men from a class of three hundred to join the Office of Strategic Services (OSS), the World War II predecessor of CIA. This is how Hayden met Dr. Wallace and later found himself in the position to recommend the two American sailors for the *Blackbird's* secret mission. Even though Hayden received several awards including the Bronze and Silver Star Medals, he maintained his nom de guerre John Hamilton and anonymity throughout the war.

Hayden selected Cole because he knew Cole's qualities first-hand from their prep school days in Dexter, Maine. It also did not hurt that Cole earned honors as the best celestial navigator of the entire 1943 class of the United States Navy Reserve Midshipmen's School in Kings Point, New York, and was celebrated for his extraordinary visual memory. Masters, a Marine, was selected because of his strength, and fitness for any difficult mission coupled with his friendly, easy-going nature, generosity, and great sense of humor – all the qualities needed for a long perilous journey with two people that should not end up hating each other at the end.

After leaving her home port in Connecticut, *Blackbird* with Cole and Masters on board sailed right into a well-established high pressure weather pattern that remained favorable for the duration of her Atlantic crossing. Strong westerlies, topping out at about 45 knots, accompanied by high but uniform, smooth swells, were the main reason for an incredibly fast crossing time, all perfectly in concert with the *Blackbird's* flawless design and construction. Miraculously, according to the testimonies of the sailors' relatives, they did not experience any northerly swell, or a low-pressure trough which are not uncommon in mid-Atlantic and can produce adverse winds. In any case, it is important to mention that, by the order of OSS, Cole and Masters did not keep a sailing log and were not allowed to leave any written record of the time spent on the schooner. Consequently, I reconstructed facts related to their journey based on memories of Cole's son Patrick and Masters' nephew Bob. Over the years, they had overheard conversations by the adults recounting *Blackbird* and the transatlantic trip. They then hesitantly, but kindly, agreed to share these memories with me.

During the crossing, to fight an inevitable boredom but also to do something useful for each other, Cole and Masters maintained a routine which was a combination of already scheduled tasks and those less expected. Notably, Cole made a goal for himself to teach his companion the secrets of navigation by the stars, and then went a step further and, passionately, taught Masters about the culture of American Southwest Indians with which he was completely fascinated. The results of these teachings were sleepless nights, gladly spent together by the two sailors, during which they stargazed imagining themselves in the fascinating buildings of Chaco Canyon and wondering why Anasazi Indians, who worshiped the Orion constellation and claimed they descended to Earth from it, suddenly disappeared without trace.

Masters, already a serious trumpet player and taking the advice of Hayden, brought with him another musical instrument he played well – a banjo! He selected it to teach Cole (who has not shown any such inclination previously) how to play an instrument, knowing very well all the benefits of making music. With surprising enthusiasm, which quickly turned to passion, Cole managed to play decently two tunes by the end of their journey – Jimmie Rodgers' "Mule Skinner Blues" and Leadbelly's "Gallis Pole". Both songs were selected by Masters, a big fan of the blues, from the popular music scores from which he was inseparable. However, he finally did give them to Cole as a present, nonetheless. Masters liked the tunes because of their uplifting quality along with plenty of room for vocal improvisation. Cole also enjoyed the tunes tremendously because his loud voice could overwhelm any chaos produced by his fingers. Moreover, the Mule's "Good Morning Captain" line, which Masters was never tired of hearing, day after day, clearly demonstrated, to all on board, who was in charge!

The two Marines, more often than not, tried to outsmart each other, fighting the monotony. Already one of the first mornings, after his nightshift, Masters descended to the cabin, stood by Cole's bed, and produced the loudest trumpet wakeup call one could possibly imagine. Cole jumped out of bed, hit his head on the ceiling, and started to curse Masters. Then, after seeing Masters laughing his head off, he started laughing himself.

The following morning, roles reversed, Cole terrorized with his banjo by Masters' bed. Masters woke up, turned his head towards Cole, and a big smile spread over his face:

"Excellent, I see you are eager to start the practice. Let's do it!"

These events started a chain of unofficial, unexpected routines to which both sailors looked forward more than to anything else and which, decades later, enormously entertained both Patrick and Bob whenever they talked about it.

According to the files I had access to, the schooner *Blackbird* made landfall in Portrush, on the north coast of Northern Ireland, on Monday, June 29th, soon after midnight. However, it is quite intriguing that Bob's testimony, based on more than one memory of his uncle's claims, states that *Blackbird* crossed the Atlantic in a little less than twelve days thus establishing an unofficial record for a private sailing boat of any kind and for any crossing route. This means that the schooner would have landed in Portrush sometime during June 21st at the latest! Although the Marines did not leave anything in writing, it therefore appears at least seven or eight sailing days of the schooner simply disappeared. At first, I did not pay much attention to this discrepancy. Later however it all became much clearer to me when I connected the dots gathered during the long research of the Alden schooner's past. Together with the dots, I acquired various connected and disconnected knowledge on later lives of the two brave Marines and do not see a reason why not to include some of it here as well.

After several months, in October 1943, Cole and Masters again sailed *Blackbird* across the Atlantic from Gibraltar, but more on that a bit later. Upon the return to the United States, they both joined the Pacific Theater (which is how, for reasons known only to them, the Americans and the British called bloodsheds around the World.) One episode deserves an honorable mention. It took place in Sasebo, the home of the third largest naval base in Japan, in September of 1945. Cole was flown into Sasebo to take command of his supply ship. As they approached Sasebo to land, he looked out the plane windows at the harbor and observed and therefore instantly memorized the layout of the harbor including where various anchored ships and landmarks were. Shortly after the landing and Cole taking command of the ship, a typhoon hit and ships were dragging anchor, running aground, and running into each other in the harbor. Cole was able to keep his ship from doing either thanks to his photographic memory of where various ships should be, where the land reference points were, and where deeper water was, all in relation to his ship. It was a huge storm and all hell was breaking loose. By starting the engine and trying to hold anchor, and then navigating to avoid hitting other ships or run aground, Cole made it through to a complete amazement of his crew and everyone else watching.

After the war, Cole became a respected lawyer in New Jersey and never pursued his short-lived banjo career but, without knowing it, he musically influenced his son Patrick who currently owns 37 guitars including the most precious one, an original *Fender Stratocaster*, and in his free time plays blues at various gigs in bars in and around Washington, D.C.

After delisting from the Marines, Masters had a professional career as a car salesman in Flint, Michigan where he also conducted a jazz big band on Friday nights and continued to play trumpet for pleasure at various gigs whenever possible. His nephew, Raymond Bob Masters, is an accomplished jazz trumpet player living in Ohio, and is in possession of several fine instruments including an *Olds Cornet* which he inherited from his uncle Steven.

Due to the *Blackbird's* voyage and information provided upon completion of her mission, Hayden worked hard on persuading his OSS supervisors and eventually succeeded in getting an assignment to the Adriatic Theater for himself in the winter of 1943-44. Because of his admirable sailing experience and Marine training, Hayden was given a command of a flotilla of sailing boats and brigs that shipped supplies from Monopoli, Italy to the Yugoslav Adriatic islands through the

German blockade in the Adriatic Sea. On the Yugoslav side of the Adriatic, Hayden earned great admiration from Tito's partisans and even received a Yugoslav commendation. For his extraordinary overall service in World War II, Hayden was awarded several times including Bronze and Silver Star Medals. The official narrative for the Silver Star reads:

> *By direction of the President, under the provisions of Army Regulations 600-45, as amended, the Silver Star was awarded by the Theater Commander to the officer named below: JOHN HAMILTON, 022085, Captain, United States Marine Corps Reserve, for gallantry in action in the Mediterranean Theater of Operations from 24 December 1943 to 2 January 1944. Captain Hamilton displayed great courage in making hazardous sea voyages in enemy infested waters, and reconnaissance through enemy held areas. His conduct reflected great credit upon himself and the United States Army Forces.*

After leaving active duty at the end of 1945, Hayden returned to Hollywood and went on to act in many memorable movies including the title character in the 1954 Nicholas Ray's cult film *Johnny Guitar*, and the role of Brigadier General Jack D. Ripper in the 1964 Stanley Kubrick's masterpiece *Dr. Strangelove or: How I Learned to Stop Worrying and Love the Bomb.*

Sterling Hayden as Brigadier General Jack D. Ripper at the Air Force Base Burpelson in Dr. Strangelove or: How I Learned to Stop Worrying and Love the Bomb directed by Stanley Kubrick. ©1964 Columbia Pictures.

Michael Cole in 1943. Courtesy of the family.

Pacific, 1944; Steven Masters on a photo produced by the War Department
for propaganda purposes. Courtesy of the family.

Chapter 8

Scandinavian Crew

Sven and Tove met in 1941 at the now famous Round Gotland race in Sweden, where they also met 25-year old Harry Hallberg. All three despised Nazis, which is one more reason they enjoyed each other's company while sharing dreams of sailing to exotic distant lands. To his new friends Harry revealed he was doing everything in his power, and despite doubts by many, to start building sailing boats in his own shipyard which he planned to open as soon as possible. The three new friends were that year members of different crews but, both before and after the race, spent all their free time together in the nice little port town Sandham on the Baltic Sea.

The Round Gotland Race is an offshore sailing race in the Baltic Sea established in 1937 by the Royal Swedish Yacht Club. The two-day regatta has become the most prestigious race in Scandinavia and the winning trophy one of the most coveted in Europe. The race takes place during June-July each year with the start and finish lines in Sandhamn on the outskirts of the Stockholm archipelago (the last several years the start took place in Stockholm). The entire race is some 350 nautical miles, around Gotland, the largest and most distant Swedish island.

Sven was born, grew up, and finished school in Stockholm after which he started working for the shipping company *Wallenius*, with the goal of one day becoming captain of an ocean liner. As his parents did not own a sailing boat, he spent all his free time, either on or around sailing boats of his parents' friends, accepting any work or assignment that came with it. Because of his utmost dedication to boats and sailing, Sven quickly became the most sought-after crew member in all possible sailing races, which were plentiful on the magnificent Stockholm Archipelago.

Tove came to Sweden from the small Norwegian town Malm on the fjord with the same name because she could not live under the German occupation anymore. She learned how to sail from her father, chief engineer at a mine established in 1906 by the *Fosdalens Bergverk* mining company. The Malm's iron ore mine, mercilessly ran by the Germans, quickly became the deepest in Europe at the time because all the ore was frantically shipped to Germany and quickly consumed for building tanks. Tove simply could not stand what the Germans did to her country and her beloved town. The daily humiliation of her father by the Germans was the last straw.

At the parting with her sad parents, who loved their only child more than anything in the world, Tove received a Viking knife from her father, which will, according to his words full of an inexplicable conviction, protect her from any misfortune and bring her luck when needed the most. The father found the knife, together with two geologists, on a prospecting trip for new iron ore deposits. The geologists, without any hesitation, generously relinquished the knife to the chief engineer who was greatly respected and loved by all miners and workers of the company.

Tove crossed to Sweden in January 1942, on skis and fighting brutal cold. Completely exhausted, with hardly any strength left in her body, she arrived at small Swedish town of Kolåsen two days after leaving Levanger, a Norwegian town on the opposite side of the Malm fjord where her father drove her with a sinking feeling in his heart. Recovering from the truly heroic winter passage of the unforgiving mountain, Tove spent two weeks with her family's Swedish friends before leaving for Sandham on the Baltic coast. There she immediately found work in the prestigious *Hotel Seglar*, first as a housekeeper and soon after, thanks to her devotion, work ethic, charm, and an extraordinary astuteness, as the hostess of the hotel's Yachting Club. In the spring of that same year she caught the attention of a certain Erik Johansen, a wealthy industrial magnate from Stockholm. He kept his magnificent sailing boat in Sandham and came every weekend to the hotel in preparation for the Gotland race. Thanks to favorable circumstances, Tove found herself at the right place and at the right moment to give the magnate a helping hand with the boat and then on a short sailing trip to which he unexpectedly invited her, not knowing exactly why. Seeing Tove in action, Johansen offered her a place on his crew for the Gotland race. Tove, more than enthusiastically, accepted the offer and, overjoyed, hugged and kissed the bewildered magnate who, in the process, flushed quite a bit.

The last weekend in May Erik was joined by a guest from England, one Larry Neal, also a big fan of sailing, who quickly befriended Tove and, for the entire time of his short stay sought any excuse to be with her.

Thus, thanks to unforeseen circumstances, but also some undoubtedly very deliberate planning, Tove, Sven and Harry found themselves together again at the end of June 1943, this time in a little port town of Kungsviken on the Island of Orust. There, they were impatiently waiting for the arrival of a mysterious sailing boat from America. The boat will be inspected by Harry and, if needed, repaired in a small shipyard he just opened with the vision to build small, fast and strong sailing boats affordable for the many and not just the rich. Tove and Sven will board the boat and take her to the Mediterranean and the exotic Yugoslav Adriatic, on a spy mission which would, even if only a bit, contribute to the fight against Nazi evil.

Preparing for the mission and talking with their Swedish sailing friends, the young Scandinavians tried to find out everything they could about the sailing conditions in the Mediterranean and the Adriatic, where they have never been before, and anything else that could help them during the dangerous trip. However, while various details about sailing along the coasts of Italy and interactions with the natives where readily available, the situation with the Yugoslav Adriatic was very different. Second-hand information they were able to obtain could be summarized in a few general, mainly useless phrases: fascinating coast and the islands, unpredictable weather even in summer, surprisingly friendly and warm inhabitants, strange, completely incomprehensible language, divine food, and wine, wine, wine!

Blackbird, under full sail, enters the Kungsviken Bay on Thursday, July 1, 1943 and docks at the shipyard. There, Harry, Tove and Sven are waiting eagerly to welcome her after being informed by radio about the time of her approximate arrival. As the Marines slowly turn the boat around to dock, Tove sees the schooner's name and starts clapping her hands with joy, jumping like a little girl:

"My favorite bird! The most beautiful song! I love it, I love it – *Svarttrost*!!!"

At dawn the following morning Tove jumps out of bed and runs to see *Blackbird* at the port, now in the light of a beautiful day. There, Harry's Chief Carpenter Frode is just about to wrap up his painting job, cleaning the brushes and putting them in a wooden box. Tove looks in disbelief at the name of the boat on the stern – *Capri*, and cries: "Frode, why did you do that?" The Chief Carpenter replies he was told to do so by Harry and have it ready by the morning so the boat can be taken out for a sail. And he even had to use a fan to dry the black paint he used to cover the old name and the rest of the boat's stern before he can paint the damn *Capri* (Frode was not happy due to the little sleep he had).

Tove, putting on the most innocent, charming smile she could manufacture, says to him:

"Dear, dear Frode, please write *Svarttrost* because that is what her name is."

Frode momentarily loses any remaining patience and almost explodes:

"Young lady, I don't even know what *Svarttrost* means and, in any case, you may discuss it with Harry."

Tove stomps her foot in anger, turns around and starts back to the house, half walking and half running, and talking to herself in a rather unpleasant way, just loud enough for Frode to hear it but not quite realizing what was said. As a clarification to this unfortunate episode, one needs to understand that Tove wanted the schooner's name to be changed to Norwegian and also an old Scandinavian word for *blackbird* (*svarttrost*) which is why poor Frode did not even know what was that all about since in Sweden the word somehow became *koltrast* long, long time ago.

Later that morning, after Harry thoroughly inspects the schooner and gives the green light, Sven, Tove, Masters and Cole board the boat so the new crew can get familiar with her while sailing on the bay under the guidance from the old crew – the friendly Marines Masters and Cole. Tove and Sven quickly take things into their own hands, becoming more and more impressed with the *Blackbird's* extraordinary characteristics with every passing minute. Left with nothing else to do, Masters and Cole join Harry at the bow and all three start to leisurely enjoy the skills of the new crew and the whole experience. At some point, Tove kindly invites Harry to sit next to her at the helm as she has something important to ask. Harry obeys with a wide smile. The conversation that follows could be described, by a bystander, as very interesting and at moments quite lively judging from various and often funny gestures of the two friends. At the end, Tove's face acquires a very satisfied expression and Harry receives a wide hug and a strong kiss on the cheek. Harry had agreed to change the name of the boat, fully accepting any responsibility for such decision. It was not entirely clear, or later documented, how Tove succeed in persuading Harry to make the decision. What is certain is that the next morning at dawn, *Blackbird* had a new name – *Svarttrost*.

The next sail on *Blackbird* stayed forever in everyone's memory. In a spontaneous celebration of the upcoming American Independence Day Cole and Masters gave a concert on the night of July 3rd. The overall joy and constant contagious laughter received a generous help from two bottles of bourbon Wild Turkey which the Marines, with great effort, somehow managed to hide from each other during the Atlantic crossing. The Cuban cigars that Masters brought from Guantanamo also made a significant contribution to this extraordinary night spent on the beautiful schooner.

After two more days of mission training (of which the first one was more of a recovery from the wild celebration the night before according to some witnesses), *Blackbird* or *Svarttrost*, (whichever you prefer), leaves Sweden not quite early on Tuesday morning, July 6, 1943.

All four crew members sail to Ulg, Northwest Scotland where Masters and Cole disembark on July 8th. All equipment installed by Edvard and Svetoslav back in the United States is removed, except for the radio, to prevent it from falling into wrong hands. Tove and Sven continue on *Blackbird* along the northern route around Ireland, on to the Mediterranean and the final destination – Yugoslav Adriatic.

At the end, a bit more information on the honorable Harry Hallberg. He started his boat building career as a boy of fourteen. By early 1960s he became the first successful Swedish builder of glass-reinforced plastic (GRP) hulls with wooden superstructure. He had an admirable export success, with most of the first hundred P-28 models sold in the United States. He retired in 1972 and his shipyard, which he moved from Kungsviken to Ellös in the mid-60's, was purchased by his rival, German-born Christoph Rassy. As the Hallberg brand was by far the most well-known in Sweden, Rassy decided to rename his company to Hallberg-Rassy. Today, Hallberg-Rassy is one of the most respected yacht design and build companies in the world.

Harry Halberg's original shipyard in Kungsviken, Sweden, where *Blackbird* had its last check before sailing to the Adriatic and where its name was changed to *Svarttrost*. Courtesy of Hallberg-Rassy.

Chapter 9

Sorceresses

In late spring of 2016, being in Europe again and after a business trip to Holland, I took an opportunity to visit a few places from my past. This brought me to Belgrade, the city of my happy childhood and youth, where I will spend some time with my brother's family and my old friends. My brother is an architect and travels frequently between Belgrade, where he lives, and Veliko Gradište where he works a few days a week as the Chief City Planer. After several days in Belgrade, he takes me to Veliko Gradište, a town in northeastern Serbia on the river Danube near the border with Romania, often referred to as "the pearl of Braničevo." He assures me I will love spending the whole morning in the sun and enjoying the Danube, the amenities of the Bijeli Bagrem resort, and sailing and fishing on the Danube's Silver Lake. During the drive in his old Lancia, my brother entertains me with a story I never heard before (although all of us from this part of the world are more than aware of the vampires).

Petar Blagojević, the very first officially recognized vampire, was a peasant from the village of Kiseljevo near Veliko Gradište. He was born at the end of the seventeenth century, and died, if my brother's memory is correct, in 1725. Immediately after Petar's death, people in the area started to suddenly die themselves, including their cattle. Rumors quickly spread that Petar turned into a vampire and started causing all that evil. Furious, the peasants opened his grave and saw that Peter's body had not even begun to rot, not even a bit, and there were traces of fresh blood on his lips. The peasants then took a sharp wooden stake, stabbed it through his heart, and burned the body. To this day, all habitants in the area claim that Petar was indeed the first confirmed vampire.

The story was entertaining and, when I later researched more about the paranormal phenomena for which this part of Serbia is well known, I discovered some documents connected with Petar and the event that made him so infamous. One of the documents is particularly interesting. At the time, this part of Serbia belonged to the Austrian Empire. Petar's case was reported officially by the Austrian Royal Governor of the Gradište Province, Mr. Frombald, in *Wienerisches Diarium*. This was the first official mentioning of "vampirism" in Europe, and since it was translated into several languages, it greatly influenced the beginning of "vampiromania" on the Old Continent:

Ten weeks after the death of subject Petar Blagojević, an inhabitant of the Kisiljevo village in the Ram County, who was buried in accordance to old Serbian customs, it was established that, in the same village, nine more persons, both young and old, died within one week following their twenty-four-hour illness. All of them, at their deathbed, claimed that the above-mentioned Blagojević, who passed away ten weeks earlier, visited them in their sleep, descended on them and chocked them, so they had to succumb to this ghost. The inhabitants of the village were very upset, including because the wife of the late Blagojević claimed how he returned to claim his shoes and then left Kisiljevo to go to another village. Since these people, to whom the inhabitants refer to as "vampires", can allegedly be recognized by various signs, such as that their body that does not disintegrate, the color of their skin is unique, and the hair, beard and nails keep growing after their death, the inhabitants unanimously decided to open the grave of Petar Blagojević and see by themselves if such signs were present.

With that intention they came to me and requested, after informing me and the local priest about the issue, that I should be present when they open the grave and examine it. Although I initially hesitated, replying that I would have to first ask for the permission of the respectful Government and wait for its divine approval, they did not agree at all, and briefly replied that I can do as I wish, but they will have to, according to their customs, leave their homes because the evil spirit, while they wait for the reply from Belgrade, could destroy the entire village, which has happened in the past during the Turkish times, and they do not want to wait for anything like that.

Since I was not able to dissuade them, using either kind words or threats, I went to Kisiljevo together with the Gradište priest and performed the examination of the freshly excavated body of Petar Blagojević. During the examination I found it entirely truthful that, before anything else, one could not sense any smell characteristic of the dead, and that the body, except for a part of the nose that fell off, was completely preserved. The hair, beard, and even the new nails (the old nails have fallen off) continued to grow; the old skin was pale white and underneath it new skin was formed. The face, hands, feet and the entire body were not in a worse shape than when he was alive. Not a little surprised, I even noticed fresh blood in his mouth, which, to the belief of everyone present, belonged to one of his recent victims. In short, all the above-listed signs characteristic of such people were present. When the priest and I concluded our examination, the mood of the crowd turned into anxiety and rage, and the subjects, with great speed, sharpened a wooden stick with the intention to pierce the body of the deceased with it. They then proceeded to lay the stick against his body and pierced it, at which point fresh blood started flowing not only from his hearth, but also from his ears and mouth, and several additional signs appeared as well (of which I would, with all due respect, remain silent). Finally, in accordance with their old customs, the inhabitants burned the body to the ashes, which I report to the praised Government, at the same time kindly requesting, if anything in this case was made in error, not to attribute that to me but to the unruly mob which was overwhelmed with fear.

In the same town of Veliko Gradište, except for a left-over vampire or two, today live predominantly Serbs, but there are also Romanians, Gypsies (or, more appropriately, *Roma*), and *Vlasi*, very gentle and quiet people who came to Serbia from Romania a long time ago and are believed to be of Roman descent. *Vlasi* preserved their culture, old customs and beliefs to great extent, and their folk clothes, dances and rituals are quite unique and interesting.

All of us originating from The Balkans have heard of the ancient *Vlasi* magic of which many are afraid because it is considered the strongest in the world, stronger than even Gypsy, Voodoo, or Jewish magic. It is passed on from generation to generation by only the family female line. It is inherited from the oldest sorceress or, as they are called, *vračka* or *rusalja*. Their hexes and witchcrafts are most often done with parts of animals, threads, fabric, parts of clothing, hair, and nails. Also commonly used are basil, mirrors, brooms, locks and keys, with fires burning until fairies or shamans are invoked. Cult places for all *Vlasi* people are the spaces in front of house doors, where ghosts of the ancestors reside. Roads also play special role in their magic, crossroads being of particular importance because it is there that the magic is administered, picked up or freed from. The sorceresses cherish the seventh rib of a dead man and water that was used to wash the deceased or to kill snakes. Perhaps the most famous deeds of the *Vlasi* sorceresses are love spells, either to connect or separate love couples. Equally appreciated is their ability to "untie" impotent men, which is by far the most common request from their female customers. Consequently, because she could not meet the demand, the most famous living sorceress, over eighty-year old Jovanka Žite from the village of Jabukovac, finally decided to uncover her secret recipe for impotence to the local newspaper, with a note that it should be followed to the last tiny detail in order to avoid possible grave consequences (it is for that reason that I am not providing it here).

While chatting about the *Vlasi* sorceresses and their witchcraft, my brother, half-jokingly or half-seriously (it was hard to tell) confided in me that his present wife Lidija gave him a thread a while ago, *when it was needed*. Two of them are laughing to this day when they talk about my brother's half-doubts, both happy and satisfied, but Lidija never told my brother if it was "yes" or "no". Whatever the case may be, we are left with a guess and future discussions if my brother's wife and her sister Maria, who have female ancestors from the village of Topolovnik near Veliko Gradište, may indeed be *Vlasi* sorceresses (my brother prefers to call them witches.) And even if they were, it is almost certain that they did not receive proper training from the oldest sorceress, as the custom demands, since both were born and lived their entire lives in Belgrade.

As we were talking and walking leisurely through the picturesque town on the Danube, we arrived to the Wheat Square where, in a nice bakery, we devoured generous servings of *burek* (cheese pastry famous in all lands of the former Ottoman Empire) and then continued our stroll on the streets until we reached the lively farmers market on the Central Square. As we were walking between the stands and just looking around with no plan to buy anything, I suddenly became aware of a granny staring at me from behind one of the stands. She waived her arms, as if chasing away spells, and addressed me:

"Hey you! Know this – you will not skip your destiny and will walk easily between the truth and dreams! You will be fine. Don't be afraid to freely follow wise Nikola who created light and watch carefully everything you see."

Farmers market in Veliko Gradište. Most likely a rusalja
sorceress in the front right of the photo.

Chapter 10

Man is a Machine

While driving back to Belgrade from the land of vampires and witches, my brother and I discuss the unusual event at the town's farmers market:

"Did you see how she looked at you with the evil eye!?"

"What made her address me out of the blue in the first place? Why me?

"She is a witch, or a sorceress, no doubt; or maybe she is just a bit crazy, who knows."

"Where did she get an idea that I am searching for something? Is it really that obvious?

Spontaneously, we both conclude that the rusalja sorceress must have thought of Nikola Tesla when she mentioned "wise Nikola who created light." The whole world knows who Nikola Tesla is. Genius, philosopher, scientist, humanist, the inventor of radio, television, X-rays, wireless control and transmission of power, induction motor, robots, and the first one who thought of cosmic rays and gravitational waves. Everyone interested in the work of Nikola Tesla can easily find this information on countless web sites devoted to the ingenious inventor.

"Yes, but what does that have to do with us?" I think out loud. But then again, if I take the message from that granny, or sorceress from Veliko Gradište seriously, an internal voice tells me that I should perhaps connect something related to Tesla with what is currently my obsession – to find out everything possible about a wooden schooner named *Blackbird*.

While the old Lancia is fighting with the uneven road full of bumps and holes, my brother suddenly hits his forehead with both hands (which freaks me out more than the hostile road) and declares how his partner from the jazz club "Jazzbina", Nikola Caranović, back in 1993 published a limited edition of a very interesting book by Velimir Abramović titled *Secret Inventions of Nikola Tesla*. The book quickly became a bestseller and then went out of print. It is now considered the ultimate work on Tesla, with a cult following. Without hesitation, my brother reaches for his cell phone and calls Caranović, paying no attention whatsoever to my loud objections how it is absolutely irresponsible to make phone calls while driving. Anyhow, he easily succeeds in securing a meeting with his old friend.

Upon return to Belgrade, we meet Caranović that same night in his favorite restaurant *Old Herzegovina*. Unfortunately, being bohemians as they were during those unfortunate times of the 1990s, Nikola and my brother did not keep any archive on the events and projects conceived in then famous cult Belgrade jazz club. Only thanks to a miracle of sorts, Nikola saved a single, broken-down and incomplete copy of the book which he hardly managed to dig out before the meeting. This, of course, does not stop us from carefully examining the poor book, while submerging ourselves into a divine beef stew, the phenomenal grilled Balkan kebab and everything else that usually follows. With every turned page, we are entering, through a widely open door, into the life and work of the genius who, according to Nikola's friend Abramović, was a true avatar with parapsychological insights.

"Of course Tesla was what in Hinduism they call an *avatar*, and in Buddhism a *tulku*" explains Nikola, recalling the words of his friend Abramović. "He did not leave behind any description of a scientific method because he was entering special psychic conditions, similar to what yogis do, when he was making his discoveries."

We continue to browse the book. There is not much on Tesla's personal life since, to this day, it remains unknown what kind of a person he really was. Abramović claims that Tesla was not just an ordinary man or a superior inventor in electrical engineering, but an embodiment of energy with a precisely determined mission; he was a true visionary and thinker of the next civilization. The last twenty years of his life Tesla worked on projects and theories that even modern physics cannot fully comprehend. Only in the future will we be able to discover the true magnitude of the genius that is Tesla, because he was way ahead and beyond current scientific methods. Tesla himself knew very well that he was ahead of his time. He announced cosmic rays and the theory of radioactivity at the end of nineteen century. One of his most important discoveries – the resonance of Earth or foundation for the wireless transmission of power, which he presented in 1899, remains a mystery. He waited nineteen years for his major patent to be materialized in form of the first electric hydropower plant at Niagara Falls. It took fifteen years for his invention of wireless control to be more widely used. Right before his 75th birthday, Tesla gave an interview to *The New York Times* in which he announced an upcoming revelation about the inexhaustible free energy everyone will have access to. Tesla considered this as his most important discovery but, unfortunately, did not live to see it through because ruthless American business and all-powerful magnates, for which the profit was everything, stopped him.

One of the key parts of the book includes excerpts from Tesla's interview for *Liberty Magazine* published in February 1935. In the interview he provided some explanations about his work on a secret weapon for which he believed would make wars obsolete:

Today the most civilized countries of the world spend a maximum of their income on war and a minimum on education. The twenty-first century will reverse this order. It will be more glorious to fight against ignorance than to die on the field of battle. The discovery of a new scientific truth will be more important than the squabbles of diplomats. Even the newspapers of our own day are beginning to treat scientific discoveries and the creation of fresh philosophical concepts as news. The newspapers of the twenty-first century will give a mere "stick" in the back pages to accounts of crime or political controversies, but will headline on the front pages the proclamation of a new scientific hypothesis.

PROGRESS along such lines will be impossible while nations persist in the savage practice of killing each other off. I inherited from my father, an erudite man who labored hard for peace, an ineradicable hatred of war. Like other inventors, I believed at one time that war could be stopped by making it more destructive. But I found that I was

58

mistaken. I underestimated man's combative instinct, which it will take more than a century to breed out. We cannot abolish war by outlawing it. We cannot end it by disarming the strong. War can be stopped, not by making the strong weak but by making every nation, weak or strong, able to defend itself.

Hitherto all devices that could be used for defense could also be utilized to serve for aggression. This nullified the value of the improvement for purposes of peace. But I was fortunate enough to evolve a new idea and to perfect means which can be used chiefly for defense. If it is adopted, it will revolutionize the relations between nations. It will make any country, large or small, impregnable against armies, airplanes, and other means for attack. My invention requires a large plant, but once it is established it will be possible to destroy anything, men or machines, approaching within a radius of 200 miles. It will, so to speak, provide a wall of power offering an insuperable obstacle against any effective aggression.

My apparatus projects particles which may be relatively large or of microscopic dimensions, enabling us to convey to a small area at a great distance trillions of times more energy than is possible with rays of any kind. Many thousands of horsepower can thus be transmitted by a stream thinner than a hair, so that nothing can resist. This wonderful feature will make it possible, among other things, to achieve undreamed-of results in television, for there will be almost no limit to the intensity of illumination, the size of the picture, or distance of projection.

And then, at the end of the dinner, as we were finishing off the traditional homemade walnut toffies, an unexpected turn of events took place which even more widely opened the door to Tesla's mind. Caranović, after learning where and when I finished high school, nervously started to curl his untidy gray beard and then took off his blurry glasses apparently wanting to clean them but stopping halfway. He seemed quite contemplative for a minute or two and then, more than passionately, suggested that I must personally plea with the famous academician Ivica Kaurić for more information on Tesla. No one before, including Abramović himself, was able to obtain that from Ivica and I may be the only one to succeed as he was my high school friend.

Before falling asleep that night I explored some more of the book Caranović generously lent me. Every now and then there was an insert, a clip from some publication, or a photocopy, in English or Serbian, or a hand-written note, and there were numerous notes on the margins written most likely by Caranović. I retyped some of that in my laptop and here it is, in no particular order (including several hand-written notes with sometimes underlined words):

Brooklyn Eagle, July 10, 1932: Nikola Tesla states: I have harnessed the cosmic rays and caused them to operate a motive device. Cosmic ray investigation is a subject that is very close to me. I was the first to discover these rays and I naturally feel toward them as I would toward my own flesh and blood. I have advanced a theory of the cosmic rays and at every step of my investigations I have found it completely justified. The attractive features of the cosmic rays is their constancy. They shower down on us throughout the whole 24 hours, and if a plant is developed to use their power it will not require devices for storing energy as would be necessary with devices using wind, tide or sunlight. All of my investigations seem to point to the conclusion that they are small particles, each carrying so small a charge that we are justified in calling them neutrons. They move with great velocity, exceeding that of light. More than 25 years ago I began my efforts to harness the cosmic rays and I can now state that I have succeeded in operating a motive device by means of them.

Philadelphia Public Ledger, November 2, 1933: A principle by which power for driving machinery of the world may be developed from the cosmic energy which operates the universe, has been discovered by Nikola Tesla, noted physicist and inventor of scientific devices, he announced today. This principle, which taps a source of power described as "everywhere present in unlimited quantities" and which may be transmitted by wire or wireless from central plants to any part of the globe, will eliminate the need of coal, oil, gas or any other of the common fuels, he said. Dr. Tesla in a statement today at his hotel indicated the time was not far distant when the principle would be ready for practical commercial development. Asked whether the sudden introduction of his principle would upset the present economic system,

Dr. Tesla replied, "It is badly upset already." He added that now as never before was the time ripe for the development of new resources.

I don't care that they stole my idea. I care that they don't have any of their own.

Let the future tell the truth and evaluate each one according to his work and accomplishments. The present is theirs; the future, for which I have really worked, is mine.

If your hate could be turned into electricity, it would light up the whole world.

Of all frictional resistances, the one that most retards human movement is ignorance, what Buddha called the greatest evil in the world. The friction which results from ignorance can be reduced only by the spread of knowledge and the unification of the heterogeneous elements of humanity. No effort could be better spent.

My brain is only a receiver. In the Universe, there is a core from which we obtain knowledge, strength and inspiration. I have not yet uncovered the secrets of this core, but I know that it exists.

We are all one.

The human being is a self-propelled automaton entirely under the control of external influences. Willful and predetermined though they appear, his actions are governed not from within, but from without. He is like a float tossed about by the waves of a turbulent sea.

If you want to find the secrets of the universe, think in terms of energy, frequency and vibration.

I salute religion even though I am not a believer in an orthodox way. All people should have some ideal, be it religious or artistic or scientific or humanitarian, to give a meaning to their life.

The ideal of religion and the ideal of science are not in conflict, but science is opposed to theological dogmas because science is founded on fact.

In nature there is basic energy behind all things, and it permeates everything. The power that directs this basic energy relates to the meaning of our thoughts. This is the power of thought, or the fifth power. By using the basic energy and the power of thought man, with his thoughts, can manage the infinite energy of Nature.

To me, the Universe is simply a great machine, which never came into being and never will end. The human being is no exception to the natural order. <u>Man, like universe, is a machine</u>.

Soon after the dinner in *Old Herzegovina*, and at the urging of Caranović, I had several long conversations with my high school friend, now the renowned academician Ivica Kaurić. All of us from the "science and mathematics program" of the Fourth Belgrade Gymnasium, every single one of us, always loved and respected Ivica immensely, from the moment he entered the classroom, on crutches and with a wide smile, on the first day of our freshmen year. From there on he helped all of us, whenever we asked for it, to finish our math homework during the long break, or any other homework we had trouble with during those four years (not to sin my soul, I must note that Rovac, undoubtedly the best mathematician in the entire school, did the same.)

I have not seen Ivica ever since prom night, until those meetings we had in late spring of 2016. I knew from before that he graduated from The School of Electrical Engineering with the highest honors and went all the way to become member of the Serbian Academy of Sciences and Arts. This did not surprise any of us – he remained Genius to us all the same. However, I was completely taken aback when Ivica confirmed that rumors, which for years circulated in Belgrade among a very narrow circle of people, were true. Yes, he saw the inaccessible documents left by Tesla. And not only that he saw them, he continues to study them to this day. And he is one of the select few that were lucky enough to hold in their hands the things that Sava Kosanović, Tesla's nephew, personally brought to the Yugoslav Kingdom years before the Americans, upon Tesla's death, gave Kosanović the remainder of Tesla's official legacy (after they kept for themselves what they thought was of "national interest" and should not be given to the Yugoslavs.) And no, not all Tesla's documents are kept in the Nikola Tesla Museum in Belgrade, at Krunska Street no. 51. And he cannot tell me where they are, and it should not interest me anyway. And yes, he will help me because of our high school days, but also because what I am trying to solve is quite interesting. And, in fact, it is very important.

After I mentioned to Ivica the Abramović's book published by Jazzbina more than two decades ago, he started to laugh contagiously:

"Many have tried, and many are still trying to figure out various claims and theories by Tesla, but no one has completely succeeded yet. Of course, I have not succeeded myself even though I am studying his legacy seriously for more than thirty years now. "

Ivica then, ever so modestly, states how he may be able to describe, using a relatively popular language, some of the more mysterious and less known discoveries by Tesla. He immediately turns to neutrinos:

"That is how Tesla called particles that can travel faster than light, which is the prerequisite for time travel. However, as far as I know, and I do know, his time machine was never completed or presented to the public. Interestingly, already at the end of the nineteenth century, I believe somewhere around 1895, he announced for the first time that both space and time can be influenced by a strong magnetic field, or I should say electromagnetic field. Although it is something completely irrelevant, and Tesla would just brush it off for sure, you should understand that there are some scientists and others out there still arguing if Tesla was talking about neutrinos or neutrons or cosmic ray particles; there are understandably many defendants of Einstein's theory and many avid opponents of Tesla's understanding of the whole gravity-particles-waves thing. Really completely irrelevant as Tesla was on a very different level than anyone else, then or now."

I listened to Ivica very carefully and then started taking notes as fast as I could to memorize some of his fascinating revelations, at least to me. The first note I typed into my laptop after that meeting was on a Tesla experiment that found its way into the press at the time. To a journalist of *The New York Herald* Tesla described how an electric thunderbolt struck his shoulder with the charge of 3.5 million volts and that he would have been dead if it weren't for his assistant who happened to be nearby and quickly turned off the power supply. Tesla also described how, while he was in contact with the electric charge resonance, paralyzed and helpless, he left his space and time bounds and saw the past, the present, and the future all at the same time.

This mentioning of time and space then expanded into lectures Ivica gifted me with over the course of our subsequent meetings. Ivica talked about transmission of power, wireless control and communication, non-Hertzian waves, an inexhaustible and free source of energy, interpretation of multifaceted dimensions of the space-time structure, and the time machine. I, of course, cannot possibly describe all of that as good as Ivica did. I can only provide here parts of my incomplete notes I managed to take.

Tesla very early on realized that travel through time can be extremely dangerous but continued to search for waves that could enable it. He first dismissed Hertzian waves named after H.R. Hertz who discovered them in 1888. These waves are useless for the transmission of energy as they progressively weaken over short distances. Tesla believed that energy can be transmitted incomparably more efficiently by interruptions of the natural electricity of Earth and atmosphere, which can be achieved using special wireless technology of extremely low vibration frequency. He patiently searched for these low-frequency static waves originating from the Earth's "volume-mass" (the best translation of the French word Ivica used, *gabarit*, I could think of). He finally succeeded in formulating this completely new type of static and multidimensional waves which eventually became known as *scalar waves*. Tesla realized they were completely different from, and in fact a negation of, traditional Hertzian waves which is the very reason he named them non-Hertzian. Tesla's waives are not electromagnetic and have zero energy as we know it. They permeate everything, at the subatomic level and the Universe level. Being static and multidimensional in both space and time, they are interconnected by default "from here to eternity" as Ivica put it.

Although the universal opinion is that scalar waves cannot be detected with any technology we currently possess, Ivica said that was of course not true as Tesla showed us in one of his notebooks written in the Serbian Cyrillic alphabet. At the time, I did not pay much attention to this remark Ivica made in passing and then continued with a brief explanation how his team demonstrated it was possible with a help of "plentiful energy and a series of Faraday Cages there in Djerdap."

The most incredible, at least to me as a lay person, was Ivica's list of what these scalar waves can produce or enable: accelerated or halted light, transfer of information at greater-than-light speeds, contraction of time, dematerialization or antigravitation, view through the Earth, and many more phenomena incomprehensible to normal human mind.

As it turned out later, the most important thing for my *Blackbird* quest was Ivica's revelation that Tesla described some of his discoveries in several notebooks written in Serbian long before his death in January 1943. He never disclosed these discoveries to anyone because he was afraid that they will be misused by the powerful. Tesla left the notebooks in care of his uncle Kosanović at the end of 1931, several months after he gave an interview to *New York Times* for his 75th birthday. Ivica, while studying these notebooks, stumbled upon Tesla's remark how he hid something very important. There were no details what and where. Ivica, however, firmly believed, based on some other things he found in Tesla's notebooks, that the genius in doing so solicited help of an acquaintance he made in New Castle Century Club where he gave one of his rare public lectures. According to Ivica, Tesla maintained and strengthened this friendship over many years. Based on Tesla's notes, Ivica believed this Club was in New Castle, Delaware, in a house named Terry House.

Nikola Tesla and his machines. Courtesy of Nikola Tesla Museum, Belgrade.

February 9, 1935 issue of Liberty Magazine with the Nikola Tesla interview. Courtesy of https://hello-earth.com/nikolatesla/amachinetoendwar/libertymagazine9february1935.html.

Ivica Kaurić, on the right, in spring of 2016. Ivica was recovering from the flu at the time I visited him with our high school friends Vuča, Dejan, and Slavka (from left to right) and Nataša who took the photo.

Chapter 11

Gift

My investigation of *Blackbird's* whereabouts on the Adriatic and the Dalmatian coast during WWII was firmly set on the right course when, in early summer of 2017, I had a chance to travel to Europe and visit Vinko in Podgora again. That was the last time I saw him.

After opening his door, surprised, and cheerfully letting me in, Vinko says he would very much like to give me some things, as a present, for memory, because my visits meant a lot to him. He goes on to say I don't even know how lucky I was to have Eddie and Joanne and that he was very happy when we all came to visit and when he saw how much Eddie loved figs. He even thought Eddie may have enjoyed the company of a lonely old man, him. Then, suppressing tears, Vinko says the following words I will never forget:

"One dies two times. The first time when one's soul leaves the body, and the second when there is no one left to remember him."

I reply that his presents will be a great honor to me and commit to bringing Joanne and Eddie along the next time, hopefully very soon, wanting him to know they often mentioned him, asking when we were going to the Adriatic again. A gentle, nostalgic smile that crosses his face after hearing my words causes in me a disturbing feeling of anxiety. Vinko wants me to follow him to Teo's room where there are presents for me. In the room, I immediately notice everything looks the same, untouched, as nearly two years ago. Things on Teo's piano are in the same position, window curtains are drawn, a sad feeling is still here.

A mischievous smile comes to Vinko's face as he takes a rather large drawing from one of the generous drawers of a nicely carved wooden cabinet made by Teo. In the drawing, Tove is sunbathing lying naked on the deck of *Blackbird*. Vinko made the drawing without Tove knowing, hidden behind grand old rosemary bush on the rocky Mljet shore and looking through binoculars (Vinko talks about the rosemary as if he smells it that very moment). He tells me with a grin on his face:

"She had beautiful eyes, just like your Joanne."

Vinko wants me to keep all the drawings he made on the *Blackbird's* voyage which he takes from several drawers. He also gives me a beautiful wooden box on Teo's piano which his son made from the dry branch of an ancient olive tree on the island of Lopud. In the box there is a somewhat irregular, almost egg-shaped, shiny metal ball which he received from Tove in 1943 when he parted with the schooner. The ball and his son Teo became inseparable. It was found on the Šunj beach on Lopud, together with several other things Teo left before his disappearance. Finally, Vinko gives me Teo's diaries which he never read, he just could not, and the Viking knife. I parted with Vinko on that 12th of June 2017 with a heavy heart, after we hugged for a long time in silence.

Upon my arrival to a hotel in Split, where I will spend the night before flying back home to the United States, I take the shiny metal ball from Teo's box and start to examine it carefully, turning it around with both hands. I notice a faint carved sign – *Dixisteel*^{TM} and instantly become aware of a strange, calm feeling which overtakes me while I continue to play with the ball of irregular shape, almost egg-like. The sight of the glowing red digits of the alarm clock by the bed suddenly shakes me out of a trance of sorts – it is close to midnight, my flight to Geneva leaves very early in the morning and I should get some sleep. Still, I keep thinking of the day's events, Vinko's words ringing in my ears: "You and my Teo were of the same age, peers. If he were alive, maybe you would have been friends today." I don't feel tired and take one of Teo's diaries hoping it will somehow put me to sleep. While turning page after page I come across a faded photograph with a caption "Reunion with my middle school friends, in Šuplja stena."

This leaves me startled. I knew the teenager standing in the photo and the two sitting. Rewinding the film in my head I start to recall various circumstances in which we saw each other in the past – in the "Technology Students Club", once famous KST, at music gigs and student parties. The one with the hat used to play basketball at Radnički for a short time and was coached by Duda Ivković; he is from Neimar, but I cannot remember his name. Yes, I knew these people, their names and nicknames are coming back. The one without shirt is Yoya from Čubura, we did crew together for a while on Ada Ciganlija. The one standing is Teo!

After that I did not even think of trying to sleep. I browsed Teo's diaries the whole night, up until leaving for the airport. Here are select entries under "M" from "The Dictionary of Words, Very Personal" (English word "my" and the Serbo-Croatian word with the same meaning both start with the letter "m"). The entries feel like something I would have written myself if someone had given me the idea, just like Teo could have been my best friend, if we only knew each other.

Mendelssohn, Felix

Because my Mother loved his music. And because I bought her a hi-fi turntable from my first sculpture commission so she could enjoy it even more. And because she made me start learning English and playing piano when I was a kid, and took my cousin and me, when I was only thirteen, to a striptease bar in Pigalle, Paris, France, and then sent me to Norway when I was sixteen, and then paid for my trip to Oxford, England to improve my English when I was twenty and where I met Teresa, after which I pretty much took my destiny into my own hands (or so I think). And because I could never lie to her, no matter how hard I tried, when she asked me to look at her eyes and answer a tough question.

My Movies

To Sir with Love (and the song, the song….) because Sidney Poitier says in it "It is scary to deal with the truth; scary and dangerous…" And because all teachers should, at some point, throw all the textbooks they recommended to a nearby basket, right there in their little classroom, or wherever they teach their little class, and talk with the kids about everything else except their little subject of which they are so proud because none of the kids in front of them knows anything about it, not even to ask a question or two.

Amarcord because it is by Federico Fellini and because we could talk about the scenes from it for hours and were not afraid to show our feelings while doing it, not even later as grownups, just like the boys in the movie.

Aguirre, the Wrath of God because it is by Werner Herzog, and it is about a group of very determined people, at the beginning of the movie, floating on a raft down this mystifying river deep in the jungle, in search of gold. And because at the end of the movie that same raft is full of small monkeys jumping aimlessly.

The Virgin Spring by Ingmar Bergman because it is so overwhelming and makes everything that is good and bad in me battle each other, and I never know which one won every time I watch the movie, again and again.

My Big Cousin

Because he was taller than me only for the first fourteen years of my life and I was a better basketball player. And because he had enough patience to help me prepare for an exam in high school after which I was never afraid of algebra again.

My Books

The Bridge of San Luis Rey by Thornton Wilder, because when I finished reading it, I couldn't stop hoping that, somehow, new pages will appear, and I will transcend the miracle of time again.

Every book by Fyodor Dostoevsky because in one of them he says something like this: "If every man opened up his soul, an incredible stench would cover the Earth and we would all suffocate..." And because (for now at least) I humbly disagree with Great Fyodor.

The Little Prince by Antoine de Saint-Exupéry, because one can read in it: "And now here is my secret, a very simple secret: It is only with the heart that one can see rightly; what is essential is invisible to the eye."

My Father

Because he married my Mother. And because he stuck with his friends when they were terrorized by the Marshall and gave them work and then left the Party. And because no money or offers of towers in the sky could change his mind. And because he took us every summer to Mljet where I was so happy wandering between magic-smelling, old pine trees. And because he experienced the Marshall's wrath, but we never knew that and felt very secure when he was with us.

My Mother

See under Mendelssohn.

My Music

Facing You by Keith Jarrett, because I love piano and there is nothing else like it.

Whenever I Seem to be Far Away by Terje Rypdal because I love daydreaming about going back to Norway one day, across the sea.

In a Silent Way by Miles Davis because it makes me feel peaceful and part of something divine.

Parce Mihi Domine by Christóbal de Morales because Jan Garbarek plays it.

Pictures at an Exhibition by Emerson, Lake & Palmer because one day my father stayed with me to hear the whole album, and then finally agreed I can paint the band on one entire wall of my room, only to end up painting most of it himself.

My Painter

Edvard Munch, because he painted "The Scream", which is exactly how I felt more than once this last year.

Photo from one of Teo's diaries with the caption "Reunion with my middle school friends, in Šuplja stena, photographed by Zoran." Teo standing in the middle.

Vinko's drawing of naked Tove, sunbathing on the *Blackbird's* deck.

Chapter 12

Terry House

After my last visit with Vinko in late spring of 2017, it seemed I had everything I needed to claim victory over the Thompsons. Nevertheless, after returning to the United States, I felt something was missing, perhaps an important detail that fell through the cracks, or a clear answer to a question or two. This feeling started to bother me. At some point I became aware that the main reason for this was the remark Ivica made last year about Terry House in New Castle, Delaware, during our conversations about Tesla. Intuition was telling me that the key answer to all my doubts must somehow be connected to this house. Therefore, in summer of 2017, I started digging through publicly available information on Terry House and the events it witnessed.

It did not take me long to locate it and learn more about its history. Terry House was completed immediately after the Civil War on a parcel bought in 1851 for 1,600 dollars by Howell J. Terry, a distinguished citizen of New Castle and cashier of the New Castle branch of the Farmers Bank at the corner of Strand and Delaware streets. Grandparents of the oldest current residents of New Castle were quoted as saying that "enough bricks went into the house to build a whole row." Architects regard the Terry House an impressive example of the Federal architectural style, characteristic of the period when it was built, the 1800's.

Terry died in 1874 leaving the house to his wife Rebecca Jane Pippin Terry and their children. In 1916 the Terry heirs sold the property to the New Castle Century Club for 3,000 dollars. The building was not in good condition but was well built which allowed a successful restoration by the Club. The lower story was used for club purposes, the second and third floors were converted into apartments for rent, and the front steps acquired an iron railing.

The New Castle Century Club was organized in 1914 by a group of women interested in civic improvement and the cultural advancement of its members. 111 members were enrolled as charter members. The programs of the Club included lectures on current events, literary speakers, musical performances, discussions on health issues, and many other topics contributing to the emancipation of its membership.

It is in this club that Tesla, on October 23, 1931, gave a lecture for a small honorarium. Tesla later, on multiple occasions and despite its relatively long distance from New York where he lived, visited the Club whenever he felt like having a good home-made meal without meat and enjoying the friendly intimate atmosphere. Tesla especially looked forward to leisurely strolls on the town streets, after lunch, because of the feeling of being in some long-gone times. Tesla looked forward to his visits even more so because of the company of a charming lucid lady that accompanied him during these walks. (This revelation will, I am sure, raise a disbelief amongst various individuals interested in life and work of Mr. Tesla, for one reason or another.)

In 1951 the Club sold the building for $25,000 due to the high costs of maintenance and moved to smaller quarters on Fourth Street. The house was again purchased in 1985 by an energetic woman which converted it into the current arrangement as a Bed and Breakfast.

A day after returning from a business trip on a red-eye flight to Washington Dulles airport, during which I could not sleep and instead thought of my *Blackbird* quest and Terry House, I jumped into our antique Ford truck on Sunday morning, June 25, 2017 and left for New Castle. After little more than two hours of a comfortable and easy drive on I-95, without any rush-hour delays typical of workdays, I took the last exit before the Delaware Memorial Bridge and automatically followed the mechanical voice instructions from my cell phone guiding me to my destination – Terry House in historic New Castle.

After I knocked and rang the bell multiple times with no answer, I opened the front door and walked into a narrow corridor at which end there were stairs to the upper floor. Hesitating, I loudly asked if anyone was there and waited for a minute or two. Still without answer, I finally decided to open a double door on the left hoping to find someone behind it. I entered a spacious room with high ceilings and crowded with old furniture and paintings hanging on the walls, somewhat chaotically. Deep in the room there was a large comfortable sofa on which, sideways, laid an elderly lady, hopefully napping (I truly was worried at the sight). Not knowing what exactly I should do, I remained awkwardly silent, for at least five minutes or so, until the lady opened her eyes and saw me standing in the door. Relieved, I politely addressed her expressing an interest in bringing my family one of the following weekends so we can explore charming New Castle. I made a point that we would very much like to stay at the Terry House as it was highly-recommended, but also because I heard a story that, long time ago, a scientist by the name of Nikola Tesla gave a lecture here.

The Lady looked at me clairvoyantly with a piercing look, not replying for a while. Then her face acquired a mocking expression, as if she saw straight through me. She finally responded, slowly:

"You are not from here. You talk like him. Do you maybe have a ball?"

Taken aback, I did not initially comprehend what she was saying. Then I muttered:

"Dixisteel?"

"I don't know, you know."

Hesitantly, not knowing why, I opened the box I carried with me and took out Teo's ball.

The Lady left me startled and speechless:

"I knew you would come. I have something for you that I kept all these years. I apologize that you will have to wait for a while until I bring it down, but my legs are not serving me very well lately."

She then slowly walked out of the room with help from a tripod cane. Utterly confused, while waiting for her to come back, I was examining all those paintings on the walls and interesting antique decorative objects scattered throughout the room.

After a while the Lady came back carrying with effort a rather large and apparently heavy leather bag, which she handed me with a sigh of relief:

"It is yours now. Feel free to open it, there are some interesting things."

From the leather bag I took out a bundle of papers, hand-written in Serbian Cyrillic alphabet, a bunch of schematic drawings, a small notebook bound in leather, three metal balls, several other peculiar metal objects, and a strange large metal box without any visible openings but with a series of what appeared to be buttons, which reminded me of a remote control of sorts. Like Vinko's present, the box also had an unreal metal luster and was equally smooth and polished. On the bottom side of the box, to my enormous surprise, there was the identical itched sign – *Dixisteel*^{TM}.

In the conversation that followed, the Lady explained how her mother received the leather bag from an elderly dignified gentleman, whom she still remembers very well even though many decades have passed since she last saw him. She remembers the most his sharp face, but also his kind smile – he was very good to her and on his visits always brought to her from the "big city of New York" a box of very tasty chocolate cookies which he, however, never tried himself. Shortly before passing away, her mother revealed a secret that troubled her for years. She asked her to do everything in her power to fulfill a promise given to the gentleman from New York. The promise which her mother gave, many years ago, before they left New Castle during WWII. The request from the gentleman was odd but at the same time very simple: "One day someone unknown, with a strange foreign accent like mine, will come to visit Terry House carrying a ball, similar to these three, and will ask about me. You will give the bag to the stranger knowing very well that he was the right person."

Mainly because of the promise she made to her mother, the Lady took an opportunity which unexpectedly presented itself and bought Terry House and moved back to New Castle in 1985. She is now immensely happy that, finally, she can fulfill the promise her mother gave to the gentleman from New York and leave this world in peace when the time comes.

Still taken aback by the whole experience and looking back and forth between the strange metal objects I held in my hands and the smiling noble face of the Lady, I started to feel an unknown, but at the same time very calming sensation. As if awakened from a dream, I discerned her words:

"Nice feeling, isn't it?"

Grinning, foolishly, I was only able to nod my head affirmatively. Then the Lady, very politely, walked me to the door and said:

"Go on now. I believe you will know what to do with all that."

On my way to our old Ford truck, before turning around the corner, I stopped to look at the Terry House one last time. Together with the Town Square and other old brick buildings she was facing, it reminded me of some long-gone, different times. Fighting a strange sense of reminiscence, I continued to walk with a heavy heart.

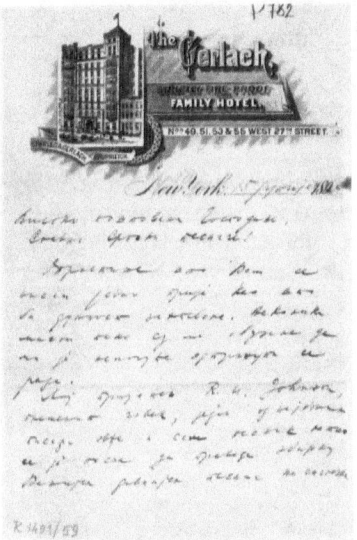 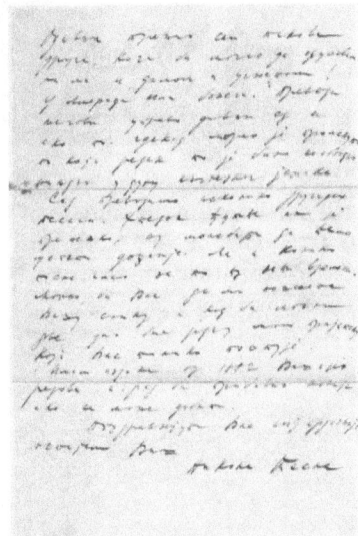

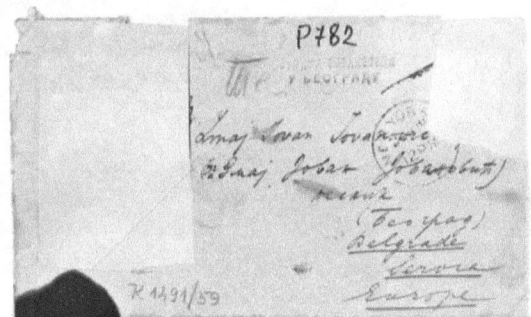

Nikola Tesla very rarely wrote in Cyrillic, and only for very important personal matters. Tesla sent this letter to the famous Serbian poet Jovan Jovanović Zmaj in 1894 from New York. The letter is kept at the National Library, Belgrade.

Young Yugoslav King Petar II, in navy uniform, during a visit to Nikola Tesla (in the middle of the photo) in his apartment in New Yorker hotel in New York. At Tesla's right-hand side is his nephew Sava Kosanović, minister of the YGE. Courtesy of Nikola Tesla Museum, Belgrade.

My Ford parked on a street in New Castle.

Street in New Castle lost in time.

Terry House in New Castle, Delaware.

Chapter 13

Lopud

Blackbird arrived at the picturesque Marina Grande on the island of Capri on August 5, 1943. This concluded the first phase of the plan conceived by Larry Neal, the gray eminence of the British SOE. The Scandinavian crew of *Blackbird* was welcomed in the port by the very wealthy Swedish industrial magnate Erik Johansen pretending to be Sven's uncle. The following two days Tove and Sven were his guests in a magnificent villa with a majestic view of the famous *faraglioni*, the gigantic rocks jutting out of the sea by the island's shore. From Erik they found out about Captain Ristorcelli who will serve as their liaison on the Yugoslav Adriatic but, unfortunately, was not able to meet them here on Capri due to some urgent and unforeseen business.

The first evening right before sunset, while admiring the view of the sea, the *faraglioni*, and the intoxicating *Barbaresco* wine which their host was constantly adding to crystal glasses, a new and challenging plan for the next day emerged. Not knowing how and why, but mainly thanks to the irresistibly persuasive Erik who promoted his idea with the generous servings of the miraculous wine, the young couple self-confidently agreed to the plan. They will impress Eric's Italian friends by taking the faithful schooner, under full sail, on a double slalom around the three *faraglioni* and will then sail through the mighty door on *Faraglione di Mezzo*, and all that in less than 20 minutes!

It was only the next morning, while *Blackbird* was sailing towards the *faraglioni* with Erik's Italian friends on board, that Tove and Sven realized the true difficulty of the plan. Namely, all five Italians burst into loud laughter, although relatively politely, when Erik told them what they were about to witness. One of the guests on board, the honorable Edwin Cerio, when the laughter subsided a bit, told Erik and the crew how that was, with all due respect, impossible.

After they heard what Edwin (of whom they learned a few things from Erik last night) had to say, Tove and Sven immediately agreed that it was of course not possible, and that dear uncle Erik was only joking. This was understandable since famous Edwin Cerio held two doctorates, one in mechanical engineering and one in ship building, and was for many years building both shipyards and ships in Italy, Germany, and Argentina. After WWI started, he concluded his career and retired to Capri, the island of his birth. Among other things, he was the city major for a while and fought real estate magnates from Milan who wanted to build and develop the island more and more. Major Cerio knew all too well how any unchecked development would destroy the traditional and unique charm of his beloved island. Because of his uncompromising views and devotion to Capri, Cerio gained the enormous respect of his countrymen and his opinions were considered almost sacred. Tove and Sven quickly became aware of that when the remaining four Italians exclaimed in concert:

"If Edwin says that, then it is so!"

As if he waited for this, the wealthy industrial magnate from Sweden, who was well known for his willingness to extend challenges and bet on them, made a proposal to one of the gentlemen. To Tove and Sven, this gentleman somehow looked the most important in the whole company.

"Alessandro, if this extraordinary sailing boat succeeds in its attempt, you will organize a ball tomorrow night, in your magnificent villa, for all of us, and please invite anyone else you wish. And if the boat is not successful, then I will have the ball in my modest house!"

I must say, however, that Erik's house was anything but modest. The dignified Italian accepted the bet with a smile and a remark that Erik must provide enough oysters and wine for tomorrow because he is certain to lose.

The next evening, at the ball in the magnificent villa of Baron Alessandro Monti della Corte, all guests were crowding around the young Swedes, wanting to meet them personally and hear, first-hand, how they managed to accomplish the impossible – to finish the double slalom around the *faraglioni* in exactly eighteen minutes and fifty three seconds, sailing on a beautiful schooner, which is something no one before was ever able to do! The guests for the evening were also eager to hear what the dear guests from the North thought of their magic Blue Grotto in which all the witnesses of the sailing miracle swam in afterwards to celebrate the incredible achievement. Everyone also wanted to learn from Tove and Sven what did they thought of many other things they saw for the first time on their sail from Sweden to Capri.

In all this it is important to note how the demand by Benjamin Foster, the natural scientist from Dartmouth, which was made at the end of the meeting in the Congressional Club near Washington, D.C., was absolutely warranted. As we all remember, Mr. Foster insisted that the woman on the boat had to be "young, pretty, and certainly blond". Accordingly, Tove looked absolutely irresistible in the evening gown generously lent to her by the Baron's young daughter Beatrice, which is the reason most of the men at the ball eagerly waited for their turn to dance with her. Among them was one Curzio Malaparte, the renowned writer and war correspondent, Amadeo Mauri, the famous archaeologist, and many other distinguished guests and inhabitants of the beautiful island. No one present at the ball in the magnificent villa of Baron Monti della Corte wanted to think about the invasion by the Allies that was unravelling on the mainland and what it meant for the future. Everyone simply tried to surrender to the magic night and enjoy every minute of it, just as their beloved island taught them to do for all those years without worry.

Blackbird left Capri on August 8, 1943 and, after two days, arrived at Licata, Sicily one month after it was occupied by the American Third Infantry Division. Tove and Sven were welcomed by Larry Neal who gave them very detailed maritime maps of the Yugoslav Adriatic and instructions for the upcoming mission. He also informed them that the mission had one informal but very important task which should not be documented. On the Pelješac Peninsula, in a monastery the location and the name of which were conveyed by Larry verbally only, Tove and Sven were to buy two jugs of red wine. One jug they would keep for themselves and the other one they were going to give directly to Larry, in person, once they were back from the mission.

Lopud

Blackbird left Licata at night on Thursday, August 19, 1943 and, on Sunday morning, August 22nd it approaches the Croatian island of Lopud. Having sailed into the shelter of Lopud Bay, Tove and Sven slowly recognize a small stone harbor in the shape of letter L. On the inward side there is a floating white rope stretched between red buoys, marking a water polo court where a game is currently in progress. The game is watched by a relatively large group of spectators, mostly teenage boys and girls, some of whom are sitting on wooden benches stacked in three rows above each other. Some are standing in small groups, and almost all of them are in swimming suits. The teenagers are creating lots of noise: laughter, frequent collective screams, and generally speaking real chaos as they cheer the match. In the water, the situation is not much different except for the absence of laughter. The two teams comprised of young men are in the serious business of swimming back and forth between the goals, seemingly following the ball but mostly interested in drowning each other. It is late morning and the crowd is feeling the heat since there are no clouds in the clear blue sky to tame the sun at least a little bit. The summer *Mistral* wind is blowing, but not helping much. This makes the teenagers jump and dive off the quay on the other side of the court every so often in order to cool down and then come back refreshed so they can scream even more and tease everyone in sight the players included.

Occupied by the game, no one at the port sees a distant boat with two masts and sails filled by the wind, approaching from the west. At some point, the boat is close enough to be noticed, first by a few and then more and more people watching the game. Finally, no one is interested in the game anymore. All eyes are looking at the schooner as she furls the sails and slows down, apparently deciding what to do next – the small port is inaccessible because of the ongoing game of water polo.

Suddenly realizing something strange is going on because of the lack of noise, and then seeing the object of everyone's attention, the referee blows the whistle and waves the players to come out of the water, addressing two of them: "Vinko and Dalibor, move the court lines so that boat can dock."

Standing at the bow, while Sven is navigating the boat, Tove clearly sees many hands waiving and apparently inviting them to enter the port. Just a few minutes earlier, she and Sven were wandering about all that deafening noise and splashing water in the distance, looking through binoculars while trying to figure out what was going on. They have never seen a game of water polo before and were quite puzzled by the scene including the strange white and blue "baby bonnets" on the swimmers' heads, as Tove later jokingly pointed out.

As *Blackbird* slowly comes to port, hoisting the Swedish flag and pretending her name is *Swarttrost*, her two-person crew is fully aware of the careful examination by many pairs of curious smiling eyes looking at them. Tove cannot help but notice the perfectly muscled bodies and wide shoulders of the young men with baby bonnets on their heads. Sven is equally pleased by the sight of tall, slim teenage girls, some of whom have long blond hair which makes him think of Sweden. After a moment or two, Tove and Sven shake off their thoughts and focus back on the task at hand – how to dock the schooner safely, without any embarrassment. After a flawless execution of the task, Tove sighs with relief and jumps off the boat with a rope in her hand. Momentarily, a young boy with a friendly grin on his face steps out of the crowd and grabs the rope from Tove, obviously eager to help her tie the boat. At the same time, another boy approaches the stern and addresses Sven in a strange language, pointing at the rope by the Sven's feet while smiling all along. Sven of course understands the gesture and hands the rope to the boy who quickly completes the securing of the boat.

Tove and Sven are finally able to relax a bit, after all the anxiety and fear of wondering how their first encounter with the locals would go. They are pleasantly surprised by the warm welcome and some sort of loud admiration that is coming almost exclusively from the young men present. This admiration is accompanied by occasional laughter, whistles and the teenagers jokingly shoving each other. Tove and Sven assure themselves how all that must be because of their beautiful *Svarttrost*.

They then see a young handsome man stepping forward and shouting and gesturing something to the crowd which makes the noise and laughter subside somewhat, but not entirely. He then quickly walks to Tove and Sven and politely introduces himself in flawless English:

"My name is Vinko Lovrić. I will be first mate on your cruise on the Adriatic which your friend Captain Giuseppe Ristorcelli arranged with my father. We were expecting you any day and I am very glad you arrived safely. Please take everything you need and come with me to our house. My father planned your stay here in detail and I am afraid it is how it must be done, without any discussion. He already arranged everything with the carabinieri, so it is not necessary for you to go to the port office. Don't worry about the schooner, no one will touch her. You will not sleep on her tonight because the most comfortable accommodation on the entire island is waiting for you, trust me."

Tove and Sven kindly thank Vinko and quickly jump back on the boat to fetch some clothes and a few necessities as commanded by their future crew member. Meanwhile, Vinko tries to defend himself from an onslaught of his curious friends who demand an explanation how is it that he suddenly knows the mysterious visitors and what is it all about anyway. His short explanation causes an avalanche of envious comments followed by numerous appeals to join the cruse, regardless of the price Vinko may ask. Vinko's best friend Dalibor offers his bicycle in exchange for Vinko succeeding in getting him a spot on the boat. This momentarily quiets everyone else as no one can offer anything as valuable. Everyone is silent waiting for Vinko's reaction, for what it seems as an eternity, only to hear finally how, unfortunately, he cannot do anything about it because everything has already been arranged in advance with his father. The gravely disappointed crowd then looks at Vinko and the Swedes as they leave the port chatting cheerfully. Slowly but surely and ever so loudly, the crowd starts to laugh, whistle and tease the *Blackbird's* crew with words only Vinko could understand.

Quite puzzled with the whole scene, Tove and Sven ask Vinko if everything is OK. He replies that of course it was and kindly asks them not to pay any attention to his friends who are just teasing him a bit, being jealous of his upcoming adventure.

After a few minutes' walk on the stone quay along the bay, the *Blackbird's* completed crew arrives at Vinko's house where they are warmly greeted by his father, Captain Ivan Lovrić. While the Swedes are enjoying tasty hors d'oeuvres brought to them, Captain Lovrić briefly explains what he has planned, together with Captain Ristorcelli, for their stay on the island. He then makes two phone calls, speaking with a melodious strange language Tove and Sven hear for the first time, not recognizing a single word. After he completes the calls, Captain Lovrić addresses the guests and suggests they immediately go with Vinko to the *Grand Hotel* where a nice clean room awaits them. Moreover, the room, actually a spacious apartment, has a private bathroom with hot water which he is sure they will appreciate after the long journey from Sicily. They can also take a swim in the crystal-clear water at the sandy beach by the hotel since the sea temperature is now ideal. Vinko will come to the hotel at 7pm promptly to pick them up and take them to a nice dinner with the Glavović family, not far from here. The dinner company will be joined by Mr. Dobrović, whom they will see in a few minutes, and several more friends, all dying to meet them.

Captain Lovrić then tells Vinko, in Croatian, that, after he takes the guests to the hotel, he should at once go with his friend Dalibor (and not alone, period!) to catch some fish with the underwater gun and gaffs that barba Giuseppe brought from Italy last summer. It would be best if they dive around the caves on the side of the island facing Mljet and try to catch a good-size grouper. He should take the fish to madame Glavović, with a kind request from his father to prepare it the way only she knows how. It is the right thing to do for our dear guests from distant Sweden. The father will bring some *Torotan* cheese from Zavala, olives, prosciutto from Stolac, and red wine from Pelješac which he keeps for special occasions and would like to share it tonight with everyone. Her son Niko, with whom the father spoke, will tell her who is coming to dinner. *And the father sincerely hopes she will join them tonight, it would be a great honor for everyone.*

Thanking Captain Lovrić from the bottom of their hearts and succumbing entirely to the overwhelming speed of the events, Tove and Sven obediently follow Vinko who takes them to the *Grand Hotel*. There they meet the architect who designed it, the renowned Nikola Dobrović. It is he who generously relinquished his own private apartment in the hotel, for the several days they will spend on the island.

View of Lopud, most likely in 1938 or 1939. Grand Hotel in the lower
right of the photo (from old postcard.)

View of Grand Hotel from the shore, shortly after its completion in
1936. Courtesy of Ms. Vlasta Pulić Glavović.

Chapter 14

Dinner

Promptly at 7pm that evening, Vinko shows up at the *Grand Hotel* garden where Tove and Sven are waiting for him as instructed. They all walk to the *Hotel Glavović* for the family dinner, with Tove noticing how they have passed by it earlier today ("It is all so near, so wonderfully cozy!"). A small company sitting at three joined tables welcomes the newcomers in the hotel's outdoor restaurant nestled by the sea. Captain Lovrić gets up from the table and ceremonially introduces everyone present to the Swedes (as we are all aware, Tove attained her Swedish identity for the mission already back in Sweden):

"Tove and Sven, I would like to introduce you to Madame Luigia Glavović, her daughter Marčela, her sons Niko and Antun, and her son-in-law Captain Antun Sesan. Here also is the architect Nikola Dobrović whom you have already met, and who designed the majestic *Grand Hotel* for our two Antuns and Niko, and our own honorable Baron Felice Luciano Nicola Mayneri."

After the newcomers are seated at the table, Captain Lovrić pours the coveted red wine into glasses for all, except not for Teo, to whom he says to help himself with some pomegranate juice. He then asks Niko to give a toast and he will translate it to the young Swedes, which Niko does:

"In the name of all of us here, and especially my mother, I wish you a warm welcome to our beautiful island in the Adriatic. You are the first guests from proud Sweden ever to come here, as far as I was able to check, and we sincerely hope that you will not be disappointed with your stay. We truly admire your courage to, in these unhappy times, sail on our blue sea and we will pray to dear God to protect you all the time. My dear mother, greatly relieved, told me when she saw you minutes ago how you seem quite normal. She believes you must be only a little bit silly in your head because of your crazy love of sailing, but she will not hold it against you..."

Having heard the last few words, Madam Glavović swiftly interrupts her son and tells Captain Lovrić not to dare translate the toast to the Swedes. This momentarily causes everyone to burst into loud laughter, except of course for Tove and Sven. To the curious guests Captain Lovrić nevertheless translates the toast, word for word, now making them laugh wholeheartedly. This marked the beginning of an unforgettable evening with laughter, jokes, incredibly tasty stuffed grouper, which Vinko caught that afternoon to the awe of everyone and madam Glavović prepared with great love, the Pelješac wine which only a select few ever tasted, the stories from seven seas, and much more.

The brief narrative that follows will never be able to describe faithfully everything that the small company talked about or felt during that evening. I have supplemented Vinko's memories here and there, when I thought it would be useful, with the details I learned of during my research. Regardless, it is almost certain that everything you are about to read was a theme of the conversation of the guests at *Hotel Glavović* at the dinner that remained etched in their memories forever.

At the very beginning of the evening, in order to satisfy the very natural curiosity of everyone present regarding the mysterious young guests from Sweden, Captain Lovrić explained the connection between them, himself, and Captain Ristorcelli whom everyone present knew. Being very modest and discrete, Captain Lovrić left out some important details about the friendship that the two captains formed over many years.

Captain Lovrić and Captain Ristorcelli got to know each other as young officers while sailing on various ships of the largest Italian shipping company Navigazione Generale Italiana, which operated between both coasts of the Adriatic Sea. When in 1923 Giuseppe took on the command of *Duilio*, the first passenger ocean liner ever built in Italy, in the Ansaldo shipyard, he immediately arranged for Ivan to get position of the *Duilio's* first officer of the deck. This of course was not difficult at all given the stellar reputation of the young Croatian officer who also came from one of the most respected maritime families on the Mediterranean. *Duilio*, of unprecedented luxury for the time she was built, was intended for the Naples–Genoa–New York City route and had her maiden voyage on 29 October 1923. She was later transferred to the Genoa–Buenos Aires route on 24 July 1928.

During his first stay in the beautiful capital of Argentina, Lovrić, still the first officer of the deck, attended a reception given to all Croatian crew members of *Duilio* by the brothers Mihanovich. His encounter with the hosts changed his life forever, dashing all the vague hopes he still had after all those years spent at the Italian company. Namely, Baron Nicolás Mihanovich, although already very weak from a grave illness, spent a whole hour at the reception personally persuading Lovrić to come over to a newly founded maritime company Yugoslav Lloyd and assume command of a brand-new ocean freight steamer *Tomislav*. Baron Mihanovich, with great pleasure, emphasized that the *Tomislav's* home port will be Dubrovnik, knowing very well Lovrić's love of and connections with the old stone city. Projecting the ultimate self-confidence, the Baron also mentioned nonchalantly that the annual salary that comes with the position should not be any problem as Lovrić can name anything he desires, no questions asked – the Baron and his brother Miho were the majority stock owners of the new company. This, understandably, made Lovrić feel incredibly honored – the name of Nicolás Mihanovich was for decades more than a legend along the coast of his beloved homeland which he left in distant 1867. Impressed and confused, Lovrić managed to ask the Baron, very politely, if he could allow him some more time to think about the offer. The experienced Baron agreed without any hesitation and reassured Lovrić that the offer will remain open as long as needed. After that, Baron Nicolás Mihanovich excused himself to all the guests because of his failing health which requires him to leave the reception sooner than he would have liked.

Ivan shared his doubts, fears, hopes, and a mixture of many other feelings with his dear friend Giuseppe during the sleepless night they spent together after the reception. From his friend Ivan heard everything that he was anticipating, but what nevertheless made him both endlessly happy and sad at the same time:

"Ivan, there is nothing to think about. This is the chance of your life and you cannot miss it! You dare not even think of that. You will see and experience everything you dreamt about. Everything we always dreamt about. You will be your own master while sailing on all the world's seas and oceans. I would give anything to join you. I hope you will not forget me, and I'd like to think that our paths will cross again soon. You must promise me that!"

The next morning Lovrić accepted the offer but, for a long time afterwards, still could not fully comprehend everything that happened since *Duilio* arrived at the Buenos Aires port on its first sail to South America. Nor could he realize what the future would hold after he shook hands with brothers Mihanovich, thus accepting the offer which simply could not have been refused.

A lot has been said and written about the man who changed Captain Lovrić's life, wealthy shipping magnate, landowner and philanthropist Baron Nicolás Mihanovich. I will therefore only briefly mention, without too much detail, what Tove and Sven learned from those present at the intimate family dinner. Very early on upon his arrival to Buenos Aires in 1868, when he was only 22 years old, Mihanovich realized how skills in diplomacy are one of the most important prerequisites for succeeding in any business endeavor. He practiced these skills with calculation but consistently with everyone who shared his values, regardless of their country of origin or strictly personal views. His business successes culminated in the formation of the largest shipping company in Latin America, *Argentina Navigation Company – Nicolás Mihanovich Ltd*. He was both the founder and the majority stakeholder together with the members of his family. He registered the company in London and commissioned all new ships from the British shipyards. This enabled him to access practically all major shipping routes around the World in which he was interested. In 1912, Austrian Emperor Franz Joseph I granted Mihanovich the hereditary title of Baron – Nikolaus Freiherr Mihanovich von Dolskidol. He also received decorations from other European monarchs, including Alfonso XIII of Spain who honored Mihanovich with the Cross of Second Order of Naval Merit, and the unfortunate Czar Nicholas II of Russia who granted him The Order of Saint Stanislaus with Stars. Mihanovich also received the highest civil medal from the Yugoslav King Alexander I. It is most likely for this reason that the newest and most modern ocean freight steam liner built for the newly established Yugoslav shipping company, *Yugoslav Lloyd*, in which brothers Mihanovich were the majority stakeholders, was named after Prince Tomislav, the newly born son of King Alexander I.

Mihanovich owned numerous buildings throughout Buenos Aires. His love of architecture was immortalized with the construction of Edificio (Palace) Mihanovich, the tallest building in Latin America at the time it was inaugurated, in 1929. This imposing structure was designed by the famous Argentine architects Héctor Calvo, Arnold Jacobs and Rafael Giménez and based on the tomb of Mausolus (a satrap in the Persian Empire) in Halicarnassus what is today Bodrum, Turkey.

The Glavović family in front of their hotel. The Matriarch of the family, Mrs. Luigia Glavović, sitting on the chair in the middle, with her daughter Marčela on the side. Courtesy of Ms. Vlasta Pulić Glavović.

Sven's photograph of Hotel Glavović.

The passenger steam ocean liner *SS Duilio* built in the Italian shipyard Ansaldo for the shipping company Navigazione Generale Italiana from Genoa. Courtesy of https://www.italianliners.com/duilio-en (the collection of Maurizio Eliseo.)

Edificio (Palace) Mihanovich. Photo published in the 91st issue of the Argentinian journal Revista de Arquitectura, in July 1928.

Chapter 15

Borges

While other guests were working diligently on the divine dinner and the intoxicating wine, Captain Lovrić turned the conversation to *Tomislav* and started talking about the ship which, by the end of his story, became a faithful friend to everyone present, just as she obviously still was to her Captain. Lovrić and *Tomislav* were inseparable for the first seven years, up until the end of 1935 when Lovrić started sharing her command with an old family friend and Dubrovnik nobleman, Captain Bunić, so he could spend more time at home with his late wife Jelena and son Vinko. The last time he saw the ship was when he and his crew disembarked her on October 31, 1941 under the threat of guns aimed at them by the Royal Italian Marines in the Chinese port of Shanghai which was occupied by the Japanese. *Tomislav* had entered the port back on April 22nd, on her way from Melbourne and Manila, only one week after the capitulation of the Yugoslav Kingdom. Anchored in the port since then, the boat was under constant threat by the Italians (allies of the Japanese), who demanded that she be turned over to them. With great anxiety, Captain Lovrić and the crew were waiting for the decision on *Tomislav's* destiny. The Japanese finally gave in to relentless Italian pressure, justifying that with a bogus statement claiming that *Tomislav*, legally and undeniably, became the property of the Italian company *Lloyd Triestino*.

Visibly shaken, Captain Lovrić stops talking and reaches toward his glass, still full of wine. At that moment, Captain Sesan comes to the rescue and, addressing Tove and Sven, continues by saying:

"Dear friends, since you will not hear it from our devoted and unreasonably modest Ivan, I will finish this story! It is thanks to him that the entire crew, down to the last sailor, safely returned to our Adriatic before Christmas that year. Ivan took good care of his crew during the entire time they were hostages in Shanghai and used all possible connections he could think of to help with their return. In the end, they all came back on various ships of the *Navigazione Generale Italiana* company, mainly thanks to the reputation and influence of Captains Lovrić and Ristorcelli, but also our own Baron Felice Mayneri who is here with us tonight. Let's toast to all three of them wholeheartedly!"

Momentarily, Baron Mayneri raises his glass of wine and reacts to the toast:

"Dear Antun, not at all, not at all! It was my pleasure to help the boys. I personally called Filippo Marinetti in Rome, I remember well, and he immediately took care of the whole thing, naturally with the necessary help of Captain Ristorcelli, always our dear guest here and in Dubrovnik!"

The Baron then quickly turns to Tove and Sven and continues in one breath:

"Our dear young guests certainly know that I helped them as well. Giuseppe very much asked me to do so, referring to the intractable Curzio Malaparte, a relative of my college friend. I presume you met Curzio on Capri. He sure is stubborn and quite unique, you certainly would agree. I hear that he even managed to get to the Russian Front and scribble something for *Corriere della Sera* from there. And was then imprisoned for a while upon returning to Rome so he can calm down a bit. Oh, not to forget – Baron Alessandro Monti della Corte also contacted me with the same request. It seems you somehow impressed him very much indeed on Capri. Curzio and Alessandro aside, what I promised I arranged, with Francesco Giunta, my dear friend who, for your information, is now the Governor of Dalmatia. Francesco assured me that, as far as he is concerned, you do not have to worry about anything while sailing on our beautiful azure Adriatic. Except, of course, for the consequences of the disgusting crimes committed daily by the communist pigs and other bandits who call themselves *partisans*!"

Captain Sesan, slightly embarrassed by the Baron's boasting, addresses Lovrić by changing the subject of conversation:

"We certainly hope everything will be OK with the beautiful schooner and her crew. By the way, Ivan, where do you stand with your translation? You first intrigued us with it quite a bit last Christmas, but then you remained silent ever since. Tell our young guests something about your favorite writer because I don't believe they know anything about him, but they sure should. Writers like that are not born every day."

Captain Lovrić starts by explaining how, during the years spent on *Tomislav* and sailing all over the world, especially to South America, he learned to read and write Spanish, English and Hindi decently (which to those that knew him meant *perfectly*). He was very lucky to meet and talk with many interesting people in Buenos Aires at parties given by Miho Mihanovich in honor of *Tomislav's* visits. Miho was the younger brother of Baron Nicolás Mihanovich who passed away in Buenos Aires in 1929. He quickly became something of a second father to Ivan who very much looked forward to *Tomislav's* sails to Buenos Aires so he could spend time with his dear barba Miho.

Five years ago, in January, only a few months before noble Miho left this world, at a reception given for the *Tomislav's* crew he introduced Lovrić to a fantastic writer by the name Jorge Luis Borges, an uncompromising fighter against all evil people. Miho and Borges got to know each other very well through joint activities in the Committee Against Racism and Anti-Semitism. Because of their open criticism of all authoritarian and nationalistic views, Miho, and especially Borges who was already a highly respected writer and intellectual, were increasingly attacked in the media and otherwise by a growing number of Argentinian Nazi sympathizers. On the day of the reception, at a lunch which the two of them now traditionally had together, Mihanovich gave Captain Lovrić a newspaper editorial written by Borges, with the following words: "Jorge Luis is an extraordinary man and a real gentleman. I am sure you will become close. I am proud to call him my friend and am very happy that you will finally meet each other tonight." Ivan remembered the following words from the editorial:

The Germanophile is anti-Semitic as well: He wishes to expel from our country a Slavo-Germanic community in which names of German origin predominate (Rosenblatt, Gruenberg ...) and which speaks a German dialect, Yiddish."

Just as Mihanovich predicted, Ivan and Borges started a beautiful friendship that night. Although the brave writer was the star of the reception, with guests flocking to him from all sides, he used every free moment to find Ivan, about whom he has been hearing words of praise from Miho for years, so they can continue their conversation about many different subjects. Subjects that, for example, included their shared views of the world, the conviction that nothing can be more important than the humanity of each person, the negative selection of people that others call politicians and who had to be corrupt by definition, the love for languages which unlocks many unknown exciting doors, exotic distant lands, and many more. Borges was particularly intrigued with Ivan's tales of his voyages to New Guinea, Australia and New Zealand, lands he did not know much about but was very interested in, especially now that Ivan described some stories he heard from the native people there.

The writer therefore kindly invited Ivan to be his guest the next day for a breakfast at the favorite *Café Tortoni*, because he is dying to continue their exciting conversation. The extremely flattered Captain Lovrić accepted the invitation, with a slight disbelief.

The delicious breakfast in the pleasant atmosphere of *Café Tortoni* ended with Señor Borges's kind request for a big favor – he is hopeful that Ivan will find some time, during his long sails on *Tomislav*, to read an unfinished story which he brought with him and provide feedback when they see each other again in the same cafe, hopefully soon. Also, he would not want to bury Ivan with his other stories although he would very much like to, believing they would both learn from them and can tell each other a lot. In any case, if he succeeds in his intention to collect his stories in one place, and add a few more, like, for example, this one named "Tlön, Uqbar, Orbis Tertius", he will be more than thrilled to send the book to Ivan before their next meeting.

Ivan then continued: "My dear young friends, that is the story Antun was talking about. I am struggling with its translation for years now, and I don't even know why. I retold it last Christmas to Antun, Felice and others when we gathered for my name day. I know exactly why they all insisted I should finally translate it – it really is fascinating. But that is not all. Two years ago, as promised, Borges sent me his first book, a collection of short stories, for my birthday of which he somehow found out, I am clueless how. The same story is in the book. To my enormous surprise, Borges slightly changed it with couple of suggestions I gave him when we again met in *Café Tortoni* on my next sail to Buenos Aires. All other stories, believe me, are as fascinating if not more, and I now don't know which one I should translate first. Although, my knowledge of Spanish is inadequate for the task at hand so I will probably forget the whole thing."

Protesting, Mayneri loudly interrupts Lovrić to the astonishment of everyone and starts to shout:

"Unacceptable! You cannot give up! Only weaklings do that. Like that damn Mussolini who cowardly turned his tail when it became scary, a month ago, and voluntarily disappeared into nothingness! I completely agree with my dear friend Filippo Marinetti who clearly wrote in his Fascist Manifesto what the future must be. The damn lazy cowardly Duce! Couldn't he read it again?! Mercilessness, courage, determination, that is what we need. Futurismo!"

Having let all that steam out, Baron Mayneri turns to Dobrović and Sesan and asks for approval:

"Nikola, am I not right? Just look at your powerful futuristic hotel, not even an earthquake can damage it! And you, Antun, you didn't light the entire island for nothing! I know, I know, everyone says my palace in Dubrovnik is magnificent! And it is, but that is now the past. Nikola? Antun?"

Completely taken aback by this eruption of emotions, the equable architect soothes the situation with the carefully chosen words:

"Dear Felice, I am sure many would agree with what you exposed to us so passionately. I am also sure our young visitors from the North will now clearly understand, if they have not already, what it means to have the temperamental Mediterranean blood. It is hot outside so it must be hot inside. Anyhow, I would like to note that my futurism, as you call it, is supported entirely by the millennia of architectural tradition from all corners of the world, with which I am permanently fascinated. Romans had already built with concrete, sometimes reinforced or even prestressed, which still only a few realize. I just repeated that with the *Grand Hotel* and *Villa Vesna*. I moved to Dubrovnik, among other things, so I could learn many useful things from the old Dalmatian builders, known and unknown. They all realized, a long time ago, the most important principle: how to build in complete harmony with the environment and how to use the sun, water, and wind, and not to fight them. Although they did not call it that way, they worked <u>with</u> the *energy* that surrounded and permeated their future buildings, instead of working against it. I will never be a real artist like my late brother Petar, who prematurely left us forever this last year, leaving behind many beautiful paintings of our Lopud, Hvar and Dubrovnik, which he loved so much. But, maybe in all that I am doing there may be a trace of an art, or something that future generations may call similarly. In the end, everything is relative. The truth is the truth, or it is not, only in the eyes of one who is looking at it that moment. However, it is certain that all of us here on Lopud agree that without our two Antuns and Niko we would have not been able to enjoy in all that electricity provides. The electricity that the three of them so generously gave us. That electric power plant in the *Grand* was just an idea of mine, until they supported it and then materialized it. Felice, I therefore join you in your demand to Ivan not to give up the translation of the story, and now the whole book by Borges, the fantastic writer whom only Ivan met personally, but whom all of us here, now including our dear young guests from the North, know. There is no substitute for persistence. Persistence that cannot be swayed by anything is a gift from God."

Waiting for Nikola to finish, and after noticing that Vinko fell asleep curled in his chair, Captain Lovrić looks at his watch and remarks out loud that midnight is long gone and that the dear Swedish friends must be dying, after the long exhausting sail, to fall into the comfortable beds that await them in the *Grand Hotel*. Shyly, Tove and Sven confirm. Then, with one voice, they thank everyone for the extraordinary hospitality, hoping they will be able to return it one day. Captain Lovrić gently wakes Vinko up and everyone rises from the tables. Architect Dobrović hugs Tove and Sven and politely directs them toward the hotel:

"Please allow me to go with you and check if everything is OK with the accommodation."

Then, not waiting for the answer, he pulls them down the quay hugging them the whole way.

Slowly drifting off to sleep by the open window, and feeling the warm night breeze which carried in the calming sound of the waves from the beach, Tove and Sven whispered to each other about the many wonderful things they experienced since their faithful schooner brought them to the small stone port of the picturesque island town. Before she fell asleep, Tove gazed at the framed painting of a grove of old olive trees hanging on the wall and lit by the moonlight, mesmerized:

"I would have given anything to have had with us at dinner those two brothers and the writer from Argentina, and Nikola's brother painter."

Incidentally, during a visit to Buenos Aires, I discovered a fascinating piece of information, at least to me. Miho Mihanovich was well known to many Argentinians as a great humanist, philanthrope and benefactor. He shared the better part of his companies' profits with the employees and was especially passionate about helping the education and enlightenment of the immigrants coming to Argentina from Dalmatia. To that end, he established a public library in Buenos Aires to which he donated 1800 books written in Croatian. I managed to track down the granddaughter of the library's first librarian, Constance Fernández. Among other things, she told me how Borges learned to read Croatian very well, incited by his great friendship with Captain Ivan Lovrić. Borges often visited the library browsing its books, before completely losing his vision later in his life. He was fascinated by the voyage logbooks kept by the seafaring men from Dubrovnik and Korčula. Among those he preferred were the travel papers by the famous Captain Marin Kanavelić. Still, his favorite remained the six leather-bound illustrated volumes written by Vinko Paletin, philosopher, theologian, cartographer and seafarer, one of very few Croats to visit South America as early as in the 16th century. Browsing the books that Mihanovich donated, Borges also found a piece of information that the Dubrovnik Republic, in 1416, was the first in Europe to abolish slavery and prohibit the transport of slaves on her ships. Borges liked to emphasize this every time he, as the favorite guest of honor, gave public lectures which the library often organized for the citizens of Buenos Aires.

Painting of the old olive tree grove which Petar Dobrović painted on the island of Lopud in 1928 and gave to his brother Nikola. At the time of Tove's and Swen's visit, the painting was hanging on the wall of the Grand Hotel apartment where they stayed. Before leaving the island, immediately following the capitulation of Italy, Dobrović left the precious painting in care of the Glavović family. Today, the painting is on display at the Gallery of Petar Dobrović of the Belgrade Museum of Modern Arts, housed in the apartment where the famous painter lived and worked.

Photograph from an old worn-out leather folder in possession of Ms. Vlasta Pulić Glavović, of unknown origin. On the back of the photo there is a handwritten note: Island of Lopud near Dubrovnik, 1928, and in the upper left corner are initials "PD". This grove of olive trees is one of the oldest on the

Croatian Adriatic. It was planted centuries before the earthquake that devastated Dubrovnik and nearby islands on April 6, 1667.

Left: Café Tortoni in Buenos Aires, where Captain Ivan Lovrić and Argentine writer Jorge Luis Borges started their extraordinary friendship (see www.cafetortoni.com.ar) Right: Book which Borges sent to captain Ivan Lovrić as a present for Ivan's birthday in 1941. I got the book from Vinko Lovrić in Podgora in 2017, the last time I saw him.

El Ateneo Grand Splendid, bookstore with a fascinating history where I met Constance Fernández. Max Glücksmann, born in 1875 in Černivci, Bukovina, in Austro-Hungarian Empire, arrived to Buenos Aires in 1890 where he managed to impress Mihanovich, a great benefactor of architecture and arts. Consequently, Mihanovich provided most of the funds for Glücksmann to purchase Teatro Nacional housed in elegant El Ateneo Grand Splendid building and renovate it to Grand Splendid-The Splendid Theater which opened in 1919. Under Glücksmann, the theatre became a pioneering venue, hosting the first radio broadcasts in Argentina and the first sound films shown in Buenos Aires, among other things. After a hectic history, in year 2000 the theater was converted to a bookstore, widely regarded as the most beautiful in the world. (https://turismo.buenosaires.gob.ar/en/otros-establecimientos/el-ateneo-grand-splendid-bookstore)

Borges

Chapter 16

Edvard and Svetoslav

It is time to explain who the two postdoctoral students from MIT were and why are they important in this story. Together with Nikola Tesla, Edvard Neumman and Svetoslav Belov were involved with a group that experimented with time and space travel. They spent lots of time with Tesla, slowly earning his trust. Moreover, the great inventor became something of an unofficial mentor to them after they promised never to misuse what he had taught them. Tesla also gave them several, as he called them, *real things* with which they spent countless hours, figuring out how they could be used.

Based on Ivica's knowledge of the information included in Tesla's personal notebooks which Tesla gave to his nephew Sava Kosanović, Edvard and Svetoslav frequently travelled from Boston, where they conducted their research at MIT, to New York. They stayed in the *New Yorker Hotel* and worked with Tesla in the laboratory that occupied an entire floor of the hotel. It is not completely clear who provided the funds for the laboratory. The best Ivica could tell from Tesla's notes, it was most likely the *Westinghouse* company which had a quite complicated relationship with its former star inventor. For the various breakthrough experiments conducted in this laboratory, Tesla and his apprentices used the energy produced by the hotel's DC power plant which was arguably the most powerful ever built for a private entity in the entire country. The plant could produce energy output many-fold higher than what was needed for the simple operation of the hotel.

Edvard and Svetoslav came to MIT from the Cornell University in Ithaca, New York where they earned their doctorate degrees under the supervision of Alexander Tukach, the eccentric professor of theoretical electrical engineering. The personal friendship Edvard and Svetoslav developed while at Cornell was strengthened and deepened at MIT.

There they first worked on both the theoretical and the applied research of fractal mathematical models of energy modulations in variable time. It seems that for the purposes of their research they even developed the first ever digital computer, of which today there are only whispers at MIT. Despite all my academic and other connections, I was not able to find out anything more about that computer or the results of their research during the many visits to Boston I made over the last several years.

What is certain is that Edvard and Svetoslav were truly outstanding scientists and engineers. It was also true that the better part of their careers they spent working for the military which secretly engaged them as "the weird geniuses." They were never military personnel however and retained their full civilian status.

Edvard and Svetoslav shared with Tesla a love for the science of new age, as Tesla called it: an obsession with the nature of time and the possibilities of time travel. They, with awe, absorbed Tesla's views on time control, founded on the technology of eternity and non-Hertzian waves which have super-luminous speeds or, when needed, can momentarily be projected anywhere in space and time. They believed that the understanding of the secrets of time would ensure control of the continuum in physical and biological processes, with no time limits. The perception of physical or local time, as we currently understand it and believe it to be the only one possible, for the two of them was only a dimension of the real (multi-dimensional) time and, in a way, a dimension of the multidimensional space-time domain which does not flow and is the arithmetic zero.

They enjoyed playing with logical puzzles, as conveyed to me by Edvard's granddaughter who still remembers the following one: "If you leave town A at three o'clock and arrive to town B at four o'clock, what is the time in town A when you arrive to town B?" The answer, of course, is that in town A it is also four o'clock. Between one point in space and another point in space time does not change at all. It is always the present, the arithmetic zero.

Edvard and Svetoslav where ready to engage in an overheated argument with a select few that were able to discuss these "esoteric things", to the point of possible physical confrontation when challenged to defend the principles they inherited from Tesla. They believed that the entire Universe was created at once because it is infinite, and the infinite cannot be composed of parts. The infinite is not a spatial eternity, as imagined by the naive human mind; rather, it is a perpetual present, the only one we have and live in all the time. It is nothing other than our own mind. From a location in space to a location in space we bounce through the zeros of time and everything is swarming with the parallel universes, phase-shifted in their parallel existence.

At the same time when Tesla and his apprentices were working on time travel, researchers at the University of Chicago were studying the possibility of invisibility using electricity. These two projects were moved in 1939 to the Institute of Advanced Studies at Princeton University in New Jersey. There, the new combined group succeeded in making some small object invisible and presented its findings to the Government. As war was clearly on the horizon, the military decided to support the research and redirected it with the goal to develop a technology which would make entire warships invisible, first to radars and then possibly to the human eye. This new project was given the code name *Project Rainbow*.

Because of constant pressure from the Government, Tesla reluctantly agreed to take part in *Project Rainbow*. In the beginning, he assumed the lead with Dr. John Von Neumann as his deputy. Edvard Neumman (Von Neumann's nephew) and Svetoslav Belov were Tesla's secret key assistants. Tesla himself was producing the majority of necessary calculations, drawings and power generators for the project, up until late 1942 when he realized that his every move was under constant surveillance by secret Government agencies. Tesla knew all too well that he would never be safe again and started to misguide and sabotage the project deliberately. He completely, although unofficially, withdrew from the project when it became apparent that the Navy intended to use the crew of one of its ships as guinea pigs in the experiment, despite Tesla's strong objections.

After that, OSS rented a room on the same floor of the *New Yorker* hotel where Tesla resided. The agency instituted a 24-hour surveillance of the inventor. What the surveillance, for some mysterious reason, failed to detect was that Tesla and his apprentices managed to remove various documents, objects, and even some equipment from the laboratory using the hotel's freight elevator and the unknown, to the agents, yet conspicuous exit from the power plant (which was located in the hotel's basement) adjacent to a New York Subway tunnel. The agents were apparently not concerned with Tesla and his two young co-workers going frequently between the laboratory and the power plant. They simply considered it a normal part of their "weird work." To this day I remember how Ivica laughed contagiously telling me all this.

On January 8, 1943, Tesla was found dead in his room by the hotel maid Alice Monaghan who ignored the sign "do not disturb" on the door and entered the room. Tesla supposedly placed the sign several days earlier. He passed away around 10:30 pm the night of January the 7th, as officially determined by the assistant medical examiner H.W. Webley.

As soon as he was informed by the hotel of his uncle's death, Sava Kosanović hurried to the *New Yorker* only to find out Tesla's body has been already removed, together with many other things the inventor kept in his room. A black notebook, of which Kosanović was aware from the earlier visits to his uncle and which had various pages marked "for government", was also missing. Two days after Tesla's death the Federal Bureau of Investigation (according to official accounts) ordered the Alien Property Custodian to seize all of Tesla's belongings. This was very unusual as Tesla was a United States citizen already for decades. It is much less known (or, more precisely, not at all known to the general public) that the whole operation around Tesla's death was handled by OSS. Soon after WWII, OSS became the CIA and the new agency quietly left the scene of various controversies and conspiracy theories surrounding the death of Tesla which quickly started to spread. The Federal Bureau of Investigation (FBI) always officially maintained that it was never involved in any search for missing Tesla documents or microfilms made of them, including the documents related to the infamous "death rays".

As more recently reported (and most likely because of his family name), John G. Trump, a professor at MIT and a technical aide to the National Defense Research Committee, was tasked to analyze the items retrieved from Tesla's room 3327 on the 33rd floor of the hotel *New*

Yorker. His conclusions can be summed up as being dismissive of any importance these items may have had for either national security or science in general. Nevertheless, in 1952, after relentless pressure from Sava Kosanović, the United States Government finally agreed to hand over to him Tesla's estate (or, rather, what remained of it). Tesla, before his death, left all his possessions to the Yugoslav Kingdom, in the intermediate care of his nephew Sava Kosanović. The estate was shipped to Belgrade in 80 trunks and has been kept ever since at the Nikola Tesla Museum, 51 Krunska Street, according to official accounts.

It is now increasingly speculated that Albert Einstein, Nobel Prize winner and Princeton professor, was initially involved in *Project Rainbow*. It is also no secret that Tesla and Einstein, although demonstrating something of a mutual personal respect (at least publicly), did not share the same views of the most important scientific questions of their and our time – the nature of Universe, gravity, light, matter, and such. Although Tesla was an excellent mathematician, unlike Einstein and as explained earlier, he did not rely much on his mathematical skills when making many engineering and scientific breakthroughs. This understanding (or misunderstanding) of the importance of mathematics was likely not the main reason for various disagreements the two geniuses had during their work on the project. Still, it is interesting that Einstein, in the years when the top-secret *Project Rainbow* was picking up steam, did not publish any scientific paper or made a notable scientific contribution. It is also interesting that in one of his personal notebooks Tesla almost sarcastically mentioned something related to the Einstein's first wife, the supreme Serbian mathematician and physicist, Mileva Marić. Namely, according to my high school friend Ivica Kaurić, Tesla wrote it as a matter of first-hand knowledge that "without the help from Mileva, Einstein would have never become famous, and it is very sad what he did to our countrywoman..."

Another man briefly involved with *Project Rainbow*, who later became quite infamous in scientific circles (especially those connected to the Government), was Thomas Townsend Brown. Officially serving as Lieutenant in the U.S. Navy, he was transferred to its largest naval base in Norfolk, Virginia in May 1942. There, he assumed position of Radar and Educational Officer at the Atlantic Fleet School and was reported to "know more about radar detection than any individual in the U.S. Navy." Under a veil of mystery, Brown was discharged from Navy service in October 1942, about the same time Tesla unofficially withdrew from *Project Rainbow*. According to official records, Brown requested to resign "for the good of the naval service in order to escape trial by General Court Martial." The official discharge exam, the final Navy Fitness Report, dated October 5, 1942, is completely blank, with hand-written "see remarks" on one page, and on the other page, in the "remarks" section, Captain Hinkamp writes "In view of the circumstances under which this officer was detached, I desire to make no comment."

As always in cases as mysterious as this one, which involve scientists-inventors ahead of their time and working on secret military projects, various theories have emerged including those purposely misleading. For example, one often-cited reason for his discharge from the Navy is that Brown suffered from a nervous breakdown. In a later official report produced by a Government agency, Brown's "self-confessed" homosexuality was offered as the real reason for his discharge. In any case, only a month after he left Norfolk in Virginia, Brown started working for the Vega Aircraft Corporation in California. He there continued *"in independent research work concerning radar detection and had concerned himself with techniques and theory more advanced than that in present use. He had his own laboratory and had purchased equipment from his own funds for use in his experimental work, and this equipment was taken by Subject when he was detached from the Fleet Service School."* (exact quotes from the same agency report.)

By leaving the Navy, Brown deliberately escaped working on *Project Rainbow* where one of his most likely assignments was to design a special radar detection antenna system on the *USS Eldridge*. However, during his short-lived interactions with Tesla's small team, Brown learned quite a few more things of which he never thought of before, even when he was obsessed with the questions of electricity and gravity during his formative years in the early 1920s.

In scientific circles today, Brown is best known for his research of "odd electrical effects which led him to believe he had discovered a connection between strong electric fields and gravity, a type of antigravity effect." Brown's claims have been dismissed by mainstream science and his "antigravity force" has generally been attributed to "electrohydrodynamics", the movement of charged particles that transfers their momentum to surrounding neutral particles in air, also called "ionic drift" or "ionic wind". However, as simply and ironically put by my friend Ivica, no one among the mainstream scientists was ever able to explain why is the so-called "Biefeld-Brown" effect observed even in the vacuum.

Despite of several key scientists leaving the project, including Tesla who passed away in the meantime, nothing could stop the U.S. military of course. In the spring of 1943, the Navy conducted the first "Live Experiment" with caged animals on board of a vessel that was briefly made invisible. When the vessel became visible again or, according to some, was materialized back, the catastrophic consequences of the experiment were apparent. Some animals simply disappeared, and some were badly burnt. The military therefore waited with another trial for a while, but the hardliners prevailed in the end. On August 12, 1943, the Navy conducted another experiment without knowledge of the civilian scientists, this time with people on board a U.S. battleship named *USS Eldridge* which was anchored in Delaware Bay near Philadelphia, Pennsylvania. This trial became known as the *Philadelphia Experiment*. The *USS Eldridge*, together with the entire crew on board, allegedly disappeared and travelled through time and, according to some accounts, through space as well. Again, various conspiracy theories regarding the *Philadelphia Experiment* have since emerged, including those purposely misleading or designed to conspire the conspiracy of the conspiracies. Even Hollywood made its own contribution with a B movie.

Less known sources I was able to uncover list the equipment used for the experiment, such as specially designed Tesla coils installed on the boat on two (or four?) towers, Tesla-designed electromagnets powered by super-generators, phase-synchronized RF transmitters, and such. All this was assembled and activated to bend the gravity and create what is today popularly referred to as "wormhole".

For our story it is important to note that Edvard Neumman and Svetoslav Below were integral to *Project Rainbow* but did not participate in *The Philadelphia Experiment,* which was not conceded by the civilian participants, at least not by most of them. Where did Edvard and Svetoslav end up? After returning to the United States from Europe in the fall of 1943 (of which I will provide more details a bit later), Edvard started working at the National Advisory Committee for Aeronautics, or NACA, which was later transformed to NASA (National Aeronautics and Space Administration). There he continued working on the project that he and Svetoslav initiated during *Blackbird's* secret mission to the Adriatic. Soon after retiring from NASA, Edvard emigrated to Israel in the mid-1980s.

After WWII ended, Svetoslav left MIT and continued his academic career at a private university also in Massachusetts. Already in deep retirement and in his old age, Svetoslav emigrated to Russia after its first democratically elected President Boris Yeltsin resigned in 1999 and was succeeded by his chosen successor, former Prime Minister Vladimir Putin.

Up until their paths diverged, Edvard and Svetoslav often visited each other to play chess, even though they lived on the opposite sides of the U.S. Atlantic coast. Although I was not able to document it yet, it is almost certain that everything they learned from Tesla, the two former postdoctoral students from MIT took with them. One to Israel, and the other one to Russia.

Edvard Neumman expecting company at a small dinner celebrating his retirement in 1985, days before his permanent departure for Israel. Courtesy of Neumman family.

Edvard (on the right) and Svetoslav (in the middle) playing bridge with friends on Edisto Island in South Carolina where Svetoslav had a modest vacation home. Courtesy of Neumman family.

Chapter 17

Delta

Blackbird and her Swedish crew spent five unforgettable days on Lopud, enjoying the hospitality of everyone on the beautiful forested island. Tove and Sven particularly cherished leisurely hours spent sunbathing and swimming on the sandy beach Šunj, "the nicest in the whole of Dalmatia" as Vinko told them, with the authority of someone who knows what he is talking about. From Vinko they also learned about exciting history of Lopud and the past glory of the powerful Dubrovnik Republic to which Lopud belonged for many centuries. The last day of their stay on the island, the *Blackbird's* crew enjoyed the sunset from Polačica, the island's tallest peak. Magnificent views of the coast, nearby islands, and the imposing limestone landscape of the Pelješac Peninsula in the far distance, were stunning. As Vinko was pointing out various landmarks on the maritime maps the Swedes brought with them, he could not hide his amazement with the maps as he never saw anything so precise and informative before.

On Friday, August 27, 1943, at 9:35 in the morning, *Blackbird* graciously left Lopud, with many people gathered in the port to wish the crew farewell. They gazed in awe at the beautiful schooner. A handful of Vinko's friends could not resist loudly teasing the schooner's crew, again leaving Tove and Sven somewhat mystified. Only one man did not clap his hands and did not have a smile on his face when *Blackbird* caught the full wind with her sails heading northwest towards the Mljet channel. Captain Ivan Lovrić, as much as he tried, could not stop tears from gathering in the corners of his gentle, sad eyes. Only he and two more people on the schooner knew the real truth behind the *Blackbird's* journey. With a heavy heart, Captain Lovrić agreed not to tell it to his son, trusting his old friend Giuseppe who persuaded him that it was in Vinko's best interest not to know anything. This agreement is what now ate at him, unbearably, as he watched the boat looking ever so smaller, taking his son Vinko away, into the unknown.

Blackbird spent the first night anchored near Kućište, a small village on the Pelješac coast west of Orebić, after sailing right by the magnificent stone towers and walls of Korčula, the medieval Dalmatian city. Tove and Sven were amazed. Although burning with desire to visit the city, seeing it lit by the sun in its full glory and hearing from Vinko that Marco Polo was born there, they resisted. They made the decision out of precaution and despite the fact that they now carried with them a permit for unrestricted sailing on the Adriatic. They received the permit, signed by the Governor of Dalmatia Francesco Guinti, from Baron Mayneri who pompously handed it to them two days earlier. Vinko of course did not quite understand why the Swedes seemed reluctant to visit the city. He even, very enthusiastically, offered to show them the house where Marco Polo was born and where the much respected Depolo family lived for centuries. (The surname Polo is linked to the Croatian name Pavao and was documented in its common form Paulovic (Pavlović), as well as in the Latin form De Paulis and Venetian Di Polo; it remains Depolo on the island to this day.) Vinko visited the house many times with his father, as their two families were close friends, always enjoying the view of the city roofs, churches, and the Pelješac Peninsula from the house's tower erected in the first half of the 13th century by Marco's father Nikola and uncle Mate. He explained to Tove and Sven what everyone in Dalmatia has been learning in school and from the elders to this day:

Marco's father and uncle started their trading business in Korčula, which at the time was part of the Republic of Venice, and the members of the Depolo family were guardians of the city's stone walls. However, for the two skillful tradesmen, the island was only the starting point of their trade and their adventurous lives. The two brothers erected a tower and founded their own trading outpost in the town of Sudac on the Crimean Peninsula. They had their main trade center in Constantinople, to which many Korčula businessmen and shipbuilders were travelling. For some time they even lived there, successfully trading with the Persians among others. Nikola and Mate eventually went deep into Asia as the first Europeans to travel the famous Silk Road trade route, stretching from the Middle East to China. They established trade contacts with the dignitaries of various Tartar peoples, and finally managed to reach the court of the Great Kublai Khan in China. Marco joined them on one of their journeys and remained captivated by the Far East for the rest of his life, always wanting to return.

Marco was taken prisoner by the Genoese in the naval battle of Korčula, between the Venetian and Genovese states. He wrote his book "Million" about his travels to China in a Genoese prison. Yet it was Marco's cellmate, Rusticello who would later produce a book "The Travels of Marco Polo" which made Marco's travelling adventures famous throughout the world.

Vinko shared his firm belief why Marco Polo and his father and uncle were so drawn by the mysterious distant lands: it was inherited from their adventurous and brave ancestors. The oldest legend of all regarding the foundation of Korčula, says that the city was founded by the Trojan hero, Antenor, after the fall of Troy. One old Venetian manuscript also points out that, together with Antenor, a certain Lucius Polus arrived here, as an ancestor of the Polo family. A well-known sculptor from Corinth, Polo, lived in Korčula in the 5th century B.C. (according to the Encyclopedia Treccani). At that time Korčula was the main Illyrian emporium in the Adriatic.

Not being able to persuade Tove and Sven to dock and visit, Vinko gave up, satisfied with their explanation which seemed logical: They would first like to finish the main portion of their official business before they could relax and fully enjoy the Adriatic. This for sure will include coming back to visit Korčula. What was their official business? As vividly explained to Vinko, especially by Sven who showcased several apparently very valuable cameras, they were first going to visit the Neretva River delta, the largest shelter for many rare migratory birds from all over Europe. There they were going to conduct an ornithological study for the Institute of Migratory Birds at the Swedish Lund University. Sven repeatedly explained the perfect attributes of one of the cameras he got from the Institute for the study. It was a modified version of *Hasselblad SKa4* which Sven characterized as "infinitely better than the two overrated German *Leicas*" which he also brought with him. Vinko was therefore quite puzzled when, from the very beginning of their exploration of the Delta, Sven started to take countless photos of everything in sight using his other cameras as often as the glorified *Hasselblad SKa4*. Sven also made many notifications and wrote various strange symbols on the marine maps Vinko admired so much. Every time he finished annotating the maps, Sven would return them into a water-proof metal box, together with a notebook in which he constantly wrote.

Unsuspecting Vinko could not possibly know the real goal of their sailing, concealed even by his father: the analysis of conditions and locations for a possible invasion of the Dalmatian coast by the allied forces which included advancing along the Neretva River valley to the strategically important city of Mostar and its airport. In any case, Vinko's intimate knowledge of every single armband of the Delta and his understanding of the significance of different marsh vegetation for the navigation of the boat was priceless.

While Sven was restlessly taking photographs and playing with his maps, even when the *Blackbird* made extended stops, Vinko was using every opportunity to draw making sketches, which Tove liked very much, praising his "great talent". Tove's warmth towards Vinko gave him the courage to ask if she would pose on the schooner's bow "and beautify a real drawing." Tove cheerfully accepted the request with a remark that she was honored by it. This marked the beginning of a series of elaborate drawings Vinko made during the *Blackbird's* journey on the Adriatic, of which the gorgeous Norwegian was often the main subject, sometimes without knowing it.

Blackbird finished her exploration of the Delta in early afternoon of August the 30th, and with that the first phase of *Mission Capri* on the Yugoslav Adriatic was completed. As the late summer sun was still relentless, Sven and Vinko, immediately and without any hesitation, agreed with the Tove's suggestion to celebrate the completion of their ornithological study of the Delta with swimming at the closest nice beach. Thus, after a short sail down the coast, *Blackbird* threw her anchor in the picturesque little bay of the Dube village. The crew then cheerfully and laughing loudly dove off the schooner and swam to the sandy beach in front of the village, to the astonishment of a few locals.

At some point, while all three of them were lying on the sand, enduring the burning sun, Vinko asks Tove and Sven if they have decided where to sail next. They reply, in one voice, that they have full confidence in him making the best choice, although they may have a suggestion as well. Namely, the last night during his regular radio communication with mission headquarters, Sven was informed that the circumstances have changed and they will have to postpone the planned sailing up the coast, to Split and Zadar, for at least three days, when they will receive further instructions. To Vinko, this was explained a bit differently: "It would be interesting if they could, before sailing north, visit Pelješac since they are practically already there, mostly because it would be great to buy several jugs of that amazing wine they tasted on Lopud so they can enjoy the sail even more."

After shortly thinking it over, Vinko makes the decision and invites them to swim back to the schooner and sail out as soon as possible so they can arrive to the destination before sunset.

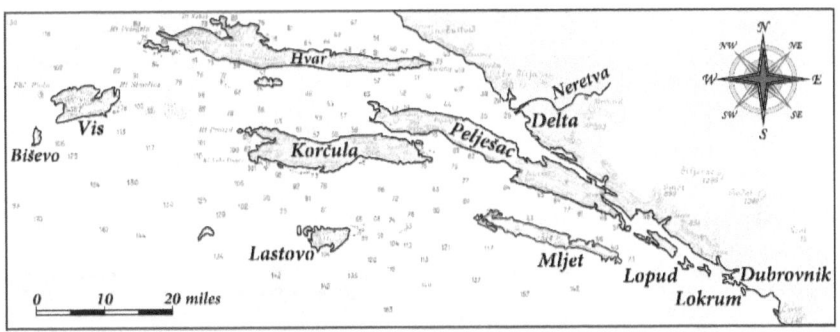

Map of Southern Dalmatia where *Blackbird* sailed between August 22 and October 7, 1943 when she left Vis for Bari, Italy.

Vinko's drawing of the Neretva River delta.

Korčula at the time of *Blackbird's* sailing on the Adriatic.
Courtesy of Croatian National Archives.

Chapter 18

Wine Cellar

Blackbird is on her final approach to the town of Mali Ston, and all five monumental stone towers of its fortification are now fully visible. After enjoying the view for a while, Vinko declares that this evening they will have a reward for the accomplished task in the Delta – dinner made of the fabled Mali Ston shells and, of course, the delicious house red wine. They will stay overnight in the town's quiet port and tomorrow continue up north, along the Pelješac coast, to the village of Drače. There they may get lucky and find what they were looking for – the rare red Dingač wine (which is what Vinko believed Tove and Sven were talking about.)

After securing the boat, Tove and Sven wait on the quay for Vinko who disappeared through a door of the nearby stone building. In no time Vinko and an imposing man with a long mustache come back carrying a wooden table with three rickety chairs on top of it and they place it right there on the quay in front *Blackbird*. The same man, whom Vinko introduces as barba Jozo, their host, then fetches a jug of red wine, glasses, and a gas lantern which he places on the old wooden table with the following words which Vinko translates to his mates: "Dinner will be ready in about half an hour, please enjoy yourselves until then and I welcome you to our little town."

Vinko, as usual, was right – Tove and Sven are elated with the taste of mussels which the friendly owner of a little hostelry brought over in a huge cast-iron steaming pot. They never had mussels that tasted so delicious and they are curious to learn the recipe. Vinko shrugs his shoulders and simply says how there was nothing to it. Everyone does it the same way in Dalmatia, himself included having for years watched how his late mother was preparing the dish. Then, at the insistence of his new friends, Vinko slowly recites the recipe:

"Clean the shells, removing any 'beards' and rinse well under cold water. Throw away the ones with cracked shells and those already visibly open. Heat olive oil in a pot and fry some crushed garlic, but just for a little bit. You don't want the garlic to turn dark brown. Once you smell the garlic real well, add some parsley and a bit of white pepper, stir and then add the mussels to the pot. Throw in a few lemon slices, cover the pot and let cook. Once the mussels have opened, add the white wine and sprinkle with breadcrumbs. Cook a little more until the mussels are wide open and then simply enjoy eating them!"

As the last few mussels quickly disappear from the pot, and the dusk surrenders to the night, the *Blackbird's* crew notice barba Jozo jump to a dinghy and paddle out of the port. Not making much of it, Sven asks Vinko about the menacing towers and heavy walls looming over the town and the port, curious when and who built them. After a rather long history lesson from Vinko, who loved the history of his favorite Dubrovnik Republic, Tove and Sven made sure to remember its key points: The Republic purchased this part of the coast from the Serbian Emperor Dušan in 1333 (an easy year to remember!) for a hefty price in gold. This marked the beginning of the prosperity for the 150 Dubrovnik families who settled here and greatly expanded two sister towns, Ston and Mali (Little) Ston. It took them 20 years to build the heavy stone walls and fortifications to protect themselves and the entire Pelješac Peninsula from the Ottoman incursions.

Just as Vinko was wrapping up his enthusiastic lecture, barba Jozo appears from the dark with a basket full of oysters he had just harvested, and addresses the *Blackbird's* crew:

"I keep these for special occasions only, and this is one of them. Guests of dear Captain Lovrić are my dear guests as well. Please enjoy every single oyster! They are the best there are on the entire coast! I will come back with knives and lemons."

Vinko, for some reason, did not care much for the oysters, which certainly was not the case with Tove and Sven. After all the shells were consumed, and the jug of red wine emptied, they boarded the schooner to spend the night tucked away in the tranquil port of Mali Ston. It remains unknown, as I did not research it much further, how and if the night on the boat was influenced by the *frutti di mare* served to the

Blackbird's crew by the friendly imposing man with the long mustache, barba Jozo. Whatever the case may be, *Blackbird* spent one more night in Mali Ston, at the firm insistence of Tove.

In the morning of September 1, *Blackbird* continues her journey, northwards along the interior coast of the peninsula. There is not much wind and the sail drags on. They finally reach the small fishing village of Drače where a few locals stare at the schooner as it docks, bedazzled and friendly. After the *Blackbird's* crew disembark, one of the locals addresses Tove, perhaps envisioning the possibility of a continuing dialogue, only to hear from Vinko, disappointed, that "Our dear guests from Sweden do not speak Croatian." Nevertheless, he quickly arranges for the guests to taste some wine after Sven reminds Vinko about it by noting that "the wine hangover is best cured by more wine." The friendly man quickly brings the wine, several glasses, and a plate of thinly sliced prosciutto from a stone tavern nearby, pours the wine for all to taste (Vinko politely declines) and remarks how "the Swede is a very wise man." This declaration instantaneously causes loud laughter after Vinko translates it.

Their host explains that the wine is the fabled Dingač, from the vine of the same name growing only here, around Janjina, and on the southern slopes of the peninsula around the village with the same name. He lists several more vines that "do not grow anywhere else in the whole world" and all produce excellent wines. Still, he "must be honest" and tell them how nothing compares to the wine made by the monks at a monastery not far from here, using their "centuries old secret recipe and the grapes that grow only in their valley." Tove, and especially Sven, are very glad to hear that, thinking to themselves about the very important assignment they got from Larry Neal back on Sicily: to bring back a jug of this very special wine, and to keep one for themselves. Sven praises the host's Dingač wine and asks to buy a large jug of it, which the friendly Dalmatian appreciates very much. After the transaction is completed, both Sven and Tove express a wish to visit the monastery and buy a jug or two of the "best wine". This makes the host chuckle: "The monks do not sell their wine; they keep it for themselves." Vinko, who had heard of the monastery before but new nothing about their wine, translates the unfortunate fact. Still, Tove and

Sven are not at all dissuaded and want to visit the monastery, anyway. The host shrugs his shoulders and wishes them good luck, with a wide smile.

After leaving the friendly village of Drače, *Blackbird* continues to sail along the coast of the peninsula, passing by the fishing village of Sreser and settling at the small stone dock of Crkvice to spend the night. One single native that welcomed them at the dock, flabbergasted with the site of the schooner, and whom Vinko asks for the directions to the monastery, shows them a narrow gravel road that "winds up over the hill and down to the village of Kuna where the Delorite Monastery is." He also confirms the existence of the "secretive wine cellar of the monks" there.

In the late morning the next day, September 2, Tove, Sven and Vinko set off on the narrow road to their destination, quickly starting to feel the effort along with the merciless rays of sun. Still, they do find themselves enjoying the beautiful views of sea and land as they climb higher, and the magic fragrance of the rosemary, salvia, and immortelle, dispersed in the air by the cheerful choirs of crickets. They finally take a long break and catch their breath at the top of the hill where the view of a gentle valley, surrounded by the rugged karst hills, opens below. The valley is full of small vineyards, gardens and orchards. The white pearl necklace of old stone houses topped by red tile roofs is lining the sides of the pretty little valley. In the middle of it all, commanding the view, is the elegant stone bell tower of the monastery's church.

The *Blackbirds's* crew quickly descends to the valley and the monastery, in desperate need of water and shelter from the grueling sun. To their great disappointment, the monastery seems closed. No sound can be heard from behind the large locked wooden entrance door. They knock on the door several times with its heavy metal ring knocker. Still nothing. Turning away and ready to leave and look for water and shelter elsewhere, they hear a sound. Turning around, they see a small shutter on the door being open. Through the opening appear two suspecting eyes, in the shadow of long shaggy eyebrows.

"No" they hear deep hoarse voice "the monastery has been closed five years, since 1938 when I took over as a civic minister and chaplain. Although, the monks did tell me they will return permanently next year and reopen the monastery. I can let you in to rest a bit and will bring you cold water if you would like some."

The visitors eagerly accept the offer and soon find themselves seated in the deep shade of the grape vine gazebo in the monastery garden, quenching their thirst with the cold rainwater the chaplain fetched from an underground cistern. Refreshed, they politely listen to the chaplain who is thrilled with the opportunity to talk with "someone new and yet friendly in these troubling times." The conversation develops in several languages, helped mostly by Vinko who keeps it going thanks to his improvised translations of quite a few subjects. At some point Sven brings up the subject of the monastery wine, "of which they've heard fairy tales from a friendly host in the village of Drače." The chaplain is very pleased with what he hears but quickly remarks how "they are not fairy tales. Please come with me to the cellar, where the air is nice and cold, to see for yourselves. We just decanted last year's wine from a barrel yesterday."

While his guests are obviously enjoying the wine, including their words full of praise for it, the chaplain tells them the history of the monastery, its church, and the precious works of art housed there. He does it so enthusiastically that it does not matter to him anymore if the young guests show interest or not; he continues more so for himself than anyone else. He is proud that the main church was inspired by the design of the Dubrovnik Cathedral and built in 1714 by the Roman Catholic Diocese of Ston. He is enormously proud that the church was consecrated by the Bishop of Stone Francesco Volanti born in Dubrovnik. And that it has five carved marble altars, the center one made of the famous pink and white Carrara marble. And not only that – the altar of St. Anton was carved by none other than Giacomo of Rome!

This monologue by the chaplain continues for a while. Everyone is happy with what they hear including Vinko who devotedly sketches the scene of the wine cellar. At some point, their host stops to catch his breath and Sven immediately seizes the opportunity to ask if it is possible to buy a jug or two of the heavenly wine for their friends back home in Sweden. In addition, they would be very happy to make a modest donation to the monastery, grateful for everything it has to offer.

In response, the chaplain's face acquires a serious, apologetic expression:

"I am very sorry, but I served the wine to welcome you. It is not for sale. I can pour you another glass if you so desire, as you truly are very nice and dear guests, but the wine is simply not for sale. I am very sorry."

An entire treatise could be written about the attempts by Tove and Sven to persuade their kind host to sell the wine, including Tove's engagement of her infinite arsenal of charms. But, to no avail. The friendly chaplain just would not budge. Until he hears from Vinko who his father is during an exchange unrelated to the topic of wine. At that point, the chaplain generously gives the Swedes two jugs of wine, as a present, absolutely refusing to accept any compensation, including a donation to the monastery:

"Captain Lovrić did so much for us over so many years, we will never be able to thank him enough. Vinko, please give your father my best wishes."

Back on *Blackbird*, while enjoying a light dinner of bread, cheese, prosciutto and figs, they bought from the farmers in the valley, and helping themselves with generous servings of the Dingač wine (except for Vinko who sticks with the grape juice they brought from Lopud), Tove asks Vinko what is his favorite place on Earth.

It was a bit silly to ask such a question of a sixteen-year old boy who never left Dalmatia, but Vinko took it seriously, nonetheless. Loosing every ounce of shyness that still resided in him, he started to evoke many memories he had of the island of Mljet, "his favorite place on Earth, without any doubts!" Vinko praised its virgin pine tree forest, the oldest in the entire Mediterranean, the ancient cultivated fields, fresh-water springs, ponds with magnificent herons and many other beautiful birds, sheltering cool caves in the heat of the summer, and much more. He also told them about the local legend of the nymph Calypso who lived on Ogygia (the ancient name for Mljet). And about Odysseus who spent seven full years in the custody of the beautiful nymph who fell in love with the Greek, put her spells on him, and did not want to let him go back to the island of Ithaca where he ruled before leaving to take part in the Trojan war. In the end, Calypso was ordered

124

by the mighty Zeus (who was persuaded by his daughter, goddess Athena) to release Odysseus of her spells and let him return to his beloved wife Penelope and son Telemachus.

Inspired by everything Vinko had to say about his favorite place on Earth, Tove and Sven decided to set sail for Mljet immediately, regardless of what they may hear from mission headquarters in the meantime. They simply could not miss setting foot on ancient Ogygia and seeing its wonders!

Mali Ston at the time of Blackbird's sailing on the Adriatic. Barba Jozo's oyster beds are visible in the front. Courtesy of Croatian National Archives.

Sven's photograph of the quay where Blackbird spent two nights at the end of August 1943. Now also hosted by TZO Ston (https://www.ston.hr/?u=povijest/hr/st/22/228)

Delorite Monastery in the village of Kuna. Courtesy of Orebić TB.

Vinko's drawing of the monastery wine cellar.

Chapter 19

Cave

As they were approaching the sheltered port of Polače on Mljet, in the early afternoon of September 3rd, the three people on *Blackbird* were each deep in thought. The Scandinavians were remembering what Vinko told them the night before about the island Mljet and its legend and were eager to enter themselves the world of ancient heroes, gods, and goddesses. As for Vinko, well, he could not take his eyes off the beautiful Tove. The minds and imaginations of the *Blackbird's* crew were now miraculously interwoven in the timeless past and the very present as the schooner was gliding ever closer to the coast of Ogygia. The ancient forest, never cut by man, emerged into view, and the magnificent pine trees became distinct.

Sven, imagining he was Odysseus, started thinking of the latest misfortune he faced after losing his only remaining ship and crew when Zeus had destroyed them to appease Helios, the god of the sun. His men stole and ate the oxen Helios kept on the Island of Sicily and the furious god demanded Zeus punish them, so Zeus did. He destroyed their ship and the men drowned. The King of Ithaca, however, managed to survive by building a raft from the remnants of the ship. He drifted and paddled for nine days before crashing on a rock by the shore of Ogygia on the tenth day. And he remembered when he saw the most beautiful immortal goddess of them all after swimming to the rocky shore by a mysterious deep blue cave. He used the very last thread of his remaining strength, before passing out.

Tove, imagining herself as Calypso, thought of the inexplicably exhausted, emaciated, but at the same time the most handsome bearded man she ever saw, climb by her cave. And how she fell in love with the man the very moment she saw him.

As he was recovering in the azure cave home of his hostess, Odysseus, the King of Ithaca, learned that she was one of nine sea nymphs, daughters of the Titan god Atlas and goddess Tethys. She was forced to come to Ogygia in exile, because she supported her father in the battles between the Titans and the Olympian gods headed by the mighty Zeus.

The nymph fell in love with Odysseus so much so that she offered to make him her immortal husband and give him eternal youth. But he refused it and kept dreaming about going back to his Ithaca and his beloved wife Penelope and son Telemachus. Having no other choice because she could not defeat herself, Calypso put the spell on Odysseus and made him her lover. They lived together for seven years on the spellbinding island and she gave birth to twin sons, Nausithous and Nausinous. Still, after sharing the bed with the goddess at night, the Greek would every day go to the shoreline, looking at the horizon and beyond, towards Ithaca where his true family was.

All along, Zeus' daughter Athena could not stand the suffering that Odysseus, her protege, was going through on the magic island. Finally, Athena gathered courage and asked her father to free Odysseus from Calypso and Ogygia. Zeus agreed and sent the messenger of the gods, Hermes, to persuade the nymph to let Odysseus go. The daughter of Atlas was devastated when she heard the message from Zeus but could not possibly disobey the mighty King of the Gods. All she could do was to say this to Hermes: "Cruel folk you are, unmatched for jealousy, you gods who cannot bear to let a goddess sleep with a man, even if it is done without concealment and she has chosen him as her lawful husband."

As the last gesture of her boundless love for Odysseus, the beautiful nymph helped him build his boat, provided him with enough food and drink, and watched him sail away towards his Ithaca, to his faithful wife Penelope and son Telemachus whom he had not seen for twenty long years.

In the mid-afternoon of September 3rd *Blackbird* arrives at Polače where she will spend the night, anchored in the nice quiet bay. Vinko explains to his friends how the small village got its name – from the remains of a Roman palace and tower they can see in front of them. In those mysterious ruins he and his friends many times played war games of Romans and Illyrians, the mortal enemies on the Adriatic. Curious Tove playfully asks Vinko which side he was on during those games. Vinko replies: "Of course, the Illyrians!" and goes on to say how they were always unbeatable when their queen Teuta was in the game. Now even more curious and playful, Tove teases Vinko: "And who would that be?"

"But of course, Andrea, my high school friend from Dubrovnik. The Romans were always frightened when she came along with us. They could never tell if she was playing the game or was serious. She is fearless, she is, I can tell you that!"

After they dock *Blackbird*, and since there is still plenty of time left before the sunset, Vinko suggests they go to see, and perhaps even swim in the two lakes Mljet was famous for – the Little one and the Big one. The three of them soon find themselves on a narrow path through the ancient pine tree forest, filled with the intoxicating fragrance of pine needles and sound of crickets. Suddenly, impatient to submerge himself in the crystal clear, warm water of his favorite Little Lake, Vinko urges them to follow him on a shortcut over some scary-looking rocky terrain full of sharp small ridges and crevices. Terrified, both Tove and Sven yell "NO!" and shout what they were told back in Sweden about all those venomous snakes hiding between the white Mediterranean limestone rocks.

This manifestation of genuine fear makes Vinko laugh like a little boy:

"Sure, there are many horned vipers in our Dalmatia, but not here on Mljet. Not anymore. You see, a grand uncle of Captain Bunić, my father's best friend from Dubrovnik, brought seven male and four female mongooses from one of his trips to India, at the request of the Austro-Hungarian Ministry of Agriculture, and he released them here. Mljet was swirling with snakes in those days and was even called "Snake Island." Well, the little fellows quickly multiplied and took care of the snakes. One cannot find a single snake on the entire island for years now. I myself am fond of the mongooses, they are so cute and clever and lightning fast. Thanks to them I can go anywhere I want, barefoot, without any fear. But people here don't like them anymore.

They became real pests and are killing birds and chickens around houses without any regrets. Mongoose is so brave that sometimes he sneaks into cellars or through open house doors and steals whatever looks tasty to him! There is a much greater chance you will be left without a sandwich if not paying attention, than to be bitten by a snake here on Mljet!"

After Vinko's persuasive explanation, the rest of the schooner's crew joins him on the shortcut and is soon rewarded with the magnificent view of the two lakes from the village of Govedjari. From there, they descend to the shore of Big Lake where several old stone houses of the Babine Kuće village greet them, with no person in sight. After a few minutes of a cheerful run along the shore, they dive into the swift current in a narrow canal that connects the two lakes. Still with no one else in sight, they let their inner children take over, screaming and laughing while being carried by the current, over and over again! Until the dusk and their neglected stomachs remind them it is time to go back to their faithful boat.

On their way to Polače, Tove and especially Sven are walking fast, eager to again have some of that incredible Dingač wine. Trying to keep up with them, Vinko proposes that tomorrow they go with the boat to the Odysseus Cave and swim in its magic blue water. Tove and Sven stop for a moment and excitedly remark that would be the second time they swim in a cave, just like on Capri a short time ago. Vinko, who had heard of Capri's famed Blue Grotto but never saw it himself, nevertheless replies how the two caves cannot even compare. Not sure how to react to this somewhat ambiguous statement, Tove confirms that they would of course love to go to the cave, but not tomorrow. She insists they must go back to the lakes, swim in the Big Lake too, including in the canal that connects it to the sea (of which they heard from Vinko earlier). And that they also must swim to the monastery they saw nestled on a small islet in the Big Lake and say hello to the monks who must be very lonely there.

Back on *Blackbird*, sipping the wine and enjoying the plentiful Dalmatian cold cuts and grapes they bought from a farmer in Polače, Tove and Sven hear another interesting tale from Vinko who explains the countless struggles between many different people who desired to claim these beautiful lands as their own. They also hear about the monastery, the oldest in Dalmatia. It was built by Benedictine monks in the twelfth century on the islet of St. Mary in the Big Lake. The islet was given to them as a present from the Serbian Grand Duke Uroš II, the ruler of Dioclie, Terbunie and Zacholmie, in what is today Herzegovina and southern Dalmatia. The monks belonged to The Abbey of Santa Maria of Pulsano in Puglia, a region in modern-day Italy. The Grand Duke, who was engaged in perpetual power struggle and brief but numerous and convoluted wars in The Balkans between the Byzantine Empire, Hungary, Bulgaria and the Serbian lands, made the present hoping to have the Rome and the Pope on his side. The Romanesque monastery and church of St. Mary were rebuilt and extended during the 15th and 16th century when Renaissance parts were added to the complex.

The next day they again enjoyed swimming in the crystal-clear waters of the two lakes and floating on the tidal currents in the canals that connect them to the sea. Tove did not forget what she thought of the day before and reminded Sven and Vinko they should swim to the monastery islet and say hello to the lonely monks. When Vinko politely replied that there are many other things they can do and see and that the monks prefer solitude, Tove dismissed him with laughter, jumped into water, shouted "Come on boys, it will be fun, catch me if you can!" and started to swim towards the islet.

What happened next completely startled both Tove and Sven. Vinko, visibly annoyed, yelled at Tove she must swim back, at once! Which Tove did, and then, after running up to Vinko and annoyed ten times more than him, yelled back right into his face:

"How dare you talk to me like that! Better watch your behavior young man!"

Then, seeing Vinko flush and lower his eyes looking down, she continued with a conciliatory tone:

"OK. What is it really? What is bothering you?"

With no answer, Vinko still looking down, Tove is now almost apologetic:

"All right, you can tell me, don't be hesitant. What is going on?"

Vinko turns to Sven and whispers something to his ear. The Swede laughs his head off, then drops on the ground, still laughing, and manages to tell Tove, in Swedish and continuing to laugh, that "The problem is her *indecent* two-piece swimsuit, and not only that, but one can even see her bellybutton! The monks would be shocked with the sight and they do not deserve that!"

Now it is Tove's turn to flush and be contemplative. But only for a few moments. She soon bursts into a cheerful laughter and starts to run around the lake, shouting:

"Come on boys, let's swim in the Big Canal! Catch me if you can!"

Following a prolonged stay in the bay of Polače, with her crew going to the lakes and back multiple times, *Blackbird* finally drops anchor by the Odysseus Cave on September 5, around noon, the best time to visit. As they were preparing to jump off board and swim to the cave, Vinko politely suggests to Sven he may want to take the *Hasselblad* with him, in the watertight box of course, "because the cave is amazingly inspiring and he will not regret it." Vinko quickly adds how he would be very grateful if Sven can also bring in the box his sketchbook and a few pencils. Sven gladly agrees and the three of them are soon on their way to the cave. Sven is swimming carefully, holding the rather large metal box high above his head, even though it is watertight, because of the choppy waves. Vinko is closely behind, whereas Tove swims wildly in front of them and quickly disappears through the cave entrance, only about three or four feet high.

As they are about to swim into the cave themselves, Sven and Vinko hear Tove screaming with delight and way ahead of them: "eventyr, eventyr!" To puzzled Vinko, Sven explains how Tove must think she is in a fairy tale. Vinko smiles widely and affirms: "She sure is. We all are!"

And a fairy tale it was! Rainbow colors quickly surrounded them, bouncing off the pink-and-white cave tunnel walls and coming from, it seemed, everywhere. A mystifying azure blue light rose from the bottomless depths beneath them. And all that light and all those colors glistening on the rocks around them were joined by the soothing sound of the waves bouncing off the cave walls. The hum of the wings of the bats welcomed them and lead them cheerfully to the end of the cave tunnel. It was there that they entered the magic and monumental chamber of the goddess Calypso's home. It was lit by the light coming from high, high above, where the ceiling was open to the heavens.

They stayed in the magic cave, swimming in the calming waters and submerged in their own dreams, for hours. Vinko, captivated, made another one of his elaborate drawings.

Back on *Blackbird*, not accepting the end of magic, Tove wants to stay overnight, anchored by the rocky cliffs and close to the cave so they can enjoy everything again the next day. Vinko, however, does not like the waves and the wind and persuades Tove and Sven to sail down along the shore and spend the night in the protection of the Saplunara Bay, at the southern tip of the island. The wind is so strong and favorable, it will take them no time to get there, just around sunset.

As the powerful schooner is cutting the waves and flying along the island's shore, sails filled with the wind to the point of tearing, Vinko, at the helm, notices that the Swedes seem to be discussing something quite passionately down in the cabin, almost arguing with each other, and not enjoying the scenery and the wind as they usually do. Puzzled, he interrupts their discussion by calling them out and telling them his second favorite sand beach in Dalmatia is only minutes away. He adds that they will even be able to enjoy the sunset right there from the deserted beach.

This does the trick and Tove and Sven emerge from the cabin in a couple of minutes, in a gloomy mood of sorts which, however, soon turns into something much more agreeable as they see the Saplunara Bay emerging over the bow. Vinko, of course, could not have had the slightest idea why his crew behaved down in the cabin the way they did. Nor could he had known that the argument was not entirely between the two of them but also with one Larry Neal, with whom they were speaking over the radio.

Larry informed the Scandinavians that the mission plan had changed, and they should be ready to sail to the island of Vis on a moment's notice, most likely already tomorrow although this is yet to be fully confirmed. They also should not, in the meantime or for any reason, sail to any village or town, however small or big, where there are Italian or Croatian Nazi troops. When Tove told Larry they were actually thinking of taking part in the Lokrum Regatta, in Dubrovnik, of which they found out on Mljet, Larry simply replied they should forget all that and just wait for further instructions and stay where they are.

The conversation over the radio really heated up when Tove, defiantly, reminded Larry how they, in their hands, have the permit for unrestricted sailing on the Adriatic signed by the Italian Governor of Dalmatia himself, and how she does not see a single reason why they would not take part in the regatta, as there was apparently nothing useful left for them to do any time soon. At that point Larry almost yelled over the radio not to sail to Dubrovnik and to wait for further instructions. This irritated Tove and she simply switched the radio off. And then it was Sven's turn to get irritated with what Tove did.

They spent the entire day of September the 6th in the Saplunara Bay area, waiting for final instructions, and going between two amazing sandy beaches where they took turns swimming in the warm sea waters. Tove and Sven helped Vinko with couple of deliciously tasty meals – a salad made of two octopuses Vinko caught with his underwater gun, and a bunch of grilled mackerels Sven caught with his fancy reel rod. Vinko marinated them in a traditional Dalmatian way and all three of them quickly devoured the meal while watching another incredible sunset on the beach. Still, Tove and Sven could not relax and enjoy their stay in Saplunara to the fullest, the stay that would otherwise be another summer dream. Their anxiety was increasing with every hour that they did not hear from mission headquarters as to what their next step should be.

All that time Tove was working on persuading Sven how they must go to Dubrovnik no matter what. This is probably their last chance, ever, to see the city with which Vinko was obviously so much in love, and he was always right about his favorite things, wasn't he?

After Helios went to bed, the hard day for him and his horse chariot now over, and as the magic horizon colors were slowly changing from one tint of orange to another, Tove asks Vinko to tell them a bit more about the Lokrum Regatta if he could. The expression on Vinko's face turns somewhat sad as he confides how he wanted to be in the regatta ever since he was a child but was always denied it by his father with an explanation that he was "still too young and impatient." And how he was so envious hearing stories from his father and Captains Ristorcelli and Bunić when they visited Lopud, about who won that year and how, all along teasing each other about what will happen the next time around. As far as he can remember, the winner was always one of the three of them, and he was so proud of that, both of his father and his father's best friends whom he liked so much because they were always very good to him. One day soon, he hopes, his father will let him be in the race and maybe even let him skipper their boat. The boat which, unfortunately, was heavily damaged this spring in a windstorm which is the reason why his father was not going to be in the regatta this year.

The horizon turned crimson and then dark blue. The yellow of the little crackling fire glowed. Sven and Tove look at each other, in silence, which lasts for a minute or two. Sven then turns to Vinko and says:

"Well, Vinko, you will be in the regatta this year and you will skipper *Swarttrost*."

Vinko, stunned, looks at the two of them and then experiences one of the most beautiful things ever to happen to him in his entire life, as he confided to me the last time I saw him. Tove stands up from the fire, goes to Sven, hugs him, and tears start to flow from her beautiful eyes.

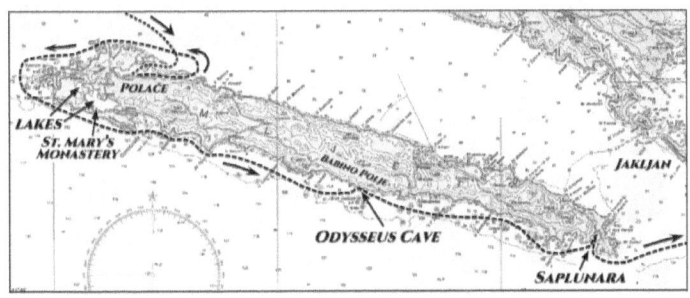

Blackbird's visit to Mljet, September 3-7, 1943.

Požurska Luka, to which Vinko and his father and friends often sailed from Lopud. Photo courtesy of Mljet National Park.

Village of Babine Kuće on the Big Lake. Courtesy of Miro Andrić.

Cove of the Big Lake with the Islet and Benedictine Monastery of St. Mary.
Courtesy of Ivo Biočina.

Vinko's quick sketch of a mongoose made during one of his many visits to Mljet.

Vinko's drawings of *Blackbird* on Mljet

Vinko's drawing of the Odysseus Cave on Mljet.

Chapter 20

Dubrovnik

Tove and Sven are on *Blackbird's* stern enjoying the early afternoon with a friendly westerly *Mistral* wind filling the schooner's sails. The island of Koločep is already far behind them and the gracious boat is sailing on windward tack. They pass the rocky limestone shore of the Lapad Peninsula.

A bay suddenly opens on the port side, together with a dense line of old pine trees and stately villas high up on the white limestone cliffs, lit by the sun. Tove and Sven are mesmerized. Vinko, who is at the helm, points over the bow:

"Look, there it is!"

The Scandinavian couple needs a few seconds before realizing what Vinko meant. But there it is, straight ahead, emerging behind a rocky point – the magnificent city of Dubrovnik, nested high on grand cliffs. Behind monumental stone walls and towers, a cheerful line of red roofs starts to peek at them as they sail closer. Sven and Tove, mouths agape, look back and forth at each other, at Vinko, and at the City, before quickly running to the bow for an unobstructed view. Somehow, they manage not to trip over each other.

Vinko does not mind that they are not offering any help while he jibes and then sails the boat into the port. The frightening fortress tower of Saint Ivan looms ahead. The Old City Port, the keys, the cathedrals, also lie ahead, behind the tower. Vinko is enormously proud of being able to show all this glory to Tove and Sven, dear new friends. And, sure enough, Tove cries with delight at the emerging sight and keeps exclaiming:

"This is like a fairytale! A fairytale!"

Sven runs down to the cabin, brings back the camera, and then starts to take photos like a madman, in every direction. Finally, Vinko proclaims:

"My friends, here it is, for your pleasure, the pearl of our Adriatic!" and then waits for a minute or two before breaking the magic with a raised, firm voice:

"Now, crew, furl the sails. We must dock safely."

Engine rumbling low, the schooner quietly passes through the Old Port Gate at approximately 2:30 in the afternoon on Tuesday, September 7. Vinko docks her at the main key, right in front of the City Café, to the delight of a rather large crowd that quickly gathers including several Italian carabineers and Croatian Nazis in uniforms. Feeling quite uncomfortable, Tove and Sven look at Vinko. He understands and reassures them:

"Everyone here admires a boat like this. They know what it takes to build beautiful boats, small and large. They built them in their own shipyard for centuries and took them to every corner of every ocean on Earth. My father was lucky to be part of that, but I probably will never be..."

As Vinko finishes the last words and looks at the men in black uniforms, a shadow descends on his handsome face.

At that moment stately gentleman with a captain's hat and a pipe in his left hand makes way through the crowd, waves and cheerfully addresses everyone on board, in English:

"Tove, Sven, Vinko, what a nice surprise. I was not expecting you and this lovely boat in Dubrovnik at all. What brings you here?"

Vinko, notably relieved, rejoices:

"Captain Ristorcelli, I am so glad to see you. Please come on board. Tove and Sven decided to compete in the regatta while we were on Mljet, so here we are."

Even more puzzled, as the boat was supposed to be somewhere near Split or Zadar up the coast by now, and Mljet was never even mentioned to him by the British, Captain Ristorcelli nevertheless manages to hide his uneasiness and, smiling, tells the Scandinavians to bring their papers with them and get off the boat:

"I understand. Follow me, I will take care of it. What a nice boat. It will be a real pleasure sailing against her."

All that time, Sven and Tove both think that this must be the Italian who arranged the sailing trip with Vinko's father.

The *Svarttrost's* crew steps off the boat and, feeling less uneasy, follow Captain Ristorcelli to the City Café where the schooner is enrolled in the regatta and Sven receives the official rules and the course map. All other formalities required of a visiting foreign vessel and her crew will be quickly taken care of in the Port office building next door, courtesy of Captain Ristorcelli and his friend, the Port's Italian Commander himself. After the paperwork is completed, the Commander invites the company for a drink at the Café, promising a table with the best view. Three Italian officers in the office promptly invite themselves as well, having a hard time taking their eyes off Tove.

As soon as the whole party is comfortably seated at two tables hastily pulled together by a waiter, a large plate full of fresh figs and a generous bottle of grappa are brought by another waiter. Only after the grappa is served, the waiters ask what everyone would like to drink. They all go for the house red wine convincingly recommended by the Commander who obviously feels at home. Vinko orders pomegranate juice while politely pushing his glass of grappa away. At that moment, Captain Ristorcelli notices a dignified gentleman with a gray beard sitting alone several tables away, reading a book. He promptly walks over and invites the gentleman to join them for a drink and succeeds in doing so after friendly persuasion. They both come back and Captain Ristorcelli introduces Captain Frane Bunić as "the most famous living Dubrovnik nobleman, an extraordinary athlete and seaman, and our generous host for later this evening."

Somewhat embarrassed by the introduction, Captain Bunić smilingly shakes hands with Tove and Sven, who introduce themselves as Swedes, and with Vinko, whom he obviously knows, and then nods to others while taking the seat. Given what Giuseppe just said, he has no choice but to address everyone:

"Indeed, it will be an honor to welcome you all tonight at my house for a modest party in celebration of tomorrow's regatta."

The Italian officers immediately accept the invitation whereas Tove, taken by a complete surprise, instinctively says to Sven, in a low voice and in Norwegian:

"What a shame. We cannot go. We don't have appropriate attire."

What Tove and Sven hear next freezes their hearts instantaneously. Captain Bunić cheerfully addresses Tove in a perfectly correct Norwegian:

"That should not be a problem at all. Both my lovely wife Lucia and my daughter Andrea will be more than delighted to let you pick any dress you like from their closets. And, believe me, how can I forget that – there are many nice dresses in those closets. By the way, for some reason I thought you were Swedish. Oh, never mind, I am obviously getting old and cannot even hear properly any more it seems."

He then turns to Sven continuing in Norwegian:

"My son Luka is as tall and slim as you and has already left for Zagreb where he studies at the university. You can pick anything you want from his closet – he cannot object even if he wanted to."

The conversation at the table then continues in English as Captain Ristorcelli starts providing some basic details about the regatta for the benefit of Tove and Sven, and then discusses every sailing boat that will compete tomorrow including his own. Seven of them, and now one more to everyone's delight – *Svarttrost*. He is curious about the boat's name and when Tove provides the English word, the poor Italian mistakes it for a crow and passionately objects:

"But why? She is so pretty and elegant, why name it after such a rather nasty, albeit clever, bird?"

The confusion is collectively resolved with the generous help of funny gestures, and Captain Bunić's whistling of the bird's song. Giuseppe is greatly relieved once he gets it, and laughs like a little boy:

"Of course, that's what she is – *Merlo*!" (For those that may have missed it, this is the Italian word for blackbird.)

Getting back to the regatta business, Tove and Sven predict they will be dead last not knowing anything about the course and seeing all the magnificent sailing boats they will compete with, especially that German boat that looks more than admirable (quickly adding – "Just like your *Genoa*, Captain Ristorcelli.")

143

"Well, you do notice things, all right. That boat is the pride of German Navy. She is visiting us after winning quite a bit this summer. Everyone says she is unbeatable, and she certainly is admirable, but I don't like that damn skipper at all. An arrogant son-of-a-bi... (quickly lowering his voice), excuse my French, if you know what I mean. I wish he somehow loses tomorrow, just for the heck of it."

Captain Ristorcelli then winks and nods at Vinko:

"By the way, you will have the best skipper."

Vinko blushes and objects, very politely:

"Captain Ristorcelli, with all due respect, you are making fun of me, please don't mislead my friends here. Moreover, Tove and Sven are as good as anyone out there, and *Merlo* is an outstanding boat, you will see that tomorrow."

Both Captains Ristorcelli and Bunić start laughing wholeheartedly at the amusement of the Italian officers and quite a few other people in the City Café. Bunić, in a very good mood, fires back at Vinko:

"Young man, that is the spirit! But, listen to my advice carefully – don't always be that modest. Especially now that you will be playing water polo for a team where arrogance is sometimes quite welcome. As you well know that team is the best in the whole country and all the players have every intention to keep it that way."

Completely taken aback by this sudden change of subject, Vinko stares at Captain Bunić in disbelief.

"Well, Vinko, I am not making fun of you – the coach told me that back in June with a little caveat, that is, if you put on some more muscle over the summer. And from what I can see, not only that the caveat is gone, but you blossomed into a truly handsome young gentleman indeed. By the way, just to make some things clear here for our dear Norwegian guests (turning to Tove and Sven) – Vinko learned how to sail from the best – his father, master Lovrić, and the honorable Captain Ristorcelli sitting here, and, if I may add, I myself had something to do with it."

Tove absolutely loves what she hears (except for the Norwegian thing as she was supposed to be Swedish) and keeps saying to herself how all this must be a fairytale. Sven is pleased as well and does not wait for the waiters – he grabs the bottle of grappa and asks if anyone else would like to have some (no one does as the red wine is perfectly fine) and then pours the hypnotizing liquid into his own glass, hands Vinko's glass to Vinko, stands up and proposes a toast:

"Tove and I thank you all from the bottom of our hearts for your incredible hospitality. Let's toast to an enjoyable regatta tomorrow and, especially, to our skipper Vinko who just learned he will be playing water polo for the first team, the best there is."

Everyone salutes, drinks bottoms up, and enthusiastic applause ensues, while Vinko hesitates with the glass in his hand and looks around sheepishly. Captain Bunić steps in with encouraging words:

"Go ahead Vinko, you are a grown man now, it is fine."

Vinko obeys causing an even louder applause that makes people down at the quay turn their heads to see what is going on.

Suddenly realizing that the dusk is about to settle in, Captain Bunić proclaims:

"I will be late! We better hurry, I don't want to have to answer to Lucia at all! Tove, Sven and Vinko, just take what you need for tonight. I am certain you will enjoy a hot bath and comfortable beds for a change. You boys also need to take your boat to the other side of the Port and dock her where you find room. Take a dinghy to the City Beach and come up – Vinko, I believe you know where our house is. And you, young lady, come with me so you have a bit more time to prepare. I do have some experience with that thanks to my own two ladies."

Captain Bunić then concludes to the rest of the company:

"Gentlemen, we are expecting you between eight and eight thirty. Please excuse us now."

Only a short walk to the boat, the crew tries, hastily but politely, to talk their way out of the party but Captain Bunić does not want to hear it:

"Don't be ridiculous! Vinko, you will have to live with one of my old suits which I cannot wear any more (panting his hardly noticeable belly). It will fit you just fine. Andrea will be delighted to see you there as she was complaining for days about all these old people at the ball that will make her feel bored to death before it even started. Girls! Everyone older than thirty seems like an old person to her. Go figure."

He then turns to Tove and continues:

"Young lady, please be quick. My car is just outside that City Gate, don't make me wait too long!"

Tove, still dazed by the pace and the whole experience of the day, fetches a few things from the cabin, jumps off the boat, runs as fast as she can, and disappears through the gate after Captain Bunić.

Vinko and Sven untie *Blackbird*, start the engine and glide her to anchor. Looking ahead, they do not see a man in Nazi uniform on the deck of the German boat, staring at *Blackbird*. Nor do they see the name of the boat on her stern – *Nordwind*.

The scene of the "modest party" hosted by the Bunić family in honor of the Lokrum Sailing Regatta which will promptly begin tomorrow morning at 10 o'clock, is a magnificent three-story stone mansion overlooking the Old Port and the City. Attached to it is a beautiful spacious Mediterranean garden sprinkled with beds of fragrant herbs, and patches of rosemary bushes, oleanders and olive trees, all crisscrossed by polished limestone pathways. A few late guests are still arriving, welcomed by friendly staff and pleasant melodies played by the favorite local sextet ensemble, grand piano included, in the large ballroom opening to the garden. At some point, Captain Ristorcelli rings a bell and positions himself between the garden and the ballroom so everyone can hear what he is about to say:

"Ladies and gentlemen! Our generous host Master Bunić kindly asked me to welcome you in the name of his lovely family and the regatta organizers. Before you continue enjoying yourselves and start dancing, which I am certain you all will do despite of the troubling times, please allow me to introduce the skippers for tomorrow's regatta. First, our surprise last-minute entry. Many of you already saw that marvelous schooner down in the Port and are dying of curiosity to find out more about her. Well, I am sure most of you did find out by now, as all of us here understand quite well there are no secrets in Dubrovnik (winking)."

Captain Ristorcelli then points at Sven and Vinko standing together in the garden close by, but cannot locate Tove, and quickly continues:

"Please welcome the crew of the boat from friendly Sweden, Sven and Vinko, son of our dear Master Lovrić who could not be with us this year, and a lovely young lady named Tove who is just about to join us."

After a nice round of applause, Giuseppe continues with the introductions:

"Captain Pasquale Pontoriero sailing from Ancona; Captain Stavros Marinos from Crete, visiting us again after many years with a splendid new boat; dear friend Luigi Passerini from San Marino; our Austrian friend Johannes von Dietrichstein sailing from Trieste; our old Swiss friend François Zwahlen sailing from his home port of Venice; Captain Bunić; and myself, the honorary Chair of the Organizing Committee for this year. And, finally, without intentions to ruffle any feathers, please welcome Herr Oberst Hans Schmelz, the skipper of the absolute favorite, *Nordwind*, sure to win tomorrow unless God himself has decided otherwise."

Interrupting a noticeably less loud round of applause, Colonel Schmelz, who wears black Nazi uniform, addresses the party in German showing no emotions:

"I will be honored to sail *Nordwind* and encourage you not to feel bad because this marvel of German ingenuity and engineering is going to win tomorrow. Just try to enjoy yourselves."

Schmelz then raises his arm for the Nazi salute and yells:

"Heil Hitler!"

While Captain Ristorcelli is translating Schmelz's address to English for the benefit of non-German speaking guests, Hans keeps his stretched right arm high in the air, joined by a few Germans and Croatian Nazis in uniforms looking at each other and scattered between elegantly dressed ladies and gentlemen. Before the translation is over, the loudest applause that night takes over, accompanied by cheerful cries coming from direction of the opposite door to the ballroom:

"Belle signore!... Bellissime!... Guardate qui!!!"

Sven, more than curious, asks Vinko what they are saying.

"Well, Sven, I think Tove and the ladies of the house just walked into the ballroom and the men like what they see."

What Vinko experienced from there on stayed permanently etched in his memory, as vivid seventy years later when he told me the story on camera as that magic, fragrant, late summer night. His voice and expressions on his face while talking were just like those of a young man, breathing life with full lungs and experiencing something new and thrilling. He remembered the colors of the beautiful dresses, the hairstyles, the shoes, the intriguing smiles, the graciousness of young women, the dancing, the fragrance of old rosemary bushes in the garden, the lights of Dubrovnik at night, and much more. I couldn't tell exactly when he was talking about Tove and when about Andrea. It did not seem to matter to him. As if, somehow, both beauties merged into one and made this boy, now a grown man, or an old man in front of me, fly to some distant mystical lands, on a magic carpet.

Historic court of water polo club "Jug" in Dubrovnik's Old Port where Vinko played for the club's junior team. Jug was the best club in the Kingdom of Yugoslavia for many years before WWII. Courtesy of dubrovnik-travel.net.

View of Dubrovnik and the island of Lokrum at the time of *Blackbird's* visit.
Courtesy of National and University Library, Zagreb, Croatia.

Vinko's drawing of *Blackbird* anchored in the Old Port of Dubrovnik.

Chapter 21

Lokrum Regatta

The following morning, Captain Bunić takes the crew of *Svarttrost* to the City Café where they join his two old sailing friends, today's crew of his yawl named *Lucia*, for a generous early breakfast. At the table, Captain Bunić tests Vinko by asking:

"Well, young skipper, what about the weather and the wind today?"

Seeing the last few clouds being quickly dispersed by the sun, and looking at the crystal-clear blue sky, Vinko replies:

"I think Mistral will be very friendly to us later in the morning, but the sunset last night seemed to have sent us some hints for the afternoon. In any case, it should be lots of fun."

The three locals smile and nod with the approval, following up in concert:

"It sure will, young man, it sure will, no question about it."

After breakfast, dinghies take the two crews to their boats which they board approximately half an hour before 10am, the official start time of the regatta. *Blackbird* leaves the port to raise her sails and take a position, admired by a crowd of small fishing and other boats outside the Old Port; many more boats can be seen lined up on either side of the pretty forested island of Lokrum, south of the City. Both Tove and Sven are quite nervous with anticipation, regretting they did not have time to study the course around the island more closely. Vinko reassures them by simply saying, with a wide smile on his very confident face:

"Don't worry at all, please do what I tell you and everything will be just fine."

Needless to say, the regatta was more than exciting and fun to watch. Importantly, however, during the race the capitulation of Italy was officially announced, first by General Eisenhower and then by the Italian government, referring to it as "armistice" to lower the level of humiliation somehow. About that same time, the friendly wind Mistral was interrupted by very strong bursts of southeasterly wind which quickly took over. Dark storm clouds could be seen far down the coast, gathering around the high Montenegrin mountains, and chaotic waves started playing with the sailing boats as if they were toys. Except for the two of them: *Svarttrost* and *Nordwind*.

The crew of *Svarttrost* is exhilarated while she sails through the finish line around 3:15 in the afternoon, closely followed by *Nordwind*. After their faithful boat is secured at the main quay in front of the City Café, Tove runs to the helm, kisses and hugs Vinko. Sven laughs in delight: "What a race! Vinko, you were simply fantastic! What you did out there, I cannot even believe it! As three of them are embraced in a big hug, the last rays of sun in the west disappear behind dark threatening clouds.

At four o'clock in the afternoon, the wind begins to howl, and a dark curtain of rain approaches quickly from the southeast. A large blackboard in front of the City Café can be clearly seen from yards away including the words written on it – "Lokrum Regatta Results". The names of six boats are listed, *Svarttrost* and *Nordwind* are not amongst them, and the lines for the first two places are empty.

Those waiting to see which boat won are finally losing patience and dispersing quickly with the first raindrops, except for the crews of all the boats and a few remaining enthusiasts. A newcomer that just entered the Port through the City Gate asks a rather annoyed man in the small crowd what is going on, only to hear the angry voice shouting back:

"Apparently, they still cannot decide because a complaint was filed. Why don't they just pick one, roll a dice or something!"

Except for the crews of the two unlisted boats everyone else loudly agrees:

"That's right! Get it over with! Make them both be the winners, or whatever!"

At that moment, several people with very serious expressions on their faces come out of the City Café and approach the blackboard. One of them picks up a piece of chalk and writes *Svarttrost* on the first line and *Nordwind* on the second. Applause breaks out but is immediately shunned by the terrifying screams of Oberst Hans Schmelz, the skipper of *Nordwind*, the pride of the German Navy:

"This is outrageous! How dare you!? What have you done!?"

As Oberst Schmelz rages, the summer storm finally explodes, and loud thunder overpowers his screams of which only a few words occasionally break through:

"Bastards…. not done yet…. hear from me…"

A few yards away Tove and Sven are overjoyed with their arms high up and start dancing around Vinko in the rain. Captains Ristorcelli, Bunić, and almost everyone else clap their hands in rhythm, while the rain keeps falling relentlessly, including on the blackboard where it quickly washes away the names of the boats.

The summer storm suddenly stops, as they usually do, and a few rays of sun peek out from behind the clouds and paint a magnificent rainbow over the almost black cloud canvas above the beautiful City. Oberst Schmelz composes himself, approaches Tove and Sven, and addresses them in flawless English:

"I do want to congratulate you on your skillful sailing. I recognize how well you skippered your nice schooner in those waves. By the way, did Alden build her in 1930 or around that time?"

Sven, without thinking, answers:

"Well, thank you Sir. Yes, I think you are correct, somewhere around 1930."

Oberst Schmelz smiles ominously, keeps looking Sven straight in the eyes, then turns to Tove with the same smile on his face:

"Thanks, that's what I thought."

He then walks away and disappears through the City Gate followed by his crew. Tove grabs Sven's shoulders with both hands, starts shaking them uncontrollably and cries:

"What did you just say? Do you know what you just did?"

Side entrance to the City Cafe (lower left) as it looked at the time of *Blackbird's* visit. The Duke's Palace is on the left and the Dubrovnik Cathedral is in the center. Courtesy of National and University Library, Zagreb, Croatia.

View of Dubrovnik from the island of Lokrum at the time of *Blackbird's* visit. The entrance to the Old Port of Dubrovnik is on the right. Courtesy of Croatian National Archives.

Chapter 22

Escape

In the evening after the regatta, while sipping the Dingač wine (including Vinko who is now a grown man according to Captain Bunić), the schooner's crew is still recounting all the excitement of the race and what happened afterwards. At some point they notice a trabàccolo maneuvering in the Old Port. They are very surprised to see the boat sail right to them, coming to rest beside them as they sat in *Blackbird*. An American, introducing himself as Edvard Neumman, comes on board carrying with him a large metal chest. He then calls Tove and Sven aside and tells them, in a low voice and looking directly at Tove, that he came from the island of Vis on this boat skippered by Mr. Mario Trumbić, a sympathizer of Tito's partisans, as arranged by one Larry Neal. He was transported to Vis from Sicily, two days earlier, on a fast, small gunboat of the American Navy. The American then hands Sven an envelope, emphasizing that it is directly from Larry Neal, and that it contains further instructions for the mission.

Without much explanation, as the rest of people on *Blackbird* watch in puzzlement, the newcomer immediately proceeds to install, on each side of the boat, two small metal objects shaped like towers that he took out of the chest. He then carefully places two shiny metal balls on the towers. Carrying the chest with him, he goes down to the cabin and connects some strange-looking instruments with the boat's ship to shore radio. Finally, he stores the chest away under the cabin table and informs the completely mystified Tove and Sven that he will finish, hopefully tomorrow, the "installation of the equipment which will enable their safe transfer from the danger zone in the Adriatic."

What did Edvard exactly have in his mind when he told this to the Scandinavians? Well, unbeknownst to the crew, it was he and Svetoslav who, during the *Blackbird's* Atlantic crossing, conducted the first ever successful teleportation experiment. The same instrument Edvard installed on Blackbird just now had also teleported the boat much closer to Portrush, North Ireland, their destination, during the Atlantic crossing.

How did I find this out? Because I was able to connect all the dots finally. Seven or eight days of the Blackbird's Atlantic crossing simply disappeared based on the testimony of the excited crew who firmly believed they set the crossing record of twelve days! This of course sounded very difficult to accept because the alleged crossing time was much, much shorter than what everyone believed possible at the time. This includes the official document I was able to obtain of the *Mission Capri* proposal, prepared by the SOE agent Larry Neal, and the notes of the OSS meeting held in the Congressional Club near Washington, D.C. in May 1943 when *Mission Capri* was officially approved. Both the group of OSS people gathered around Dr. Wallace at the meeting, and Larry Neal, the gray eminence of SOE, concluded that the minimum time required for *Blackbird* to cross the Atlantic was around twenty days, and only if the weather conditions were ideal for the duration of the trip.

After the experiment, Edvard and Svetoslav finally confessed to Loomis, the head of the MIT Radiation Laboratory, what were they working on and why were they so proud of their invention – because it would change the course of history! Loomis first scolded the two young scientists, because of their insubordination, and then proceeded to congratulate them. Edvard immediately seized the opportunity to ask Loomis for "a big favor": to send him to the Adriatic where he would like to implement an additional piece of instrumentation, on which they were currently working, together with the modified original equipment, which would all significantly improve the experiment. Loomis agreed and this is how Edvard found himself first on Sicily, which was liberated by the Americans, and then on the island of Vis which was liberated by Tito's partisans couple of days ago, and now in Dubrovnik where he had just joined the surprised crew of *Swarttrost*.

Vinko, understandably, was quite puzzled by the appearance of the American. He still knew nothing of the secret mission in which he was participating unknowingly, although traces of doubt about some things

Sven and Tove were telling him started to appear. These doubts only grew stronger when he saw the American and witnessed the strange things he was doing on the boat. So, Vinko gathered his courage and approached Tove with questions. After some hesitation, Tove revealed to the young Dalmatian the real nature of their sailing trip on the Adriatic, knowing very well that they will soon part with him.

To Tove's great relief, Vinko did not show anger. On the contrary, he expressed gratitude for everything they had done because he had always wanted to fight evil fascists and Nazis, regardless of where they came from or to whom they belonged.

This revelation from Tove, the excitement and the adrenalin rush he felt realizing he was in danger, the pride of being on the beautiful schooner and fighting against the occupiers of his beloved country, and the feeling of relief that the mission was nearing the end, all contributed to Vinko's resistance awakening which culminated with him joining Tito's partisans when the mission was over.

The next afternoon, on September 9th, while the late summer sun was keeping the old stone city hot, most of its inhabitants were sheltered in their homes in the shade of the awnings, or inside the stores lining Stradun and Široka streets. No one paid any attention to a wooden schooner quietly leaving the Old Port of Dubrovnik.

Conditions for sailing were excellent and they entered the welcoming port of Lopud just after sun set into the sea leaving a brilliant red and orange sky behind. Vinko invites his mates to come to his house for good wine and a farewell meal. His father, happy that they are back, will be more than glad to cut some prosciutto and cheese so they can comfortably spend the evening before leaving for Vis that same night, as announced by Sven.

After the tasty supper, washed down by wine made of grapes from the family vineyard, Vinko offers to Tove and Sven to choose from his sketchbook three drawings of their choice which he made on the trip. Tove is again full of praise for Vinko's talent, whereas Sven is not all that interested, being eager to sail out because of a feeling of unease he had after the episode with Oberst Hans Schmelz, yesterday in Dubrovnik when he so foolishly blew their cover. At Sven's urging, they rush to the port after saying goodbye to Captain Lovrić, who also receives a hug and a kiss from tearful Tove.

Sven's fear soon proved to be more than justified. Vinko, on board the boat with Edvard, notices a group of armed carabinieri and Croatian Nazis led by Schmelz, yelling and running towards the port. He warns Tove and Sven about the danger and they shout back to Vinko to start the engine. They quickly untie and jump onto the boat, continuing to shout in panic: "Take us out, take us out!" Vinko does, and under a shower of bullets that start raining on *Blackbird*. He cannot sail safely to the northwest and the open sea in the direction of Vis because of the gunfire. He is forced to turn south, back towards Dubrovnik.

Once out of gunfire range, and safely behind the island's horn, everyone on the schooner has some time to catch their breath and begin to think of what to do next. Tove and Sven immediately agree with Vinko who confidently states that the best option is to continue southeast towards Dubrovnik and then turn back, under cover of night, and sail around the island's south side and on to Vis. As *Blackbird* is catching wind in her sails, and adrenaline rush receding, Vinko realizes he has been shot in his shoulder. Clenching his teeth in pain, Vinko manages to turn the boat around issuing orders to his crew and navigating by the stars, just like he did many times before with his father, sailing at night in these very waters. He hopes to avoid a likely sea posse by taking the boat as close to the island's rocky shore as possible and sail by the cove of Šunj beach which he knew like the back of his hand.

After the main fear has passed and while the schooner is gliding quietly through the night, Edvard frantically starts to install metal cables and strips on *Blackbird's* masts and booms in the darkness. Sven is at the helm, and down in the cabin Tove tends to Vinko's wound by candlelight. The touch of her hands and tender calming words create an unknown, indescribable feeling in the young man and he does not feel the pain anymore. The wound, however, takes its toll – the entire cabin spins around Vinko's head and he blacks out.

Chapter 23

Flight

Blackbird is approaching the southeastern tip of Lopud, the Horn of Poluge, with Sven at the helm. She is sailing right by the rocky shore with only her mizzen sail up. The wind is ebbing, and the sail starts to sag, slowly at first. As the boat sails closer to the Šunj Beach cove, the sail starts to flap helplessly. At the same time Sven realizes that the beach is lit by powerful searchlights and full of armed enemies! In a panic, he manages to furl the sail onto the boom, but cannot momentarily think of anything that would stop the boat from drifting into the open. He quickly steps down into the cabin to alert his mates, only to see the unconscious Vinko lying on the bed. He tells Tove what is happening and gently shakes Vinko who regains consciousness and quickly grasps the gravity of the situation they are in. The three of them come up from the cabin but Vinko passes out on the deck. Tove and Sven, feeling cold sweat spreading down their spines, start to pray for a miracle which will help *Swarttrost* drift across the bay, unnoticed.

Just like Tove and Sven, who are now seated by the helm, Edvard is completely dazed near the schooner's bow where, only seconds ago, he was trying to hang the last few metal strips on the fore boom. For a moment, which seems like an eternity, the three of them feel they might be able to make it, the rocky end of the bay becoming discernable in the dark.

And then, as the faithful schooner inches toward the Bay's end, a searchlight spots them. Loud shouts from the beach are instantaneously followed by rapid gunfire. Two gunboats, full of armed ustashas, leave the beach in pursuit of *Blackbird*. Terrified, Tove and Sven can only watch the boats quickly catching up with them. They start to feel an enormous sorrow that the mission will end this way, the two of them resting dead on the sea bottom so far away from their homes.

But NO! The Scandinavians snap out of the paralysis of sorts, remembering times when they conquered even the most dangerous winds and waves taller than the highest mountain! The fearless Viking blood did not entirely leave their veins and they are not going to surrender!

Tove takes the helm and shouts at Sven to start the engine. *Blackbird* is now in the race of her life, the motor rumbling with full power. Still, the enemy gunboats are mercilessly closing in, searchlights and bullets streaking through the night. Edvard, in as much panic as anyone else, somehow manages to concentrate and then cross-connects the densely coiled cables along the schooner's masts with metal balls on the two small towers he erected on each side of the boat. He then connects the metal cables on the booms with the bases of the two balls and jumps to hang the last remaining metal stripe on the fore boom.

Under a shower of bullets, at nine o'clock and thirty minutes, Edvard finishes the installation of all the equipment he brought with him and checks the connections between the instruments down in the cabin one last time. As everything seems right, he frantically starts to push buttons on a shiny metal box by the radio. This engages one, and then another super electromagnet. Almost instantaneously water and air are agitated by the ultrasonic waves which create sonoluminescence. The boat becomes enveloped in a dense green fog. At the same time, all those vertical and horizontal metal cables and stripes on the schooner's masts and booms start to emit an unearthly glow.

Blackbird's crew and men on the gunboats then experience terrifying lightning and thunder. The electric discharge produces a strong magnetic force which bends gravity and creates a rotating field. The gravity and magnetism become unified in mass and energy and a thermal field emerges. Then, suddenly, a deafening silence replaces the thunder. Vinko is lying on the deck unconscious while the others are frozen in awkward positions. As if they are wedged somewhere outside the limits of their immediate space, they cannot make the slightest move or say a word to each other. They are fully aware of their surroundings and yet cannot do anything.

And then *Blackbird* simply disappears.

The gunboats stop the chase in disbelief. The gunfire stops. The searchlights from the beach keep piercing through the dark for a while longer and are then switched off. The armed men slowly leave the beach.

Only one brief account of what had happened that night was left in Schmelz's report to his command, which he filed the following day, September 10, 1943, stating:

The boat we pursued was hit with our gunfire and about to be seized but it suddenly disappeared. I do not have an explanation for this event.

On September 10, an hour and a half past midnight, the schooner suddenly appears, in the exact same place where she disappeared four hours earlier, at the western end of the Šunj Beach Bay, on the island of Lopud, still enveloped in green fog.

Sven, Tove and Edvard are standing on the deck, speechless, and for a few moments, clueless as to what just happened. As if awakened from a dream, they notice Vinko who starts to moan and shows signs of regaining consciousness. They are alone by the deserted beach. The thunder is gone, the Croatian Nazis are gone. Everything around them is motionless. The stars glitter in the night sky, beautiful but indifferent.

Suddenly, a young slim tall man in a wet swimsuit comes out of the cabin, tottering. He steps on the deck, obviously bewildered, and looks around in disbelief. Everyone else is equally mystified with his appearance, not having the slightest idea who the stranger is. As the people on the deck keep exchanging stares with each other, in silence, the water dripping from the wet body of the tall stranger creates a small puddle around his feet.

Edvard, utterly confused like the rest of them, nevertheless gathers himself and gives the stranger a towel to dry. He then leads him back to the cabin, helps him put on some clothes, and prepares hot tea for the perplexed man. The two of them remain in the cabin, engaged in a conversation for a long time.

Tove and Sven are aware they must leave Lopud as soon as possible. Sven helps Vinko stand on his feet and looks at him closely – Vinko's shoulder wound is bleeding, his face is very pale, and he seems quite battered. Sven asks the Dalmatian if he will be able to help them reach Vis as planned. Vinko confidently replies that he of course will do it, but his trembling voice reveals the extent of his weakness and the seriousness of his gunshot wound. Tove insists that he at once must go home, to the care of his father, and seek urgent medical help.

Without thinking, she then takes one displaced, lose shiny metal ball from the Edvard's tower and gives it to Vinko with the following words:

"I hope you will keep this a reminder of the time we spent together, but also of me."

Tove also gives Vinko the Viking knife she got from her father before leaving Norway:

"And this Viking knife will protect you from all woes."

Vinko reluctantly accepts the gifts. He explains to Sven how best to keep the course to Vis. The two of them jump into the dinghy. Sven quickly takes them to the beach and helps Vinko disembark. He wants to walk Vinko home, but Vinko insists he does not need any help and can make it home just fine. He urges Sven to return to the boat and sail out as soon as possible. Sven hugs Vinko, jumps back into the dinghy and returns to *Blackbird*. The scene is quiet and tranquil. The surface of the sea resembles an endless mirror reflecting millions of stars on the night sky above.

A few minutes later a favorable wind picks up and Tove and Sven raise the sails, putting *Blackbird* on her course towards the open sea and the island of Vis. The schooner's crew stand on the deck in silence. They are listening to the only sounds that can be heard – the hum of the full sails, the splashing of water cut by the schooner's bow, and the voices of two men talking in the cabin below.

On the beach, Vinko is holding his arm below the wounded shoulder and presses the metal ball and the Viking knife against his waist with the elbow. Watching the beautiful schooner disappear into the dark night, he remains motionless for a very long time. Only after lowering his head and smiling softly, does he become aware of the tears running down his checks. That was the last time he saw *Blackbird*, Tove and Sven.

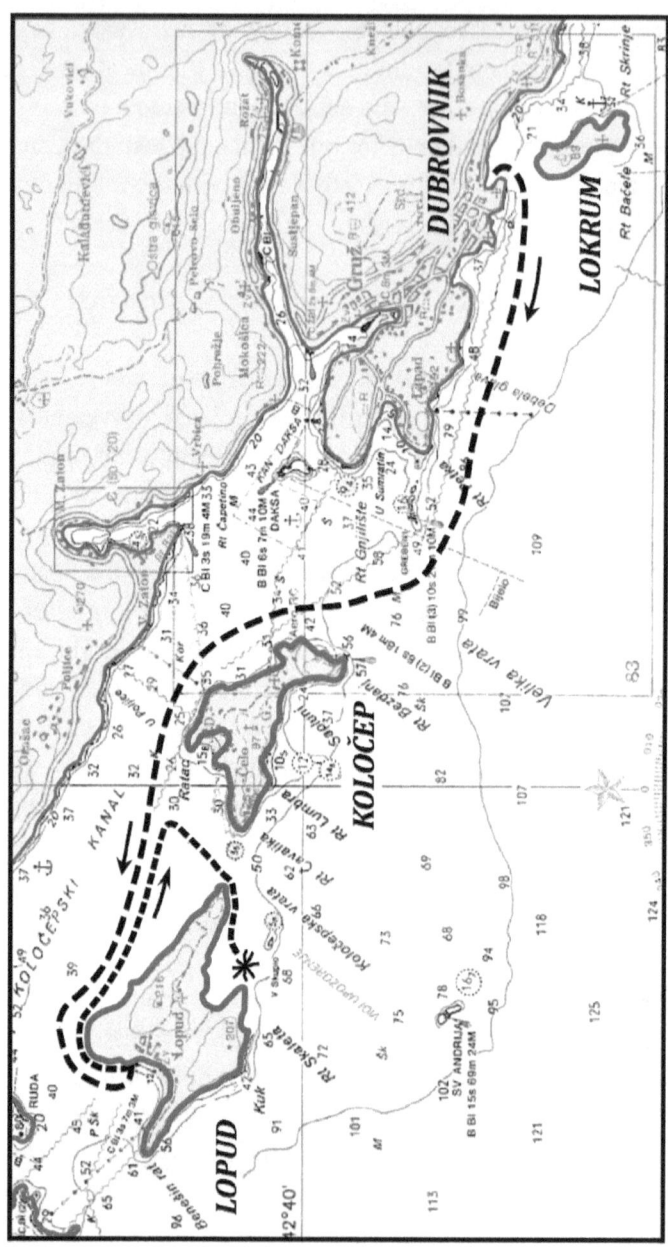

Blackbird's sailing route on September 9, 1943, day after she won the Lokrum Regatta.

PART TWO

Chapter 24

Vis

Mussolini was arrested, and the allied troops were in southern Italy after the successful invasion of Sicily. On the other side of the Adriatic, as the *Blackbird* was sailing to the island of Vis, the situation was chaotic. Even before the armistice was officially announced and Italy capitulated, the partisans gained control of several islands and most of Vis, fighting the Italians. After the capitulation, the Italian soldiers, those that could, fled the islands in panic, fearing revenge. The less lucky ones surrendered *en masse* and some even joined the partisans. On Vis, the Croatian Nazis and the Serbian nationalists aligned with the Italians were in hiding, trying to flee the remote island.

From the deck of *Blackbird*, which was about to sail into Komiža harbor on the morning of September 10, the Swedish flag flapping on top of her main mast, the four people on board were witnessing all the chaos, screams and noise on the island. Smoke rose from several burned houses. Local civilians, soldiers in different uniforms, military motorcycles, and donkeys pulling carts, could be seen swarming everywhere in the small town and on the docks.

As soon as they reluctantly disembarked from *Blackbird*, Tove, Sven, Edvard and the mysterious man were surrounded by a squad of suspicious partisans and escorted to the town command. The uncertainty and the anxiety in the small crowded room full of cigarette smoke ended by the appearance of a British intelligence officer Larry Neal. In anticipation of the Italian capitulation, he and a squad of British commandos arrived in Komiža from Sicily six days ago to connect with the partisans and lay the groundwork for the arrival of allied troops. Larry's clear orders were to collaborate fully with the communists and no one else. Churchill's government finally broke with the Yugoslav royalist Mihailović and his Chetniks. The British general MacLean who, under the name Safford Cripps, previously worked in the British embassy in Moscow, played a crucial role in this decision. The allies were fully aware of the strategic importance of Vis after the fall of Italy and, within weeks, with the permission from Tito, started to transport personnel, provisions and military equipment to the island, eventually creating an impregnable fortress in the Adriatic. McLean himself arrived in January 1944 to oversee the process.

The stay at Komiža started with two very embarrassing episodes for Tove. First, Larry Neal was bewildered by the name of the schooner displayed on her stern, which made him explode, to the astonishment of the partisans who escorted the Scandinavian crew and Larry back to the harbor.

"For Christ sake, what the hell is this?! Who did it? I was not told anything. Absolutely unacceptable!!!"

Thanks to Tove's exceptional charm, and her irresistible smile, she managed to calm the enraged Brit, explaining why, already back in Sweden, she "suggested" the new name for the schooner to Harry Hallberg. And how Harry's approval proved to be invaluable for their sail on the Adriatic and various encounters with the Italian authorities.

In addition to her charm, Tove pulled another ace from her sleeve, which undoubtedly helped in winning Larry's good will, "And please, do take both jugs of the amazing red wine we were able to wrestle, with an enormous difficulty, out of the monastery on Pelješac."

After calm returned to the group, the American Edvard Neumman, who started to unload his equipment from the schooner, noticed that both the metal towers and the super electromagnets they housed had disappeared. Stunned, he then realized that the metal balls were also missing. When he found out from Tove that one ball was intentionally left at Lopud, as her present to Vinko, Edvard completely lost his mind. His piercing shouts made the partisans witnessing the event remark to themselves how the nice-looking schooner brought to their island a bunch of lunatics.

Edvard demanded to have a private meeting with Larry. At the very beginning of the meeting, the American and the Britt first passionately complained about the inexcusable actions of the "wild Norwegian." The conversation then turned to a much more important topic. Without elaborating, Edvard informed Larry that the mysterious man who appeared on *Blackbird* out of nowhere the previous night is of utmost importance to OSS and the War Department. As such, he is now the subject of special attention, must be placed in permanent custody, and transported to the United States. Larry acknowledged the importance of the request and had no objections. He suggested however that Edvard sail to Bari on a fast gunboat, scheduled to leave in four days, and prepare there the necessary logistics. And that he and his commandos would personally take care of the *subject* and his custody here in Komiža, before the schooner is repaired and ready to sail to Italy.

Blackbird's crew and Edvard were accommodated in an abandoned tavern on the ground floor of an old stone house by the town church. There, they would await the continuation of their journey in the company of an old fisherman, Mate Kalafatović, the only occupant of the house. Their free time while waiting would be spent largely between the walled herb garden in the back, a stone bench in front of the main entrance, and the interior of the house which was kept comfortably cool by the thick limestone walls and heavy wooden window shutters. The fisherman Mate proved to be an exquisite chef, preparing for his guests delicious *frutti di mare* meals with great enthusiasm, happy to have company willing to listen to his favorite stories. Only gloomy Edvard, who just could not forgive Tove for what she did, would leave the tavern as soon as he devoured the food, not uttering a single word during the entire time.

The following several days Sven and Tove worked with Larry, explaining the findings of their mission in detail and using heavily annotated maritime maps, sketches and notes. The last meeting Tove and Sven had with the Britt, just before sunset on September 14, involved a brief study of the countless photographs taken during the trip and carefully produced by the local photographer Frano Lasić from the films Sven shot with his coveted *Hasselblad SKa4* and two German *Leicas*.

Edvard boarded the gunboat headed for Bari at 10 pm on September 14, in a lousy mood, still angry as a hungry lynx, and without saying goodbye to anyone. The partisans had simply ignored his repeated demands to return the metal towers and the electromagnets. He left Vis

167

carrying his heavy metal chest, backpack, and a large sealed waterproof metal box with the *Mission Capri* materials he received from Larry, who requested that the box be turned over to the SOE office in Bari.

Tove and Sven unexpectedly spent almost a full month on Vis, waiting for *Blackbird* to be repaired which proved not to be that easy given the extent of the damage from the Nazi bullets and the lack of skilled locals who were consumed with other "more important" tasks. Still, they were thoroughly enjoying the time spent wandering around the island, the company of barba Mate, the meals, the plentiful wine, and stories so vividly told by the old fisherman. One of the stories left a particularly strong impression on the speechless Scandinavians:

> *A month or so before they were defeated, the Italians tried yet again to destroy the Blue Cave on the neighboring island of Biševo because it is prettier, or at least as pretty, as their famous grotto on Capri. The Italian Governor of Dalmatia decided, after realizing that capitulation is inevitable, to destroy the entire cave this time around, with two tons of dynamite.*
>
> *This second attempt of the Italians failed again. An Italian, who simply could not stomach such barbarity, revealed the plan to the partisans, including the exact date and time of the hideous crime to be committed. Then an armed partisan boat under the name Partizan, hiding at Živogošće near Makarska, on the coast, sailed to Biševo at night. There it ambushed and sank the Italian gunboat which was sent to destroy the cave.*

During their stay on Vis, Tove and Sven witnessed a constant flurry of activity. Only a week after their arrival from Lopud, British aid in the form of food and military equipment started arriving on fast small boats. In time, the Allies brought tons of food, medical supplies, gasoline and diesel, thousands of rifles, heavy machine guns, large-caliber guns, tons of ammunition, and various types of radio equipment. English instructors started training the partisans in handling weapons, and especially anti-aircraft guns, preparing them for what was coming that winter of 1943-1944, including the arrival of hundreds of Allied troops. Among them would be an American with the name John Hamilton. But, this is another story and I will not cover it here.

At the end of September, while walking on a beaten path to the top of the hill northwest of town, where she was going to watch the sunset, Tove stumbled upon architect Nikola Dobrović, their generous host on Lopud. Apparently, he arrived at Vis just a few days after the capitulation of Italy and joined the partisans. Now, that the fighting is over, he is looking to get to Bari, but without much success. Tove immediately offered to take the architect with them, on *Blackbird*, as soon as the schooner is ready to sail out. He would just have to be packed and ready to leave on moment's notice. Later that night Tove told Larry about the architect and the arrangement, more as if it were done deal than a request. Larry agreed, without thinking much of it; the Norwegian seemed to have gained complete control of the poor agent of SOE. All that Larry said is that he did not want to be bothered with any paper trail:

"Do with him whatever you want, I am not responsible for him and... In fact, come to think of it, you did not tell me anything and I did not tell you anything."

Finally, on Wednesday, October 6, 1943, at five o'clock in the afternoon, Larry showed up at the old tavern and informed Tove and Sven that *Blackbird* is ready to sail out to Bari, Italy, promptly before dawn next morning. They will be joined by the mysterious man whom he will personally escort to the schooner from custody. The Scandinavians were somewhat surprised to hear about the mysterious man whom they did not see since arriving to Vis, including that he was in custody, but did not say anything.

The last night before leaving Vis, Tove, Sven and the architect Dobrović spent in the company of barba Mate, enjoying another meal he prepared and a long monologue he had on the history of his beloved island. Moreover, barba Mate served them the famous red wine, preferred by the Austrian emperors to any other, as he proudly emphasized. Dobrović's presence proved to be invaluable as he was helping with the translation and every so often inserted details he thought would help in keeping the interest of the Scandinavians. The combined effort and the genuine enthusiasm of the two Yugoslavs resulted in a beautiful gift to Tove and Sven: they heard an extraordinary tale of the island which saw millennia of different Mediterranean and

European people battling over its natural wonders, resources and unique location. The Illyrians, the Greeks, the Romans, the Slavs, the Venetians, the Austrians, the French, the British, the Italians, all left their mark and blood here.

As scheduled, *Blackbird* sailed for Bari before dawn on October 7, with four people on board – Tove, Sven, the architect Dobrović, and the mysterious man who was as silent as when he appeared on the schooner out of nowhere, almost exactly a month ago. From the beginning, the Scandinavians were very cheerful and talkative, and laughing every now and then. Their ordeal was all but over, they managed to save their heads, everything could not be looking better. A minor disruption to their optimism, which also infected architect Dobrović, was Sven's realization that the jug of red wine from Pelješac was missing. The enraged Swede promptly accused "traitorous partisans" for the theft, only to hear from Tove what had really happened with the wine.

After this brief exchange, everyone on board quickly turned to admire the sunrise behind the rugged Dinaric mountains, visible far across the sea in the east. Except for the mysterious man who kept looking over the schooner's bow, at the horizon that laid ahead.

I found out much later who the man was. He was Teo Lovrić, son of Vinko Lovrić.

The schooner *Blackbird* flew through time and space, on September 9 in that distant year of 1943, in the cove of the Šunj Beach on the island of Lopud. The flight was enabled by a frightening release of magnetic energy and the limitless force of the rotating magnetic resonance created by the two Tesla super-electromagnets, mounted on metal towers on each side of the *Blackbird's* hull. Teo was the only one in the immediate vicinity of the boat, enjoying an early night swim, after sunset, as he very much liked to do. But for him, it was September 9, 1980. Suddenly, out of nowhere, a ferocious storm unleashed a downpour of rain, thunder and lightning. Just as he turned to swim back to the beach, a lightning strike hit the sea near Teo. A wave of energy bounced off the water surface and connected instantaneously with the metal ball he left on the beach. The ball which Teo always carried with him, because, as he often remarked, it made him feel nice and peaceful.

The moment the electric arch touched the ball, Teo disappeared.

Where and if Vinko's son Teo really drowned and died, no one knew. I uncovered the truth many years later, searching for answers about the wooden schooner *Blackbird*. Teo appeared on the boat, at that very cove of the Šunj Beach, but on September 9, 1943. When *Blackbird* flew from the Croatian Nazis and Oberst Hans Schmelz who were pursuing her, Teo flew with the schooner to his new future where he remained for the rest of his life.

Armed motorboat Partizan, together with the motorboat Pionir, was the nucleus of the Partisan Navy formed in Podgora on January 23, 1943. Courtesy of Archives of The Yugoslav People's Army.

Marshall Tito, The Supreme Commander of Yugoslav Partisans, visiting his troops on Vis. Courtesy of Archives of The Yugoslav People's Army.

Chapter 25

Rebus

My European days are long gone but I still cannot get used to the daily grind here at home. Neither my professional duties nor frequent business trips can take my mind off the pursuit I started. The pursuit which consumes me more and more with every passing day. Yes, I did uncover quite a bit about the schooner including when she sailed to the Adriatic. That was the goal but, along the way and unexpectedly, much more had emerged. Slowly but surely, another mystery materialized – an unknown, unclear, and perhaps crucial role of the great Nikola Tesla.

Fighting exponentially progressing troubles with airport security and customs officials, which I do not want to describe here, I finally managed to bring home the presents I got from Vinko Lovrić – the Viking knife, and the shiny metal ball left behind by Teo. At the time, I could not imagine what the ball was all about, but it was obvious to me that, somehow, it had to be related to the history of *Blackbird* in an important way. I did not know what a connection between Teo's ball and the three identical balls I received from the owner of Terry House in Delaware could possibly be either. Or its connection with any of the other things in the large leather bag she gave me – the shiny metal box and other metal objects, Tesla's drawings, notebook and notes written in Cyrillic.

I am constantly puzzled with all of Tesla's things that ended up in my possession, including the question – why me? Why was I chosen to be the beneficiary of the pledge the Terry House owner's mother gave to Tesla many decades ago? And, in any case, although I can read what Tesla wrote, I do not understand any of the technical details, various equations, scattered symbols, and numbers. It is clear that I need help from someone knowledgeable, an engineer or scientist.

That would be Ivica Kaurić, professor at Belgrade University and my old high school friend, who else? Ivica immediately accepted the invitation to be my guest here in the United States, as soon as he finishes with the exams.

"Ha-ha, it will be an easy term for them, including the lazy ones. They will have to thank you a lot, ha-ha-ha. I will probably let everyone pass, except for those notoriously ignorant; I want to have enough time studying the things you described, as much time as we need. And I may also try to postpone the beginning of my lectures next semester. Who knows, I may even succeed; it would be super. I will let you know the flight details, just please pick me up at the airport. See you soon."

Upon his arrival, Ivica asked not to be disturbed for several days. He withdrew to my study and used the sofa to catch up on some sleep. He left the room only during quick visits related to his bodily functions. He probably would forget to eat anything if I had not brought him food and drinks regularly. When he finally emerged from the room, Ivica had an introduction and plenty of explanations.

"Tesla, it turns out, left us an unpublished patent, its physical model, instructions how to use it in his diary, and an incredibly important note!" Ivica said. He then went on to explain how Tesla himself wrote why he was so secretive:

I do not want and cannot fight against magnates, companies, agencies and ruthless capitalists, but I do hope that future generations will know better than us how to use my patents and ideas for the benefit of mankind. More than once an immeasurably important patent was forcefully destroyed, such as the case of all the results achieved by the respectable Mr. Rife, using my advice and formulae for targeted resonances. He succeeded in eliminating, in a non-surgical way, virtually all pathogens and even viruses, and was able to inhibit growth of cancer cells, but all this work vanished without trace. I also will never forgive them the viciousness with which they sabotaged my project of free inexhaustible energy for all.

Ivica then continues with how Tesla, in this unpublished patent, first explained the principle of Unified Field Theory and then described one of his experiments. According to Tesla, gravity and magnetism are connected in the same way as mass and energy in the famous Einstein equation, because they exist in two different dimensions between which there is a constant frequency. The genius explained how the mind also reacts to interdimensional travels. He provided a formula for certain alternating transformations of the boundless frequencies which enable directional mind travel forward and backward in time.

Although clearly a genius, a gentleman, a wizard and everything else, Tesla, still just a human, could not resist emphasizing, at the end of his notes, that Einstein, in fact, never resolved the Unified Field Theory. Tesla's remark, written in Cyrillic, was short:

A portion of this patent was utilized by the Ministry of War in the Eldridge Experiment. Using my two resonators they sent a physical object and live organisms into another space and another, future time, and returned them. This was an uncontrolled process with many awful consequences. The Ministry of War then used my idea, illegally and without my consent, in other experiments that followed. I did not give them the second, much more important, part of the patent. It provides for control of a multidimensional transfer through both future and past times. They will likely remove me but I, Nikola Tesla, write this patent in Cyrillic so they cannot read it without help, and am hiding it as a covenant for some future, more humane time.

Ivica points out a drawing of a model in Tesla's patent which shows four steel balls of irregular shape, almost egg-like, and a metal object with surfaces designated as "ideally polished." The object consists of four narrow steel cylinders resting on four ceramic cube bases. The small metal box from the bag is incredibly smooth and has shiny surfaces, without any visible openings or slits, but with a row of buttons resembling a remote controller of kind. One side of the box has an engraved number 3210. There is no explanation in the notes as to what it means.

The small notebook from the leather bag is apparently Tesla's diary, also written in Cyrillic. Exactly in the middle of the notebook, on the two center pages, there is a brief hand-written instruction with rather simple commands – connect the bases and the four metal balls on their respective cylinders, connect all of it with conductors, the charge will self-induce, direct physical or thought transfer with the switch, select the direction using buttons on the box, and so on. At the end of the instructions is a seemingly random string of Cyrillic alphabet letters and several numbers: 5дсеоз5пħрттст5хħтосфрсвħзне. It is obviously a code of some kind, but we are clueless as to its meaning, and even more so how to break it.

The buttons on the remote controller are set at 37 forward and 37 backward. Why 37? Because, as Ivica explains, Tesla's waves of which he talked about earlier, are based on the number 37 and its simplicity as the ultimate expression of perfectionism. For mathematicians the number is unique because it is the only one among natural numbers that can be numerically evenly multiplied, arithmetically and geometrically, by cyclic permutations of its numerals.

Sensing that all this information causes certain chaos in my head, Ivica continues in a simplistic manner:

"To be clear, I must tell you that not everything is exact and precise. However, I believe I managed to comprehend most of it, as it is closely related to some of my projects which utilized focused electromagnetic fields with the potential of tens of millions of volts. I was also involved in creating instrumentation for measuring, recording and amplifying various waives. Granted, all that was happening long time ago, including building electric power plants in support of the experiments, but enough about that...

The main point is this—it looks like we have uncovered the secret of Tesla's rumored time machine! Its key is four metal balls and you have them all: the three you got in New Castle and the one Vinko gave you; they are exactly the same as these balls in the drawing. The machine uses induced static waves with negative wavelength I already told you about. They are Tesla's non-Hertzian waves. Since their frequency is endless (I explained that as well), their transmission is instantaneous. I can illustrate to you what it all means in space dimensions. Their wavelengths as they travel through natural materials are proportional to distance. If, for example, we want an instantaneous transmission to twenty kilometers, all we have to do is emit them precisely at that wavelength. Since the transmission is instantaneous, it means that the negative wavelength halts the series of physical reality moments in the dimension of time.

More detailed technical specifications probably would not mean anything to you, but let me tell you that the machine excites neutrinos (I told you about them in Belgrade – they are particles with super luminous speeds first mentioned by Tesla) because the wave vibrations cause electrical charge disturbances, transmission of energy through the Earth and multidimensional oscillations. These oscillations create 37 cyclical, alternating, spiral electrical vortices with a pronounced effect of time contraction and transmission of information at super luminous speeds.

In other words, so you can understand better, Tesla's machine can lead to a fourth dimension of the multi-dimensional space-time structure via this complex form of non-Hertzian waves. It can instantaneously send something, perhaps an object, perhaps ourselves or our projections, or anything, to different reality, that is to three new dimensions of space and another dimension of time!"

Although, after Ivica's words, my mind now seems to be spinning at super luminous speed making me almost dizzy, I realize that, between the two seemingly unrelated stories, one about the wooden schooner *Blackbird* and the other one about the secret patent of Nikola Tesla, a third story emerges that finally connects them.

The key for *Blackbird's* time flight was a device installed on her in June 1943 in Boothbay Harbor, Maine. This device, or machine, was a secret prototype created by Tesla and implemented by two postdoctoral students at MIT, Edvard Neumman and Svetoslav Belov. Tesla was undoubtedly deeply involved in teleportation experiments in late 1930s and early 1940s. He also guided preparations for sending a Navy vessel on a time travel experiment until, in protest, he completely withdrew from *Project Rainbow* alarmed by the Navy's recklessness. Edvard and Svetoslav, to whom Tesla revealed most of the time travel secret, continued to work with the prototype after his death in January 1943.

The device on *Blackbird* was activated for the second time on September 9, 1943 when the schooner, facing grave danger, jumped to different time and after four hours returned to the same location where it disappeared. The different time was September 9, 1980 and the location was the Šunj beach cove on the Dalmatian island of Lopud. There, *Blackbird* picked up a swimmer who was enjoying an after sunset swim and took him with her back to the year 1943. I discovered later that the swimmer was Teo, son of Vinko Lovrić who was a mate on *Blackbird* during her secret WWII mission on the Adriatic.

After this event, I could not find anything else unusual when it comes to *Blackbird's* whereabouts. Upon her arrival to Bari from the Dalmatian island of Vis she stayed in Italy until October 8, 1943, then crossed the Mediterranean and sailed across the Atlantic back to the United States where she was returned to her owner, Hubert Toppin, Commodore of the Essex Yacht Club in Connecticut. After 1950, the schooner changed hands several times until 1993 when Peter and Sandy Thompson bought her.

As it turns out, Tesla hid his final patent of controlled travel of mind and body through space and time, and we are now in its possession. We can try to build Tesla's apparatus from the parts we have and understand what happened with *Blackbird* and Teo.

Except, we do not know exactly how to do it, at least not yet.

Chapter 26

Halloween

My research of the voyages of the wooden schooner *Blackbird* during World War II is finally over. The bet made with Peter in 2013 I undoubtedly won, and the day came to declare victory officially. Exactly at 10 o'clock on the morning of October 27th, 2017, I inform him of this fact, announcing I will, together with all the evidence, show up at their house next Tuesday evening unless he and Sandy have other plans. Peter laughs and replies I am always more than welcome, especially on Halloween, just like all other kids that will, dressed in scary costumes, ring and knock on their door asking for candies. I, of course, do not hold back and confirm that I love candies, especially those made of chocolate, but do expect something in addition that is rightfully mine, certain he understands what I am talking about. Momentarily and with loud laughter Peter says,

"Don't you worry, a bet is a bet. An unopened bottle of a 23-year old *Pappy Van Winkle* will wait for you together with a pack of our favorite IPA, chilled to the right temperature."

I thank Peter very much in advance and warn him the whole story is incredible, so much so that I am bringing along my high school friend from Belgrade, now a renowned scientist and academician, to confirm everything because they certainly would not believe me. And there is no need to worry about accommodation as the two of us will stay in nearby Bath, in a cozy little hotel named *Daniel*, and will bring with us some lobsters and backup drinks. The story is so unbelievable, good food and drink will be more than needed to digest it.

Peter is now completely intrigued, and I hear him calling Sandy to explain what is going on, and then telling me they cannot wait for our visit.

Our flight from D.C. lands in Portland little after 5 o'clock in the afternoon of October 31st, just in time to pick a dozen freshly caught lobsters at the Freeport Marina where the Thompsons keep their beloved schooner. In the Marina, I point out *Blackbird* to the amazed Ivica who cannot take his eyes off the boat. She is anchored in the distance and lit by the setting sun, happily rocking on small waves. On our way to the Thompsons, we make a brief stop at a liquor store where Ivica selects a bottle of white Bacardi and a bottle of his favorite Scottish malt. I add the largest jar of cashews to help with all that drink and, just in case, two packs of newly crafted IPA from the nearby local brewery, wholeheartedly recommended by the extremely friendly store clerk. Ivica's unique Duncan & Taylor malt with the interesting name *Dimensions* is very expensive, but they both assure me it is worth every penny.

Peter and Sandy open their door dressed as witch and Dracula. Ivica, not knowing anything about the Halloween tradition, is confused and, for a moment, I guess a bit scared. This causes a general laughter during which I introduce them to each other. We have not yet settled comfortably in the living room, by the fireplace where the flaming wood was cracking cheerfully, when Peter points to the trophies displayed on an old wooden captain's chest under the window and declares the drinks will become my possessions as soon as I present proof. I suggest we first toast to our reunion, and especially to our guest from Serbia who, for the occasion, brought his favorite malt as a present. And, it would be perfect if we first take care of the lobsters so we can relax afterwards, our stomachs pleased, and then leisurely look at the evidence which is on this jump drive (which I pull out of my pocket and raise above my head, theatrically.) That huge TV screen in the corner will do just fine. Peter replies that we should wait with the dinner a bit before all the kids from the neighborhood claim their candies. Trick or treat it is usually over by eight o'clock.

After the toast and collective admiration of Ivica's favorite drink (which really is worth every penny), Sandy fetches a big plate with snacks from the kitchen and leads us to their backyard garden where awaits a humongous express pot on gas. Peter fills the pot with a garden hose and water, by some miracle, boils in seconds whereas lobsters, one by one, become victims of a ritual that terrifies poor Ivica. I try to divert my friend's attention, to no avail, and desperately cry for Peter's help. Peter quickly comes to rescue and explains to Ivica how lobsters almost do not feel pain and momentarily leave this world as soon as their tiny heads are submerged in the boiling water. He adds something about their famous cruelty which justifies ours. Like, for example, that they devour each other. And that everyone he knows agrees the unbelievable taste of lobster meat requires no discussion. Based on all these facts, Peter then politely asks Ivica to relax and tell Sandy and him how he likes his stay in America so far.

Somewhat persuaded, Ivica replies there were not that many chances for sightseeing because, since coming to America, he spent all his time studying the fascinating documents I gave him – they were, after all, the main reason for his trip. Only yesterday he saw little bit of Washington, D.C. which, surprisingly, he liked very much, especially the National Gallery. He sincerely hopes there will be little more time to tour the capital and its other museums, before returning to Belgrade where the lectures at the University he managed to postpone are awaiting. Also, he hopes one day to come back to Maine because he instantaneously fell in love with its rocky coast, picturesque bays with boats, lovely little towns and everything else he saw during the short drive from the airport to their beautiful house full of nice paintings and interesting antiques (Ivica's curious eyes did not miss numerous boat equipment pieces and instruments scattered all over the house and furniture, without any particular order.)

According to an old proven recipe, the unfortunate creatures, now bright red color, are extracted from the pot after exactly 18 minutes. While waiting for the lobsters to cool down a bit, Peter uses the opportunity to proudly explain Ivica the origins and purpose of all those things Sandy and he passionately collected over many years visiting countless antique shops and New England harbors: sextants, octants, small and large boat compasses, chronometers, sandglasses, nocturlabes, and other contrivances. At one moment Ivica pauses in front of a large framed poster on the wall and, surprised, remembers that he saw the painting yesterday in original, in The National Gallery, in room 73 (Ivica has an extraordinary photographic memory). Peter confirms:

"My favorite painting. Reminds me of power of Nature and our vulnerability, but also brings hope when we need it the most – I am sure you notice the sun light emerging from behind the frightening storm clouds."

After the last of the lobsters are wrestled out of their shells only to end up in our delighted stomachs, the time came to present the evidence to the Thompsons and claim my victory. I hand the jump drive over to Peter, ceremoniously, with the words:

"And now, here is the crown of my efforts of these past four years. Please let us all sit around the TV and you will open the file, there is only one. I assembled all the evidence in a short video. It will be more than interesting for you to see it, believe me."

While the scenes I recorded in Podgora, and the islands of Lopud and Mljet are being played in front of us, Peter and Sandy every now and then look at each other in disbelief and exclaim:

"Absolutely unbelievable! Oh my God! Impossible!"

In the first scene Vinko, in excellent English, remembers Tove's explanation about the schooner's name – how she managed to persuade someone in Sweden to change her name from *Blackbird* to *Svarttrost* instead of *Capri*. In the second, Vinko shows to the camera the drawings he made during the cruise. Following are the shots I took on Mljet in which there are the same landscapes from Vinko's drawings but this time without the beautiful boat. There are also Sven's photos from Lopud and the Adriatic, then the schooner anchored in the Old Port of Dubrovnik, again a clip with Vinko admiring the boat's capabilities, and finally a story how *Svarttrost* defeated the unbeatable *Nordwind*. The video is over, the screen turns black, we all sit in silence for at least several minutes. Peter finally stands up, goes to the wooden captain's chest, takes the trophies of the bet, comes back and hands them over to me with the words:

"Now, you must explain all of it in detail!"

I joyfully open the bottle of the 23-year old bourbon *Pappy Van Winkle* which I earned with great effort, pour everyone a glass and toast to the late Vinko, brave war crews of their beloved schooner, and to the

181

two of them for restoring *Blackbird* at the delight of all that ever sailed on her. We empty the glasses bottom up and Ivica fails to hide a tear or two. I hug my dear friend.

"That is why I love him so much."

Ivica quickly reacts to my gesture:

"Sentimentalities aside, I am here to tell you everything you saw and heard is only the tip of the iceberg. Namely, your incredible schooner almost certainly took part in something immeasurably more important than a spy mission. As it is, based on all the documents and testimonies I witnessed, I am ready to put my scientific reputation on line and confirm that *Blackbird*, together with her crews, at least on two occasions, travelled through space and time during World War II! The first time it was through space, when she crossed the Atlantic in only twelve days, and the second it was through time when she literary disappeared during a pursuit near the Croatian island Lopud. I, of course, cannot persuade you, at least for now, that my claim is not some kind of science fiction. However, I learned a long time ago that *fantasy*, for lack of a better term, is more than desirable in science. In fact, it is necessary. Most helpful to this belief was my decades-long study of the research of scientist Nikola Tesla, of whom I am sure you heard before. My belief was only reinforced when, over the last few days, I examined previously unknown Tesla's documents. Tesla's unique, special waves and an enormous electromagnetic field are exactly the things responsible for the time travel of your schooner. It is a miracle that all the people involved survived without any physical harm, as the resulting temperature, if something goes wrong, can easily and instantaneously melt any known material. "

Aware of the absence of any reaction from our hosts and seeing their very tired faces after the flood of incredible information, I realize that midnight had passed long a time ago. I tell Peter and Sandy we will now go to the hotel to get some sleep before tomorrow's sail, to which we very much look forward. And that we hope they will be able to get some rest as well. We both thank them for the unforgettable hospitality and, especially, for the bet they lost. If there were no objections, we would also like to continue the story after the sail tomorrow, around the grill. The Thompsons, in one voice, enthusiastically welcome the request, with a remark that they expect as many details as possible because this whole thing reminds them of an exciting science fiction movie!

Ships in Distress off a Rocky Coast. 1667 painting by Dutch master Ludolf Backhuysen. Ailsa Mellon Bruce Fund, National Gallery of Art, Washington, D.C.

Chapter 27

Instrument

The next morning, during the first few minutes of our sail on *Blackbird*, there were two new surprises.

Immediately after stepping onto the immaculately polished deck of the schooner, Peter invited Ivica and me to follow him into the cabin, because he wanted to show us something. He said he hadn't slept a wink the night before thinking about what he had heard and seen. He seated us on a mahogany kitchen bench and placed six photos on the table in front of us. He then proceeded to point out one of them, explaining that the twelve notches visible on the photo are dates written in the US Navy code:

"This is a photo of the underside of the bench you're sitting on, taken during restoration in my workshop. Feel free to look at it yourself, I haven't touched that surface. Here, take a flashlight so you can see better."

That was the first thing!

Next, Peter started explaining the remaining five photographs, taken from different angles. They showed a large iron beam – a ballast at the bottom of *Blackbird*, with traces of something Peter had not been able to logically explain to himself until then. The ballast gap had a regular web of grooved lines on it, which could have been formed only by the melting of the metal. The lower edges of the gap took the form of displaced bulges, with about half inch radius (just over one centimeter), which also strongly indicated that the metal had been melted. Peter removed all these imperfections and smoothed them out with a very powerful grinder that he rented, at great expense, in Portland.

The three of us concluded almost at the same time that these "regular imperfections" must have been due to the thermal field that occurred on September 9, 1943, when a complex configuration of metal balls and steel cables on *Blackbird* was activated by the mysterious instrument of Svetoslav Belov and Edvard Neumman!

The unforgettable day out sailing on *Blackbird* thus began with precious discoveries that confirmed everything I had either heard directly from the descendants of the wartime American crew of the schooner or reconstructed with Ivica's help. But that was not the end of it! About half an hour later, the Thompsons had raised the sails on the schooner. Ivica and I went to the bow to enjoy the indescribable experience. After a while, he started talking, looking at the waves all along.

"I haven't told this to anyone outside the project so far. Ever since you invited me, I've had this overwhelming feeling that everything that has happened to me since then, everything that had happened to me before, is by no means accidental. I don't know how to explain it, but I can't shake off the feeling that all we have come to know about Tesla is in some way closely related to my work as well. You see, a long time ago, back when I was his assistant, my Professor assigned me to a project classified as top secret. Later, when I became Assistant Professor, around the time when you left for the States, the Professor retired, and I took over the management of the project. I don't want to bother you with the details, but you will certainly find this extremely interesting. We were working with the Romanians on the development, recording and use of telepathy for military purposes, all under an agreement Tito and Ceausescu made a long time ago. We used a secret army facility inside the Djerdap Gorge as headquarters for that part of the project. We obtained all the energy we needed by a direct underground transmission line from the Djerdap 1 hydroelectric power plant, and later from Djerdap 2, because we needed huge amounts of it. At one point we even experimented with rusalja witches, can you imagine? Anyhow, we managed to get some amazing results. And not only with the telepathy.

Just before the breakup of Yugoslavia, word got out that the entire project had been leaked to the English, which means to the Americans as well, and probably also to the Russians. The military was alarmed, and the project died out immediately. None of us who worked on it heard anything about it ever again, and they threatened to eliminate us all if we didn't keep our mouths shut. It's been almost 30 years since then, nobody ever found out anything about the project, no one told anyone anything, we were scared and silenced. I've kept my silence all these years.

But let me tell you something. Now, today, at my age, I am no longer afraid of anything. Besides, this thing I'm working on with you is completely original, challenging, motivating, at least for me it is. I hope that something will come out of it and that we'll be able to let the whole world know about it. I don't give a damn if it's classified, I don't care about secret services and all that nonsense anymore. Remember Tesla and what he went through. They thought they had silenced him, the FBI, the magnates, his opponents, all those men in power! But they were wrong – his message reached us, it reached me.

Completely confused and not knowing exactly what to say at that moment, I patted him on the shoulder, and so we silently stared at the bow of the beautiful schooner for a while, as it cut the surface of the water before us.

Back on land that evening, we sat around the fire in the garden until late into the night, enjoying a barbecue like a bunch of kids, trying to rationalize, if at all possible, what Ivica and I had told the Thompsons. One thing was for sure: it all started as a seemingly naive and simple bet, just for the fun of it, and then we went on digging through various archives, spending our nights searching the Internet, travelling and having countless conversations and meetings with various people in both America and Europe, making the bet eventually develop into a completely new, mysterious, unsolved and unexpected story. And then, halfway through all this work, we were faced with a new ordeal. All that we were able to anticipate, all that Ivica explained, together with all my knowledge and objects that were now in my possession, all of that was not enough for us to understand how *Blackbird* was able to travel through time. How did Tesla's device, or indeed some other device that was created at MIT and that the sailboat was equipped with, allow the controlled travel of objects through space and time? How exactly do Tesla's unpublished patent and the metal objects in my possession work, and what effect do they produce? So many questions and not a single answer yet.

I remember it as if it was yesterday, the very beginning of our conversation around the fire, that night with sparks flying everywhere around us, not only from the embers over which burgers, sausages and corn were cheerfully sizzling. The first sparks took off when the temperamental Sandy almost cried out that a return to the past was impossible – disrupting the chronology, or history as we know it, could lead to fatal changes in the historical course of events, and to temporal paradox.

Ivica answered politely how Einstein had proven that, once we went out into space and were moving in it at about the speed of light, our clock would slow down compared to that on the Earth. Therefore, once we came back to the Earth, the future will already have happened. Ivica claimed that the famous genius explained, admittedly only in theory, that time travel would be quite possible at some point. He also used exact calculations to demonstrate that if we stayed close to a powerful source of gravity, such as a neutron star or a black hole, time would flow extremely slowly for us, and therefore upon our return to Earth we would find ourselves in the distant future. Thus, Einstein argued, we would be able to time travel into the future.

He ended his exposition with what was, according to him, the most important claim made by the famous scientist: there are "wormholes" in the space, or tunnels that are shortcuts between two distant points in time and space. Theoretically, if we go in one direction, we will travel back into the past, while the other direction will take us into the future.

Sandy gazed thoughtfully into the embers and we all went silent for a while. Suddenly, Peter presented us with a new challenge:

"This is all very well, it makes for interesting reading, it spurs the imagination and can work well in the movies, and the Internet is full of hoaxes and popular theories about traveling to the future and the past. But, I mean, come on, can something like that happen for real?"

Ivica felt he was challenged. He didn't want to claim that it could or could not happen, but if Tesla personally presented something as his discovery, theory or hypothesis, who were we to mock or ignore him? Everything that this great man ever invented has now become an inevitable necessity and a lasting achievement of civilization.

Ivica then briefly explained what he had learned by interpreting Tesla's instructions and drawings, and comparing them to the strange, shiny metal objects I got from Vinko and the owner of the Terry House. The first part was relatively clear to him: we should assemble the several simple parts we have into a single "machine" according to Tesla's instructions. The energy required should be self-induced.

The second part, the manual, was also clear to him, but not entirely. The information was sparse, and no detailed explanation was provided. The "machine" should act on an intertwined network of space and time with two forces. One was gravity, the other was electromagnetism, and the switch connected them. A constant frequency was created between these two forces and between the different dimensions of space and time through which one could travel, either physically or mentally or both.

The third part was a control panel with switches. The number 3210 was etched on the board, but there was no explanation as to what it meant. The marks below the switches indicated that they were probably meant to be used for travel into the future or back into the past. Switches changed the frequency. However, Ivica didn't understand whether Tesla was referring to physical or mental transfer, to the mind or the body, or both. By all accounts, Tesla made no particular distinction between our minds and our physical beings. The instructions ended in an arbitrary string of Cyrillic letters and several numbers:

5дсео з5пħрттсг5хħгосфрвсвħзне.

What we all agreed about with Ivica that night, without a single doubt, was that, even if we somehow managed to assemble and start up the "machine" according to Tesla's instructions and drawings, we would still be facing a great and unknown danger. How can we prevent this danger if we don't even know what it is? Are we going to be in control throughout the process? Do we travel physically or mentally? If it is our minds that do the traveling, how do we control it? Which one of us dares to venture into the unknown? The switch-control itself presented a danger: where, when and how much? What determines our journey into the future or the past? How do we know the passage is over, how do we stop it, who will be operating it if our minds or bodies are elsewhere, how do we return? So many questions and not a single concrete answer yet.

And then, suddenly, a thought popped into my head that would, later, prove to be the right solution for the conundrum. Both during our ongoing conversation and earlier that day on *Blackbird*, when Ivica confided in me, there was a lot of mentioning of the human mind. Maybe the solution to the riddle can be found, at least in part, in a more complete understanding of the secrets of the human brain? I knew immediately who to call for help. I'd call Magdalena first thing in the morning. If the experiment we were working on was an adventure of the mind, we needed her knowledge and lucidity.

Blackbird's ballast keel being smoothed with a grinder (left) to remove imperfections; right: cleaned and coated with Interprotect.

Chapter 28

Dialogue

Magdalena Birnbaum is an anthropologist, psychiatrist and a psychologist. She completed her PhD studies at Universidad Nacional Autónoma de México (UNAM) in Mexico City by defending her thesis on the physiological functions of the brain under the influence of psychotics. As a successful and original researcher, she worked at major Mexican institutes and then relocated to Washington, D.C. in 2004 to pursue her research career in the United States. She married a good colleague of mine, Allen Fintch, which is how I became acquainted with her and her scientific work. She studied the culture of Native Americans, especially Mexicans, and their secrets, including the five-millennia-old tradition of spiritual enlightenment through the solemn and religious use of Peyote Cactus, their sacred deity. Magdalena's scientific interest was deeply related to her roots – her Native American grandmother and her Spanish grandfather – who met and started a family in Mexico at the beginning of the last century. As far as she was able to find out, her grandmother belonged to the Cora people, a tribe of Indians in the Juto-Aztec family that used to live along the Río Santiago River, in Nayarit, Mexico a long time ago.

Notwithstanding the generation gap between us, our families enjoyed each other's company and we spent a lot of time together. We were also happy to accompany Magdalena on her missions, wandering around southwest Texas and New Mexico. She traveled on business to the American Southwest, and the rest of us, we traveled for pleasure, always in awe of the mystical setting of the fantastic landscapes and of the ancient inhabitants of the magical high plateaus of New Mexico.

However, after Allen's tragic death in a car accident that left her a widow, Magdalena sold their apartment in D.C. and moved to a large, old, two-story house in Sarasota, Florida, where she devoted herself entirely to research, scientific work, and writing.

I quickly agreed with Magdalena about the amount of time she would spend with us, especially since I awoke her motivation for play and curiosity from a slumber (as she put it). Unfortunately, Peter and Sandy were unable to come with us because of their job obligations, and they wished us success on our quest. Ivica was more excited and curious than I was. It was out of the question for him to leave anything to chance. He decided he must accompany me to visit Magdalena. He just asked me to help him come up with an important reason for extending his stay in the States. He would have to postpone his lectures at the University of Belgrade again, and that might cause him some inconvenience.

So, I called an influential friend of mine in a high place at Princeton, who told me to let Ivica know that the problem was solved: he will be giving a lecture there next Wednesday on a topic of his choosing, as part of the university's "Meetings with Mysterious Researchers" program. Hearing all this, Ivica was all at the same time, scared, surprised, and honored. I told him not to worry and that he just needed to be himself when he delivers the lecture. There was more than enough time left to prepare for it, and he can surely come up with some framework for the content that would be discussed informally. The whole point of these meetings was to encourage students to ask questions and discuss them, as vehemently as possible, and that's what he excelled at.

We flew out of Portland that afternoon to Tampa, Florida. We met Magdalena at her home, on the Gulf Coast, ten miles south of Sarasota. She seated us in cozy armchairs in a gazebo, next to a small pool, a fountain, and a pond, served us some cold fruit cocktails, and started a small talk so that everyone could get to know each other.

The conversation turned to the books by Carlos Castaneda that Ivica spotted lined up on Magdalena's desk. After he admitted that he knew very little about them, she instructed Ivica thoroughly in these philosophical works and the profound meaning of the teachings of Don Juan Matus and the knowledge of the Toltec and Jaki Indians. She also spoke with great zeal about Castaneda's interpretation of the practice of raising awareness about the energy, existence, and worlds that exist outside the perceptual field of most people on this planet. She particularly lingered on movements we make while dreaming which increase the power of perception and were discovered by shamans from the same tribe as Don Juan.

Castaneda's first book that Magdalena read way back as a student was the biggest "culprit" for her career choice and this tireless pursuit of hers that she, however, was slowly losing interest in. Even though she had had some encouraging results over the years, she was unable to reproduce them the way she wanted. She also commented on the fact that Castaneda was accused by usual sceptics of inventing the whole story, but that she did not mind that at all since she herself attested to its truthfulness. Ivica solemnly declared that he was finally able to gain deep and clear understanding of why we had come to Magdalena for help.

I then recounted to her my research into *Blackbird's* history including all the unexpected, surprising and mysterious facts, data, and discoveries. The focus, of course, was on Tesla's unpublished patent, but we couldn't help but tell her everything about our speculations and dilemmas regarding the mysterious disappearance of Teo, the man whose trail I kept running into every step of the way.

Magdalena, who was listening to the entire story for the first time, was unable to hide her mild disappointment. Yes, she was open-minded, willing to accept and validate findings by analysis, but it seemed to her that we had come with a slightly exaggerated story, and that it all looked more like a fairy-tale and a stretched-out story than science. It was impossible to start from the premise that the movement of body and mind through space and time was possible. Well, she and her team had been experimenting with psychotics for over two decades, and she was still not quite convinced that the mind would actually be able to fly through space, let alone through time.

"In psychology, consciousness is the totality of experiences and psychological processes in an individual." she said.

"It all starts with the consciousness and the state of thought and is all controlled by the brain. The brain supports consciousness, emotions, and makes humans sensible, intelligent and moral beings, at least most of them as I would like to think.

The brain connects our entire body as if by cables, selects and simultaneously accurately sends out and receives countless signals from all parts of the body and the environment. The left hemisphere of the brain is associated with sensory experiences and logical thinking, the right one with spiritual experiences, and it is supra-logical.

Our thoughts are indeed a series of biochemical and biophysical events. Some of them may in certain cases be partially or completely controlled by medicines, psychotics or drugs.

The path from thoughts to cells looks like this: a mental image triggers a sensation, the sensation stimulates brain cells, brain cells send nerve impulses, they act on hormonal glands, hormonal glands secrete certain hormones, and hormones chemically affect the state of cells.

The mind understands time, and the senses understand space, so space and time are an expression of our sensations and our reason. Our every thought triggers chemical and physical reactions in the body, primarily in the brain, nerves and glands. So, we ourselves, or our minds, are the bridge between the spiritual and the sensory dimensions.

Generally speaking, consciousness means a state of alertness and reactions to events in our surroundings, as opposed to sleep and unconsciousness. In this sense, it is closely related to the phenomenon of attention. The mind is consciousness. We can have only one, and it can only change its state, it cannot move or multiply. Therefore, it cannot travel through time on its own."

After this brief but discouraging analysis, Ivica slowly revealed his rich knowledge of Nikola Tesla's life.

"I studied everything about Tesla I was able to find, whether it was his patents or private letters. I read his letter to a friend of his, Johansson, who was a poet actually, and it clearly states that he discovered what the mind is in his scribblings about high-frequency electromagnetic discharges and how soon he, this man Johansson, would be able to read his poems to Homer, while Tesla would discuss his inventions with Archimedes.

Tesla later stated in a magazine that he had made a connection with alien civilizations by constructing a device for tuning the electromagnetic oscillations in his brain and controlling his mental activities, so that he was easily able to move into the parallel existence of micro and macro worlds that fill our cosmic space. In one of his last interviews, in 1942, in The New York Times, Tesla stated that he had figured out the relationship between the souls of the dead and the souls of the living, and was able to communicate with Twain, Westinghouse, and others whenever he wanted.

When he talked about these things, he was rarely taken seriously, and many laughed at him. I think that's why Tesla did most of his research into "parallel worlds" in seclusion and in silence, without publishing the results. By pure chance, having done nothing to deserve it, we got our hands on Tesla's precious letter and an unpublished patent of his, with the message that his machine made it possible to synchronize movement and communication through the unity of space and time. This machine Tesla has left us obviously works based on his general principles, because it uses resonance, magnetism and electromagnetic oscillations.

Are we then to be hostages to the generally accepted interpretation of the world, like physics that describes time in its classical sense, the sense that we come across in our ordinary, everyday lives? Why should we doubt in advance the Tesla's thesis that nature's energy is part of us, that it is our energy, so that our thoughts can coincide with physical manifestations?"

Magdalena remained silent for a moment and then introduced new, slightly more conciliatory, premise.

"Then let us suppose we can go off the beaten track here. If, contrary to everything I have told you, we suppose that Tesla's machine can direct the mind to a place, it would be logical for the consciousness to remain in its physical space – the body. We can also suppose that our soul, or psyche, somehow creates an image of a new kind of matter, and projects itself into it.

Jung, whom I have studied for a long time, argued that the existence of a soul or psyche is an objective psychological fact that does not need scientific proof of existence. The nature of the soul is extremely complex, it is constantly on the move, multitudinous, multifaceted, layered, alive, and full of creative potential. Psychological energy is the entire living energy that allows a person's mind to work. According to him, psychological images and imagination are where a person's inner and outer world are unified. He argued that the soul is made up of images and that the world of psychological reality does not refer to the world of the material, but to the world of images. Further, the way we experience the reality comes from the soul's ability to create images and the psyche creates reality every day, so our reality rests on fantasy as the imaginative capacity of the soul.

If Tesla's machine stimulates the processes through which our fantasy and imagination can create a new reality for us to project into, then the visual perception during that projection, as well as any perception, is probably supplemented by parts of our mental experience. If we could somehow control the psyche's imagination with that machine, the images we would see would not be a new fictional reality, but a vivid and clear reality at another time. Therefore, we would be able to project ourselves into the past, because we have the collective unconscious experience about it. We can then set the thesis that the processes in our brain cells and nervous system, and the movements of our body that can increase our power of perception, as they do during sleep – are in fact, our time machine.

Is this thesis acceptable for future analysis?"

After listening to this long monologue by Magdalena, I was admittedly tired, and maybe even disheartened. I suggested that we continue the discussion in depth another time. After that, we scheduled the second reunion of our little workshop, tasking ourselves with preparing an actual experiment, on Saturday, November 11, 2017, in the garden of Magdalena's house. That left us with plenty of time for Ivica to make all the arrangements back in Belgrade, and to deliver his lecture at Princeton.

Chapter 29

Princeton

After returning to Washington D.C. Ivica spends two full days preparing for the lecture at Princeton scheduled as part of a more than original program named "Encounters with Mysterious Researchers." The program was open to all interested students and faculty, without exception. For it to be truly a mystery, only one or sometimes two people at the entire University had an idea of what a mysterious researcher would be presenting, but even that was not always guaranteed. Ivica had never heard of anything quite like that and, despite my encouragements that the whole idea gave him complete freedom to talk about anything he wanted, was increasingly nervous and full of anxiety. Finally, he chose a topic that would certainly encourage everyone who will be attending to ask questions and participate in discussions (neither Ivica nor I had a slightest idea about possible number of attendees). Ivica would talk about the secret military project he mentioned to me on board *Blackbird* while we were sailing with the Thompsons the day after Halloween. In the spirit of the whole concept, he also tells me that he expects questions and challenges from me as well since he had no intentions to reveal what the talk will be all about, not even to me: *It is not easy to digest, believe me.*

At Princeton, in the Office of the Provost in Nassau Hall, we are welcomed by Professor of Engineering Pilar Mirabel de Vasconcelos. She was selected by the administration to be our host during the entire visit. Surprisingly young and exceptionally cordial, always with a nice big smile, she immediately confides to Ivica, with a big apology:

"Professor, I cheated a bit while preparing for your visit and beg you not to get mad at me. Although I still do not know what the subject of your talk is going to be, I managed to find out where you are coming from. The administration, very reluctantly, revealed it to me as I am your host. But, to tell you the truth, I believe they finally caved in because I was relentless with my inquiries, ad nauseum. Then, unfortunately, I shared the information with my students which apparently spread it around. It now seems I may be in a big trouble. After the lecture, you shall be our guest at an informal dinner. I truly hope that all this is acceptable to you. And now please give me your PowerPoint presentation so the technicians can check it and prepare everything needed."

Somewhat taken by surprise, Ivica greatly apologizes because he did not have any PowerPoint presentation with him and expresses a hope that there will be some markers and a board available that he would like to use from time to time. He then wholeheartedly thanks Pilar on her hospitality, declares that he was enormously honored and humbled by this unique opportunity to meet the students and the faculty of the best university in the World, at least when it comes to his own profession, and proceeds to give many thanks in advance for the time we will spend with her, and her students, after the lecture, at the dinner.

After catching his breath, Ivica confesses that he spent quite a bit of time over the last couple of days familiarizing himself with the work and achievements of her School of Engineering and Applied Sciences and will try, as best he can, to better focus his presentation and provoke, hopefully, interesting questions and, why not, even some sort of polemics. It is his understanding that the Program he will now be a part of is conceived to do exactly that. This, however, is quite the opposite from his own school where students have something of a fearful respect for their professors. Although, Ivica emphasizes quickly, he always encourages polemics from his own students, aiming at establishing a friendlier relationship with them.

Pilar laughs cheerfully and replies that there are plenty of markers and a large board in the lecture room and, when it comes to questions and polemics, there was nothing to worry about – students, and certainly professors that will attend his lecture today are not shy at all, on the contrary! Her advice, therefore, with an apology that he certainly knew that already, is not to be upset if some questions were deliberately provocative or seemingly disrespectful, especially because his lecture will be attended by students from other departments, those non-technical included.

After this lively exchange of common themes, our hostess asks if we would like to see something in particular at the University before we all go to the lecture room, located in the Von Neumann Hall, a five minute leisurely walk away, where the lecture was scheduled to start promptly at 4:30 pm. This leaves us with a bit less than two hours of available time.

Ivica immediately expresses a wish to visit the School's Machine Shop where students and faculty can make instruments of their own design. In addition, he would like to see the library and some of the laboratories if possible. Our friendly hostess, Professor Pilar Mirabel de Vasconcelos, confirms that there was no problem at all to accommodate his wishes — the Machine Shop and the library are very close to our final destination where there are numerous laboratories as well. She suggests that we first go to the library, which is closer, and leave more time for the Machine Shop, which is in the complex called Engineering Quadrangle, because it is indeed very interesting. So, that is how it was.

Pillar shows us to the lecture room five minutes before the start of Ivica's presentation and smiles when she sees us exchanging glimpses in awe. The room is completely packed, and good number of students are standing along the walls. She points me to an empty chair in the middle of the first row, but I politely decline telling her I would rather sit somewhere else hoping it will not be difficult to find a willing student to swap places. With a smile, she simply shrugs her shoulders and takes Ivica to the podium where, exactly at 4:30 pm, she introduces the mysterious researcher to the audience and officially opens the lecture.

In the interest of complete transparency, I must say that for all sixty minutes, which is how long the lecture and the questions that followed lasted, I did not blink. I was at the same time fascinated, shocked, and at moments full of disbelief, just like everyone else in the room.

The following is written from memory, months later, and I am sure my testimony is incomplete, although every attempt was made to describe the talk faithfully, including Ivica's exact words.

First, I wholeheartedly thank your University for this exceptional honor given to me and the opportunity to share with all of you some aspects of my life and work. I am especially grateful to our kind hostess professor de Vasconcelos for everything she did and showed us since we came less than two hours ago. I immediately fell in love with your Machine Shop and my first advice to all of you is to take full advantage of it whenever you can. Of course, you must always be in the best possible relationship with its kind and interesting Master, Mr. McIntosh (laughter in the room).

Do the same with your extraordinary library. The internet is certainly necessary, but nothing can replace the feeling of holding a good book in your hands and realizing that it can become your best friend, pets aside (loud laughter).

I am proud of my university and its School of Electrical Engineering named Nikola Tesla, which are in Belgrade, Serbia of which some of you probably never heard before, although the name Tesla is now more or less known to everyone. Nevertheless, I was very pleasantly surprised when I saw Tesla's bust by the entrance door to your School. I am sure that all of you are proud of Princeton and your own School, probably the best in the World, at least when it comes to electrical engineering which is what I have been interested in for almost forty years now. Looking at all of you and guessing that many were not born on this continent, gives me great hope that you will, together, make this World a better place for all of us, and those yet to be born.

Honestly, I have never heard of anything similar before. Namely, that not even professor de Vasconcelos knows what I am going to talk about for the next forty minutes or so. It is an enormous trust your University awarded me with, but at the same time also a great personal challenge that has been haunting me for days. However, I now feel very calm and inspired, possibly owing to an amazingly positive energy I can feel all around us, including the very name of this hall we are in. Of course, I should not forget the ghost of one Albert Einstein, for which my secret sources told me is wandering all over the place, aimlessly, and may even be in this room right now (laughter).

Although I can deviate from it at any moment, because everything is relative, I will first try to convince you, experimentally and momentarily, how the knowledge of mathematics is absolutely necessary for everything you do here. I am positive that some of you are still not aware of this – primarily those that are not from the School of Engineering and Applied Sciences or the Department of Mathematics. By the way, how many of you belong to this category? (two dozen or so hands are raised).

Very good. I will now close my eyes and randomly state the row and seat number, starting from my left side, and kindly ask those sitting at those seats to stand up and remain standing, there will be five of them.

Ivica later told me he deliberately selected three students from other departments: three beautiful female students because he could not resist, rotten bastard. He did this without any effort because of his extraordinary visual memory of which we all at 4th Belgrade Gymnasium knew very well, such that his closed eyes did not mean a thing.

Please tell us a single word, the first that comes to mind.

What follows are *hypertension, resonance, quantum, fear, semi-conductor.* Ivica then speculates that *hypertension* and *fear* must have been selected by students from other departments, probably medicine (Ivica did not know Princeton does not have a medical school) and psychology (which is confirmed), while the rest of the words relate to scientific fields of his own interest and therefore were most likely chosen by the students of this School (which was not entirely correct since word *quantum*, somewhat unexpectedly, was chosen by a student from another department but Ivica of course knew that and concealed it slyly).

I will now write a somewhat extensive system of mathematical equations that connect these five words. Based on that I will design a device, instrument, or machine (to me these words are synonyms). This is a game we play during postgraduate studies at my School back in Belgrade. Students, at the end of the course, must have physically completed at least 25% of the equation-machine in order to obtain a passing grade. We, professors, are well aware of the fact that the grading is subjective and therefore provide students a chance to improve on the grade if desired, through a legitimate argument.

To me, personally, words hypertension *and* fear *do not pose a mathematical problem, but I presume this may not initially be the case with some of you. Because everything is relative, as we have agreed long time ago, I will describe* hypertension *as something that functions under extremely high pressure, or perhaps vacuum, which is the same just with the opposite sign (there are plenty of such equations of course). I will describe* fear *as a kind of energy that can have negative consequences for the user of the machine, for example if she or he did not read the operating instructions carefully.*

Ivica then, for some 3-4 minutes, scribbles on the board mathematical symbols (many of which I have never seen before), in several chains and at different parts of the board, and then connects all that with a bunch of lines, more symbols, diagrams, and schemes. He finishes by writing several words and short sentences *"to explain better to those that do not consider mathematics and electrical engineering to be their strongest suit."*

While this magic is taking place, every now and then I look at the audience and what I see is mostly disbelief. Some students comment loudly between themselves; some are doing it intensely, and some laugh in addition. Some, including several professors, just stare at the board, and some look rather mystified.

I hope that, to those of you who understand what is on the board, or at least most of it, I have demonstrated how mathematics is useful and very beautiful too. To me, it is a tool with which one can literally make anything imaginable. To those of you who cannot decipher what I scrambled, I sincerely apologize but kindly ask you to believe me. Of course, you can always ask your colleagues for an explanation, hopefully a layperson's one. I see that quite a few of you are taking photos of the board with your phones so it will be easy to remind yourselves.

However, even more important than knowledge of mathematics is that you never lose a desire for scientific and exploratory fantasy. Many differentiate between the words fantasy *and* fiction, *namely* science fiction. *For me, honestly, there is no clear difference between these two words. I would not worry or become upset if someone qualifies some of my work as science fiction. I will repeat to you something I said a few days ago during a very interesting discussion about the thing that made me came to the United States in the first place: "If Tesla personally presented something as his discovery, theory, or hypothesis, we today are not the ones that should ridicule or ignore him. Everything this giant discovered and invented is now a necessity and belongs to the eternal achievements of our civilization, so much so that everything, and I repeat, everything he ever worked on, wrote, made or just suggested we must analyze and study with the utmost care."*

I often think of one thing I unfortunately never had chance of experiencing since the country in which I grew up, former Yugoslavia, was not rich. It is the knowledge that in the former Soviet Union there existed a fund for scientific fantasies of which we were very envious. Literally, fantasies! Everyone could apply, nothing was forbidden or predestined to fail. There were no prerequisites or requirements as to who can apply. According to my Soviet colleagues at the time, approximately seven percent of the fantasies were funded, generously, and out of those only three percent would result in something concrete and useful. The whole thing was not about profit for someone, or about military, or some narrow interest of the Communist Party. Only the most recognized, proven scientists and engineers were the ones judging and selecting the proposals, anonymously. They themselves could never apply or later work on the projects in any capacity. Everything was coded and no one knew who was behind a proposal. Very rare attempts at corruption were punished such that the whole process was recognized by everyone as honest. Can you even imagine something similar today, anywhere in the World?

This little introduction leads me to the main topic of my lecture today. For the first time I will publicly talk about some results of a secret project I was part of more than thirty years ago. Even to my dear high school friend, whose guest I am here in United States and who is with us today, I did not reveal everything (most in the audience turn toward me and I nod back smiling politely). *The most precious experience I gained from the project is the understanding of the existence of unbreakable, often unexpected and incomprehensible, connections between different scientific fields. Because of that, if I may, I am giving you more advice. Do not be afraid of the unknown or what you don't understand. On the contrary, seek such challenges. If you succeed in maintaining passion for new knowledge, which you undoubtedly have since you are here, everything is possible.*

The secret project I worked on, first as a doctoral student and assistant to my professor, and later as Chair of the Cathedra after his retirement, was funded by the military for its purposes. As you must know, militaries around the world, and certainly here in the United States, work on various secret projects with generous multiyear budgets. I believe that the astronomical costs of our project were split in half with one of the neighboring countries which was included from the project's inception: a part of the project for which I had direct responsibility required enormous quantities of energy. Because of that, our two countries jointly built a very powerful hydropower plant, and then another one. Several completely unexpected discoveries, utilized for other aspects of the project, were direct results of using this vast energy supply. Among other things, we developed instruments for measuring, recording and amplifying quantum (aha, our word from today!) gravity, light, and magnetic (yes, magnetic) waves. A small example is the first-ever wave nano-gravimeter, of which there were only theoretical discussions around the world at the time (as far as we could tell). It was built thirty years ago with help from mathematicians and geophysicists from our University. This instrument was later utilized for practical purposes, mainly by the military, such as for deep underground works, but also for detecting various natural cavities including those quite small, even smaller than one cubic meter, at depths up to several kilometers. For the reduction of focused electromagnetic fields with the potential of tens of millions of volts (the most we were able to record was around 87 million volts) to the quantum sensitivity of our nano-gravimeter, we have developed a unique technology based on absolute vacuum. This technology itself required enormous initial energy. For the miniaturization we utilized organic conductors which were self-organized under the influence of the energy field (for us completely unexpectedly), into something that resembled very rare crystal lattices (these were later deciphered to us by colleagues from the Department of Crystallography at our School of Geology).

For me personally, the most interesting part of this truly multidisciplinary project were the instruments we developed for detecting, recording and transmitting brain waves to great distances. We were able, by using triangulation, to concentrate brain waves onto any location on the Globe. In other words, we could target any person anywhere in the World by utilizing three strategically positioned human media who were using miniature amplifiers. With the help of one instrument based on magnetism, in an energetic concert with the nano-gravimeter and an additional instrument developed at our Institute for Copper and Rare Metals, of which I do not know much, we were able to target subjects located at depths of up to two kilometers below ground surface (for these experiments we were using deep underground mine works.) It was frightening that some of the psychosomatic functions of the targeted subjects could be manipulated by the operator since the transmitted brain waves were easily adjusted at quantum levels. Unfortunately, these adjustments were not sufficiently studied at the beginning such that undesired consequences were not rare. Because of that the project soon conscripted psychiatrists and psychologists from our School of Medicine.

I remember well the expressions on the faces of people listening while Ivica was talking about the secret project. Everybody was still, there was not the slightest sound or movement in the audience, none. Disbelief is a weak word to describe the whole scene. Ivica concluded his talk with a note that the project was abruptly terminated right before the breakup of Yugoslavia and everyone involved was told not to talk about it or any of the results. Actually, everyone was warned not to talk at all. He then repeated he is not an enemy of science fiction and opened for any questions.

Were there questions? Professor of Engineering Pilar Mirabel de Vasconcelos could hardly maintain order in the room. The whole event had to be over exactly sixty minutes after the start since the room was reserved for another lecture. There was no discussion about this strict schedule and the remaining twenty minutes for questions were quickly disappearing. At some point, our kind hostess politely asks those that may not be able to take turn, and everyone else that wishes to do so, to contact professor Kaurić with any questions directly as he kindly committed to answer all of them via e-mail. She also kindly asks all interested not to hold up our distinguished guest after the lecture because his official program at the University requires him to attend several important meetings.

The last question was certainly provocative, together with several others, as predicted by our young hostess. This, of course, was not surprising at all given everything Ivica wrote or spoke about. Although, only one question was about the heavy mathematics and schemes on the large board in front of us. All other ones, completely understandably, were either about the unbelievable instruments or brain waves, including questions about special warfare, connections with Russians, and even aliens. Ivica's very polite answer to the last question was:

"Again, to me, science fiction is not a negative term. However, if you do not believe what you heard from me today, I nevertheless kindly ask you to believe that all is possible. I am convinced the day when someone will achieve the same, maybe even with your own help, is not far away. And why am I convinced? Because I already saw it all with my own eyes."

After Ivica's answer, and despite the pledges from our hostess, a bunch of students quickly surrounds Ivica and blocks the path to the exit, shouting various questions and thanking him for the presentation. Everything looks like an unruly mob after an end of a rock concert, such that the unfortunate Ivica, in all that pandemonium, drops the leather bag he always carries to his lectures. Out of the beg slides a handful of papers among which is a copy of Tesla's instruction manual with the puzzling lines written in Cyrillic. Ivica now carried it everywhere with him and used every free moment to try and find the solution.

From the crowd emerges a young woman who drops to her knees to help collect the scattered papers. She has messy short black hair, a tattoo on her shoulder, bracelets, and chains on her wrists, and is dressed in a rather colorful hippie jacket with strings, jeans, and tall untied black leather boots. The same one that provided word *quantum* for the Ivica's mathematical experiment.

"Please, let me help. Ooh, what is this, some interesting text, appears foreign?"

In a hurry and modest panic not to lose sight of professor de Vasconcelos, Ivica replies that he does not know himself but is trying to find the answer. The student laughs cheerfully and says:

"A professor of your caliber should be able to recognize an encrypted text immediately."

Ivica quickly composes himself and equally cheerfully replies:

"If that is what you think, then you must be correct. But, if you could help me a bit and spare me more suffering over that text, I would not mind at all."

The student with the messy hair, of course, has nothing against the request. Yes, she would be happy to help, but notes that, unfortunately, it is hardly possible to do so because of the official obligations waiting for him at the University, doesn't he remember what the professor said? Although, it is not that terrible, it happens to older people...

Ivica nods his head seriously and confirms that this indeed happens to him from time to time, and then smiles, somewhat mischievously, asking her to follow him as he will try to arrange something.

Hence, at a dinner after the lecture, in the restaurant of our hostess' choice, we are joined by the astute PhD student Bavishni Panday. After we all are comfortably seated at several joined tables, professor de Vasconcelos remarks that the name of the restaurant we are in may not be a pure coincidence given everything we heard from our distinguished guest this afternoon. This name was *The Alchemist and Barrister*.

Everyone laughed including, of course, Ivica, who proclaimed that nothing is coincidental, but can be relative. There was no lack of food or drink, up until we were politely kicked out of the restaurant as all other patrons already left long time ago. Ivica did not mention Tesla's puzzle the whole evening but, after I reassured him it is OK and guaranteed the same for Magdalena, he invited the student with a tattoo to join us in Florida where we were going to meet next weekend and try to solve the crypted text.

Bavishni Panday accepted the invitation excitedly and without any hesitation.

Photographs taken by Ivica Kaurić before his presentation at Princeton. Top: School of Engineering and Applied Sciences. Bottom left: Bust of Nikola Tesla by the entrance door. Bottom right: one of many laboratories in Von Neumann Hall. Courtesy of Ivica Kaurić.

The Alchemist and Barrister, the pub in which Princeton PhD student
Bavishni Panday joined our team.

Chapter 30

Clue

As promised, Bavishni Panday joined us at Magdalena's house in Florida. Ivica introduced the host to the guest, and we had a little chat as it was expected for reasons of politeness. Bavi ("that's what everyone called her and so should we") briefly told us about who she was, where she came from, how she came to Princeton and what she chose as her PhD thesis.

Yes, yes, she confirmed to our astonishment, she was a doctoral student, everyone was deceived by her youthful appearance.

"I don't like having people touch my hair and I don't go to the hairdresser's, my tattoos are my existential diary, my lifestyle is hippy, I don't care if its old-fashioned, I wear my boots both in the summer and winter, so what?"

To say that we were all more than interested would be an understatement. Bavi was the daughter of an Indian and a Corsican (not French, not Italian, her mother always said she was Corsican), and she was born in San Jose, California. Because of her mixed origins, she had this exotic physiognomy, and therefore people were seldom able to guess which part of the world her genes came from. Her parents were students at Delhi University (DU), at the Faculty of Mathematical Sciences in Delhi, specifically New Delhi. There, at South Campus, they met and fell in love with each other, to her great delight. Her father was Indian, he was one of the Vaishyas, the third caste, so they were able to develop their businesses and provide their sons with an education, which they wouldn't be able to do if they were the Shudras, or the untouchable Paraiyar caste. Her maternal grandparents were originally from Corsica, immigrants to India, and her mother was also born in India.

Her parents came under severe pressure after they got married because of their adamant opinions on the caste system and resistance to the still persistent belief in India that not all people are born equal. Because of that, they relocated, or perhaps better said, fled to America. They completed their education here and continued to specialize. They now work in the Silicon Valley, so she grew up with math, computers, and intelligent machines, and it's only natural that she continued on that path.

She completed her undergraduate and master's degrees at Stanford. Although her doctorate thesis was virtually guaranteed there, at her father's insistence, she applied for doctoral studies at several other universities "to widen her horizons". This is how she sent her application to Princeton, where she was admitted to The Princeton Human-Computer Interaction Group.

"But I see there is no end to it! Ever since I sank into this vast and complex area, I have been even more intrigued by the mysteries of the human mind, the issues of ethics, existence, and meaning. So now I am seriously considering taking two courses in philosophy, probably gnoseology and ethics. Although both myself and my mentor are still struggling to find a title for the main topic of my research."

In her spare time (we all marveled at the fact that she had spare time) she listened to contemporary jazz (none of us had heard of John Hassell, whom she adored, only I had heard about Albert Mangelsdorff and only Magdalena knew who Barre Phillips was) and went mountaineering. She even did some diving for several months with her ex-boyfriend, who was a diving instructor. Plus, she had her hobbies, cryptography, numerology, and more. That's why she immediately recognized the encrypted text on Ivica's papers.

We arrived at the main theme of the evening when Bavi asked:

"How did you come by this message anyway, whose is it? That will certainly help me figure it out sooner than later."

We looked at each other and hesitated for a second, but then decided, why not, to recount her, leaving almost nothing out, the story of the sailboat, the bet, the tracks of the schooner on the Adriatic, of Vinko and his son's disappearance, of the spy mission about which I was able to uncover fascinating information, about Tesla's patent and message, and all of our assumptions and guesses. And finally, about our intention to assemble, start and test the mysterious machine!

Our conversation was becoming louder, and our excitement grew exponentially. The challenge of leaping into the unknown excited the children in us. We discarded the cloaks of serious scientists and adults, rational people.

Now with a whole new motivation, she looked again carefully at the text at the end of Tesla's instructions, an arbitrary string of Cyrillic letters and a few numbers. She looked at the paper in front of us, turning it over in her hands several times. Yes, she was sure it was coded. In her opinion, it was a simple transposition cipher, probably columnar. All she needed was to find the key to the cipher, likely a series of numbers indicating how many character spaces from the encrypted original shift according to the alphabetical order. Which, in our case, was the Cyrillic alphabet. However, as it was the Cyrillic, "she wouldn't be able to do it alone, she wasn't familiar with the writing of the Russians, or whoever used it."

We wrote for her the 30 letters of the Cyrillic alphabet:
АБВГДЂЕЖЗИЈКЛЉМНЊОПРСТЋУФХЦЧЏШ

Magdalena was the first to assume that we also needed to consider the four numbers on the metal box, which, in the absence of a better term, we called the "remote control". Bavi immediately agreed, concluding that the key to the cypher was probably a number from the "remote controller", a series of digits, 3, 2, 1 and 0.

Bavi then counted the letters and numbers of the coded text. There were 28 in total. Her assumption was that the rectangle containing the text is probably composed of either a 4x7 or 2x14 matrix. She tore a sheet of paper into 24 pieces and wrote all the letters of Tesla's code individually on each one of them.

She then explained, talking to herself out loud rather than to us, that if it was a four-digit code, she was sure that it was to be found in fields of the matrix 4x7. She then sorted out all the letters and numbers from the mysterious word into 4 columns and 7 rows, with 4 fields in a row: 5дсе, оз5п, ђртт, ст5х, ђтос, фрсв, ђзне.

At first, she tried to decode the letters backwards, but didn't come up with anything meaningful. Finally, she used the 3210 code to arrange the letters from the encrypted text in forward alphabetic order, shifting them by the number of character spaces determined by the code. Her transformation was: 2время4простор4хпросторвреме.

The spaces weren't part of the code, she said. When she added spaces in logical places, it became:

2 време 4 простор 4 хпростор време.

She couldn't read Cyrillic, of course, so Ivica and I wrote it in the Latin alphabet and translated it for her: 2 time 4 space 4 hspacetime

"This x is not h, 4 hspace doesn't mean anything, I'd rather say it's an X, like a cross mark, maybe multiplication?"

Her final solution was:

2 time 4 space 4 x space time.

She then copied the coded text and the solution, and we had a sheet of paper with a vivid illustration of the decoding process of a relatively simple columnar transposition code:

3	2	1	0		+3	+2	+1	0					
5	д	с	е		2	в	р	е		2	v	r	e
о	з	5	п		м	е	4	п		m	e	4	p
ħ	р	т	т		р	о	с	т		r	o	s	t
с	т	5	х		о	р	4	х		o	r	4	x
ħ	т	о	с		п	р	о	с		p	r	o	s
ф	р	с	в		т	о	р	в		t	o	r	v
ħ	з	н	е		р	е	м	е		r	e	m	e

2 v r e m e 4 p r o s t o r 4 x p r o s t o r v r e m e

(2 t i m e 4 s p a c e 4 x s p a c e t i m e)

And then suddenly it all became clear to us. 2 balls mean traveling through time. The body or the mind travels through time. 4 balls mean traveling through space. Teleportation. 4 cross-connected balls mean traveling through space and time. Both the mind and the body can travel through space and time!

At that point, we all realized that Bavi had definitely become a member of our small group. She herself told us in one breath, with a disarming smile, that she *loved us, that we were great and that everything was cool, but there was no way on this Earth for her to leave before finding out everything that we knew, because if, for whatever reason, we failed to satisfy her curiosity and thirst for discovery, she would do something she was as yet incapable of imagining, for example, she'd be eternally camped in a tent in front of Magdalena's house protesting from dusk to dawn, every day with a new banner, until she would eventually burn herself in the yard and then turn into a sad palm tree, or a frustrated raccoon, so it was up to us really...*

Bavishni Bavi Panday

Chapter 31

Workshop

By all accounts, we now had everything we needed to use Tesla's unpublished patent and open his strange world. This gadget we had could instantly send something, maybe an object, and maybe us, or our projection, to another part of reality. That is, as the genius himself wrote – in the other three spatial and one temporal dimension!

Do we really know how to do it and dare we do it? What should we try, two balls, four balls or four cross-connected balls? None of us were sure about how this would affect the participants. We were even less sure about the choice of time and place. How do we schedule our tasks and what exactly does each of us do in the experiment? Can the machine connect us with the people who were part of the exciting story of the sailing boat's war days on the Adriatic? And if it can, how does it work? Would we be able to use the machine to communicate with them, through space and time?

Ivica, Bavi, Magdalena and I were the ones who had to find the answers to all these questions. We spent the next few days and nights in discussion, often running in circles and accumulating unsubstantiated conclusions, only to refute them immediately. To recount all this would take too much effort for both me and the reader, so I will reduce the story down to the main dilemmas that plagued us and that we sought to eliminate.

If, according to what Bavi deciphered from Tesla's message, two balls were to connect, the machine would allow the body to move through time. *Blackbird*'s flight on the beach in Lopud was done using the two balls and was obviously movement of an object through time. It was both uncontrollable and dangerous, because on this occasion it was completely unplanned and done by accident. As "collateral damage", one man, Teo, got picked up from his present to be lost forever in the past. In any case, it was one thing to travel through time, but controlling the machine afterwards and making the return journey was a completely different thing. How can we master an unsolved issue of our return through time, or, more precisely, from another time dimension?

Four parallel connected balls were designed for teleportation: they should be able to move or transport the body through space. According to everything we were able to gather, this was the case in that old Philadelphia or Eldridge experiment. But the experiment was also uncontrollable and dangerous because many people were badly hurt in it. Admittedly, we knew that there were no human casualties in the second case, the one when *Blackbird* made the jump to shorten its voyage across the Atlantic. This experiment was in all likelihood operated by Edvard and Svetoslav. The period between the Philadelphia experiment and *Blackbird's* sail across the ocean was too short to assume that, in the meantime, some major changes or improvements had been made to the newly discovered and still secret technology. Consequently, it seemed unwise we should assume that teleportation was sufficiently perfected to make it safe. While we knew that back then nothing terrible happened to either the sailboat or the people on it, Masters and Cole, it still proved nothing. It may have simply been an exception to the rule.

By using the four cross-connected balls, Tesla's apparatus sends both the body and the mind, through both space and time. If we concluded that the activation of the first two options was both uncontrollable and dangerous, was the third option, as a combination of the two, a double danger? Didn't Ivica say it clearly and loudly that Tesla himself knew that time travel was dangerous and that these multidimensional non-Hertzian waves with infinite standing longitudinal oscillations produced by his machine were difficult to understand. Except for Ivica's team, one couldn't even measure them or otherwise detect their projections into our reality. In addition, the effects of stopped light, dematerialization or anti-gravity, and many other things that are incomprehensible to common sense are apparently possible. What would happen to us in the physical sense if both our minds and bodies were to move through a jumble of complex and immeasurable sensations and effects defined in such manner?

Even if we assumed that all these dangers could be eliminated or put aside, we would still be facing the very real dilemma of whether the whole patent was realistic and feasible at all from the point of view of science and common sense. If the experiment is feasible, how could it be possible that Tesla's instructions to operate such a complex and powerful machine were so simple? They were very much like a vacuum cleaner instruction manual – assemble, attach, plug in, push button – and yet the machine should initiate a complex form of energy flow that will, by some miracle, take us to the fourth dimension of the multidimensional space-time structure.

Ivica wouldn't allow anyone to doubt his scientific idol. He reminded us that Tesla never used to work with complex formulas, equations and theories. All descriptions of his inventions were straightforward, his formulas were simple, his calculations short and mostly intuitive, so it was natural that this was the case with this machine. The simple instructions by no means meant that the genius had made a mistake. No, he was always right, we could trust him freely and unreservedly. Whether we dared take the experiment ourselves or not was a completely different question as articulated by Ivica:

"So, this formula for infinite frequency transformation, which allows the direct movement of the body and mind back and forth through time, is certainly correct. I am more concerned that his message does not say anything about what is happening to people and what dangers they are exposed to, if any, if they take part in the process."

Magdalena had another very real problem with the idea that a physical transfer between different realities at different times was possible.

"I can accept the thesis that runs through all of Tesla's messages, which is that our consciousness determines the shape and size of everything in the universe, such that time and space don't actually move, that this is only the way we interpret things, what's going on in our heads. OK, if we accept that space and time are only constructs of our brains, the conclusion is that the space and time are unlimited in the world that we inhabit. Let's say that that's OK.

But then, question is raised, what is the objective reality, the one we all share? Let's take two consciousnesses, for example, Ivica, yours and mine, they create two realities. If our two consciousnesses were having a dialogue, then that interaction of our consciousnesses would be like a synthesis of those two realities. Using this logic, what we call objective reality in our common daily lives is the interaction of many consciousnesses and the synthesis of their realities. It is the intersection of the common elements of all our individual realities and it exists only through the multiplicity of our continuous communications, interactions or dialogues. But if our consciousnesses don't communicate, there is no objective reality either, each of us has only their own, you have yours, and I have mine.

So, tell me now, what reality does an individual mind then travel to? Perhaps into its own imaginary reality?"

Bavi then interfered with a very fresh outlook on the topic that has baffled and annoyed the rest of us for a long time, and told us that we might be losing focus and ability to think clearly:

"It is not our physical bodies, but our consciousness or minds that engage in this dialogue or communication you are talking about." (except for sex, Ivica interjected).

"Okay, well, please, come on, let's get serious, we are all in the middle of a difficult task, a problem, call it whatever you want, so let's try to make some progress. Here, let me set a hypothesis, too. In fact, let me illustrate how I see our overall existence as human beings. I think, but I don't think so only because a lot of scientists today say that our existence is an energetic synthesis between our physical bodies and minds or consciousness. This physical body, made of flesh and bones is changeable, they have proven long ago that every seven years it is completely transformed and nothing, no atom of the old body remains. It is matter, powder, and it does not interest us, it is irrelevant to this experiment, it does not participate in communication. It is the consciousness that communicates. So, that is why I would like us to discuss what consciousness essentially is, and then we will discover how Mr. Tesla managed to send it through time and space."

Magdalena didn't exactly frown, but she obviously wanted to skip the subject:

"That, my dear colleague, is the broadest topic of an entire scientific field, and let us conclude briefly for our internal purposes as follows:

consciousness is the synthesis between a living body and personality. Personality is created in the first years of an individual's life and developed by having role models and by learning. A living body collects everything starting from our childhood, adolescence, youth, maturity and old age. It makes no sense to talk beyond that. I would have to mention values, judgments, experience, morals, ethics, culture, and more, so it wouldn't get us anywhere."

When Magdalena mentioned values, morals, and ethics, my thoughts went past science, physics, magnetism, and psychology. If we can really move through time and space with this machine, are we indeed going to do it and what would our motivation be? Do we only intend to find out what happened with the sailboat and the people on it, or did we have something else in mind? What if we succeeded, would it be a one-off party for the four of us or do we give humanity another one of Tesla's spectacular discoveries and thus change the world forever? And will this change be for the common good, or will it open up a whole new field to the rich, powerful and malicious for abuse and manipulation? Do we, the four ordinary and powerless people that we are, have any assurances that the great scientist's desire to let the patent fall only into the hands of well-intentioned people will be honored, and will we have the strength and wisdom to defend it from all sorts of armies, states, terrorists, spies, politicians, fanatics, conspirators or just lunatics?

As I spoke about my misgivings out loud, our little workshop turned its course to various conspiracy theories. Ivica added to our concerns by recalling that paradox when someone went back into the past and murdered their own grandfather, the logical result of which was that he had never existed which meant that he would not have been able to travel back into the past and kill his own grandfather.

"Although it looks like mere mental gymnastics, it is not a naive question at all: imagine the possibility that anyone can change the past or affect the future, and then convince me that everyone has good intentions, as if what happened with Nagasaki and Hiroshima might persuade us that atomic fission and nuclear energy were invented with good intentions and only for the benefit of humanity!"

It no longer matters who said what on the subject, it suffices to underscore how we firmly agreed that we were not ready to be the ones assuming any responsibility for the potentially dark destiny of humanity! In other words, we agreed that we would never release any information about the balls, clamps and other objects from Tesla's leather bag to the public, nor would we ever disclose to anyone any technical details regarding the startup, operation and use of his machine. In doing so, we have eliminated the moral dilemma or doubt, leaving that burden to some future generations and some happier times. This is the reason why this story will include no information, apart from the general description, about the assembly, startup and operation of the machine.

At the end of the day, we reached the strange fate of the missing Teo, about whom we had gathered by that time a lot of information from various sources regarding the places he lived, things he did, what traces he left behind. When we cross-matched all of them, we concluded, without any doubt, that his existence in the past was an irrevocable fact, that he had really lived and existed. It was indisputable that clear trails and testimonies about him could be found from 1943 to 2000 when he died, at the age of 81, according to his own previous calculations, which meant that he may have been born sometime around 1919.

However, the irrevocable fact is that he lived at another time, as Vinko's son, who was certainly and irrefutably identified as having been born in Belgrade in 1957 and was 23 years old in 1980 when he disappeared never to be heard of again. The first Teo himself claimed that he was on a beach in Lopud in 1980 when, all of a sudden, he found himself on *Blackbird* in 1943, on that same beach on the island of Lopud.

Did he really physically transition from one time to another?

We were completely confused by one detail in that calculation – if both facts were true and irrevocable, it would turn out that Teo himself existed twice between the time of his birth in 1957 and that of his disappearance in 1980.

Could it be possible that he simultaneously existed at two different times?

219

Did he originally belong to the past, the past of that past, or to a present of his own?

However, there was nothing but the claim made by this older man that could prove the fact that they were the same person. There were, admittedly, numerous coincidences and co-occurrences, but they were not clearly measurable and could be purely accidental. But then it was quite unclear how the older man could have known anything about the future in which the other, the younger Teo, would appear, as if he knew it? Did he continue to travel through time? Was he actually alive at some point and then reincarnated? And if he was reincarnated, how could he have done that during his lifetime, because reincarnation and migration of the soul, in the religion of the Indians, Egyptians, Buddhist and Pythagorean philosophy, with Plato, Empedocles and Heraclitus, was the return or continuous restoration of the spirit or soul to the body that took place only after death?

Ivica, who at one time seemed to be a little dormant, came to and livened up when he heard this subject:

"Aha! Does the fact that Tesla believed in reincarnation, in the eternity of everything in existence, including the consciousness, mind and energy, which periodically disappear and re-appear, have anything to do with these events, so that when a person dies, the spirit and soul do not disappear and they reappear physically on Earth to live in another body and sometimes in the bodies of animals or as plants? Even his death was a kind of personal ceremony, and more like a conscious relocation of the soul to a different plane of existence than the death of an ordinary famous man, confused and scared of self-liberation – three days before his disincarnation, Tesla stopped working and retreated behind the closed doors of his hotel room, asking that no one disturb him. When the maid and hotel director finally entered the room, they found him elegantly dressed, lying dead, his arms folded across his chest, fully ready to leave."

"Pardon my expression, but it's totally stupid to even think about reincarnation here!" Magdalena snapped at him, cutting off further improvisation on the subject. "With all these general issues, wouldn't it be wiser, before attempting to do anything on our own, if we were to analyze the technical route to successful or unsuccessful attempts, and experiment with various subjects, for example with a lizard and tortoise, and then with a mammal, mice work best in these cases don't they? So, when we have studied and mastered it all and eliminated all doubts, maybe we could try something with humans as well?"

I was not surprised by her reaction, what did surprise me was the ferocity with which Bavi lashed out at Magdalena at the slightest thought of mistreating any animals in any way:

"Who are we to put in harm's way a living being who was given the gift of life by the sublime spirit of the nature? No life is less valuable than any other. We are not gods; we have no right to do that!!"

I do not need to stress out that Bavi immediately and definitively and irrevocably made the unalterable decision that no attempt would be made to experiment on innocent living beings. *At the same time, her message was quite clear: there was no way that the experiment could involve anyone but herself and the machine, she wanted to experience it, she was not afraid, it would be great for her PhD, it didn't matter if the rest of us objected to it and it didn't matter how much we tried to dissuade her, she would have none of that nonsense.*

Overwhelmed by her torrential arguments, we took a vote and decided she would be the one. I voted against it, because I was dying to be the first traveler in time and space, but being a tolerant democrat, I eventually agreed to it.

All the doubts about what happens to the body and mind of people when they go into the unknown were removed the next weekend, November 18, 2017, when we dared to try the device and send Bavi into the uncertain.

Chapter 32

Dream and Reality

We made the decision. We wouldn't try anything with two or four straight-connected balls. If Bavi were to fly through time physically, she could get killed, everything was uncertain. If we used four balls to physically move her, we would be tempting the fate by taking the same risk. The only thing that made sense was to activate the machine with four cross-connected balls and move both her mind and her body through time.

Ivica and Magdalena were in their seats around the cross-connected four balls (and a few other objects in the middle) that were resting on their stands. Bavi was reclining in a garden chair in the middle, and I was holding the control panel. We arranged our laptops around the setup and enabled their cameras to record the whole experiment. Magdalena placed small wireless detectors all over Bavi and attached a plastic cap with electrodes on her head and nape, as she was planning to record Bavi's brain activity, pulse, pressure and other physical reactions throughout the experiment. We read Tesla's instructions once again and then firmed them up together.

After hesitating for a short while, filled with anxiety, we connected the machine according to the instructions. Immediately, everything was activated, we didn't know exactly what and how, but some self-induced low-frequency and extended hum begun, almost below the audible level. When it stopped, a little white light on the controller came on. I took that as a sign to push the button, first in the back row, as we had agreed. As soon as I did that, the power went out and we were left in the dark, as if I had caused this by pushing the button. Only the monitors on our laptops remained bright. Later, we learned that electricity had disappeared throughout the city.

But the machine remained active and developed a new energy felt by me and everyone else surrounding Bavi. It was in form of a subdued slow vibration. I lost my sense of reality, and later found out that others had a similar sensation. Bavi herself shook for a moment and then relaxed and calmed down. Her eyelids were half-closed, and her eyes moved uncontrollably underneath, as if she were constantly looking around.

Magdalena monitored the electroencephalogram and the visual record of her body's reactions on the screen with an increasing excitement:

"Global brain bioelectric activity has jumped dramatically, but this is quite unusual! At the same time, the frequencies of both alpha and beta waves have increased, and delta waves are constant! A relatively uniform image with a fast beta rhythm in the anterior regions and a slower alpha rhythm above the posterior areas would be normal, while delta usually lasts only a few seconds. But with Bavi there are huge deviations from this image, which happens only during sleep. Apart from that, I have never before recorded anyone with these continuous low-frequency delta waves!"

There was nothing going on after that, or at least we had that impression. Bavi was still lying down, her eyelids fluttering. Magdalena's screen kept displaying the same values. We were sitting in the dark, there was still no electricity, and indicators on the laptops began to show that our batteries were running critically low.

Exactly four hours after I pushed the first button, another light on the control panel turned on and I pushed the forward button. That instant, the electricity came back on, the lights turned on. Everything went back to normal and still nothing was happening. After a minute or two, the machine emitted subdued vibrations again, and then there was complete silence.

Bavi opened her eyes slowly. We stood around her, confused, ready to be disappointed that nothing significant had happened. She was a little dazed, quietly moaning. After a while, her eyes cleared up and she told us, in a very quiet voice, that she had a strange headache.

"But everything is alright, I came back, we made it!"

And then, visibly excited, she told us about what she had experienced. She was sure that she had left us both physically and mentally, her impression was clear and unambiguous. We were looking at each other. We told her she definitely did not leave us because her body was here all the time, all of us saw it very clearly, there was no doubt, and maybe she just lost consciousness. She was completely confused and asked to see the video immediately, as proof that it had happened exactly that way.

"Yes, I see it now, I believe the video, I really was here, but at the same time I find this impossible! I was traveling, moving, talking to people, though I somehow didn't hear my voice. I remember everything, I was in this house, but there were some other people around me, I saw the furniture, not this one, though, I saw something else. Here, in this corner, the TV was on, not this plasma TV, rather, a smaller CRT, and Big City Comedy was on. There was music playing from an older analog receiver, "Upside Down / I am Coming Out," by Diane Ross. According to the short news I heard, Jimmy Carter was President. I could see different surroundings through the window, there were billboards out there that are not here now. One advertised *Stardust Memories*, directed by Woody Allen, as the most watched movie in 1980. The other advertised Digital Equipment Corporation, Intel and Xerox announcing the launch of their DIX standard for Ethernet, the first to support 10Mbps which would be its first deployment outside Xerox. There was a book on the table titled *Bellefleur* by Joyce Carol Oates, and it said on the back that it had already become one of the bestsellers. There were two boys playing video games, Fishing Derby and then Compu-Spel.

If you say so, and I believe it because I saw it myself that I was physically here all the time, then I must have dreamed it! If so, it was like a compelling dream that you don't forget as soon as you wake up, because all the details remain clearly in my memory. I also had the feeling that I was awake and dreaming I was dreaming at the same time!

I really spoke to all these people straight away, but no voice came out, it was as if we exchanged all our thoughts right away. They wondered where I came from, and I told them we were doing an experiment and that I had travelled through time! They didn't immediately understand me, so they showed me a daily newspaper with a date. The most attractive political topic was the difficulties and struggles that surrounded the formation of Solidarity trade union in Poland. The front page also featured news about several smaller ash jets that erupted again from an opening near the base of the lava dome at Mount St. Helens. Each volcano eruption lasted about 30 minutes, with only a few cubic meters of ash, but still, as reported, everyone was scared because the national trauma was still fresh after the first big explosion."

Since this other news seemed extremely important, just like everything else she read related to it, not even knowing why that was so, Bavi recalled a peculiar way of exploring the topic through some sort of deeper communication with the people in the house.

So, she learned and remembered everything, to the smallest detail, which surprised her completely, including the fact that the numbers were expressed in both the metric and standard systems: the terrible eruption of Mount St. Helens, in the massif of the Cascade Range in Northwest Washington, happened several months earlier, more specifically on May 18, 1980 at 20:32 hours. The top of the mountain that had been 2,950 meters high was blown up and a horseshoe-shaped crater, 2 kilometers long and 4 kilometers wide, with a circumference of 2,549 meters, appeared instead. An earthquake measuring 5.1 on Richter scale caused a huge landslide on the North side of the mountain and two cubic kilometers of deposits slipped downhill. Hot volcanic gases and vapors burst horizontally through the cracked mountain, torn ridges and flattened forests up to a distance of 28 kilometers. The Northern slope was blown up in the explosion that ensued, the air blast that followed had an initial speed of 300 miles per hour and a temperature of 660 degrees Fahrenheit. It scattered a cloud of glowing ash and rocks within a 25-kilometer radius of the summit of the volcano. This was followed by minor side explosions, avalanches, streams of glowing lava and silt. All river basins within a radius of 27 kilometers were covered with deep sediment deposits. At the same time as the eruption, a vertical cloud of glowing gas and ash rose up to some 26 kilometers, 400 million tons of steam and dust ended up in the atmosphere, with ash falling all the way to central Montana. Even the city of Spokane, Washington, some 400 miles northeast of the volcano was covered in darkness in daytime. 57 people died, thousands of birds and wild animals were killed, even fish. All trees within a few miles were destroyed by a gust of hurricane-force wind that caused the explosion. About 300 homes along the Toutle were flattened or badly damaged by floods and silt flows of melted glaciers. The ash reached farmlands far to the East, covering fields and crops, clogging up traffic and leaving in its wake a depressing and dismal atmosphere.

Bavi saw all this as in a movie and could spend hours recounting it to us. Her journey, we concluded in the end, was a leap through time and space, but at the same time just an incredibly compelling dream.

Chapter 33

Communication

We were reunited on January 15, 2018, when Ivica returned to the United States during winter break at his university and Bavi had her days off at Princeton. It was cold. We were with Peter and Sandy in Maine. They were grateful, because they finally got the opportunity to attend the long-awaited unusual event, which, who knows, may prove to be historic.

There were five of us at the Thompsons: Bavi, Ivica, Peter, Sandy and me. Magdalena had definitely given up and left the team as she had long ago planned a trip to Taos, New Mexico for Christmas and intended to spend the next few weeks on research there. In addition, she said, she had seen that frightening electroencephalogram and was afraid of the possible grave consequences. She also explained why – a patient on whom her mentor experimented with psychotics eventually went completely insane, so even though she was just an observer, she still couldn't get rid of guilt which constantly tormented her conscience. She didn't want the responsibility for similar situations and decided not to be directly involved in our experiments, despite her curiosity. This came as a blow to us, we tried to persuade her, we begged her, but she remained firm and so we parted with our hearts heavy.

We already knew, or at least we thought we had understood, how to operate the machine reliably. We were ready for another try, and we were better organized. We didn't have Magdalena's instruments to monitor brain and body activity, we just re-deployed the laptops with cameras on. We installed the balls, stands and other parts of the device. Peter, Sandy, Bavi and Ivica were standing around the machine, and I was reclining in a chair in the middle. This time, in this second attempt with four cross-connected balls, I was to be the one who would travel instead of Bavi, I insisted on it! It was finally my turn, my body and mind, that we would use for our new experiment.

The first experiment showed that space and time are images formed in our minds. We know that Bavi had been physically there all the time, which means that the mind responds to an interdimensional journey by projecting an image of matter at some point in time. The speed of time flow probably changes depending on how the machine acts on the state of our consciousness. Changing the state of consciousness probably affects the function of the brain cells and so we ourselves start up our own time machine. What may be past or present to one state of consciousness is a future event to another state of consciousness.

Maybe we'd be able to use the machine for me to go into the past in full consciousness, to look at it, feel it and maybe find out the answers to some questions, who knows? We discussed the possibility to choose 1943 as the year of my trip, at the time of the *Eldridge* Experiment, in Philadelphia Bay. We also discussed the possibility to use the four balls to make a jump to Lopud beach, where *Blackbird* had briefly disappeared. However, we immediately rejected both ideas: it was clear that we would not be able to pinpoint a place if we were not physically there, and so we remained at the Thompsons' house. Besides, it was clear that Lopud would additionally have no purpose or meaning, since we would find ourselves there just at the time of the transfer of the boat, after which it would be gone. We finally agreed that we didn't care about where and at what time, but that our primary goal was to get to know the machine, its processes, its effects and its range.

We didn't change the controls on the box, so my jump was also back into 1980. As the second experiment took place at their house, my "new" space was also the Thompsons' home. However, my body and mind were the body and mind of a living girl. I was very much aware of myself both in the present and at that time, because in my dream my mind had moved into that other body. I felt I was really here, and I also genuinely knew that I dreamed I was there. My physical body remained in the present, and my mind moved through time. I was at the same time me and that girl.

So it seemed that the machine worked by integrating the mind into an existing body; I was in the body of a girl in the past, but also here in my body at the same time, as I was able to see in the video after the experiment was over. Apart from that, my companions were explicit in claiming that I, like Bavi, had been there all along, right in the middle of the stable installation of Tesla's device. Therefore, it was more than certain that I hadn't travelled there physically – my mind had moved and materialized there!

The entire experience was like an uncontrollable mix of dream and reality. I was asleep, and at the same time aware of my physical self. And because at the same time I knew I was not really there, it felt like a dream to me. But even though it was a dream, it was also an alternative reality for me. This dream of mine involved the events, people and places in other people's lives, and the complex life situations of active participants in that dream.

Dreams are said to reflect the events, people and places in our lives. Dreaming does important work for us, it is an existential message of the dreamer to himself, a testimony of who he is and what his situation in life is. It is believed that we never see ourselves in our dreams, but my new experience told me it was not true.

Specifically, I saw myself, but not as in this reality. My dream was of a different kind, it was a lucid dream. I knew that I was dreaming that my mind was in another mind, in a body from the past. The dream was a synthesis of the interplay of my consciousness, mind and energy that produced some new form of existence in me. I suddenly knew this mind as if it were mine, but I knew that it wasn't, and I knew whose it was. I was someone else and had internal communication both as that girl and as myself.

In our ordinary sleep, we can look like someone we know, or like a complete stranger we once walked by on the street. The girl whose character I took was part of my personality, and I was constantly discovering similarities. My memory of everything I went through was flawless down to the smallest detail, even though dreams usually fade away easily and often disappear immediately once we are awake.

When we wake up from a dream, we may not even know if something was a dream or a real experience. It is clear to me to this day that my experience from both dimensions was real. I was able to experience everything physically as that person, I was able to take actions, talk and do everything else. This is what this person and I did at the same time. We were also able to communicate with each other. I knew all about myself and I knew all about the girl. I had both experiences at the same time. My thoughts were both my own and hers. I was both her and me. I had a sense that we were close. My brain was constantly suggesting that I had experienced all this before. The details were not from my memory and I was constantly receiving new information. They included elements that were different from everything I had ever experienced in my former reality.

When it was all over, we analyzed and discussed the whole strange process that took place and the situation I found myself in, until we had digested it all and understood in detail how the migration took place. The first flight that Bavi had in November, and this second flight of mine in January, may not have been sufficient for some specific targeted knowledge about someone from the past, including Teo, but they were helpful in understanding the effects of Tesla's machine. Thanks to this trip, we got a better understanding of the whole thing and became familiar with the wide range of options on how to operate the next transfer, when and if we decided to start up the machine ever again. Another important conclusion we agreed about was that we, subjects in the experiment, might be able to engage the metal balls ourselves, without the help of the others, because we were physically present.

Chapter 34

Rock

During the sail from the Croatian island of Vis to the Italian port of Bari everyone on board *Blackbird* was extremely kind to the silent young man who finally realized he was now in distant past. Tove, Sven and Nikola were doing the best they could to relieve the unrelenting shock he felt. Tove was especially attentive during the two-day crossing of the Adriatic, explaining repeatedly and with a soothing voice what had happened to them back on Lopud while trying to escape Croatian Nazis. Teo's startled gaze toward the horizon, across the sea, revealed what he felt while listening to the story.

Blackbird arrived in Bari on October 7, 1943 where the U.S. Military Police immediately took Teo into custody, not giving him a chance to say goodbye to his new friends. After a short-lived anxiety caused by couple of abrasive policemen, the architect Nikola Dobrović was quickly escorted to the Yugoslav Mission but not before receiving a big hug from Tove. The fast pace of events following the *Blackbird's* arrival ended abruptly with the departures of Teo and Nikola, leaving the two Scandinavians somewhat bewildered and standing alone on the dock by their faithful schooner.

At the OSS Headquarters Teo was met by Edvard Neumman and two OSS agents who arrived by airplane directly from the Marine Corps Air Facility Quantico near Washington, D.C. three days earlier. The agents informed Teo where he would be going next and then gave him an hour and a half to "rest and gather his faculties." The four men, under heavy security and after sunset, boarded a U.S Air Force B-17 Flying Fortress and took off from the Bari Military Airfield captured only a couple of weeks earlier by the British Eighth Army.

Meanwhile, Tove and Sven hardly managed to have any downtime before receiving instructions for the continuation of their trip including the tight schedule for replenishing the schooner's water and food supplies. *Blackbird* left Bari at noon on October 8th, under the power of the engine since there was no wind to speak of. Soon, however, as they were leaving the Strait of Otranto, a strong wind picked up, filling *Blackbird*'s sails. The schooner was fearlessly flying on 10-foot tall waves, with her exhilarated crew screaming in delight when the silhouettes of Sicily and Malta appeared on the horizon. The sun was setting in the churning October Mediterranean Sea behind a long string of heavy gray clouds. Suddenly, Tove and Sven were overcome with a feeling of dread. The darkness that was falling reminded them, without mercy, of what laid ahead. Almost five months ago, *Blackbird* left the Atlantic and sailed through the Gibraltar. The fear of Italian warships and German submarines was constant. Italy did capitulate in the meantime and her ships were gone, but the Germans were still around and posed a very real threat. Gibraltar was far, far away and the German *Kriegsmarine* campaign was as vicious as ever. Its goal was the isolation of Gibraltar, Malta, and Suez and the disruption of the Allied shipping supply convoys. Admiral Karl Dönitz deployed more than sixty submarines in the Mediterranean starting in June 1941. By the time *Blackbird* was on its way back to Gibraltar and the Atlantic, his U-boats had destroyed close to one hundred Allied merchant ships and many U.S and British Royal Navy warships.

Fortunately, the luck that followed them from the start of the mission did not turn its back on Tove and Sven. Did the schooner look harmless? Did the U-boats search for targets elsewhere? Did the regrouping of armed forces following the capitulation of Italy play the role? Blackbird's return sail across the Mediterranean was completed safely and successfully. By the coast of Tunisia, they saw an armed fishing boat which ignored them altogether; they peacefully sailed by Sardinia and even made a short stop in Cagliari to replenish the supplies. No one paid any attention to the schooner as it passed Algiers. Between Majorca and Ibiza, they struggled with some rough waves but that was it as far as any troubles go – U-boats were nowhere to be seen.

When, in early October, they approached Malaga, they sighed with relief knowing the danger had passed – Spain was neutral in the ongoing ravaging warfare. Still, they were completely exhausted by a day-long storm with skin-piercing gusts of wind and bone-chilling rain. This torture ended right before Gibraltar when the wind changed direction, and blew as *Poniente* from the west, bringing warm, dry air. Finally, at about 3am on October 7th, all clouds gone and under the bright moonlight, they saw it. First as a dim speck in the distance, and then growing bigger and bigger, a huge shadow wrapped in fog – The Rock!

The Rock is a small peninsula on the southern tip of Spain or, more precisely, a huge limestone rock massif rising above the sea for about thirteen hundred feet or so and surrounded by a narrow coastal strip of land. It guards the strait that separates Europe from Africa. Legend says that Heracles, while returning from the tenth of the twelve labors imposed upon him by Eurystheus, stumbled upon a huge rock. The rock prevented passage of the cattle he seized from the three-bodied giant Geryon who ruled the island Erytheia in the far west, by the coast of Libya. The greatest of the Greek heroes simply split the rock in two, creating the passage and, at the same time, the strait connecting the Atlantic Ocean and the Mediterranean Sea. The two pieces of rock, on either side of the strait, were thus named The Pillars of Heracles in the ancient world. For a very long time an engraving on the Rock could be seen from far away: *non plus ultra* ("nothing further beyond"), signifying the end of the known world.

It is now October 1943 and the role of Gibraltar, British Protectorate, has changed significantly since *Blackbird* last docked there in June 1943. Back then, the port and the bay were swarming with Allied ships engaged in the invasion of Sicily, including British Royal Navy *Force H* warships. From the beginning of war, the British were continuously working on reinforcing Gibraltar, turning it into impregnable fortress guarding access to The Mediterranean. They evacuated women and children, built a military airport, and expanded the huge stone and concrete underground water storage reservoirs. After the capitulation of Italy, Gibraltar turned more into a support base for shipping convoys, but it was still heavily defended and home to Allied submarines.

To their enormous surprise, the crew of *Blackbird* was greeted with open hostility when it entered Gibraltar Harbour the morning of October 18th. The schooner was escorted by two navy patrol boats. Tove and

Sven were literally dragged off the schooner upon docking and taken to prison despite their explanations. Any likely messages about their arrival to Gibraltar simply fell through the cracks. The prison was part of a tunnel sealed with heavy iron bars. They were taken through a labyrinth of underground passages and tunnels carved into the Rock. They remained locked behind bars until the next morning, in company of a flickering gas lamp which slowly went out after couple of hours. Before complete dark took over, they were able to discern a few more cells along the sides of the tunnel and hear the moaning and cursing of several drunken sailors brought in to cool down for the night. The tunnel itself was crowded with heavy tools and pieces of equipment used to cut deeper and deeper into the Rock. The tunnel, as they learned later, was part of a vast underground labyrinth – the War Tunnels.

The arrest of Tove and Sven was not unexpected as the British had many reasons for suspicion. Gibraltar was a constant target of German air raids and everyone was on alert for any signs of possible subversions, espionage, and hostilities. They were committed not only by the Germans but also by the Spanish who greatly resented the British presence on Gibraltar. For them, it was Spain's own soil.

Just as much as Spain, if not more, Hitler wanted to control this strip of land because of its utmost strategic importance. Wehrmacht generals did manage to persuade Hitler not to launch an airborne attack or landing because of the inevitable heavy casualties and little chance for success – The Rock was armed to the teeth and truly impenetrable. Instead, the Germans turned to Spanish fascist dictator, Generalissimo Francisco Franco, hoping he would take sides and help them overrun Gibraltar, since they were the ones that turned the tide in the Spanish Civil War and helped him win. The German plan for taking over Gibraltar was given the code name *Felix* and involved amassing German troops north of Gibraltar, with Franco's permission, and its ground invasion. Except that Franco never ended up giving permission and the plan simply fell apart. He was a skillful negotiator as it turned out, a master of suspense and passionate actor in the diplomatic theater, outfoxing the Germans. He knew that siding with Hitler and the Axis would bring doom on his country and he firmly resisted the enormous pressure. Left with no choice, the Germans turned to other means to possibly gain control of Gibraltar including relentless air raids, sabotages, diversions, subversions, and underwater attacks.

Because of the continuous, unpredictable hostile German activities, conducted by Abwehr spies, saboteurs, and Spanish collaborators, it was only natural that the unknown couple, both blond and appearing out of the blue on a sailing boat, would be promptly arrested and interrogated.

The morning after the night spent deep inside The Rock brought great relief for Tove and Sven. The beautiful Norwegian had managed to charm the young officer Lance Corporal Durant, assistant to David Scherr, who agreed to involve his high school friend from Portsmouth, now a military radio operator on the second floor of the Defense Security Office building where the interrogation was taking place, in resolving the situation. The radio operator succeeded in contacting the SOE office in London and then Larry Neal himself. *Blackbird's* crew received a big apology for the wrongful imprisonment from Lance Corporal Durant, a considerable number of British pounds as "pocket" money, and friendly advice how to spend their time on the peninsula while waiting for two American Marines who will join them in sailing *Blackbird* back to America. Tove and Sven truly rejoiced after learning the names of the Americans who will arrive by plane in two or three days – Michael Cole and Steven Masters. They vividly remembered the cheerful, entertaining and musical Marines, including all the bourbon and Cuban cigars they consumed together with them back in Sweden.

When Cole and Masters landed in Gibraltar on October 21, Tove and Sven were already well acquainted with various places worth visiting and recommended to them by Lance Corporal Durant who also generously offered to show them Gibraltar's taverns and similar establishments. The Scandinavians enthusiastically welcomed the Marines and informed them they will be their exclusive guides on a tour of the port which must start without delay as dawn was just around the corner and there is lot to see and taste, like incredible local stews, assortments of genuine English beer, grog and such. Moreover, one tavern they liked a lot was featuring a guest flamenco dancer visiting that week from a neighboring Spanish town, and she was something else! So, they better hurry and try to get a table because the place is sure to be packed, just like last night. Masters and Cole did not need any further persuasion, and yelled in unison "But of course, let's go!"

From the docks they almost run through Commonwealth Park, Cathedral Square around the Holy Trinity Cathedral, up George's Lane to the intersection with Main Street, south on Main, past the intersection with Convent Place, and laugh loudly the last fifty yards or so before entering the tavern on the corner of a small square paved with polished limestone. The tavern, which looks like a strange hybrid of a run-down Spanish cafe and a fancy Irish pub, is already packed like a new box of matches. The old-new crew of *Blackbird* elbow their way to a long wooden bar table, almost black with patina, and join the crowd composed of sailors, officers, locals and other colorful characters who are all shouting, laughing and cursing to get their glasses refilled first.

Dim lights scattered on stone walls are rather unsuccessfully trying to penetrate a heavy fog of cigarette smoke filling the long narrow room. Only one corner of the room is somewhat better lit. In it, an old Spaniard with a wrinkled face and a deficit of front teeth is sitting on a tall bar stool and ripping strings of a poor guitar that has seen much better days since it first came to life.

In the opposite corner of the room, a British officer and a civilian are sitting at a small round table and drinking beer. They are leaning into each other as they talk. Sven notices the two men and, at the same time, witnesses something peculiar: the officer surreptitiously looks around before passing an object under the table to the civilian. Sven immediately thinks of the scene as none of his business – today Tove and he are here, tomorrow somewhere else, life goes on. But then, he couldn't ignore what they learned since setting foot on Gibraltar, including the imprisonment deep inside The Rock. He decides to alert Michael who is standing next to him:

"Look at those two sitting in the corner. We were told about all those spies and saboteurs trying to inflict damage here. For all we know, there may even be German commandoes somewhere around as we speak! The two appear quite suspicious to me, an officer and a civilian conspiring to something. We better report them to someone, have them interrogated, or something."

Quickly, however, Sven and Michael agree that time is of the essence here – it would simply take too long for someone to run to the port and fetch military police. The patrol, which regularly checks for drunken sailors in joints like this one at night, may or may not show up soon. It is therefore up to them to come up with a plan, fast! Tove and Michael, with drinks in their hands, will stroll by the spies' table, pretending to look for a seat. The gorgeous Norwegian will certainly catch their attention, enabling Steve and Sven to sneak up on them from different sides, unnoticed. They will confront them and restrain if needed. Sven will take care of the civilian and Steven of the officer. They will then search them. If it turns out it was all one big mistake, they will apologize, all good. If they do find something, they'll confine the bloody bastards until the patrol shows up. The others in the joint will help for sure once the truth is revealed.

Unfortunately, the hastily dished out plan turned out badly, as they often do. While Tove and Sven were approaching the small round table where the suspects were likely plotting some bad deeds, the British officer, with the corner of his eye, noticed Steve and Sven trying to sneak around. He abruptly jumped off the table, knocking down his chair in the process. He pushed the civilian with one hand and drew out a pistol from an inside pocket of his uniform with another, waiving it in circles high above his head.

This commotion quickly drew the attention of everyone in the tavern including the Spaniard who stopped torturing his beaten-up guitar. All heads turned towards the scene in the corner, those sitting at small tables jumping up to see better what was going on. Taking advantage of the confusion, the civilian ran to the entrance, savagely burst open the door, and disappeared into the darkness. The man in British officer uniform, while nervously looking around him, started to retreat slowly towards the broken door, continuing to wave his pistol. Then, suddenly, he started shooting after seeing Tove make a move towards him. Tove grabbed her shoulder with a cry and fell on the floor. In split second, the shooter flew out of the tavern and disappeared in the labyrinth of narrow streets circling the small square. The Marines and Sven rushed to Tove in panic, fearing the worst. But, the brave Norwegian, holding back pain, reassured her faithful friends she will be fine and urged them to go after the shooter and bring him to justice. Hesitating, the Marines looked at each other, at Sven, and back at Tove. Finally, Cole ordered Sven to stay with Tove and the two Marines left the tavern in search of the two enemies, followed by an angry mob.

After a short chase on narrow winding streets leading to the steep face of The Rock, the posse caught up with them resulting in brief shootout near La Línee de la Concepcion. The conspirators were seriously wounded, incapacitated and handed over to a motorized military patrol which soon showed up.

As it turned out, *Blackbird's* crew did witness a major spy affair. The British officer impostor was indeed a German spy and the civilian was supposed to take information collected by the German to someone across border in Spain. The British Command was ecstatic with the German spy capture by the Scandinavian-American team. However, although all four of them were flooded with praise, attention and care, the Marines were informed there were no major changes – they were still going to sail as planned, except that since Tove was wounded, she and Sven will remain on The Rock, in the care of the British. Steven and Michael will sail *Blackbird* alone.

Unlike their last sail on *Blackbird*, the Marines encountered bad weather most of the time, with high and erratic winds, storms and dangerous waves, and no help from Edvard Neumman and Svetoslav Belov's device (of which they did not know anything). Unphased, the two sea wolfs completed the Atlantic crossing and returned the beautiful schooner to her home port, The Essex Yacht Club on the Connecticut River.

Initially, I have not been able to find many details about destinies of Tove and Sven. I first learned that they both ended up in the United States near the end of the war, being brought first to Chopawamsic Recreational Demonstration Area near Washington, D.C. because of what they experienced when *Blackbird* disappeared near the Croatian island of Lopud. There they even saw Teo briefly, but more on Teo's whereabouts a bit later. After week-long interrogations by the OSS agents, the Scandinavians were free to leave. Sven immediately returned to Sweden where he became a diplomat after the end of war. I did not research his life further. Tove settled in New York.

Since the bureaucracy is same everywhere, Tove had to officially apply for residence in the United States and for that she needed some kind of official documents. To avoid any delays and complications, she decided to use her fake Swedish passport. This was just fine with a State Department official who promptly approved and processed her application, after thoroughly enjoying a personal interview with the charming young lady. Tove's heroism on Gibraltar and fearless execution of Mission Capri played key roles in her being more than welcomed to the United States. She was given a generous financial support and the freedom to select a vocation of her choice in her new home country. After finishing a nursing course, Tove worked as a nurse in The Mount Sinai Hospital in New York until the end of war. After the war she took various short professional courses and frequently changed jobs. Eventually, she settled at a local TV station and had a successful career as commentator.

Unwavering in her love of sailing, Tove saved enough to buy a pretty yawl and became an enthusiastic member of the Yachting Club of America. She sailed along the coasts of Florida and on the Mexican Gulf whenever an opportunity presented itself, until late 1990s. Thanks to her cheerful spirit and strong body kept vital by sports, Tove stayed in good health, full of energy and enthusiasm, long after she retired.

I discovered these details about Tove while investigating the history of *Blackbird*. My search often branched in different, unexpected directions. For example, when I stumbled upon an old newspaper article on a challenging regatta in Florida and a sailing boat entry with the familiar name – *Swarttrost*. This track helped me find Tove in a retirement community near Florence, Florida and, in turn, a bounty of additional information about what happened to *Blackbird's* crew on their WWII spy mission, and to Teo after he appeared on the schooner one peculiar night in September 1943.

Bari Airport, captured by the British Eight Army on 23 September 1943, from which Teo was flown to the United States on October 7, 1943. Photo by the U.S. Air Forces. Courtesy of Center of Military History, United States Army, Washington, DC.

Tove (shown in the middle) gave me this photo of sailing on her own *Swarttrost* off the coast of Florida in 1990s.

Rock

Chapter 35

New Life

The United States Air Force aircraft, which Teo boarded in Bari, landed on the runway of the Marine Corps Air Facility Quantico near Washington, D.C shortly after nine o'clock the evening of October 8, 1943. From there Teo was immediately taken to Area C, within nearby Chopawamsic Recreational Demonstration Area, what is today Prince William Forest Park. Area C was part of an OSS complex where agents were, among other things, instructed in various techniques of communication including interrogation of human *subjects*. The complex, some nine square miles, was enclosed by either a fence topped with barbed wire or a solid wall. The entire perimeter was, day and night, patrolled by armed Marines accompanied by dogs.

The second day of his interrogation Teo was given an unofficial code name WTF by the agents conducting long exhausting interviews with him and having crazy fun while doing so. Because of the extraordinary facts connected to Teo, the number of mystified agents interviewing him the first three days, including those that just wanted to be present out of curiosity, was rapidly growing. This trend was suddenly interrupted from the highest level on the fourth day of Teo's arrival. From there on only one agent was assigned to Teo, exclusively. His code name was Ostap Bender. Agent Bender joined OSS from the very beginning and before that, for many years, he worked in the Government and for Joint Chiefs of Staff on secret operations and other activities related to Soviet Union. He did his work with great success and was continuously promoted with astronomical speed, earning his official code name along the way. That fourth day, agent Bender, to his enormous surprise and disappointment, was urgently dispatched to Area C from Washington, D.C. The last thing he expected, given all the accomplishments and high qualifications he possessed for performing even the most complicated tasks, was to be sent to conduct boring interviews of some *subject*. However, already after the first session with Teo, agent Bender realized that nothing about the *subject* was going to be either boring or simple, and he enthusiastically immersed himself into the challenging task ahead.

While Teo, exhausted beyond belief, was still asleep in a strictly guarded room in a similarly strictly guarded building in Area C in distant Virginia, on October 23, 1943, something happened at the Massachusetts Institute of Technology in Boston that no eyewitnesses, then or later, until now, were able to explain. Exactly at eight o'clock in the morning six, or according to some sources eight, covered military trucks, escorted by several motorcycles and two jeeps, pulled in front of Building No. 4. A rather large unit of Marines in uniforms emerged from the trucks and, for the next three hours, completely emptied and loaded on the trucks the entire contents of various rooms, laboratories, and machine shops used by Edvard Neumann and Svetoslav Belov. When the two stunned postdocs, upon arrival to work that morning, asked what was going on, no one replied. Instead, they were separately shown to the jeeps, taken to their apartments, and instructed to pack everything they needed for a trip lasting several weeks.

Nauseated after two days of the sleepless non-stop drive from Boston, Edvard and Svetoslav found out what was going on only upon arrival of the truck convoy to Area C. For the next six days, with all necessary help from the Marines, they reconstructed their work environment from MIT, to the last detail, in one of the OSS complex buildings which, temporarily, got its new name – Building No. 4. Starting in early November Teo's interrogations included frequent visits to Building No. 4.

Teo remained in Area C until Christmas of 1945 when he moved to a charming 19th century brick house in Georgetown, the oldest part of Washington, D.C. This is where his new American civilian life began. Together with the nice spacious house, he was given a new identity which included a new name as well: Wilbur Thomas Fletcher. Except on three occasions, during the visits of Yugoslav President Josip Broz Tito to the United States, and during short official trips to New York (linked to jazz, as explained a bit later), Teo, until retirement, never left the American capital, the city in which he lived for the rest of his life. This does not include regular visits to Area C, at first every three months and then less frequently. In January 1950, he married Ingrid Swanson, an analyst at the State Department. Teo met Ingrid at one of the informal parties organized for the members of the Interagency Group for Strategic Forecasting.

According to secret documents kept at several locations in Washington, D.C., to which I had access, including testimonies by rare personal contacts I was able to establish, Teo's work and contributions within the Interagency Group for Strategic Forecasting were immeasurable at the beginning. Everything he either learned or read about a long time ago was again taking place in front of his own eyes. Teo's impressions were clear and convincing, just like the prognoses he was making, soon to be fully confirmed one after another. Nevertheless, Teo could not quite channel his own feelings, consisting mainly of memories of his private life and unimportant details that mattered only to himself. Then, with the passage of time, even these little details started to pale. During exhausting questionings, Teo was much less able to provide the detailed information about the future on which the agents insisted. As a result, they were increasingly frustrated and, slowly but surely, becoming disinterested in working with Teo.

Although Teo could still clearly remember important events from his past and thus predict the future, these were generally known to most people or seemed inevitable, at least to the professionals. Because of this, confusion and suspicion descended upon Teo who started to question if his travel through time was real or nothing more than a dream or illusion. He even interpreted, to himself, that his ability to predict the future was likely only a consequence of an uninvited, constant *Deja vu* experience. The feeling that he already saw or experienced something was crystal clear even though his mind was telling him that was not possible. Teo's *Deja vu* often made him convinced that the reality is only a mirage, and his ability to predict the future only a dream or invention of the time travel that never took place.

According to my personal contacts, the ability of Wilbur Thomas Fletcher to foresee the future returned, almost entirely, in 1970 and 1971 when he intensely worked on the Vietnam War. During this period, he frequently spent time at Quantico, sometimes staying there for weeks. One of my Washington, D.C. contacts, in order to illustrate these two years, told me, among other things, how both he and his colleagues laughed when Wilbur, very persuasively, informed them that Yugoslavia will win the 1970 World Basketball Championship after defeating the United States. Unfortunately, about the same time, Teo started to experience excruciating headaches which, by the end of 1971, became completely unbearable such that Teo was declared "useless". My contact speculated that this qualification was the main reason for Teo's early retirement at the end of 1972. Interestingly, in the written top-secret documents I reviewed initially there was no mention of any headaches or other reasons, health or personal, for Teo's retirement. Only at the end of my investigation of the whereabouts of the schooner *Blackbird* did I stumble upon additional documents and solved the mystery.

My persistent attempts to reconstruct Teo's life in America where greatly rewarded by a series of conversations with Teo's daughter Margo in the spring and summer of 2018. These meetings later grew into a real friendship although I struggled quite a bit for them to even take place initially. After I tracked her down and made multiple attempts to establish communication with her, by e-mail, phone and regular mail, Margo avoided me for a long time. She later confessed that my persistence and phone calls annoyed her greatly, but her own curiosity finally prevailed.

With Margo's help, my picture of Teo's new life crystalized completely. She provided me with several critical missing details needed for completing this story and, in turn, learned from me many unbelievable and unknown things, not only about her daddy (Margo always referred to Teo as "daddy" and it was more than clear to me she truly adored him, just like her "mommy".) We often laughed in unison when solving certain puzzles together which, years ago when they appeared, she did not even view as such, taking them for granted. Many times, during our meetings, her eyes teared up, sometimes of laughter, sometimes of sorrow, and sometimes of both at the same time.

First time I saw Margo was in a cozy intimate French restaurant near Washington National Cathedral which she personally suggested.

Margo came to it after "thirty minutes of a nice leisurely walk from her house in Georgetown where she was born." She immediately told me that she finally agreed to meet me after hearing certain things from me that no one, except for her mother and herself, could have possibly known. "She is certainly much afraid what I can tell her about her daddy. She was afraid ever since daddy, a few months before he passed away, revealed certain things to her mommy and her, and only hinted about several more. It seemed to her that, after such experience, nothing else would be able to astonish her but, it now looks, she was wrong."

I saw Margo several more times after that evening. The first time it was again where she could comfortably come on foot, near her beloved Georgetown, and the second time she invited me to come to her family house where she lived alone after her mother's death, "for almost ten years now." It is then that I found out why our previous meetings were always relatively near her house – she did not possess an automobile, just like her parents. After I explained that the most likely reason for this was the fact that Teo (by now she already learned from me the real name of her father) was under constant surveillance by the Agencies which did not want to risk anything, she simply shrugged her shoulders:

"We never missed having a car. Georgetown has all that is needed including good public transportation to downtown and everything worth visiting."

The story about her father's coming to the United States ten or so years before the war, which I heard from Margo for the first time, I attributed to special agent Ostap Bender (which was later proven true). When I explained that the agent's code name was after a character from the hilarious comic novels by Ilf and Petrov, Margo nodded approvingly, with a smile. The secret agent had wild imagination, indeed, just like the character after whom he was named! Both Margo and her mother believed that Wilbur Thomas Fletcher arrived in America with his parents from Paris because his father, a Jew with the name Viktor Laffite, wanted to leave Europe in time knowing very well the horrors yet to come were inevitable. The mother, a young countess named Ekaterina Pavlovna, came to Paris from Russia immediately after the 1917 October Revolution brought to power Lenin's communists which started to tyrannize the aristocracy showing no mercy. Teo's parents fell in love at first sight and married only nine days after their encounter which happened by chance at a concert of classical music. Teo learned fluent Russian from his mother and it is questionable if French could be referred to as his mother tongue. Although he arrived in the United States relatively young, Teo never managed to lose the strange accent. The accent which his daughter completely adored, especially when Teo was pretending to be a clown, trying to cheer up Margo when she was little and sad for some reason.

Upon arrival in America, directly to Washington, D.C., the grandfather changed their family name to Fletcher wanting to distance from the past completely. Teo's name was changed to Wilbur Thomas marking the beginning of a new free life for their beloved son, in the land that opened endless opportunities for him, welcoming the family with widely open arms. Sadly, she never met her grandparents as they both passed away before mommy and daddy married.

When Margo mentioned she still greatly regrets daddy never went to a real vacation with mommy and her because he was always prevented by "an official business" from doing it, I gave her the real explanation which made her feel even more sad. The Agencies simply did not want to risk anything and leave Teo without complete surveillance. I also told her the reason behind their only three times together as a family away from Washington, D.C., providing exact dates and locations they visited. Naturally, neither her nor her mother were aware of the constant presence of agents which were continuously and masterfully observing the family, unnoticed even in the vast open desert of Big Bend, Texas. After hearing my explanation of their two-week long visits to Texas, Margo, yet again that evening, was left speechless, staring at me with an open mouth.

One week before Marshall Tito's first visit to the United States in September 1960, when the Yugoslav President made a speech in the United Nations and afterwards met, in the *Waldorf-Astoria*, with President Eisenhower, Teo, his wife Ingrid, and seven-year old Margo were taken to a ghost mining town Terlingua, near the Mexico border, in the most remote part of Texas where river Rio Grande forms a tens of miles long bend, Big Bend. The only reason for this temporary exile was the presence of Teo's father, Vinko Lovrić, in Marshall Tito's escort as one of the select top Yugoslav Secret Service agents. These agents were, as part of the security preparations, sent to the countries and cities Tito was about to visit at least a week earlier, and sometimes a lot earlier. The Americans wanted to prevent any chance, either intentional or unintentional, of father and son meeting each other. Thus, Teo and his family were removed to the remotest possible location, hours drive away from the closest airport, even the smallest one.

The same happened two more times: because of the Tito's first official state visit in the United States in October 1963 when his host was President Kennedy, and during Tito's return visit to President Nixon in October 1971. Only during the last visit of the Yugoslav President to the United States in March 1978, when his host was President Carter, the Fletcher family did not have to leave Washington, D.C. because Teo's father was not in the Marshall's escort this time around.

Both times, in 1963 and 1971, Teo was offered two alternatives for his temporary exile but the entire family expressed desire their "annual vacation" again be in Big Bend. This because all three of them completely fell in love with the desert, mountains, plants, animals, hardened and somewhat wild individuals that lived there either temporarily or permanently, as well as in everything else Big Bend had. Margo was the most vocal in these decisions which was not surprising at all. Ever since their first visit she relentlessly and ad nauseum pressed her parents with the question "When will they again see the real Indian and the mountain lion?"

This story about an Indian and a mountain lion I heard from Margo on my next visit. This time I was the one left speechless.

During one of the exhausting hikes, at least for her as she was still small, they suddenly came eye-to-eye with a mountain lion. The lion emerged from behind a rock or a bend in the trail, she could not remember exactly. Mommy and daddy froze in place after placing her in the middle, daddy in the front, mommy in the back. In contrast, she started to jump with joy clapping her hands, exhilarated and shouting, "What a big kitty, pretty kitty!" Mommy and daddy hardly managed to quiet her down, probably in a complete panic. The lion did not take his eyes off them for a long time, standing motionless just like three of them. Finally, he very slowly turned around and, walking equally slowly and somewhat leisurely, disappeared where he came from.

When that night, in a joint in Terlingua, we reflected again and again, often excitedly and probably too loudly, upon our encounter with the mountain lion, an old Indian with a wrinkled face approached our table. He apologized for overhearing parts of our conversation and asked is it that we saw a mountain lion only a few feet away from us. When we confirmed it, the old Indian remarked, with certain awe, that we are extraordinary lucky experiencing something like that, it is very, very rare, it happens only to the chosen ones. Then he suddenly quivered after looking directly at daddy's eyes and started to murmur a song of a sort, in half-voice, his arms stretched in front of him.

The next day, while we were waiting for dinner in the same joint, the old Indian appeared from nowhere and again approached our table. From a small leather bag, he took out a figure of a mountain lion made of stone, with an arrowhead tied to it, and gave it to me: "I made this fetish today to keep you all safe from the evil spirits. Take good care of it, it is yours now."

Daddy then invited the old Indian to join us for dinner which he gladly accepted. "One-that-talks-with-animals" was his name. He came to Big Bend as a young man, from the Zuni reservation in New Mexico. He grew up with the legends of his tribe, but also the legends about wild Apache for which Zuni had great respect. He was sick of living at the reservation and wanted to experience real freedom and the spirit of wilderness. Here he met his deceased wife from the Apache Mescalero tribe. He never regretted coming to Big Bend.

At the end of 1971 daddy's headaches became unbearable and mommy arranged for a visit to Johns Hopkins where he was examined by top neurologists. They immediately ordered him to stay at the hospital where he remained for ten days. The doctors tried to help him doing everything in their power (they were, and still are, the best in the country), but daddy's condition was worsening rapidly. Then, out of desperation, and not knowing why, one day I brought the little figure of a mountain lion made of stone and left it on a night table by daddy's bed where he laid unconscious. The next day, upon returning from the hospital visit, mommy ecstatically told me how daddy was suddenly feeling much better. After two days he was dismissed completely recovered and without any headache. The mystified doctors did not have any plausible explanation for what has happened. I only told my mother what I have done and why I believe, from the bottom of my hearth, daddy recovered because of it.

When I revealed to Margo the reason for Teo's headaches, she remained silent for a while and then stood up from her chair and invited me upstairs to second floor where there are numerous paintings on the walls. Paintings she loves so much and which her dad "painted only from his imagination, beautifully, over many years." That is how it was. While we were going from one room to another, walls packed with Teo's oils on canvas and aquarelles, Margo suddenly said:

"I want to think all that suffering daddy went through was not for nothing."

I replied that it certainly was not the case and she must be proud of her father who did everything he could for the bloody Vietnam War to end. I did not tell her, at the time, that the agents working on Teo at Quantico during that time and exposing him to different machines and energy emissions completely unknown to them were absolute laymen, carrying out orders because they had to. They were relying on brief, incomplete notes and movies filmed in distant 1943 and 1944 when, among others, Teo was handled by two postdocs from MIT, Edvard Neumann and Svetoslav Belov, who did that against their will and under enormous pressure. Edvard and Svetoslav refused to do it again when approached at the beginning of 1970 and the Agencies never forgave them, turning their lives into constant nightmare. Because of that they finally left the United States: Edvard went to Israel and Svetoslav to Russia.

At the end of my visit (it was already late night), a sight of single photograph among all those paintings prompted me to ask Margo what did Teo love the most, excluding of course her and her mommy. She laughed immediately and replied:

"Everyone knew that, the music of Miles Davis, no doubt about it!"

I saw Margo again in Vermont where she invited me to stay in an old cabin her mother and she bought together soon after Teo passed away. She wanted to show me some very interesting things they immediately brought there from Georgetown. The last several years, upon retirement, she spent whole summers in the cabin together with her three dogs, running away from the unbearable heat and humidity of the South. There she had many invited and uninvited guests or, better, dear friends which would appear suddenly and unexpectedly since she encouraged it completely, very much looking forward to a surprise. The same happened this time. A day before my arrival two of her best high school friends came to visit, one with a son. Margo granted me the largest room and apologized if I felt a bit cramped, but it is summer and most of the time is spent outside anyway, in the nature or on the porch. There is no electricity, everything is powered on gas from the bottles. The water is perfect, cold, from a nearby spring. The nights are cool, it is nice to fall asleep under a blanket, she hopes I will get used to all that.

Margo also immediately asked me not to mention anything about the conversations we had, or who I am, or why I came to visit her (she will think of something). She needs time to digest everything, not even knowing if she would share that with anyone, not even with her best friends. I, of course, promised her that and kept my promise. After three wonderful days spent in an interesting company, in the wilderness of Vermont, I returned to Washington, D.C. without seeing anything Margo wanted to show me and why I came in the first place. We left this to some other time.

Then, at the end of June 2018, completely unexpectedly, Margo called me on the phone, wished me happy upcoming 4th of July, and invited me to come to Vermont again because she believes I can help her greatly with Teo's files stored in one of the chests in the cabin's attic. Hopefully, I would come visit before the end of the summer because the next time it would be possible is after the winter is over (usually not before the end of April). The chest has been gathering dust ever since mommy and she brought it from Georgetown years ago. The notes in the files are written in alphabet and language she does not recognize (it is not Russian, she already checked, so it must be Serbian?) I instantly promised I will come to visit her, now more than intrigued.

After a short pause and silence at the other end of the phone line, Margo informed me that, actually, she brought back one of Teo's notebooks and also that I have her permission to write in my book everything she told me, including about herself if desired, for the authenticity.

That is how it was.

Teo's parents as conceived by the OSS special agent with the code name Ostap Bender. Left: French Jew Victor Laffite; right: Russian countess Ekaterina Pavlovna. These and many other family photos illustrating the life of Teo's imaginary parents were assembled by OSS in a series of attractive leather-bound albums and handed over to Teo upon his departure from Area C. These two photographs of her imaginary grandparents are Margo's favorite.

Margo's mother Ingrid, avid amateur photographer, took these photos on their second trip to Big Bend. Top: crossing of Rio Grande filmed with a strong telephoto lens from a bluff above the river. Bottom: scenes from Terlingua, Texas.

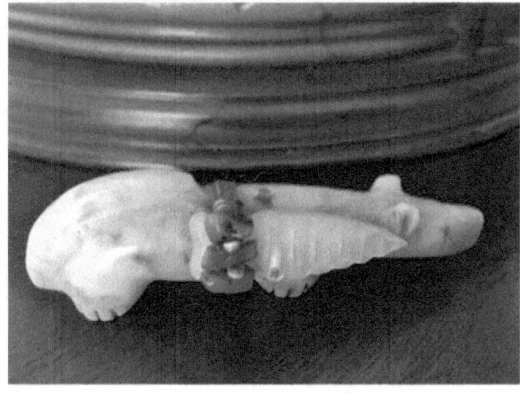

A mountain lion fetish given to Margo by an old Zuni Indian in Terlingua, Texas in 1960.

Teo's watercolor of a stone house in Old Podgora, Dalmatia where his mother Jelena was born. He painted it from memory in his atelier on the top floor of the Fletcher family house in Georgetown. Courtesy of Teo's daughter Margo Fletcher.

In company in front of the Vermont cabin in summer of 2018. Margo kneeling in the middle with her three dogs.

Duke Ellington School of Arts in Georgetown where Teo gave complimentary piano lessons in the evenings as a favor to his friend Jonathan Arthur, the school's music teacher.

Margo's favorite place: Bishop's Garden of The National Cathedral where her parents often took her to play.

Street in Georgetown where the Fletcher family home is.

Chapter 36

Miles

There existed a real but confusing, dangerous possibility that Teo, in his new present, would consciously influence something from his old past thus creating an absurdity. Or that he may even redirect an important course of history in a wrong direction. The Agencies were well aware of this and so was Teo, both very much afraid of negative, and possibly even catastrophic consequences. In any case, the Agencies did not want to take any chances and Teo was sentenced to some sort of quarantine in Washington. He was forbidden contact with any official of the Yugoslav embassy and could not come closer than 2 miles to the embassy building (it is not entirely clear why this particular distance was selected). Teo was also immediately informed that his phone was under constant surveillance and that "means exist to prevent any written or other communication he may attempt with overseas." Together with several similar examples, he was advised, rather ominously, to "think twice before succumbing to any temptations, which are sure to come sooner than later." The Americans, being true capitalists, also warned Teo to not even think of becoming rich by playing the stock market. In return, they did provide him, and later his family, with a comfortable lifestyle.

However, completely unavoidable when considering all the weaknesses of human nature, Teo soon started to toy with a thought he could perhaps influence something that would, to all involved, bring nothing but benefits. Something small, unimportant, under the radar of even the mighty Agencies. He decided to change a tiny, to most people absolutely irrelevant, outcome. He decided to do everything in his power for Miles Davis to give a cancelled concert in Belgrade in 1971 after all. Crystal clear in Teo's memory was an enormous disappointment his big cousin and other jazz fans in Belgrade and the entire Yugoslavia experienced when it was announced that the legendary jazz trumpet player will not come to Belgrade. Namely, everyone was expecting Miles will take part in the first European tour of the Newport Jazz Festival in communist (or, more precisely, socialist) countries. That year Belgrade saw one Duke Ellington, Dizzy Gillespie, Thelonious Monk, Art Blakey, Ornette Coleman and other jazz giants, but great Miles Davis was not among them, inexplicably.

Teo approached the whole plan very meticulously, considering it as a game of chess which will, he knew, last for a long time, be exhausting and extremely challenging (Teo loved chess and played it very well). No one in Teo's future team, including the chess pieces he started to gather, realized they were going to play in a game. The only exceptions were Teo's two colleagues from the Interagency Group for Strategic Forecasting who were permanent employees of the State Department. I cannot reveal their names because they are still alive, rather vigorous in their early nineties, and quite frightened by the current events in the American capital where no one is secure given the ruthless grab for power at any cost. Although, one of them did show a lighter side and a good sense of humor regardless of all the fear. He told me about this bumper sticker he saw the same day we met (in April 2018), laughing: "Elect a dangerous clown, expect a dangerous circus." In any case, for the purposes of this story, they are given the names Anonymous 1 (a bit higher in rank) and Anonymous 2 (a bit lower).

Anonymous 1 became well respected in the State Department when he proposed that, as the most powerful propaganda means in the fight against the Warsaw Pact (countries of the Soviet Block) they start using jazz. The idea came from Teo, but our hero knew very well that the best tactics always was to target a *subject* in such a manner that, at the end, the *subject* accepts the idea as his/her own and then starts to promote it him/herself. Teo did not need recognition or some promotion at work. All he wanted was the final victory in the Game of Chess. Anonymous 1 thus received all accolades for the brilliant idea. The State Department, and other Agencies when needed, started to invest significant amounts of money into the promotion of jazz, not only in eastern European countries which found themselves behind the Iron Curtain. Yugoslavia, of course, was not behind the Curtain, but it always flirted with both The West and The East which were therefore doing everything they could to win it for their cause. Teo took full advantage of this fact and succeeded in placing Yugoslavia first in line for the ambitious promotion of jazz. Although, this was almost natural as jazz was quite popular in the Balkan country already before WWII.

With the full support of Anonymous 1, Teo often travelled to New York, with an escort and a task to acquaint himself, thoroughly, with the jazz scene as part of detailed preparations for the secret project of breaching the Iron Curtain with jazz. For the bureaucrats of various Agencies, Yugoslavia was gotten over so to speak, for its political system but also many other things, and it was placed behind the Iron Curtain instead in front of it. Teo, however, did not object to this erroneous decision, it was not worth the effort. Teo's escort on his visits to New York was usually Anonymous 2, himself a big fan of jazz, and everything started moving in the right direction.

Preparations for the Game, following a very detailed plan, began with Teo's first visit to New York in late fall of 1950 when he met a passionate jazz fan and big friend of Miles Davis, Buddy Gist. Buddy then personally introduced Teo to Miles on February 17, 1951 during Teo's second visit to New York. Both encounters happened in famous Harlem club *Birdland* which became a household name around the country thanks to direct radio broadcasts of performances of famous jazz musicians but also those yet to make a breakthrough.

Buddy and Miles immediately found a common language with Teo and continued to socialize with him during frequent short visits of "the European with strange accent" to New York. On his part, Teo did not miss any opportunity to hear, firsthand, Miles's bands and everything new and exciting they were bringing to the world of jazz. Teo, together with Buddy, thus personally witnessed history in making, following Miles around the venues that became part of the history themselves – *Cafe Bohemia, Vanguard, Village Gate* and many others.

Teo, of course, also went to concerts in Washington, D.C. where he liked two venues only a few minutes' walk from the Georgetown house where the Fletcher family lived. He went mostly by himself to a cult club *Blues Alley* where jazz and blues were played exclusively. To *Cellar Door*, a renowned venue for pop and rock groups and musicians, he often took his wife Ingrid, and sometimes daughter Margo as well. The club did prefer popular music, it was certainly important to make a profit, but when it featured jazz, it was always a good jazz. Hence, in December 1970, the club hosted one of the later legendary Miles's sextets (Gary Bartz, Keith Jarrett, Michael Henderson, Jack DeJohnette, Airto Moreira and Miles) when Margo saw and heard the trumpet player for the first time. All four sessions, from Wednesday to Saturday, were recorded for a possible album.

Teo introduced Margo to Miles on Saturday, December 17th. The band was wrapping up their D.C. visit and the sextet was, at the invitation from Miles, joined that evening by an English guitar player named John McLaughlin (which caused a not so small turmoil in the band, with Jarrett being the most vocal). The audience, some 150 strong (the club was tiny, crowded with tables, and the stage was too tight, especially for a sextet) became part of the magic. Select short parts of the four sessions appeared on the legendary album *Live-Evil*, and the complete recording was finally published much later, in 2005, as *Cellar Door Box*.

Seventeen year old Margo was bored during the concert as the music sounded very strange and at moments chaotic, but she comforted herself by a thought that her presence made daddy very happy, knowing how much he wanted her to start appreciating jazz (Margo loved classical music, perfectly played cello, and enjoyed listening to rock.)

After the music ended, Teo suddenly grabbed Margo's hand telling her he wanted her to meet someone and pulled her towards the door through which the musicians disappeared a moment ago. Margo was completely taken a back not having the slightest idea daddy and Miles, or any of the musicians that played on the stage that night, knew each other. Immediately recognizing Teo, the security folks opened the door themselves and let the father and the daughter enter a small room behind the stage. In the room, the members of the sextet, with Miles, were rather loudly arguing about something, occasionally laughing and swearing. At some point Miles noticed the newcomers and addressed Teo with his raspy voice:

"I thought you would not show up at all. You don't like my new gang? You are probably right, they don't give a damn what I say, especially that *motherfuc...* (nodding towards Jarrett). What do you think about the English? Not bad. He plays some good shit."

Miles then became aware of Margo's presence and asked Teo: "Who is this?" When he heard the answer, Miles started to apologize for the inappropriate language (which was completely uncharacteristic for him as he never apologized for anything like that.) During a short conversation that followed, Miles learned from Margo that she liked classical music the most, especially Bach, played cello, and the music she heard that night sounded interesting, perhaps even a bit puzzling. Before parting, Miles told Margo he liked Bach's music himself, that she should be proud of her father, and then advised Teo to watch carefully after his beautiful daughter because the world is full of "*mother fu....* that will want to take advantage of her." At the end, he invited both to visit him in New York whenever they felt like it, as that would make him very happy.

The second time Margo saw Miles was in New York, on June 20th, 1978, years after Teo's Game of chess ended. The Game which, to everyone involved, remained a secret until now. This time it was Margo who took her father to a debut recital of her good friend, violinist Cecylia Arzewski, which was taking place at Carnegie Recital Hall. She hoped a little change of routine would help her father come out of a mild depression he suffered ever since his early retirement. This hope was fulfilled entirely. The Agencies informed Teo they did not have anything against his trip to New York and, moreover, he was free to go without any escort! As far as they were concerned, Teo was declared useless years ago. Unexpectedly, Teo therefore found himself completely free for the first time since coming to the United States decades ago and started to look forward to both the concert and the upcoming trip he will spend in the company of his beloved daughter!

Margo could not remember exactly how the idea to take advantage of being in New York and visiting Miles was born. She heard from Teo that the trumpet player fell into deep depression and, for two years now, lived completely alone, withdrawn from society, and overwhelmed with health and other problems that kept piling on one after another. Maybe even she herself (Margo was not exactly sure) suggested they should take Miles to the recital hoping it would shake him out of his misery a bit. Isn't it true that he himself told her, eight years ago when they met in *Cellar Door*, how he also loved Bach's music? Cecylia will play tomorrow, unaccompanied, Bach's Partita No. 1 in B minor, Sonata No. 1 in G minor and Partita No. 2 in D minor! She will ask Cecylia for one more ticket, not revealing for whom, in case Miles does not want to join.

Miles was more than glad when he heard from Teo he was in New York and would like to come visit together with his daughter. When around 10 o'clock in the morning, dressed in house gown and slippers, he looked through the second floor window of his brownstone at 312 West 77th Street and saw who was ringing the bell, Miles quickly came down the stairs, let Teo and Margo in and immediately locked the door after them. Then, faithful to his good old habit, he addressed Teo without choosing words:

"You look like shit! What the hell is wrong with you?"

Margo, visibly annoyed, immediately came to her daddy's defense and replied herself instead:

"Sir, it would be better if you first looked yourself in the mirror before starting to offend someone like that."

Margo later learned from her father how everything that followed was completely unlike Miles, even during the times when he was on the very top, free of drugs, sober, polite, meticulously dressed up and cleanshaven, and when his parties and gatherings were attended by various jetsetters including biggest Hollywood stars, painters, musicians, writers, and alike. Namely, after hearing Margo's words, Miles countered with nothing but praises ("Your daughter is something else! She is for real! I love it, I love it, shit!") and then "just for her" played a tape he got from Keith Jarrett on which the "genius" plays Bach, on electric organ.

At the beginning of the tape, before the music, the jazz pianist addresses Miles with the words: "Stop that s… and come back, so we can all fool around again, a bit." Miles immediately tells the guests he "never played the tape to anyone before and will not do it again for anyone." (Margo remembered how Miles said that, with a voice that seemed to her a bit more hoarse than usual, perhaps holding back tears.)

At some point, while the Fletchers were listening to the magic, unreal sounds of the organ, Miles excused himself and went to the kitchen, from where he returned after five minutes or so, carrying a tray with three rather large cups of steaming fresh coffee, sugar and cream, which he placed on a coffee table in front of them:

"Buddy brings me this coffee personally and claims it is the best there is. Supposedly, he is the only one that gets it, directly from Africa. I don't know if I should believe him at all, you know how he likes to shamelessly praise himself. But it is good, I cannot deny. I may even start to like the damn coffee!"

Teo, of course, knew very well what Miles was talking about, but did not reveal it, not even with a single gesture. Buddy Gist was a mutual friend but Miles, nevertheless, did not know he was much more than a good friend to Teo. Buddy was the most important piece in Teo's incredible, secret Game of chess that ended almost seven years ago, in November 1971.

Somewhere around 11:30 am, after patiently listening what her father and Miles had to tell each other (actually, this exchange was more like a series of long monologues) and, to her surprise, finding out how and where they met, Margo gathered courage and out of the blue addressed Miles, in one breath:

"We came to invite you to join us for a debut recital of my very good friend, violinist, tonight at Carnegie Recital Hall. She will play Bach solo, I do not accept "no" for an answer, be ready at seven, we are coming to pick you up by taxi, please dress in something decent, and I kindly ask you to shave."

Startled Miles, uncertain what he just heard, first looked at Teo, then at Margo, then again at Teo, and eventually started to laugh turning his head and rolling his eyes. Finally, after minute or two of general silence, he addressed Teo:

"Man, she is something else! Did you hear that? Can you believe it? How can I refuse? She will kill me; I am not kidding!"

That evening Margo, Teo and jazz trumpet player Miles Davis, right before start of the program, literally sneaked in and sat in the last row on the balcony of the small recital hall hoping not to draw any attention to themselves. Miles wore large dark glasses and a funny big hat pulled over his forehead (because of the hat and the glasses Margo cheerfully teased him from the moment when, at seven o'clock sharp, just like they agreed, Miles came out of his house.) During the taxi ride Miles told Teo's daughter, not without certain warmth, how he could not possibly imagine going to damn Carnegie Hall again after experiencing there the worst stage humiliation in his life: "Damn cockroach (note to the reader: Max Roach, famous jazz drum player) during the break came on the stage and started cursing that African Research Foundation in which Buddy involved me!" Margo, not having the slightest clue what Miles was talking about, did not know how to react and kept quiet while her father simply said:

"I know exactly what you mean, and you are right."

Miles, motionless, watched the entire recital without blinking. After the end, when they were parting on the street (Miles was going to take a taxi by himself, it was late and he felt tired), Margo heard the words she never forgot, words that fill her with happiness to this very day:

"Thank you very much for everything. But don't you dare tell anyone I was here. Not even your friend Cecylia. And she will do some great things, no doubt about it."

Miles's prediction came true and much more than that. After her breakthrough to a position of Assistant Concertmaster of the famous Boston Symphony Orchestra, followed by advancement to Associate Concertmaster of the equally famous Cleveland Orchestra, Cecylia became first female Concertmaster in American history after joining the Atlanta Symphony Orchestra where she stayed until retirement.

Teo has not seen or heard Miles until April 1980 when, impulsively, he called him up on the phone and told him he must return to playing music, he owes it to him and his daughter Margo. Margo, standing by her father, grabbed the handset, repeated the same words and went on to declare he will be more popular than ever before, even amongst teenagers, when he comes back, as soon as possible, she will not accept "no" for an answer. On the other end of the line a croaky voice, laughing, answered stopping in the middle:

"You, little..." and the call disconnected.

Miles's triumphant comeback started on May 1st that same year when he entered a recording studio after struggling during four full years of hiatus. Album *The Man with the Horn* was recorded between June 1980 and May 1981, and the producer was again legendary Teo

Macero. In June 1981 Miles returned to the stage, for the first time after 1975. The rest, so to speak, is history.

Building in Georgetown where cult music club The Cellar Door once was and where Teo introduced his daughter Margo to Miles Davis on December 17th, 1970. The building is today occupied by Starbucks.

Carnegie Recital Hall in New York where Miles Davis, incognito, together with Teo and Margo attended debut recital of now famous violinist Cecylia Arzewski (on the right) on June 21st, 1978. Courtesy of Carnegie Hall.

Photograph of Miles Davis taken by William Culhane (friend of Cecylia Arzewski) in 1988 in San Sebastian, Spain. He dedicated it to Cecylia knowing how much she liked Miles' music. Cecylia gave the precious photograph to Teo's daughter for memory after hearing from Margo, for the first time, that Miles attended her recital in the Carnegie Recital Hall on June 21, 1978.

Chapter 37

Chess Game

Teo decided to approach the task of bringing Miles Davis to Belgrade to give the concert that was canceled in 1971 as if it were a challenging game of chess. In part, this approach was Teo's tribute to his cousin who was so disappointed with Miles' cancellation and who played chess very well. Although a young teenager at the time, not attracted to jazz at all, Teo never forgot the great sorrow his beloved cousin felt. Because of his cousin, Teo later developed a great passion for chess and gradually for jazz as well.

So, who will be the players in this chess game? Teo, of course, who more than anything else wanted Miles to give at last the cancelled concert in Belgrade. Teo's opponent was not always well defined. The only thing certain is that, for a long time, Teo's main opponent was the ruling Yugoslav communist clique and their sympathizers. Since the end of World War II, the communist party viewed jazz as a decadent product of the West, not suitable for the proper development of socialist youth and society.

Most of the pieces Teo selected never realized they were participants in the Game. The notable exceptions were Anonymous 1 and Anonymous 2, career employees of the State Department, as explained earlier.

Teo decided that his most valuable pieces will be the queen and the two rooks. Nominally, the *White King* was his most important piece simply because everyone had to deal with him. The *White King* had several other titles he liked to use interchangeably, such as Supreme Commander, President of the Socialist Federal Republic of Yugoslavia, Secretary General of the Communist Party, and three-time War Hero (he was the one and only official bearer of three war hero medals awarded to him by his subordinates.) The name of this extraordinary person was Marshall Josip Broz Tito. Paradoxically, Tito was Teo's fiercest opponent in the beginning because he did not like jazz music at all, initially. However, with the generous help of his other pieces, Teo slowly but surely won over his *White King*. In turn, the *White King*, when the Game was in its final stages, managed to persuade the *Black King* to change sides. Who was the *Black King*? It was Richard Nixon, the 37th President of the United States.

If all this is starting to sound complicated and convoluted, it is because it was. Teo's Game lasted two full decades and he played it masterfully. He engaged some truly colorful pieces, including President Nkrumah of Ghana and his Ambassador to Yugoslavia, and a real African emperor, the Divine Haile Selassie. Teo used the world-wide influence of the *White King* to the fullest, without the king's knowledge. He faced relentless attacks of the opponent's pieces including the rival's powerful agency, the CIA. He even repelled, what could have been the defining move of the Game, the sacrifice of the *Black Queen*, no one else but the most famous of them all – Queen Elizabeth II. Teo was also severely challenged by the *Black King's* servants such as the Secretary of State of the United States. In any case, I will do my best to distill this truly phantasmagoric chess masterpiece to just a few crucial moves by Teo. The key pieces that played for Teo were:

The *White Queen*, the glamorous Italian movie star Sophia Loren. I will describe her key move a bit later.

The *First Rook*, Miles' best friend Buddy Gist, himself not a musician.

The *Second Rook*, the fabled Yugoslav war hero General Koča Popović, Tito's man of confidence.

Teo recruited Buddy in late fall of 1950 on his first trip to New York, with Anonymous 2 as his escort. Thanks to favorable circumstances, Teo, Buddy and Anonymous 2 found themselves at the same table of the famous Harlem jazz club *Birdland*. There, Teo served the Americans his imaginative story about how he came to love jazz and good music in general. He was born in Paris, the story begins, where, before World War II, his father took him to jazz clubs with real Americans. His mother taught him to play piano and he sometimes went to jam sessions to play with "real jazz players", developing his love of jazz even more, and so on and so forth… Buddy then insisted that Teo must play something "original" from Europe during the break. Teo sat at the piano, produced several test notes, hesitated a bit as if he was contemplating something, took a deep breath, and then resolutely started to play something no one present had ever heard before. When Teo finished, for a few moments there was complete silence in the club. Then, a roaring applause broke out. Buddy quickly got up, went to the piano, firmly hugged Teo and addressed the astonished guests:

"My friend from Paris, what do you say!"

What was that roaring applause all about and why Buddy hugged his "friend from Paris?" Well, the explanation is simple. First, Teo played, with his own syncope, a Yugoslav piece "Little Girl" (*Devojko mala*) sang by Ivo Robić. He then ended his short performance with his own version of *Aber Dojde Donke*, a Macedonian folk song played by his favorite Yugoslav band "Bread and Salt" (*Leb i sol.*) Everyone present was mesmerized by the unique Macedonian rhythm (five fourths and seven eights) and an unbelievable Phrygian scale. This amazement was completely understandable as no one heard anything like it before. This display of virtuosity was how Teo won Buddy's loyalty.

Teo's *Second Rook* General Koča Popović had many roles, and not only in Teo's Game. His responsibilities included the purchase and sale of weapons around the World, command of the armed forces (he was Tito's Military Chief of General Staff for a while), diplomacy (he was also Tito's Foreign Minister for many years), and secret meetings with numerous World leaders from all pacts and blocks. The *Second Rook* tirelessly jumped all over the chess board, often replacing other pieces, and was not ashamed to help even the poor pawns when needed. Namely, he believed in the highest communist ideals, fighting for workers first and foremost, but also for the peasants and all other citizens, without exception. Moreover, he spoke several foreign languages perfectly, which enabled him to have easy communication with the World's working class, and their leaders. Interestingly, General Popović, who grew up in a very wealthy, well-educated and cosmopolitan Belgrade family, studied at Sorbonne University in Paris before WWII. There he became involved in the surrealist movement.

For his *Second*, Teo selected grandmaster Svetozar Gligorić "Gliga" who was born in Belgrade just like Teo. In 1950s and 1960s, Gliga was the World's best chess player outside the Soviet Union. Although he never became a World Champion (he did come close three times), all World Champions at the time, Max Euwe, Mikhail Botvinnik, Vasily Smyslov, Tigran Petrosian, and Mikhail Tal, lost multiple games to Gliga. The Yugoslav Grandmaster led his country to one gold, six silver, and six bronze medals at the Chess Olympic Games. In Münich, in 1958, while playing at the first table, he won the individual gold medal ahead of Botvinnik himself. Therefore, as the Soviets will not take part in the game officially, Teo selected the best possible second.

Teo wanted to thoroughly prepare Gliga for the upcoming challenges and completely win him over for the cause of jazz, at the same time not revealing himself to the Grandmaster. Consequently, during Gliga's first visit to the United States, or more precisely to Los Angeles and Hollywood, in 1952, where he attended a tournament, Teo, via an intermediary, gave valuable advice to the Yugoslav Grandmaster regarding a purchase of JBL stereo loudspeakers. Gliga listened to the advice and, after quite a few obstacles, including at customs, the loudspeakers were delivered in Belgrade. Gliga complained to his friends how the loudspeakers cost him a fortune, not knowing that he got them at half price. Together with the best loudspeakers there were, Gliga also received 67 jazz records which astonished him.

Over the years, the Grandmaster accumulated the most extensive private collection of jazz records in the entire country. Many of them he brought home from travels abroad, but the largest chunk he ever acquired was again thanks to Teo. Gliga received, as a present, 128 jazz records from a record store on Wisconsin Avenue in Washington, D.C. after his simultaneous game at Georgetown University in August 1963. The simultaneous, which Gliga attended after participating at the U.S. Open in Chicago, was arranged by Teo and his friends from the State Department.

Most important for Teo's own Game was the fact that Gliga generously shared his record collection with Radio Belgrade which very successfully promoted jazz across The Balkans.

Last but not least, Teo engaged a group of extraordinary pawns. For those that are not well versed in the game of chess, it is important to emphasize that sacrifice of pawns, or proletaries, is not all that uncommon; in fact, it is necessary for the final victory.

The Game, which I am about to describe, was a rare variant of the Nimzo-Indian defense in which the *White* plays the fabled Rubinstein System with original moves. This is the system in which Gliga, Teo's *Second*, was unbeatable against every single opponent.

Buddy Gist (on the left), and Miles Davis after a gig in the New York club Birdland. Buddy sent the photo to Teo for a memory after their first meeting in the fall of 1950.

Teo's *Second*, Yugoslav Grandmaster Svetozar Gligorić "Gliga", during first
Capablanca Memorial in Havana in 1962 where his every game was closely
watched by revolutionary Che Guevara, Gliga's great admirer.

White King and *Second Rook* (sitting next to each other on the left) often
played other chess games on the World stage. Here they can be seen in
conversation with Che Guevara (front right) while discussing a possible sale
of much valued Yugoslav arms to Cuba. Courtesy of Museum of Yugoslavia.

Chapter 38

Opening

Teo started the Game with an unusual opening. More precisely, he and his friends from the State Department tested the whole idea of tearing down iron and other curtains with jazz by sending the famous jazz trumpet player Louis Armstrong and his All Stars Band to Accra, the capital of the British colony Gold Coast (which was renamed Ghana after gaining independence from the British Empire). On May 23, 1956 Satchmo and his wife Lucille were welcomed as royalty by ten thousand cheering fans and thirteen African music bands that played and sang "Everything for you, Louis, everything for you!" Satchmo, deeply moved by this welcome, took his trumpet from the case and joined the thirteen bands playing. This caused an eruption of joy and noise never experienced in Accra before or since. Satchmo was then officially welcomed by Prime Minister Kwame Nkrumah, the soon-to-be first president of the newly independent, and very socialist, country of Ghana.

After this successful test move, Teo opened the Game with Satchmo's first visit to Belgrade, again with his wife Lucille, in early April 1959. This marked the official start of the State Department's operation named "Iron Curtain Jazz." In Teo's Game, the main target of the operation was the *White King* who was given the code name "CS" (Comrade Supreme.)

Immediately following Satchmo's spectacular concert in Belgrade, Teo continued his clever opening by activating his first knight, Vojislav "Bubiša" Simić, the legendary conductor of the Belgrade Radio-Television Big Jazz Band. The first knight jumped over couple of white and black pawns and positioned himself to ask his own *White King* a very sensitive question, on the very day of the king's birthday, May 25,

1959. The position at the time of the jump is best described with the conductor's own words which he remembers to this day:

We were in company of big stars – Ivo Robić, Gabi Novak, Lola Novaković. At one point I found myself face to face with Tito and said loudly: "Excuse me, may I ask you a question?" All eyes of the known and unknown Secret Service agents in the room turned towards me.

Tito calmly replied, "Go ahead, ask", and I uttered it: "Is it true that you don't like jazz music?" The entire room went dead silent. Aleksandar Ranković made a move towards me, and the subordinate smiles of the people in the room quickly changed to grim ones.

The tense, unbearable situation ended with Tito's laconic explanation: "I do like jazz, but only the real one from Africa. I recently returned from a visit to Sudan where I listened to excellent jazz. The Americans ruined it." Everyone started to laugh and affirm Tito's words, and I realized with whom I was talking about jazz.

For Teo and the State Department officials, Anonymous 1 and Anonymous 2, this was an impatiently awaited move. The *White King* was finally pointed in the right direction. Satchmo reinforced Teo's position later in the Game when he visited Belgrade again at the end of March 1965. On the occasion, The New York Times published an article in its April 1 edition, with the title "Thousands in Belgrade Cheer Louis Armstrong."

Photo of Louis Armstrong and his wife Lucille after his first concert in Belgrade in 1959. Courtesy of Ilustrovana politika.

ЛЕГЕНДАРНИ »САЧМО«

Луис „Сачмо" Армстронг опет је, после шест година, гостовао у Београду. На концертима у Дому синдиката и у хали Сајмишта одушевио је преко 5.000 Београђана свирањем на својој златној труби, коју је, као и увек нежно али и енергично држао белом марамицом. Велики аплауз добио је и за певање, својим тако карактеристичним гласом. И остали чланови његовог ансамбла „Ол старс" су музичари високог ранга. Због поодмаклих година, али за би и осталим члановима ансамбла пружио шансу, „Сачмо" се чешће, него раније, на бини из клавира одмарао уз цигарету (прва фотографија). Иако је озбиљан музичар, Армстронг не запоставља шоу интерпретирање. Али само као „гарнирунг" браunurозних интерпретација (друга фотографија). Џуел Браун, млада и талентована певачица такође је заслужна за успех концерта ансамбла „Ол старс".

Текст и снимци
Жика Милутиновић

Бр. 335 ИЛУСТРОВАНА ПОЛИТИКА 17

Second visit of Louis Armstrong to Belgrade at the end of March 1965 additionally strengthened Teo's position in the Game. Courtesy of Ilustrovana politika.

Vojislav "Bubiša" Simić, legendary conductor of the Jazz Orchestra of Radio-Television Belgrade. I took this photo on March 18, 2019, Bubiša's 95th birthday. He is holding one of his most cherished photographs: the official welcome of Duke Ellington at the Belgrade Airport in 1971. Bubiša is in the center front, Duke is on the left of the photo.

Teo's room in his family apartment in Belgrade, with the Emerson, Lake and Palmer painting he painted as a teenager with his father. A painting of Teo playing chess is on the wall. Before his disappearance, Teo earned the title of National Master Candidate. Photo is from one of Teo's diaries I got from his father Vinko.

.

Chapter 39

Pawns

Teo engaged the most extraordinary group of pawns. They were dirt-poor proletaries that could be sacrificed. As mentioned earlier to those that are not well versed in this ancient game, it is important to emphasize that sacrificing the pawns, or proletaries, is not all that uncommon. In fact, it is necessary for the final victory.

The main stronghold of Teo's pawns was in the Belgrade district of Vračar, in Neimar, where Teo grew up. The pawns' headquarters were in a small rundown apartment building at 4 Kornelije Stanković Street, minutes away from the legendary Chess Club Obilić on Maxim Gorky Street. Also not far away from the Club was the Embassy of Ghana, sitting across the street from the primary school Svetozar Marković which Teo attended. The intimate knowledge of the history of this rough Neimar neighborhood, including tales about the Club where he perfected his knowledge of chess, helped Teo execute the pawn attack effortlessly.

The pawns, or more precisely the punks of Kornelije Stanković street, one October night in 1960, easily persuaded the best unranked player of the Club with the nickname Cale to lose a game of chess to the Ghanaian Ambassador (who was frequent visitor to the Club.) In fact, Cale lost two consecutive games to his Excellency the Ambassador. As a result, everyone present in the cigarette smoke filled room (which was tiny, less than 300 square feet) started to express their admiration for the Ambassador and suggest that he, perhaps, may even be able to challenge Grandmaster Gligorić because Cale once managed to pull a draw from Gliga.

All this theater staged by Teo's punk-pawns culminated in a game between the Ambassador and the Grandmaster that took place the following week in the smoke filled, overcrowded room of the Chess Club Obilić. Completely inexplicably, the great Grandmaster lost to the Ambassador who was overwhelmed with joy. He exhilaratingly accepted the invitation to celebrate this incredible achievement in the nearby restaurant *Sokolac*.

The Ambassador was treated like a king in *Sokolac* where tasty meats from the mixed grill were overflowing, together with plum brandy *šljivovica* and white wine chilled with soda water. The poor Ambassador became delirious with joy while listening to *Romanian Lark*, which was expertly played by Gipsy Ratko and his band. The culmination of the evening for his Excellency, already a bit drunk, were the following words from a young man who wore an impeccable dark suit and a tie:

"Your Excellency, it is my great honor to be in your secret security escort. I was appointed by General Popović, as ordered by Marshall Tito himself who highly respects you. If you allow me, I will convey to you a kind request for great personal favor. Our Marshall would be enormously grateful to your respected President Nkrumah if he, with a concrete move, can start helping our black brothers and sisters in America in their just fight for equality, and by extension to all our repressed comrades around the World, just like the two of them discussed last month in New York. For the beginning, a small gesture would be enough. However, since it is all very sensitive because of the Americans, this kind request cannot come from our Marshall directly, as I am sure you understand. If you agree, I will provide more details tomorrow afternoon when you come to the Club. General Popović is of the opinion that your participation in this important fight for justice can bring you great recognition and even greater respect from Marshall Tito and President Nkrumah."

The Ambassador, overwhelmed with boundless joy, replied to the young man in the impeccable dark suit that he is extremely honored by this confidence from Marshall Tito and will assiduously wait for further instructions. The following day, after receiving the instructions, he personally wired a message to Accra putting in motion the conclusion of Teo's attack.

Capitalizing on the sacrifice of his pawns (after the battle one of them spent a month in Belgrade's Central Prison and one was only beaten up a bit by the secret police), Teo closed this part of the Game at the beginning of November 1960 in New York. There, he and Buddy Gist went to a gig at *The Village Gate* to hear some good jazz. At the end of the evening, Buddy fully embraced an idea suggested by Teo and made firm a decision to start a new business: *Mt. Kilimanjaro Coffee Company*. Buddy was more than excited by this new endeavor which will allow him a more comfortable life since, unfortunately, he always came up short when it came to nice suits and other small luxuries.

Buddy also pledged he will never reveal, to anyone, the origin of the coffee, as well as the cocoa he will be getting directly from Africa, with Teo's help. Finally, he also agreed that, as a sign of great appreciation for generous African brothers and sisters, he will donate a hefty percentage of the proceeds to the African Research Foundation, recently formed by noble medical doctors who were going to provide medical supplies, medicine, and all other necessary help to former African colonies, now independent countries, very poor but with bright futures.

Thus, in 1961, *the Mt. Kilimanjaro Coffee Company* started receiving substantial shipments of coffee and cocoa directly from Ghana, at bargain prices. With this series of complicated moves, Teo earned unlimited loyalty from Buddy Gist, his *First Rook* and best friend of Miles Davis. The very loyalty he will need to win the Game.

The main supplier of both coffee and cocoa was a middle-aged farmer Mwambe-Abeiku Annan who inherited a decent plantation from his father and was in a good relationship with the new, progressive, socialist (almost communist) government of the young country. Interestingly, Mwambe-Abeiku also happened to be a very distant cousin of the future (now former) Secretary General of the United Nations, Kofi Annan.

Teo's *Second Rook*, General Koča Popović (left) and *First Bishop*, President of Ghana Nkrumah (right) in the Royal Locksmith Shop with the *White King* where he taught them secrets of the trade. Courtesy of Museum of Yugoslavia, Belgrade.

The very cosmopolitan *Second Rook* enjoyed company of World's celebrities. Shown here with famous Italian actress Gina Lolobrigida. Courtesy of Legacy of Konstantin-Koča Popović and Leposava-Lepa Perović, Historical Archives of Belgrade.

Chapter 40

Queen's Gambit

The Game got stirred up quite a bit when Teo's opponent from the shadow made an unexpected move. Namely, The United Kingdom, very concerned how the situation was developing in her former colony Ghana, decided to activate the Queen. And what a queen it was! The very charming, young Queen Elizabeth II offered herself as an "illogical sacrifice" as it is commonly referred in the game of chess. When the Queen, in official capacity, visited her former colony, she offered to dance with the bewildered President Nkrumah. This was a death dance of sorts, all in the hopes that Teo's first bishop will, perhaps, abandon all this nonsense of spreading communist, revolutionary ideas all over the chess board and instead go back to the shelter of his former masters.

However, the *White King* already had a countermove which he prepared in advance, before the Queen even offered her sacrifice. In September of that same year of 1961, Teo's first bishop Nkrumah was welcomed in communist Belgrade with the highest state honors. The *White King* took the first bishop for a ride in a luxury limousine manufactured abroad, from which both, standing, enthusiastically waved back at seemingly delirious subjects of the *White King*. During the ride in the luxurious, spacious limousine manufactured abroad, the first bishop asked the *White King* if he were pleased with his coffee move. At the same time, the first bishop expressed his fascination with the amazing plan the *White King* had for the entire World. The plan that will start with the conflict on the opponent's own turf where the ingenious coffee move will admittedly play a small part, but, hopefully, an important one.

The *White King*, clueless as to what the first bishop was talking about, thought to himself how his *First Rook*, General Popović, must have again played something useful, although obviously of his own accord (the latter part of the thought shook the *White King* a bit.) The *White King* therefore resorted to an answer that always worked like a charm:

"Very good, very good."

Unfortunately, as it usually happens, and perhaps because of a premature celebration, Teo was shocked by the next move of his new unexpected opponent. Although, for the truth's sake, this move was highly irregular, against all known rules of the ancient game. One arm of the opponent, with the name CIA, decided to apply sheer force and turn the situation around. Notably, however, it is also undoubtedly true that Teo's first bishop, President of Ghana Nkrumah, overplayed a bit by flying all over the chess board and not listening to the *White King* who warned him more than once. He, the first bishop, started imagining how, one day, it is he who will become the leader of the independent World and replace the *White King*. He decided to visit the most populous country in the World, the communist China, and in the same move visit its smaller neighbor, also very communist North Korea. In retaliation, while President Nkrumah was visiting the two countries in the Far East, on February 21, 1966, he was simply removed from Teo's chess board by a coup organized by this arm of the unlikely opponent called CIA.

The understandably traumatized Teo then failed to anticipate a very logical next move by the opponent and bore all the consequences. That same year, on April 22, in New York, in the *Village Vanguard* where he went with Buddy to watch Miles' new gig, Teo heard very bad news from his visibly shaken friend. Buddy told him that all deliveries of coffee and cocoa from Ghana suddenly stopped, without any explanation. At one point, Buddy even mentioned something about suicide because of the mounting debts.

After some hard thinking Teo, in early-October, orchestrated a miraculous series of moves. No one before or after has seen such a series of chess moves. Teo threw his previously neglected second bishop, the Ambassador of Yugoslavia to the United States, his Excellency Bogdan Crnobrnja, into the middle of the fight. He then reinforced the attack with his always active *Second Rook*, Tito's Foreign Minister General Koča Popović. Together, they engaged the *White King*, without his knowledge, and succeeded in something completely impossible – Teo's team was joined by one real African Emperor. The Emperor of brotherly Ethiopia, no one else but Divine Haile Selassie!

The emperor, out of utmost respect for the *White King* and his plan for World affairs, listened to the Ambassador Bogdan Crnobrnja and General Popović, and agreed to supply coffee to this dedicated, although secret, organization in the United States named *Mt. Kilimanjaro Coffee Company*. Thus, Buddy Gist started receiving shipments of the best coffee there is, the Ethiopian Yirgacheffe. Buddy was happy again, enormously indebted to his European friend for help in securing the coffee (but not cocoa) deliveries. Buddy of course was curious about the whole arrangement but did not push when Teo nonchalantly waved his hand and said it was not a big deal at all, no need to talk about it.

According to Teo's very logical, best estimate, all his chess pieces were now in place for the final victory.

Rival Queen Elizabeth II in a foxtrot dance with Teo's *First Bishop*, President of Ghana Nkrumah. Courtesy of The Washington Post.

White King (Marshall Tito) organized a magnificent welcome for Teo's *First Bishop* (President of Ghana Nkrumah) in September 1961 in Belgrade. Courtesy of Museum of Yugoslavia, Belgrade.

Close ties between *White King* (holding spears in the photo on the left) and Teo's second bishop, Yugoslav Ambassador to the United States Bogdan Crnobrnja (in photo on the right) with the Emperor of Ethiopia Haile Selassie played a key role in the Game. Both photos Courtesy of Museum of Yugoslavia, Belgrade.

Chapter 41

White Queen and Black King

Suddenly, the Game turned beyond intense and complicated. A ferocious attack by the opponent forced Teo to engage his sleepy queens (there were two queens playing for the White) – the real *White Queen*, the famous Italian actress Sophia Loren, and the wooden queen to which the *White King* was officially married. On the day of the crucial move for Teo, the *White King* was finally pointed towards the final goal of the Game. It all happened on the beautiful island of Vanga in the Adriatic archipelago Brioni. The weather and everything else on that June day in 1969 was just perfect and the *White King* did not hesitate a bit – he finally accepted the American jazz as something he can learn to live with. According to the confidential sources, things fell in place during a conversation in an electric golf vehicle operated by the *White King* personally (he did not tolerate gasoline fumes on his paradise island, full of exotic animals from Africa and Asia). What follows is a concise transcript of this historic conversation I was so lucky to lay my eyes on.

Escort (official husband of the *White Queen*, Italian film producer Carlo Ponti):

"Honorable Mr. President, I am very impressed with your playing of the piano and knowledge of classical music which you demonstrated after the divine lunch you personally, and so generously, prepared for us. Sophia and I are equally fond of jazz and are interested in what you think about it?"

White King (partially remembering the reply he gave, long time ago, to the famous conductor of the Belgrade Radio-Television Big Jazz Band):

"I was earlier dissatisfied with the American interpretation of the original, genuine, and excellent African jazz, but am now under the impression that American jazz did improve somewhat."

Carlo Ponti, cordially:

"It seems to me that you came to terms with American jazz; things certainly can and do change."

White Queen, famous, gorgeous Italian Actress Sophia Loren:

"But Carlissimo, Marshall Tito was always renowned for his progressiveness! I completely understand and support him. The American jazz is fine, but the phenomenal Miles Davis is something else. His records are not a simple repetition of the American jazz tradition but a complete turn, the revolution, and even the American youth adore him. And you, dear Marshall, you are exceptional! How do you manage to always stay so young, in body and soul!?"

White King, quite satisfied and playfully:

"Dear Sophia, thank you, thank you. I must admit that, sitting like this, next to you, I do feel as a twenty-year old youngster."

After these words by the *White King*, everyone in the electric golf vehicle laughed, including the wooden queen (who, however, did it somewhat sourly.) Later that evening, in their royal bedroom, the wooden queen threw a jealous tantrum for which the *White King* never forgave her.

The following day, when Anonymous 1 received a confidential wire about the above-described event, he raised his hands high above his head, triumphantly. He then immediately informed Teo and several colleagues in the State Department (including, of course, Anonymous 2) that they can put in motion the next phase of the operation with a code name *Iron Curtain Jazz*. Anonymous 1 then phoned the White House Chief of Staff Haldeman and conveyed the important news. In turn, he received praises, with an assurance that President Nixon will be briefed about the very favorable turn of events. That same evening Teo, with a glass of Champaign in his hand, silently thanked his Italian friends in New York (with whom he developed strong personal friendship during his many visits to the city), and especially members of a very powerful *famiglia* with strong connections in Sicily and across Italy.

Thus, through a wide-open door, the *Black King*, 37th President of the United States Richard Nixon himself walked into Teo's Game of Chess. Ever since January of that year when he became a resident of the White House, Nixon witnessed how all his plans sailed through smoothly and now it happened to yet another one – the breach of Iron Curtain can finally commence! Naturally, thanks to skills Anonymous 1 possessed, Nixon started to consider the jazz plan as his own, emphasizing ever so often his own ingenuity, and not being embarrassed in doing so, not even a tiny little bit. In rare cases when Nixon's Secretary of State William Rogers tried to get a partial credit for the incredible plan, he was promptly cut off by the *Black King*. All along, Anonymous 1, very cleverly, kept his mouth shut in the company of his supervisors, and continued to advance his career to Teo's delight.

In fact, the *Black King*, at the beginning of his involvement in the Game, was some sort of an ally to Teo. This is best illustrated with him hosting, only three months after he moved to the White House, the 70th birthday party for the most respected American jazz musician Duke Ellington. On the occasion, Nixon presented Duke with the highest civilian honor, the Medal of Freedom. The Game for Teo thus developed in the best possible way – he had the complete personal support from the *Black King*! This then brought in all necessary means for the final victory including generous financial resources.

It now seemed nothing could stop Teo on the path to final victory, especially because the *Black King* and the *White King* seemingly formed a pact of mutual understanding regarding jazz music in general. Namely, Richard Nixon (*Black King*) made the first visit by a United States President to Yugoslavia and to the *White King*, Marshall Tito. As the occasion dictated, the *Black King* received a true royal welcome in Belgrade. According to the custom, tested many times by the host, both kings were driven on the streets of Belgrade in a large, luxurious, convertible car manufactured abroad. From it, the two kings were bravely, in the pouring rain, waving to seemingly delirious subjects of the *White King*. The citizens, workers, students and other youth were all happy because the working day was cut short for the occasion. Despite the unfavorable weather conditions, the bystanders were all patiently waiting for the presidential motorcade to pass so everyone can go about their own business for the rest of the day.

The exhilarated *Black King*, before the state dinner that evening, cordially conveyed to his host how several famous American jazz musicians are looking very much forward to the concert they will give in beautiful Belgrade in less than a month, thanks to his personal efforts (Nixon was, as usual, taking full credit for another event organized by the *Iron Curtain Jazz* folks.) Of course, the *Black King* did not miss an opportunity to thank the *White King* on his amazing hospitality and then express the great pleasure that the two of them share the same passion for jazz music and both play piano perfectly, if he understood correctly.

White King addressed the *Black King's* comment about jazz as follows (partially remembering the exchange he had with the famous conductor of the Belgrade Radio-Television Big Jazz Band long ago, but more importantly the very nice words he heard from the beautiful *White Queen* during a ride on the equally beautiful island of Vanga, not that long ago):

"I was earlier very dissatisfied with the American interpretation of the original, genuine, and excellent African jazz. I am, however, now under the impression that the American jazz did improve somewhat. I especially like the trumpet player Miles Davis and his progressive music. I myself was always supporting young courageous people, and the revolutionary changes they were bringing to society."

The two monarchs then joined the *White King's* subjects at the reception and the state dinner that followed.

White King (with the hat) and *White Queen* (Italian actress Sophia Loren.) On the back seats are wooden queen (Jovanka Broz, official wife of the *White King*) and Italian film producer Carlo Ponti, official husband of the *White Queen*. Courtesy of Museum of Yugoslavia, Belgrade.

White Queen and *White King* very much enjoyed each other's company. Courtesy of Museum of Yugoslavia, Belgrade

Black King, President of the United States Richard Nixon (on the right) and famous jazz musician Duke Ellington at his 70th birthday party in the White House in April 1969. Courtesy of The Richard Nixon Presidential Library and Museum.

Festive welcome of the *Black King* (standing on the left in the Mercedes Benz and waving to the onlookers) in the Yugoslav capital Belgrade on October 1, 1970. The host, *White King* (Marshall Tito, with the hat) is standing on the right. Courtesy of Museum of Yugoslavia, Belgrade.

One-on-one conversation between *White King* and *Black King* before state dinner in honor of the first President of the United States to visit Yugoslavia. Courtesy of Museum of Yugoslavia, Belgrade.

Chapter 42

Time Trouble

Teo's time trouble started in early April of 1971. As it often happens in the game of chess, he did not even realize it was there, until it was plainly and painfully obvious. Almost accidentally, he learned about it from his friend George Wein, the renowned music impresario and the key founder of the famous Newport Jazz Festival. Wein was now the organizer of the upcoming First Newport Beograd Jazz Festival in Belgrade, in November that year.

The cooperation between George Wein and the *Iron Curtain Jazz* operation started more than a decade earlier at Teo's initiative. In late fall of 1970, it was Teo who insisted that Wein not give up on Miles Davis and keep persuading the trumpet player to agree and give the concert in Belgrade (Miles never travelled to a communist country since he could not stand any kind of tyranny.) It took Wein several months to succeed, but only after Buddy Gist joined the effort, all to Teo's great relief.

Unfortunately, Miles Davis was, in January 1971, taken off the list of jazz musicians that will be playing in Belgrade later that year. The bureaucrats at the State Department, including Anonymous 1 (but not Anonymous 2) and the Secretary of State William Rogers, qualified Miles as a rebel and "disturbing element" who poses threat for legitimate law and order and who, under certain circumstances, could incite dissatisfied masses of young people, to riots. The bureaucrats therefore rejected any possibility of Miles traveling to Belgrade and promoting him there while paying for his travel expenses and an honorarium on top of that.

After learning about this, Wein had to apologize, painfully, to the trumpet player for the unfathomable decision by the State Department to leave him out. What Wein inexplicably failed to do was to inform Teo what had happened, until their meeting in April.

In a not small panic Teo, in June 1971, decided to do something very risky. Via a confidential messenger, he asked for advice and help from his *Second*, Grandmaster Svetozar Gligorić Gliga. Gliga firmly promised he will do everything in his power to work on the move directly with the *Second Rook*, General Koča Popović, as a sign of great appreciation for what Teo did for him in the past. Coincidentally, the *Second Rook*, a former wealthy sympathizer of the International Surrealist Society headquartered in Paris, France before WWII, had the second largest private collection of jazz records in former Yugoslavia. He also was the proud owner of the largest private collection of classical music records not only in his own country but in The Balkans. As a result, the *Second Rook* and Teo's *Second* quickly found common language.

The *Second Rook* communicated personally to the United States Ambassador to Yugoslavia, William Leonhart, a direct message from the *White King* to the *Black King*. In addition to some general diplomatic language regarding the improving relationship between the two countries, the message explicitly emphasized the hopes of the *White King* that any misunderstandings or ambiguities about the Miles Davis' highly anticipated presence at the upcoming First Newport Belgrade Jazz Festival will be put to rest by the *Black King* himself.

When Nixon's Secretary of State William Rogers received this message from his Ambassador in Belgrade, he could not believe it. He was mystified why the "crazy commie" would spend his time on stupid things like that. However, Rogers knew he had to pass the message from Belgrade to his boss no matter what. While doing so, he did not hide his inexplicable animosity and disgust for Miles and all other "commies". Rogers bluntly advised the *Black King* to ignore the part of *White King's* message regarding the jazz trumpet player.

Nixon, who was a much more skillful diplomat than his own head of diplomacy, did not take the advice. He needed Tito's help and mediation in the planned new approach to the relationship with Soviet Union. He also certainly did not want to unnecessarily offend the sly leader of the Third World because of such a trivial thing. He therefore ordered Rogers to fix the problem with the trumpet player and do not bother him again with it. Consequently, Miles was put back on the list and impresario Wein was told to inform the trumpet player of the new development.

Poor George Wein was struck by lightning from a clear blue sky when, on October 19, he personally called Miles, who was on a previously arranged tour in Europe, to tell him the good news that he will, after all, travel to Belgrade and give the highly anticipated concert there. The famous jazz trumpet player replied to Wein how "*he was not interested at all anymore, and that he can tell motherf... from the State Department to go and f... themselves until eyes pop out of their f.... heads!*"

Chapter 43

Endgame

The same lightning that struck poor Wein had an extended duration and path because the following day, October 20th, it also struck Teo who was a few thousand miles away, in the ghost town of Terlingua north of Big Bend, Texas, in temporary exile with his family where they were sent because of the Marshall Tito's visit to the United States. Our hero almost fainted after the phone call he had with the renowned music impresario. After recovering somewhat from the devastating blow by the completely new, illogical opponent, Teo asked Wein not to talk with anyone about the catastrophic turn of events as he will try to do something about it, with God's help. Of course, this was easier said than done. The following two days Teo spent going feverishly over possible moves and countermoves, until he decided to make the ultimate bluff and again activate his exhausted but still fearless *Second Rook*, General Koča Popović.

This risky move had an immediate impact. Already at the very beginning of their first one-on-one meeting during the return state visit of the *White King* to the *Black King*, in the White House, on October 26, 1971, the *White King* expressed great dissatisfaction with the exclusion of revolutionary Miles Davis from the Belgrade jazz festival. It is here important to emphasize how the *White King* that year still had unbreakable trust in his *Second Rook* and did not question his best judgement, especially when it came to the just fight of poor fellow Americans, and their brothers and sisters in Africa.

The *Black King*, President of the United States Richard Nixon, was shocked by this expression of rage from his guest. He quickly composed himself and replied how there must be a misunderstanding of sorts, and that he will immediately correct the inexcusable mistake, if there was a mistake. After their first one-on-one conversation ended, the *Black*

King, hiding his anger, demanded an explanation from his Secretary of State. Secretary Rogers replied that he will check the whole thing at once while, at the same time, offering an opinion that probably no one was able to make the crazy trumpet player interested in giving the concert to the Yugoslav commies.

Approximately thirty minutes after leaving the room where the monarchs were mingling in the company of their few confidants, Secretary Rogers returned with a pleased expression on his face. He approached his king and whispered to his ear that Miles Davis was indeed on the official list of jazz musicians that was sent to the Yugoslavs and that it is all simply a misunderstanding, or lack of basic knowledge of English language or something similarly unintelligent on the part of Yugoslavs. Visibly relieved, the *Black King* addressed the *White King*, making sure everyone present can hear what he had to say:

"Mister President, Miles Davis, your favorite jazz musician, will most certainly give a concert in Belgrade next week, because I personally took care of it!"

The *White King*, in the same old proven manner, replied:

"Very good, very good" but this time went further and assured his host, during their second one-on-one, long conversation that, in return, he will gladly arrange a meeting next year with the Secretary General of the Soviet Communist party comrade Leonid Brezhnev, for which the *Black King* so kindly asked him.

What the *White King* promised, he delivered. Richard Nixon was the first president of the United States to visit the Soviet Union, in 1972. This marked beginning of the official detente between the two superpowers, grave adversaries in the Cold War.

Regrettably, the visible satisfaction of the two kings with their fruitful interactions did not mean anything to Teo anymore. He was deeply disappointed and sad because of the inevitable defeat in the Game of chess that started two decades ago. Miles was not going to Belgrade after all, his flag on the chess clock by the Game Board was about to fall, the position on the Board was hopeless, and he felt the excruciating pain in his stomach, just like during countless, inescapable visits to the Marine Base Quantico, where he was exposed to dreadful energy waves.

On October 31, while walking aimlessly between sad dilapidated tombstones in the graveyard of the ghost town Terlingua in southwest Texas, Teo suddenly had a moment of enlightenment. He remembered his *First Rook*, Miles's best friend Buddy Gist. With a superhuman effort, Teo forced himself to concentrate and think if and how he could use his most important piece in the remaining few seconds of the Game, before the flag falls. And then it all became clear to him.

Reinvigorated, Teo ran to the only store in Terlingua and from an old candlestick phone asked for help from the operator for a long-distance call to New York. When on the other side he heard Buddy, Teo, with a trembling voice, begged his old friend to do whatever he can to help him out and explain to Miles how the Yugoslavs deserve to see and hear him, how they are not hardcore communists, how they fight for justice and equality for all people in the World, how they were not afraid to say no to the Russians when it mattered the most, how they take from us and then give to the poorest of the poor elsewhere, just like Robin Hood did, how they build roads and dams for our brothers and sisters in Africa, and a lot more. And of all jazz musicians in the World, they like him, Miles Davis, the most.

Teo's Game of Chess ended, two exhausting decades after it started, when the Miles Davis Septet:

Miles Davis – trumpet
Gary Bartz – alt and tenor saxophone
Keith Jarret – electric piano and organ
Michael Henderson – electric bass
Ndugu Leon Chancler – drums
Charles Don Alias – conga and percussion
James Mtume Forman – conga and percussion

gave their historic concert in the overcrowded *Home of Labor Unions* performance hall in Belgrade, on November 3rd, 1971.

Miles Davis at the First Newport Beograd Jazz Festival in Belgrade, on November 3, 1971. The photo is made from a scanned 6x6 slide film Kodak Highspeed 22 Din taken and processed by Belgrade photographer Dušan Milijić. It is made public for the first time. No other official photographs or film footage of the event are available from any sources, including any Yugoslav or Belgrade media.

Epilogue

In the early fall of 2018 all of us, observers, direct participants, or collaborators in the story of the schooner *Blackbird* and the time travel experiments, returned to our usual lives. Ivica returned to Belgrade because his semester at University was about to start. He supplemented his personal technical archive with the analysis of our experiments and photographs of Tesla's apparatus, promising to keep the secret from the eyes of others.

Magdalena was still working on her research in New Mexico. She, however, replaced the Pueblo Tesuque with a more comfortable winter accommodation in Santa Fe. Bavi, with whom I kept in frequent regular communications, intensified the work on her doctoral thesis, spending most of her time in the library and machine shop at Princeton.

More than winning the bet and celebrating with a bottle of twenty-three-year-old *Pappy Van Winkle* bourbon in the company of dear friends, I appreciated the fact that I was able to shed light on the unbelievable destiny of a man who vanished in the labyrinth of time. I still could not fully accept that our adventure was over. I kept reflecting on the experiments we conducted, relieved that nothing went wrong. I had the apparatus and it was my responsibility to keep it safe in an undisclosed place, the location of which only I knew.

For the sake of transparency, I must admit that, on two occasions, I could not resist the challenge of having the apparatus. The first was when, impulsively, I drove to Princeton one weekend and had Bavi test what she called an "improvement" on Tesla's concept. I will not elaborate on this event, other than stating that not everything went as she hoped. Of course, this experience did not discourage the always curious and unstoppable Bavi. On the contrary. The second occasion presented itself when I learned of the most famous schooner festival in the country, held every year in Gloucester, Massachusetts. After some friendly persuasion, I managed to have the Thompsons enroll their beautifully restored schooner in the race.

In *Good Morning Gloucester* that year one could read how "With 29 schooners participating and a three day stretch of perfect weather, the Annual Gloucester Schooner Festival was a magnificent success. Congratulations to all the schooners, to the captains, crew, festival committee members, and to all the volunteers and organizations who make possible this most stellar of maritime sailing events."

Blackbird won its class, and not only that. She had a better time than any large, medium, or small schooners, except for the two of them. One was a legacy *Malabar II*, a legendary schooner designed by Alden. Until now, I did not reveal to anyone, not even to the Thompsons, how *Blackbird* achieved this amazing feat, after decades of leisurely life, without wear and tear. Personally, I was not all that happy with the result because, again, I did not do something quite right with the Tesla's apparatus.

The last time most of us were together was at Peter and Sandy's, enjoying time on *Blackbird* after the festival. I can't remember who exactly suggested that we bring all of it out in the open, tell the scientists, the media, or at least intrigue someone. This prompted heated discussions about who would believe us. Some expressed great concern that we may come across as laughable charlatans. Still, we did reach a consensus at the end. Everyone pledged to keep the most important details about our experiments secret, and I was tasked with putting the narrative together, being the one who started the whole thing. Others helped me as they saw appropriate, but it was mostly up to me. Those who wanted to remain anonymous were free to do so. Everyone was given an opportunity to review my first rough draft, volunteer to expand on something of their personal interest, or withhold information I included without any explanation. Ivica sent me an email telling me not to elaborate on his scientific work. It is enough that he must fight with some of his conservative colleagues; he does not need additional conflicts.

The final product, everyone agreed, turned out to be a decent one (although some of us thought it was perfect.) And so here it is.

Restored *Blackbird* at the Gloucester Schooner Festival.
Bottom: Peter receiving the prize.

Old Fox Books

The meeting I had with Margo right before the English edition (which you hold in your hands) was ready for print resulted in several last-minute additions, a few changes here and there, and most importantly, this additional chapter (to which my publisher graciously agreed.)

We met at Old Fox Books in Annapolis, Maryland at Margo's suggestion: *It is my favorite place in the whole metro area, you must see it!* I was going to show her the Belgrade edition I had just received in the mail from my brother and tell her about some fascinating things I found in Teo's remaining diaries. She gave them to me last month. There was one story I would have loved to include in the book if it were not too late. I picked Margo up in Georgetown and drove us to Annapolis. In the bookstore's cozy Coffeehouse, we both ordered mocha and various chocolate goodies (Margo apparently loves chocolate as much as I do) and my "expose" began. After several hours and more chocolate, I decided to hold the English edition because of Margo's feedback on the book and everything else she told me.

The following day I reached out to all the people involved and those that generously helped me with the book, kindly asking them to provide anything they could think of, including any photos or "visuals" they would like to see in the English edition. Magdalena, Cole's son Patrick, and Masters' nephew Bob sent photos they felt quite attached to. Others simply replied how everything was just fine, no need for additional stuff (and "exposure" as a few of them put it).

Magdalena's explanation of the photos she sent was straightforward and touching: "My best friends, filling me with love and joy every single day." Patrick's explanation was as inspiring: "This is Benjamin, my guitar student. I've known him since he was a newborn and I now feel responsible for his love of guitar. Every time he came to visit us with his parents, he would politely ask if he could see my guitar collection. He dropped playing piano and trumpet (which he was quite good at) last year and is now completely devoted to playing guitar. I am helping him with it a bit. I recently gave him my Stratocaster which he adored as some kind of deity. He was so happy it made my day. And he deserved it, no question about it. I just hope he will not drop playing guitar as well." Bob simply wrote "Me and my uncle's Olds so he can see, if he is watching from somewhere, how I am taking good care of it."

I started telling my story to Margo by prefacing it, unnecessarily, with a general statement about how it seems nothing is coincidental: past and present and future are one and the same, it is only us who may or may not perceive it that way. Not everyone is operating on the same level, and it would be boring if that were the case anyway. She understood it all along and was kind enough not to tell me how I am stating the obvious. Then I continued by dissecting Teo's love for the arts and why his talent was never fully realized in, what others would consider, a "normal, expected manner."

Teo was classically trained at the Belgrade University's Academy of Arts to become a sculptor. In his senior year he spent a semester at the Academia di Belle Arti di Bari in Milan, Italy. There he learned about works of the Academy's famous contemporary alumnus, Ruggiero Morigi, including the amazing achievements of his team of stone carvers working on the National Cathedral in Washington, D.C. He instantly fell in love with the Cathedral's best-known sculpture, *Ex Nihilo* after seeing its life-size reproduction at the Academy. Once in D.C., Teo befriended Morigi and later Morigi's favorite protégé Frederick Hart of Baltimore.

In 1967, Teo encouraged Hart to take a job as a mailroom clerk at the Washington National Cathedral suggesting he could then "push his way up from the inside and one day work directly for Morigi, as a stone carver and then a sculptor, and why not, think big, the sky is the limit." Hart reluctantly applied for the job and the rest is history. Morigi eventually caved into relentless pressure from Hart and accepted him as an apprentice, so the story goes. From everything I read however, it really was mainly thanks to Teo's doing, from behind the scenes as always. With his exceptional talent and hard work, Hart earned every bit of fame that finally came with his most celebrated work, *Ex Nihilo*, the tympanum above the main entrance to the Cathedral. The story how the sculpture came to life is truly fascinating. Morigi, with Teo's decisive help, eventually succeeded in persuading the Cathedral's Building Committee to break with tradition and go for something truly avant-garde by accepting Hart's submission. Most interesting and intriguing to me is what Teo wrote about it in his diary, including a vague hint about beautiful sculptures of naked women emerging from the overarching spiraling form of *Ex Nihilo*. I of course fully understand why Teo was so vague even in his own personal diary written in Serbian Cyrillic – it is because of the involvement of his beautiful daughter.

Teo would sometimes spend time hanging out in Hart's garage studio near Dupont Circle, watching him carve miracles in stone. Sometimes he would grab carving tools and do it himself, more out of nostalgia than anything else as he now preferred painting and drawing just like his father did. Hart, more than once, tried persuading Teo to devote his energy to sculpture since he was "really, really good at it." Each time Teo would reply how he was not a good thief, even though he tried hard... Eventually, he explained to Hart what he meant. Morigi once told Teo he cannot teach him how to carve. Teo can *steal* from him and his team of carvers as much as he wants by watching what they do, for as long as he wishes. "You can steal a little bit from one, a little bit from the other, but at the end you must develop your own way. It is as simple as that."

One day Teo brought Margo to Hart's studio to show her the amazing sculptures his friend was creating. After a while, the visibly nervous Hart finally gathered enough courage to ask Teo if he had anything against his beautiful daughter posing for a sculpture he was planning for this "damn composition" for the Cathedral's contest. He has been struggling with it for months but is now convinced that having his daughter help may do the trick. Teo simply shrugged his shoulders and told Hart "Why don't you ask Margo yourself; it is none of my business."

So, Hart did. Margo was understandably taken aback by the question. She flushed, looked at her father sheepishly, and managed to reply how she is not really sure; it may be embarrassing; she never did anything like it before; she loves art and sculpture and everything, but still. After a pause, she offered a suggestion instead, telling Hart how some of her high school friends (Margo was eighteen at the time) are very beautiful. One is a ballerina and two are swimmers; she can ask them if they would pose for him.

The following week, while they were enjoying a round of drinks at a cafe near Dupont Circle, Teo spotted a beautiful young woman passing by. He alerted Hart "Here she is again; why don't you finally ask her; stop suffering like this; it cannot hurt, you can only gain, there is nothing to lose." Hart replied, "What the hell, you are right." and then rushed to the beauty. This act of courage lead to the marriage of Miss Lindy Lain and Mr. Frederick Hart seven years later, in 1978. In the meantime, Miss Lain was immortalized in *Ex Nihilo*.

After I told the story to Margo, I confronted her by noting how, a few days before our meeting, I went to the Cathedral, took numerous photos of *Ex Nihilo* including with a powerful zoom, and then processed them on my computer, looking at every single detail. This led me to the conclusion that not all the female figures are of the same woman and is there anything she has to say about that. Margo flushed and simply said I was correct. We were quiet for a minute or two after that, me staring at Margo with a slightly mocking expression on my face. Finally, I said "Yes?"

"Well, I can give you my favorite photo of my best friends. We were so young and happy then. You can put it in your book if it is not too late. What I remember the most from it are the words my grandfather said when he gave you my father's diaries for gift:

"One dies two times. The first time when one's soul leaves the body, and the second time when there is no one left to remember him."

Old Fox Books in Annapolis, Maryland, Margo's *"favorite place in the whole metro area."*

Magdalena and her pets, tabby Nick, little Igor (a Russian Blue),
and dog Millie, all-time favorite.

Left: Patrick's student Benjamin with Fender Stratocaster he got as a gift from Patrick. Right: Raymond "Bob" Masters with the Olds Cornet he inherited from his uncle Steven Masters.

Teo took this photo of Margo and her best friends in 1988 after a retirement farewell for their favorite high school religion teacher Mr. Wood. From left to right: Theodora, Monica, Margo, and Laura.

Detail of *Ex Nihilo* by Frederick Hart, central sculpture above the main entrance to Washington National Cathedral.

THE END

About the Author

Nestor M. Kaminski is a pseudonym (nom de guerre) and still under a veil of mystery. The author insists that remaining anonymous is of the utmost importance. The reasons for this secrecy are many, including the circumstances surrounding the mysterious documents of Nikola Tesla and the controversial military projects in former Yugoslavia. It is our understanding that Mr. Kaminski is currently working on another book with an expanded team of researchers. It will provide more detail about events after WWII and up to the present day, and key characters connected to the original story.

Blue Ridge Press LLC

www.ingramcontent.com/pod-product-compliance
Lightning Source LLC
Chambersburg PA
CBHW030155200626
46812CB00017B/2081